Jihadi

A Love Story

YUSUF TOROPOV

ORENDA BOOKS

Orenda Books
16 Carson Road
West Dulwich
London SE21 8HU
www.orendabooks.co.uk

To Safie

First published in the United Kingdom by Orenda Books 2016

ISBN 978-1-910633-31-1

Typeset in Garamond by MacGuru Ltd
Printed and bound by CPI Group (UK) Ltd, Croydon CR0 4YY

SALES & DISTRIBUTION

In the UK and elsewhere in Europe:
Turnaround Publisher Services
Unit 3, Olympia Trading Estate
Coburg Road
Wood Green
London
N22 6TZ
www.turnaround-uk.com

In USA/Canada:
Trafalgar Square Publishing
Independent Publishers Group
814 North Franklin Street
Chicago, IL 60610
USA
www.ipgbook.com

For details of other territories, please contact *info@orendabooks.co.uk*

CSA
5/16

PRAISE FOR *JIHADI: A LOVE STORY*

'Smart and searing … a deeply felt depiction of morally fraught choices that result in devastating outcomes' *Publishers Weekly*

'Toropov writes an utterly fantastic tale, which does so many different things so well. The author captures the very essence of the "war on terror" and its psychological and moral complexities. It is a book of our time' **Edward Wilson**

'*Jihadi* is a gripping tale of a clash of cultures and individuals told with panache, dazzling wit and remorseless intelligence. More please' **William Ryan**

'An exquisitely drawn debut, that twists and turns to its stunning conclusion. With echoes of Bellow, Pynchon and Kafka, Toropov's tale is a modern classic that challenges our perceptions at every turn' **Cal Moriarty**

'If it was Yusuf Toropov's intention to leave us pondering good and evil, right and wrong, love and loss, wondering who the good guys were, he certainly succeeded. I know one thing for sure, he's a wonderful writer and a born storyteller' **Mari Hannah**

'Intelligently written and multi-layered … with its gorgeous language, rich detail and gentle wit, *Jihadi* is simply enchanting' **Qaisra Shahraz**

'A bold and skilfully executed novel that bravely tackles a complex and timely subject in accomplished and precise prose' **Frankie Gaffney**

'Timely and spookily prescient, Yusuf Toropov's *Jihadi: A Love Story* is a magical mystery tour through a labyrinth of competing ambitions and motivations, wherein truth and justice are matters for interpretation' **Texas Booklover**

'It is not an easy story. It is, at times, complex and demanding. Some parts are harrowing. But two things grabbed me at that early stage: the quality of the writing, which is quite outstanding, and the intriguing setup. A US intelligence agent, accused of terrorism, is held in a secret prison. The decoding of his memoir is the starting point for a novel that has as its theme th̶e̶ ̶v̶e̶r̶y̶ ̶n̶a̶t̶u̶r̶e̶ ̶o̶f̶ ̶t̶r̶u̶t̶h̶ ̶a̶n̶d̶ ̶h̶o̶w̶ ̶i̶t̶ ̶i̶s̶ ̶p̶e̶r̶c̶e̶i̶v̶e̶d̶' Saf̶i̶e **Maken Finlay**

ABOUT THE AUTHOR

Yusuf Toropov is an American Muslim writer. He's the author or co-author of a number of nonfiction books, including *Shakespeare for Beginners*. His full-length play *An Undivided Heart* was selected for a workshop production at the National Playwrights Conference, and his one-act play *The Job Search* was produced off-Broadway. *Jihadi: A Love Story*, which reached the quarter-finals of the Amazon Breakthrough Novel Award, is his first novel. He is currently living in Ireland.

You can visit him at: http://yusuftoropov.blogspot.com

Or follow him on Twitter: @LiteraryStriver

From the Desk of R.L. Firestone

This is no love story, though the late author would have had it so. A sad tale, a tale of treason, *Jihadi*, an encrypted memoir posing as a novel, is the work of the terrorist Ali Liddell, upon whom the justice of God descended on July 3, 2006. This date marked both his forty-fifth birthday and the fourteenth anniversary of the star-cursed day that I recommended we hire him. I here seek formal immunity against prosecution for his death.

Although my detractors never fail to note that the terrorist's last name rhymes with 'riddle', the case against him could not be clearer cut. Much has been made of the imagined legal and moral dilemmas presented by Liddell's American citizenship. Yet the three facts driving his case remain indisputable.

- First, that Liddell received briefings on classified material of the most sensitive kind on an almost daily basis.
- Second, that he suffered a nervous breakdown prior to writing *Jihadi*.
- And third, that he was the first and only senior staffer in our history to convert to Islam. This travesty occurred after his final overseas mission, during which a series of unpardonable security breaches resulted in his being targeted, seduced, renamed, and reprogrammed by a female jihadi, now in custody: Fatima Adara.

We may expect more such attempts at subversion, not only from overseas operatives, but from stateside religious extremists as well – see my essay *The Liddell Syndrome*.

Thelonius Liddell drafted *Jihadi* during his final months, in the demented script of a masochist, using an ink of water and charcoal, and occasional specks of his own blood (minute amounts of which served as some kind of thickening agent). The work is thus attributable solely to him via DNA, graphological and forensic evidence.

The facsimiles from which I work correlate precisely with Liddell's original pages, each now encased in Lucite and held within a temperature-controlled basement at Directorate headquarters in Langley, Virginia. The sheets were impounded by Operations only minutes after I discovered them in Liddell's cell.

A full embargo on this material has been set in place, and for good reason, yet my detractors — emboldened, perhaps, by the recent resignation of Mr. Unferth — now debate, with apparent seriousness, whether this should be lifted. In so doing, these misguided simpletons aid and comfort the (obvious and unseen, late and living) enemies of our nation. And enemies is indeed the proper word.

Why does the manuscript even exist? A difficult question. Enemy combatant Liddell, under surveillance at Bright Light, a technically nonexistent resort for violent religious extremists, was, per our protocols, forbidden writing implements. He somehow obtained several reams of letterhead from an unauthorized source. Post-mortem, a syringe, repurposed to create his book, was found in his quarters. Such was his arsenal.

To date, the manuscript has been seen by less than a half-dozen persons, all senior members of the Directorate. Some argue that we are this book's only intended audience, or that its message is merely an extended, largely incoherent insult, not worthy of deep classification. I offer, with this commentary, my respectful dissent.

The reasons for this dissent begin with the work's now-infamous opening page: Liddell's dedication. It has attracted almost as much attention as the similarly obscure reference within the work to a mythical 'hundredth chapter'. Is the dedication a call to action — or some harmless literary ruse? Until we can answer such questions with certainty, we must not risk compromising our assets or our nation's security. For the sake of the innocents, not to mention the ideals of democracy, free enterprise, and good sportsmanship that we are sworn to protect, Liddell's hidden fatwas, his paranoid ravings, his absurd accusations, must never reach their intended audience: terrorists in training.

A few more words are in order before I close this prefatory note. This commentary is not merely a personal defence, but also a labour of love. It is dedicated to the nation and the Directorate to which I have sacrificed more than can be recounted here. I hope and pray that that nation, that Directorate, may yet see fit to show me some compassion.

It pains me to ask for this. I feel entitled to do so because I took a stand. By dedicating my expertise to the cause of freedom — I was the only official assigned to interrogate Liddell privately — I did my duty. Not always perfectly, but always out of a profound love for our country and its values.

I saved lives. I do not deserve prosecution for having done so. Those who claim I do, those who challenge my love for America or for the Directorate because a terrorist died, are wrong.

You who accuse me of murder and torture (hateful, hateful words!), know that I did all of this for you, too, even though positions such as yours are unlikely to be softened by appeals such as mine. Know that the terrorists count on our uncertainty, on our wasting time on debates like these before we take action.

A question for you. You must choose between: A) flying on a plane whose route and security procedures benefit from intelligence gathered by means of 'torture'; or B) flying on a plane whose crew have no such intelligence.

Would you ever choose the latter? You clear your throat. You turn the page. You press the button and summon the stewardess for another coffee.

We who cared for you, who risked our lives for you, and who occasionally erred in the service of your journey's sacred tedium, who put your well-being before our own, we selected for you the sweet boring (A) that we knew you would select for yourself, over the potentially more eventful (B). We seek absolution now because we did our duty. Because we took care of you. Took Care Of You.

We ask now only for the same security and respect that our detractors within the Directorate enjoy each day, and barely notice.

A final housekeeping note: Our condition appears to have occasioned some intermittent loss of short-term memory. (Never, as far as we can tell, long-term.) This has complicated the project somewhat and necessitated multiple careful inspections of the material. We apologize for the delay in forwarding this.

R.L Firestone

DEDICATED TO KHADIJAH – You know I limp now, and move slower than I once did. One way or another I will get out of here. Get home.

I am the dead guy telling you this story. Stories are all I have left. Stories will get me out of here, get me back where I belong. Once upon a time, you believed that man who said, 'Justice is the first virtue of social institutions, as truth is of systems of thought.' Justice will have to do for this story, because none of what follows is true. It is all one long lie. If you come across something seemingly true in these pages, remember this: Only the Word of Allah is true. I pray that Word guides us.

i. Khadijah.

Bucharest, United 101 last night. Didn't get much sleep until the layover at Kennedy. Passport viable after all. And then that exhausting drive through the desert! To the purpose: Liddell's text is in English, as is the transcript from which I work, but readers embarking upon this text must nevertheless note two points: first, that the English phonemes KH and H are expressed by precisely the same letter in the language of the Koran; second, that the reproduction of vowels within the written text of the Muslim Holy Scripture is forbidden. KHADIJAH thus becomes an anagram for JIHAD, which Ali (aka Liddell) personifies and invokes here. Look at these swollen feet.

This story begins with a prayer and ends with a prayer, Khadijah. I pray our destinies may yet intertwine to our benefit. I pray we may forgive each other. I pray our trials in this world may benefit us in this life and the next. And despite my falsehood, my guilt, I pray the Lord liberates us both, guides us to His Straight Path and spares us the fires of Hell.

1 In Which the Terrorist Describes his Surroundings

ii. (lacuna! Almost missed my own index card on this, only saw it while reviewing materials on plane)

. The next passage of the manuscript is, my notes remind me, marked 'Chapter One' in parentheses set within Liddell's ample margins. This faint but visible two-word notation, confirmed by personal evaluation of both the facsimile and the Lucite-encased originals, does not appear in the otherwise faithful official transcript compiled by the Directorate. The attentive eye of an editor has been wanting! All ninety-nine of the terrorist's chapters are *numbered*, but no text from Liddell *describes* them.

I have supplied, or am in the process of supplying, all of the present chapter titles.

He tried not to write this book, but, as a dead guy, felt he had an obligation to do so. He owed her that.

He counts as a dead guy, even though his heart beats, his blood flows, and his mind races, six out of every seven days, within a ten-metre-by-ten-metre cell in the containment unit he calls The Beige Motel. He used to live in a place called Salem, Massachusetts. Now he lives here.

They pride themselves on consistency at The Beige Motel. They see to it that your fluorescent lights never go out. They make certain the brittle, E-flat hum of the place never varies. They follow a strict time scheme, confirmed daily by whether or not you have just been served scrambled eggs on Styrofoam. The plate of scrambled eggs is set on a tray that they place in a creaking, rotating compartment built right into your locked door. Scrambled eggs mean morning. Anything else means later.

He supposes they could switch things up and serve him scrambled eggs at dinnertime to mess with his sense of time. If they wanted, they could. They do mess with his sense of time. So far they have never done that, though.

He misses his wife.

Every seventh day he hears the door groan: Sunday. It opens, and someone leads him away. He inspects a soundproofed enclosure of linoleum and echoes called the Yard. In the Yard, he discusses world affairs with the other guests and reconfirms that morning remains morning by staring at a rectangular sheet of glass set so high into one wall that the place feels, to him, ever so slightly like a church. The glass is probably bulletproof. Only sky is visible through it.

He has concluded that this sheet of glass in the Yard's wall happens to have exactly the same length-to-width ratio as the nineteen leaves of blank paper AbdulKarim smuggles to him each week. Sometimes, when he is writing, he imagines he can see the gold of early dawn through the window in the Yard. He imagines this sheet, on which he now writes, as that impossibly high-mounted window. He imagines it has just lowered itself and opened for him. He imagines golden light, imagines flying toward it.

Whatever he actually sees through that big, inaccessible, rectangular window in the Yard – sleet or clouds or, lately, swirling dust – means a new week has begun. Ten hours into that week, his day has vanished, and he makes his way, escorted, back to his own little corner of the Beige Motel. There are two beds there, but no one lives in the tiny compartment with him. Strictly speaking, he doesn't live in it, either. He died months ago, or might as well have.

Somehow, he got on the bad side of a network of unjust institutions. These institutions interrogate people and make them disappear.

He just wrote, 'somehow'. But he knows how he got on their bad side, why he was interrogated when he arrived, why he will be interrogated again. It was because he spoke justice. When you do that, they say you are gone. When they say you are gone, you are gone; you're simply waiting around for a muscle in the middle of your chest to stop sending spurts of freshly oxygenated blood through your arteries. You are a dead guy in an orange jumpsuit, sitting in a room, patiently waiting for scrambled eggs, strolling one day out of seven among other patient dead guys in orange jumpsuits, who are also sitting in a room waiting for scrambled eggs. All of you are dead.

iii. patient dead guys

Liddell, as noted above, created this manuscript while confined at Bright Light. He did his work in a remote corner of that beige cell of his, during daily six-hour periods when the video surveillance system, more primitive than the American unit one would have preferred, was set to 'stationary' rather than 'scan'. This was meant to permit sleep for those who had earned it. He imagined he could elude our system of controls. Patient patient.

The dead guy telling this story remembers Fatima, in a gold head-scarf, her weeping eyes wide, begging him to tell the truth.

iv. Fatima.

No comment. Yet. Haven't the energy. Need to nap. Errors likelier when tired. Note about control systems goes here?

(Continued) I still recall with a chuckle the first active Jihadi I interrogated at Bagram Air Force Base. The dusky, defiant Habibullah, an unreliable front-line informant, proved as taciturn with me as he had with his three previous interlocutors. I administered a series of peroneal strikes as he hung by both wrists from the sturdy ceiling of his questioning room (one area of my expertise is compliance blows). I later learned that a pack of imprudent, thrill-starved Green Berets imitated my technique and took turns delivering careless strikes to the limp, increasingly exhausted Habibullah. The story goes that they kept this up for twelve or fourteen hours (a statistically ineffective application), and found his cries of 'Allah! Allah!' amusing. Boys will be boys. True to his own wish, Habibullah passed away in captivity. A simple duty to circulate best practices compels me to record here that my avoidance of any paperwork connected with this episode spared the Directorate involvement in the (minor) legal flap and so forth that ensued stateside. *A pasting error. But retain last sentence?*

⊠⊠⊠

It isn't so much that he started writing this book in order to keep himself from going crazy, which is what AbdulKarim, who smuggles him paper in the Yard, always says. Everybody goes crazy somewhere down the line. Writing a book won't stop that. Writing a book can repay a debt, though. Writing a book can confirm one's guilt.

The dead guy telling this story remembers two human bodies of contrasting sizes, face down on busy Malaika Street. A spreading pool of mingled blood. The sound of an approaching siren. A gun in Thelonius's hand.

Thelonius made a promise, not to Fatima, but to himself. To cut through the bullshit. To plead guilty. The book does that. 'Hi, Becky,' he writes now.

The dead guy telling this story remembers redflowinghaired Becky recruiting him into the Directorate in 1992. Smiling green eyes from behind the barrier of her desk. His certainty that she would soon touch him. That she would take good care of him. That there was no shame in that. That there could be honour in being taken care of, a home in that. Becky came from a long line of caretakers. Her mother, Prudence, had been a caretaker. Prudence's husband had needed taking care of, too, having been raised by alcoholics.

Becky's caring, green eyes smiling at Thelonius. Making everything okay. He only killed people when specifically instructed to do so by the United States of America.

See how the small white milk carton on that breakfast tray is vibrating?

2 In Which Liddell Engages in Fashionable Howling

During the first hour of September 9, 2005, he showered, dressed, ate his breakfast in the middle of the night, gathered his things, stared out the window to make sure his limousine was there, and, after a suitable delay, climbed into the back. He enjoyed making the limousine wait, then making it hurry. He told the driver he preferred to do at least eighty on these predawn jaunts to Logan.

When his plane touched down in the Islamic Republic, nineteen hours later, Wafa A—, a twenty-one-year-old pregnant mother-to-be, had not yet begun her breakfast. Wafa happened to live in a disputed region of the Islamic Republic. She did not have an appetite. She was thinking about her sister Fatima.

Wafa reminded herself that she must call Fatima and congratulate her for being hired as a translator for the Bureau of Islamic Investigation. Wafa sat on a plastic lawn chair in an overgrown green area, at a bone-white plastic table she shared with her husband and mother-in-law, drinking tea with them in the sun, thinking this thought of reaching out to her sister Fatima, of warning her again about the dangers of working with men, when hundreds of tiny metal darts, their points tight and sharp as needles, tore into her flesh and the flesh of her unborn baby.

According to Wafa's husband, the tea drinkers heard a strange collapsing sound. Almost an inhalation.

PLOOF.

Followed by screams. He turned in his chair, intending to see whatever it was that had made the odd noise, but never had the chance. He only heard the sound of metal projectiles finding their way, at high speed, into his body, leaving him in a state of shock.

THWOCK.

There were not enough darts embedded in Wafa's husband's flesh to kill him. Nor was Wafa's mother-in-law hit by enough darts, in the necessary points, to lead to major organ damage or blood loss. Wafa, however, facing that wave head-on, strafed by that barrage of tiny darts, saw herself and her unborn, unnamed daughter shredded.

The miniature metal darts were called flechettes. Flechettes are less than an inch in length, about the size of a finishing nail. Pointed at the front, they carry four fins in the rear, designed to accelerate their speed. To the casual observer, they resemble small sporting darts.

On that warm, pleasant morning in the village of D—, seven thousand five hundred flechettes had been packed into a shell which was fired from a tank rolling behind a stand of trees near Wafa's home. The shell disintegrated in midair with that PLOOF sound, the sound of air sucking into itself.

The shell scattered its darts in a conical pattern over an area about nine hundred feet long and three hundred feet wide. Only about four feet of that three-hundred-foot-wide arc had disrupted the tea drinkers.

Flechettes are designed to maim and kill concealed enemy soldiers: soldiers hiding in dense vegetation, for instance. Flechettes will pierce a pine plank or a thin sheet of steel. Once they reach high velocity, they curve and hook into every available surface, including human flesh. When flechettes reach maximum speed, they travel with such force that sometimes only the fins at the back are left sticking out from walls.

At the moment Wafa and her unborn child were being peppered with flechettes, Thelonius Liddell was not yet ready to deplane. His aircraft was coasting to a stop on a runway no one was supposed to know about. He was reading, scribbling in the margins of a long briefing about his mission in the Islamic Republic. Thelonius, uncertain about this mission and preoccupied with it, read his brief for the third time. He found something in it unpersuasive, and suspected it contained factual errors.

A few miles away, Wafa and her daughter were preoccupied with dying.

As Wafa died, another shell from another tank penetrated the room where laughing Hassan D., aged two and a half, sat with his taciturn eight-year-old brother, whose given name will not be repeated here.

Their father, Atta D., an attentive man, had spotted two American soldiers on a hillside, gathered up both boys, and escorted them inside for safety's sake. When Thelonius Liddell's unnumbered plane touched down on its unnamed runway in support of its classified mission, Atta's boys were preoccupied with learning a new board game. Atta was teaching this game to them when he noticed a large hole in the side of his home.

The shell that made that hole in Atta's home disintegrated and released its own thousands of flechettes, hooking into the toddler, his brother, and his father.

KA-THOK.

Little Hassan, who resembled his late mother, was the closest person to the brand-new hole in the wall. Despite being the smallest one in the room, he accumulated the largest number of flechettes. Hassan, who was Atta's favourite, was preoccupied with dying, too.

Of the three, Atta, the father, took the fewest hooks. None of his flechettes was fatal.

Much later, investigators from the United Nations examined the bloody wall near which Hassan was killed. They noted that it was studded with flechettes, but that there were some blank spots. Some of the investigators conjectured that these blank spots on the wall corresponded to the positions of the two boys as they had crouched on the floor.

The game they had been playing there was called *Sorry!*

Sorry! is an American board game adapted from something Muslims invented and started playing in about the year 1400. *Sorry!* was first sold in 1940 by Parker Brothers, a company based in Salem, Massachusetts.

v. *Sorry!*

And awake. Here, the first of many fatal discrepancies. There are scores, hundreds of examples of Liddell's clinical disregard for plain fact from which to choose, but the one offered here, his embarrassingly verifiable ignorance of the datum that the British version of the board game *Sorry!* was patented in 1929 and marketed in the UK under that title the following year, is worth examining closely. *Sorry!* was first sold, under licence, in the United States in 1934 – *not* 1940, as Liddell claims. On such slips empires fall. The sheer volume of such factual errors in the manuscript, many of which take the form of seditious libel, gives rise to a host of grave security concerns. Note that Liddell used verifiable names for all his main characters, and then, lacking internet access, simply made up whatever information he could not research properly in captivity. I operate under no such constraints. This telling *Sorry!* slip is brought to you by our Wi-Fi-enabled Motel 6, to which we are warming. Here, inexhaustible white stacked sugar packets attempt to atone for the execrable coffee. Clean white sheets, clean white sink, postcard-perfect view of the pool: loving shades of aquamarine and deep blue, colours Mother favored.

At the moment Thelonius's plane landed, sixteen-year-old Islam D., Atta's third son, was walking home from a friend's house. Islam knew the road well and was staring into space, not attending to where he was going. He was preoccupied. Focused as he was on the physical beauty of the female human form, he did not hear the PLOOF or notice any of the nearby tanks.

Islam happened to be standing at the very furthest edge of a vast wave of incoming metal projectiles. At the moment he was struck by his flechette, he was thinking of a pretty girl he liked. That girl was Fatima A——, Wafa's sister, the one who had just gotten that job at the Bureau of Islamic Investigation. She had visited yesterday. Islam had seen her. He had never spoken to her.

Fatima was out of Islam's league and he knew it, but he liked thinking about her just the same. He'd been thinking about her a great deal lately. The very last thought he had before getting hit by his flechette took the form of a question mark and an exclamation point about Fatima.

Islam had posed a question to himself, and answered it for himself, in less than a hundredth of a second. The question concerned the quality and placement of Fatima's hair. Because she wore a headscarf, usually gold, Islam had never seen it. That was the question mark.

vi. Islam

Presumably Islam Deen, eldest son of a known terrorist leader. Liddell's straight-faced claim to have insights into this (dead) young man's amorous longings during his final moments suggest the scale of his, Liddell's, broadening problems with schizophrenia.

Islam imagined Fatima's hair as fine and silky, straight black and very long, extending down to the precise midpoint of her back. He imagined a small mole on the small of Fatima's back, just below the point where her hair stopped. That was the exclamation point. He happened to be right about all of that, which was remarkable.

In Islam's case, there was only one wound. A single flechette struck a vulnerable spot in his neck. He began the process of bleeding out from a tear in his jugular vein, which takes less time than you might think. Within just a couple of minutes, Islam was preoccupied with dying, too.

There was something different about this mission. Something wrong with it. Thelonius couldn't quite put a finger on what it was. He got off his plane.

3 **In Which Liddell Hallucinates**

On the morning of October 14, 2005, Thelonius Liddell, having just returned from the last overseas assignment of his career, noticed that the milk carton on his dining-room table was vibrating.

This was forty-three years, three months, and seven days after Thelonius Liddell was born – thirty-six days after the unpleasantness with the flechettes – and exactly two months before he would be escorted into the Beige Motel.

Thelonius tried not to think about why a gallon of milk would be vibrating all by itself.

Ever since he'd returned from the Islamic Republic the previous day, things had been vibrating inexplicably. In the garage, a clear, tightly capped plastic jug of antifreeze had shaken long after he kicked it away. He saw it waver for ten full seconds, heard it shiver, still half-full and still insistent, from behind a rake that had fallen in front of it. Becky walked right past. Antifreeze is not supposed to vibrate at any time. He took a deep stress breath and walked away.

And a framed photo of Child the Cat. That had been vibrating, too.

Tough it out, kid. Tough it out. Stick with Sarge.

Becky did not need to know about the vibrating. Not yet. He recorded these incidents in a tiny book he might or might not decide to show Becky.

I know something is happening, Thelonius wrote.

vii. *I know something is happening*

A ludicrously inappropriate Bob Dylan reference.

He wrote a sentence with quote marks, *'Where then are you going???'*

He scratched that last sentence out. Then he put the little book in his back pocket.

In the kitchen, Becky could be heard but not seen. She was on the phone, negotiating something complex. Becky was good at negotiating complex things.

⊠⊠⊠

The dead guy telling this story wants you to imagine Fatima's neighbours.

He never met them. He has to imagine them, just like you do. Every day, he writes this book you're reading. Today he wants you to imagine them drinking tea, opening their discussion about how scandalous Fatima did not spend any time grieving her pregnant sister, Wafa.

The two had been quite close, her mother always said, but the women on the block insisted that one would never know that. For the neighbours, Fatima's lack of emotion was troubling, and her lack of propriety more so. She was nineteen, a woman now. Her sister had passed. Her niece had passed. She had obligations to her family. Yet she appeared to live only to mount stairs and close doors. She lived for solitude. Why?

The neighbours had many conjectures. They settled on a theory put forward by Mrs. H., who lived directly across the narrow street from Fatima: She preferred the company of lustful men, conversed with them online for hours at a time. She sat in her room staring at the computer, no doubt typing out and receiving messages from unwholesome fellows.

Her typing was visible from Mrs. H's bedroom window: the distracted girl neglected to close her blinds. The messages themselves were not legible from that distance, but Mrs. H had opinions as to their content. At any rate, no one had seen her weep.

Fatima had always been regarded as unusual. It was not surprising to them that she would avoid doing what a woman should do.

viii. Fatima had always been regarded as unusual.

Now regarded as a captured terrorist and a major operative within Liddell's network in the Islamic Republic. Bitch.

Through my window, I note a family of Brazilians congregating by the swimming pool for what appears to be some sort of musical reunion. Barking orders between verses, feigning unawareness of the late hour, their drunken, overbearing paterfamilias sings badly and too loud, and spouts occasional English profanities. Makes passes at the help. Points to where his daughter must sit.

It is ever thus.

Abominable.

Wait until I get him back. Fucking control freak.

4 **In Which Victory Is Defined**

Thelonius was trying to decide whether he wanted Becky's insights on that rattling milk container, a persistent blur of colour and a wash of sound that was increasing in volume and raising the stakes of his morning, when he saw the word CHANGE writing itself in milk in midair. The word collapsed into a puddle on the dining-room floor. He put down his coffee cup and covered his mouth with his palm.

Whenever something is vibrating, you're supposed to stop and look at it, according to the weirdo back in the Republic: 'Vibration is change.'

ix. the weirdo

Another member of Liddell's cadre. Entered in the prison records as one Abd'al Dayem, 'slave of the eternal'. Codename Raisin. Died December 2005, of lung cancer.

The Plum, for instance, is change.

Complicating everything that follows (the guilty dead guy telling this story acknowledges) is the deepening illness of Thelonius's wife.

Becky has a grey tumour, larger than a plum by now, surely, that the Directorate's physicians isolated. They reported a clear pattern of accelerating growth. This type of tumour mimics schizophrenia with increasing accuracy. It culminates in blindness and, some unknown number of weeks later, death. It is located alarmingly near the centre of Becky's brain. No one can get at the Plum. It has been expanding with dark purpose, they guess, for about five years.

Doctors caught the Plum during an MRI for a nerve problem Becky inherited from her mother, Prudence. This was an entirely separate problem that also required periodic monitoring. As it broadens, that Plum, Becky's behavioural and mood swings become more pronounced. A change.

What to write next.

The guilty dead guy telling this story decides he doesn't feel like writing anything else on this page. He plans to start fresh with a new sheet tomorrow.

X.

Dad opted to make Becky's final years count. Thelonius went along. He justified this silence by thinking, 'We decided not to tell her.' But whenever Thelonius thought 'we' about that kind of thing, he meant Dad.

Thelonius called Becky's father Dad. He could've pushed Dad on certain secrets, could've objected earlier and harder. But Dad always had the final word on secrets.

xi. the final word on secrets

Diagram here of the human heart, wounded.

The dead guy telling this story notes that Dad is dead now. Another change.

'Everything changes,' the Raisin said, 'except the face of God.'

⊠⊠⊠

'Whenever something changes, the first moral and legal imperative is to consider the new development closely; simply look at it without preconception,' Fatima typed in a message box on the website IslamIsPeace.com.

'We must stop and look in order to determine whether that which is new is halal or haram. Not everything new is haram. Not everything familiar is halal.'

xii. halal, haram

One means illegal, the other legal. I forget now.

Ever with the patient and blah, blah, blah. All on your own now, though, aren't you, bitch?

The discussion thread in which she posted was called SORRY, SISTERS. A man had started that discussion thread. Fatima was defending her right, as a Muslim woman, to use the internet to organize public protests, a right some members of the group had questioned.

Fatima reminded herself that Allah was ever with the patient and struck the Enter key.

⊠⊠⊠

Thelonius looked at his hands, so as to avoid looking at the milk carton. Then he didn't want to look at his hands. So he looked at the floor.

Well. Maybe it would stop that shaking. If he just stopped and looked at it. Like what that wacko back in the Republic promised.

No, kid. Eyes front. That's an order. Stick with Sarge.

Well. Suppose he just tried it. Once. To see whether that would do anything to slow down that freakish rattling noise.

No.

Well. He had to do something. The noise hurt his knee now. It was spreading through his body. Why not look? What was the harm in looking?

Just no.

The ache broadened. He grabbed his knee. As he did so, he looked at the milk carton. He didn't know whether he meant to look or not.

The noise stopped. The milk carton calmed itself to stillness.

There, on the panel of the plastic jug facing him: a still colour photograph. It was clear, remarkably high in resolution. It showed his peach-and-black bathrobed wife Becky, in their kitchen.

Becky wearing that robe. Becky in that kitchen. Becky having a conversation on that landline, its actual cord leading to Becky, stretching and bobbing as she spoke. In the photo: Becky's pale, delicate profile and long, bare neck, exposed. Becky's massive wave of deep-red hair, slung motionless over one angled, robed shoulder.

The picture on the carton had to have been taken within the last minute or so. It stopped his breath.

Look away, kid. Machine.

Thelonius did not look away, though. He waited for the photo to vanish, as certain elements of dreams vanish upon inspection. It refused. He felt a dark tightening and buzzing in his chest.

Thud. Then a smaller thud. What the hell?

Of course: the sound of Becky bumping into something, then recovering.

Her field of vision was receding.

When Thelonius looked toward the direction of the noise, he heard the carton begin rattling again. In the kitchen, he saw only that taut, white, trembling phone cord, parallel to the floor. Becky stood, certainly, on the other end of it. She had in fact been wearing that very black-and-peach patterned satin bathrobe, his gift to her on her most recent birthday. Thelonius had seen it flash as she spun past him to answer the kitchen phone. Now he could only hear her.

He looked back at the carton. The shivering stopped.

The photographic image of Becky was so clear, so impossible to refute, that it made his mouth go dry. The plastic jug showed Thelonius his own kitchen in high definition, and Becky's profile playing soft in its shadow against the green, butterfly pattern of the wallpaper, and Becky within it, on the phone, her eyes narrowed in concentration.

'You can count on him,' Thelonius heard his wife say from the next room. 'We all know how much the banquet means.'

Above the photograph was a headline: LOST WOMAN.

xiii. LOST WOMAN

Whatever. These crude personal attacks – many more follow – constitute a special category of strategic misdirection, a tactic in which Liddell specialized. We politely decline the invitation to hurl ourselves down such rabbit holes. Every war is a puzzle, an unbroken code, a kind of chaos waiting to be put in order, and this war more than most. In warfare, my distracted colleagues, victory does not come on the battlefield. Not victory that matters, anyway. Real victory comes to the side that creates and sustains the most persuasive solution to the puzzle. I raise a glass of wine. A toast. To victory.

5 In Which the American Embassy Is Very Nearly Stormed by a Mob of Terrorists and Terrorist Sympathizers

The dead guy writing this story ponders the timeline and concludes that two long, busy days after the passing of her sister Wafa and her unborn, unnamed niece, Fatima attended a big protest at the U.S. Embassy in Islamic City, one she had helped to organize.

Islamic City was, and may still be, the capital of the Islamic Republic.

This protest took shape quickly. It had been arranged in less than forty-eight hours by just under a dozen people. As the crowd gathered, Fatima was veiled and (she hoped) anonymous. She did not want to jeopardize her new job as a translator for the Bureau of Islamic Investigation, also known as the BII.

The Bureau of Islamic Investigation was, and may still be, the national intelligence-gathering apparatus of the Islamic Republic. It was full of spies and military men who lacked basic English skills. Fatima's English was perfect. She and her sister Noura had dual citizenship. They spoke English like Americans because that's what they were: Americans.

Fatima's new boss, who did not speak English, wanted her to help him keep an eye on the Americans. He would probably have put her in prison if he'd known about her work organizing the protest, his own organizing principle being that no one should organize anything he didn't know about.

⊠⊠⊠

In *SERGEANT USA #109, THE HERO THAT WAS* (the dead guy recalls), Sarge takes down the Mutant Machines. The Mutant

Machines are part of an evil plot spun by the enemies of America. Sarge disables all seven by flinging his Expand-A-Shield at them.

PLOOF. THWOCK. KA-THOK.

⊠⊠⊠

Before her promotion to translator, Fatima had been a typist for the BII. With a little help from Ummi, who worked part-time in a fabric shop, Fatima had been (barely) supporting the family for more than a year. She had to work, at least until she got married, and she didn't feel like getting married. She was fine with work. She didn't like Ummi working at all. Ummi's back was giving her trouble.

When Fatima was ten, her Baba – an obstetrician from Massachusetts who prayed all mandatory and optional prayers, who read the Koran aloud every day to his daughters, who told Fatima Paradise lay beneath the feet of her Ummi, who knew Fatima was destined by God to be a good girl and a patient woman and a true believer, and told her so every night – was in a car accident. The accident was serious, and he passed. They set him into his grave, to be questioned by angels there.

A few months after Fatima's Baba died, Ummi returned to the Islamic Republic, dragging her three daughters along with her, saying, 'That's where family is.' Ummi had never liked Massachusetts much. Fatima didn't like the Islamic Republic much.

Fatima withdrew into herself and prayed and read the Koran.

The guilty dead guy telling you this story does that now, too.

In Islamic City, Fatima's schoolyard opponents had called her the Ugly American. This was before she grew into her features. Fatima told her sister Wafa about the insults, and Wafa reminded her that what mattered was not what people called her, but what she answered to. It was something Baba would have said.

xiv. the Ugly American

A grim joke at our nation's expense. But I might add that it's quite correct concerning Fatima's physical appearance.

Baba had also said Fatima should take her time getting married.

In her Koran, Fatima kept a photograph of Baba kissing the top of her little-girl head. After each evening prayer, when she was alone, she took out the photo of that kiss and studied it.

Ummi always said she wanted her girls to get married, just not to Americans. There were a lot of American soldiers since the invasion, but Ummi considered none of them appropriate son-in-law material. These days, her mom had taken to introducing Fatima to total strangers. She brought them right in the house. Fatima waited until her mother left the room on some imaginary errand, then, whispering, threatened to pour boiling water on the man's private area while he slept. This was something she never would have done, but lies in warfare are permitted. The man always left, never to return.

More people now. Fatima prayed no one would die at the demonstration.

⊠⊠⊠

Thelonius, who had only killed people when specifically instructed to do so by the United States of America, sipped his coffee, closed his eyes, took a deep breath, then said to Becky, 'Honey, have you seen Child?'

xv. Child

Meaning the cat. As Mother used to say: Good Gravy. We here encounter one of the subject's favorite themes, betrayal. I am still asked, will apparently always be asked, whether Liddell's US citizenship gave, gives, or ever will give me pause. My concise answer: no. He betrayed our nation, not vice versa. This position's unassailability is detailed in notes xl and xlv, the latter for mature audiences only.

⊠⊠⊠

Within fifteen minutes, the protest Fatima helped organize had drawn about twenty thousand people, double what she had prayed for.

She stood chanting *Allahu Akbar* with everyone else. *Allahu Akbar* is one of those hard-to-translate phrases. You hear people saying it means 'God is great', but that's wrong. In fact, it means, 'God is greater than anything that might have ever happened, or is happening now, or could happen in the future'. That's too long for a translation, though.

Fatima took deep breaths each time she said it, used it to avoid crying tears of rage.

xvi. breaths

She breathes now only sour air, our Fatima.

xvii. tears of rage

The name of a Dylan composition recorded by The Band, based loosely on (I swear) *King Lear*. Relevant because the title inspired 'track twenty-eight', one of John Lennon's endearing experiments in Carrollian wordplay, of which more in due course. Liddell wept to that track.

More noise outside from that damn grey-haired tyrannical Brazilian. I have plugged in the CD player, donned my earbuds, and placed the earphone jack in its little black socket. This jack yields a satisfying click whenever I insert it. A powerful, indescribable sense of being in control of events can occasionally, as now, render even the insertion of a CD unnecessary.

6 **In Which Liddell Provides Inappropriate Biographical Detail**

The dead guy telling this story wants you to know Thelonius was born in 1961 in Los Angeles, California, the only child of a suspicious, hard-working, well-read, bourbon-loving, wife-beating truck driver, George, and a homemaker with low self-esteem, Irene. Back then, you called a homemaker a housewife. They moved to San Francisco. Made a home there. George said he was tired of the road.

By 1966, Thelonius's father, now a suspicious, hard-working alcoholic, had used the savings of five years to buy himself a small bookstore. In which he cut his wife's throat. Thelonius happened to observe that, which wasn't in George's plan.

Thelonius moved in with his grandparents Hal and Louise B. in La Pine, Oregon, right after what his grandparents agreed to refer to as The Accident, when they referred to it at all. Which wasn't often.

He kept asking when he would be able to go home. They always changed the subject. When they did, he read his copy of *SERGEANT USA #109. THE HERO THAT WAS.*

Nine months after Thelonius arrived in Oregon, his father went to prison. Read a lot there, according to the initial, and only, letter. Didn't write back when Thelonius responded to that letter nine times.

In La Pine, Thelonius craved approval, created a series of alarmingly violent hand-drawn comic books, and described himself to teachers and everyone else who would listen as a 'bright, active, and curious child'. Whoever heard that had to agree.

At some point during the confusing years following The Accident, Thelonius established a certainty: the necessity of victory. Everything else became a blur. The more things Thelonius made happen, the dead guy recalls, the more chances there were for winning. Winning mattered.

Two of his teachers, Miss Tokstad (Arts and Crafts) and Mr. Hess (Everything Else) described him as 'extremely competitive'.

He blamed others with a deep ferocity, and was always in a hurry. Preventing him from attaining goals, or being perceived as doing so, was dangerous. He devoured a book on memory techniques, with the aim of always securing the highest grades on tests. Coming in second on an exam produced an unwholesome expression on the boy's face. One recess, during a foot race, he elbowed a much smaller, younger boy, who had scored one hundred on a math test, out of the way, causing a fall that broke the boy's wrist.

Thelonius insisted, with apparent seriousness, that his opponent was an android.

Mr. Hess did not send his star pupil to see the principal – Thelonius had, after all, reported the collision – but he did suspect some kind of problem. Back in the early seventies, students with excellent grades who had extreme competitiveness issues were not referred to psychologists.

Thelonius finished first in that race, got more A's, made more things happen. He refused to wait for anything. He became a bright, active, curious boy scout, then a bright, active, curious class president, then a bright, active, curious high school swimming star.

Thelonius worked out a lot, developed serious upper body strength, made All-Everything, made the Honor Society, and was extremely patriotic. His grandparents told him how proud they were about the way he'd bounced back from The Accident. Thinking his grandson was sleeping, Hal said to Louise late one night that George had no right to see how well his son was doing, that George never inspired anyone, never won anything, and never amounted to anything but a killer.

George died in prison, trying to kill someone who'd threatened him. Thelonius was nineteen when Hal and Louise sat him down to tell him. He went to his room and reread *THE HERO THAT WAS*.

A voice said, *If you kill, make sure you kill for America, kid.*

Thelonius captained the winning swimming team in the 1980

Oregon State High School Championships, a special moment of triumph. It was followed by enrolment in the army in 1982, an even bigger triumph, given Hal's status as an army veteran. That was followed by winning a spot in the Special Forces in 1983: the biggest triumph of Thelonius's young life. That was followed by a vasectomy in 1985 by an army doctor who had been nervous about performing the procedure on a twenty-four-year-old. Thelonius said, 'Just get started.'

xviii. nervous

Needlessly so. A vasectomy is reversible, with some clinics reporting a 97% fertility rate.

Thelonius had almost gotten somebody pregnant. That was not going to happen again.

Two years in Special Forces. Then off to school to study international relations, which the army paid for, because they saw potential in Thelonius. Then more time in school, also paid for by the army. Then, on an application form, a request that he 'briefly summarize' his 'life philosophy', which he shared and, later, framed.

Followed by certain members of the intelligence community seeing potential in Thelonius, like the army had.

And falling in love with Becky.

Followed by his entry into the exciting world of espionage. Followed by a fast track at the Directorate, which he loved. Followed by various hush-hush assignments.

Followed, in 2005, by the mess he ran into in the Islamic Republic, which got complicated both for himself and for Child the cat, a mixed-breed whose uncertain parentage Becky could never excuse.

Followed by his murder during an interrogation session in (he predicts) the early summer of 2006.

xix. early summer of 2006

A sober mystery yet to be unravelled, and certainly beyond the realm of the civilian justice system. It pains me to be forced to reiterate that everything – absolutely everything – I did while interrogating T had ample operational precedent.

7 In Which the Reader Is Assumed to Have Access to a Track List

The grey-suited man with grey hair, reduced to shouting from the hood of a black Lincoln Continental and clearly not used to this kind of duty, was a friend of Thelonius Liddell's.

He flicked off the bullhorn by accident, then flicked it back on. It popped, too loud, as it reawakened. The embassy, he informed everyone, had investigated the incident with the flechettes. It had been a tragic accident. People should return to their homes.

Sorry!

No one returned home.

The crowd had grown to thirty thousand now. It surged with firm, unintelligible purpose against three of the four massive iron gates that surrounded the embassy compound. No one paid attention to the man in grey. They all kept chanting *Allahu Akbar*.

The earnest man on the Lincoln, having reached the limit of his effectiveness, asked if there was anyone in the crowd who could translate for him so that he could do a better job of clarifying the situation. Fatima did not even think about raising her hand.

She found herself in a corner, pushed by the throng's ceaseless, expanding geometry into an obscure convergence of two angles of the embassy gate. There were many such nooks surrounding the embassy. This particular nook had a locked service entry. It barricaded a dumpster.

A heavyset woman next to Fatima jabbed her in the side.

xx. A heavyset woman

Ringo Starr appears dancing with such a woman on the *White Album*'s photo-illustrated lyric sheet. *Provide* White Album *track sequence here for ease of reference in later chapters? (No, don't think so, too much information, but see if this omission still makes sense on next pass.)*

8 **In Which Liddell Abuses Certain Confidences**

Fatima assumed at first that the jab in her side was just an over-energetic spike in the chaotic, respectful movement of the huge crowd, but when the heavyset woman elbowed her a second, and then a third time, Fatima turned and glared. The woman's eyebrows arched upward in alarm, and she pointed toward a segment of the immaculately manicured embassy lawn before them.

Adjacent to that lawn was a small rectangle of concrete, right behind the dumpster: a flat place that looked like a loading area. The rectangle was cut off from the view of the rest of the crowd. There, a few feet away from them on the rectangle of cement, a U.S. marine, his back to Fatima, stood above a large, open Koran.

He was urinating on it.

xxi. urinating

That cat pissed all over the house whenever Liddell was on assignment. And left great tufts of fur about.

⊠⊠⊠

No answer from Becky. The milk carton was still, but it bore her picture.

Thelonius and Becky had been married since 1993, which was twelve years now. In all of that time, Thelonius had refused to have a baby with her, his reasons not always open for discussion. She had certainly worked them all out for herself by now. Both Becky and Thelonius, of course, had lost their mothers at a young age.

'I don't understand why you're so worried about repeating your father's mistakes,' Becky had said on their honeymoon, her smile wide. 'Just don't make *my* father's mistakes. Don't disrespect me.

Don't betray me. Don't micromanage me. Don't screw the help. Or I'll kill you.'

They laughed at that, raised their glasses of red wine, clinked them, drank to his promise, laughed at Dad, and (Thelonius having sworn credibly enough that he had no intention of screwing the help) made love.

Becky talked a lot during sex, something Thelonius didn't and couldn't do. She even told fitful, whispered stories that focused him while he was inside her. She was all about stage management, all words and knees and words and elbows and words and green eyes to die for. He did what she told him to do. Why not? She made him feel, for a moment at least, like he was home.

⊠⊠⊠

The whirring blades of a helicopter sent to monitor the crowd drowned out what would have been the splash of a stream of urine hitting the Koran's open pages.

When he finished, the marine rearranged himself, picked the Koran up by a dry corner, heaved it into the dumpster, and stalked away in an arrogant, loose-limbed manner that made Fatima's flesh crawl. He had kept his back to them the whole time. Neither Fatima nor the heavyset woman could have accurately described his face.

Fatima fought a powerful urge to flee. Given the crowd, she could not have run away, even if she'd allowed herself to try. She stood her ground.

Perhaps she was brave. Or perhaps the moment was structured in such a way as to instil courage.

xxii. courage

These hagiographic passages make me physically ill. An airplane roars overhead, and into my temple, presaging synchronistically the all-important note xl. A need for a lie down.

Naked Becky held Thelonius in her arms in 1993 and said, 'Big boys don't cry.'

It was a night of stars, counted through a big window overlooking a broad, unnameable Massachusetts lake happy to reflect starlight. Becky, whose mother had read her Shakespeare, pointed out the constellations she knew, of which there were many: the lesser lights, the greater ones, and even her slim hand, the same shade of even flame as the moon. She counted that as a constellation, too. The night was luminous. She was luminous. Her story of Prospero. Her kiss on his forehead. Her love.

'We won't be talking about this again. Time goes in one direction. Do you hear?'

He nodded.

'Say it out loud, Thelonius. Time goes in one direction.'

'Time,' Thelonius said, 'goes in one direction.'

He closed his eyes and tried to believe it. His face was still wet all over. In La Pine, Oregon, his grandmother Louise wiped his face, told him that his mother had loved him very much. Told him he would be fine. The boy was not so sure. He had begun to have flashbacks, found himself, without warning, watching his father cut his mother. He was terrified he would have one at school.

'Say it out loud, Thelonius,' his grandmother Louise said. 'Everything is going to be all right.'

'Everything,' Thelonius said, 'is going to be all right.'

Haste and hard work, he found, stopped the flashbacks.

The era of Just Getting Started had begun.

⊠⊠⊠

In the late spring of 2000, Thelonius, sleeping poorly, exhausted with Becky's lectures on the subject of parenthood, Just Got Started. He brought a little charcoal fluffball of a kitten to their ample Salem foursquare. He unboxed him in the living room for Becky's inspection, announcing him, mock-pretentiously, as Child.

Becky refused to call him that at first, but everything she proposed over the next week or so – Marx, Stalin, Castro, Lenin, Lennon

– brought unacceptable cultural and geopolitical baggage that Thelonius rejected as unsuited to the animal's genial, baffled personality.
So he remained Child.

xxiii. unacceptable cultural and geopolitical baggage

And back. How much the traitor Liddell papers over with these five words! He was, of course,
a serious Fab Four devotee before the virus overcame him, however much he may attempt to
conceal the fact here.

Child, Becky said, played into Thelonius's 'deep need to be responded to'. Child saw things that were not there and expressed
his concerns about them until Thelonius stroked his furry back to
calm him. Then he purred in gratitude. Child noticed when Thelonius was not around, and, more often than not, went to whatever
room Thelonius occupied. Child became skittish and anxious whenever Thelonius went off on assignment, relaxed again when he came
home. Child was family.

xxiv. not around

I myself have been forced to take an extended leave of absence from the Directorate. Sitting in my
nowhere land, waiting for absolution, I note that Thelonius here describes behaviour he admits to
not having observed.

xxv. Child was family.

Nonsense.

At the time Child died, Thelonius and Becky had not made love
for a long time, but it was best (he decided, sitting there at the kitch-
en table) not to think about things like that. Time might collapse
on him.

9 **In Which Liddell Turns Down the Chance of a Lifetime**

Fatima, who had never met the heavyset woman, suggested it might be best to leave unspoken what they had both seen behind the dumpster. She appealed to her as a sister in Islam, said life was complicated enough at the moment. The heavyset woman didn't respond. Instead, she scowled, averted her gaze, edged away from Fatima, and melted into the crowd.

---

xxvi. what they had both seen

Claimed to have seen, rather. No hard evidence ties anyone in American uniform to this incident. Room service – actually Clive, the vacuous middle-aged front-desk clerk who appears to live onsite – has knocked. He bears pizza. Waits a moment when instructed, as now. He will, I hope, do something about that cadre of noisy Brazilians. Their elderly leader, not content with having re-infested the pool area, has just cranked up another infernal macarena. *Check carefully and delete all refs to Brazilians etc. on final pass through manuscript.*

⊠⊠⊠

For the sake of compromise, for the good of the marriage, Becky made a point of noting, once a month or so, that she had gone along with Thelonius's gag name of Child – 'but only as a reminder,' she insisted, 'that the subject is not closed.' Five years later, Thelonius asked his unseen wife: 'Becky. Where is the cat?'

The sound of Becky taking a deep breath. The sound of Becky saying 'Goodbye'. A flash of peach and black. The sound of the phone being dropped on the cradle. The sound of a familiar argument that had not yet started.

Then from the next room: 'You'll be making a speech at the Freedom Banquet, T.'

'The Freedom Banquet. I'd forgotten. Who's setting that up?'

'Dick Unferth,' Becky's voice answered. 'Your new boss.'

Thelonius felt cold rain, pinpricked with hail, piercing his veins.

'According to Dick, whom we now *trust*, T, that heroic return from the Islamic Republic won us the keynote slot. Keynote! Oh, don't wince. I mean, you are *home*, aren't you? You are still *alive*, aren't you? You are *proof of concept*, right? Keynote means we are top of the heap. Dad or no Dad. It means we get a strategic vision theme, if we want it. Which we do. We get all the big themes we want from now on: freedom, courage, respect, democracy and so forth. Justice, your favourite. If we want that. Also sacrifice; can't forget sacrifice. Whatever we want. Quite a coup, T. Oh: you'll love this. Your pal, Carl Arnette? The dispenser of all the good gossip? The Directorate's embodiment of neutral Switzerland? The one who claims he has no ambitions? Turns out he coveted, and I mean *coveted* coveted, a slot at the Freedom Banquet. Tried to persuade Dick to let him speak right before you. Wanted Dick to give him the First and Fourth Amendments, their ongoing relevance to the mission. Good Gravy. *That* came under serious consideration for about ten seconds. We can go anywhere we want now. Anywhere. *Anywhere.* If we follow the script, and follow the Law of Appearances. So much for us to work toward, you know. If we just work together. Say something, for Christ's sake, T.'

The Law of Appearances.

Becky's latest obsession held that, to the degree you managed people's perceptions, you managed reality. Control the message. Unferth stuff. She had been on this for weeks before he left for the Republic. He had been hoping it would have worn off by now. The ice in Thelonius's veins ran colder, sharper.

'I suppose I constitute some kind of internal trophy now.'

She still had not made her way into the room. Her shadow rearranged its hair.

'Oh, stop. You aren't really serious about making difficulties. You aren't going off the reservation *now*. I know you aren't. Consider the possibilities. There are some big victories in store for us, some wonderful things, wonderful, if we market ourselves properly. Some respect. If we control the variables. Even heroes have to follow the rules, T, once they get home.'

Market ourselves. Control the variables. Follow the rules.

Icy rain outside, too.

'What about Carl? He was held hostage, back in '94, you know. Why shouldn't he say a few words?'

He already knew the answer. Too pre 9/11.

After the deluge of words, another drought. That disapproving silence of hers, designed to intimidate: there was an art to avoiding it. Like sidestepping her occasional ethnic jokes. You just change the subject the instant you see it coming.

xxvii. deluge of words

Clive wonders: What's on all those index cards? How in the world did I learn to write so neat and so small? What am I so busy typing all the time? Offers unrequested details of his failed marriage to Twyla Jean, or Tammy Lynne, or Tina Mae, or whatever her utterly inconsequential name is. Then, after I give an imitation of condolence sufficient to generate another of his long-suffering smiles, he predicts that I will be wanting to rest, asks if I need anything (I don't), and skitters away on a repair errand of some kind.

'By the way,' Thelonius said, 'I couldn't find Child this morning.'

Becky stepped into the dining room.

Having shaken the phone's vague imprint from her hair, having made it symmetrical again for him, she opened the blinds. She settled into her customary chair, opened the most recent Sunday *New York Times Magazine*, shielded the bottom of her face with it and flashed her green eyes across the top.

'You couldn't find Child,' Becky said, 'because I drove him to the pound last week while you were still in the Republic.'

Thelonius's abdomen tightened. The milk carton trembled.

'That animal no longer made sense here, T. Too many scratches. Too much shedded hair in too many corners. And the litter box. You gone. Who knew how long. Some decisions make themselves. Why are you staring at that?'

The back of Thelonius's milk carton rattled to a halt. It showed him a colour image of Child, terrified, backed into a bleak cage, eyes wide after having seen too much, his great tufts of dark fur matted with blood and urine. The caption above the photo read: LOST CHILD.

Thelonius backhanded the carton, watched milk spray in a dense arc across the dining room, barely missing Becky. She frowned at him.

'That was not closed,' Becky said, calm but firm. 'Deep breaths, T, from the diaphragm.'

xxviii. not closed

The subject is not closed, not by a very long shot indeed. During the riotous summer of 1968, as the masterpiece now known as *The White Album* evolved in-studio, conflagrations in Poland, Hungary, Romania and, yes, even our own American college campuses coalesced into a single crisis. This metacrisis underlined the deep divide between Western values and those of the Other Side. We face a graver, more lethal metacrisis today, one playing out on a far larger global stage, encompassing an exponentially greater universe of conflagrations. Yet some in our Directorate dare not call this metacrisis by its true name. My own case (fortuitously, I believe) requires a clear understanding of the true nature of this Great Challenge, dark older sibling to the Communist menace! This commentary, at least, calls it out explicitly and without apology: The Islamic Threat. Referring to it as 'post-war' misses the point. It has always been *the* war. It is not at all new. It has plagued us for fourteen centuries.

My friends, my colleagues, my peers, I ask you: After all I have sacrificed for this nation, all the dark trails I pursued, all the evildoers I identified, interrogated, and neutralized, do I deserve her fate? Is that to be the precedent? Can our nation afford that? Before you answer, consider: I have uncovered, thanks to patient, persistent and unyielding evaluation of the evidence, invaluable new intel on the 9/11 attacks, outlined for the first time by any analyst, anywhere, in my note xlv, below.

But to the point. Of course, the reference to respiration here ('Deep breaths') is contextually appropriate, but it may also be intended to alert members of Thelonius's terrorist cell to the importance of performing certain bizarre Islamic breathing rituals strongly associated with suicide attacks. Note Liddell's equally bizarre insistence in the next chapter that a puddle of milk is breathing!

This passage foreshadows the critical 'let it in and let it out' passage of *Jihadi*, which presents (see note xxx) a synchronistic rephrasing of a key lyric from the Fab Four's biggest global hit single, released during the fateful late summer of 1968. See, see and see again note xl.

Thelonius obeyed. He had been trained, in moments of crisis, to do what he was told.

The guilty dead guy writing this, recalling his countless misplaced obediences, spots a big expanse of nothing below his scribbled words, finds this nothing preferable, reaches for a new sheet of paper.

10 In Which Liddell Falls Prey to a Characteristic Fit of Blind Rage

A convoy of tanks approached, each equipped with water cannons. Fatima took a deep breath and found cover behind a van. She drew herself into a ball.

In the end, the van did little to protect her from the jets of water, but it did separate her decisively from a photographer she had noticed. She had no desire to show up on the front page of the newspaper the next morning. The tanks dispersed the crowd, pummelling protesters with high-velocity torrents. Order vanished. A cascade of water, stray garments, and lost objects overtook the street. The tanks belonged to the Islamic Republic. The Americans paid for them, though.

People scattered like leaves. Everyone began to head home. The tanks withdrew. When the street was empty enough, Fatima emerged from behind the van.

The next morning's papers explained that the Americans had apologized for the flechettes. The problem was an error in intelligence. Their troops had believed they were firing those flechettes at insurgents. The story in the paper explained how sorry the Americans were for being wrong about that. Fatima scanned the paper for another news item, but did not find it. She breathed deep and gave thanks to the Creator. It seemed no one besides Fatima and the heavyset woman – whose name Fatima never got – had seen the marine do what he did. An end to it, then.

xxix. end to it

It will not end here in the desert, I can promise that much.

⊠⊠⊠

'Blind rage?'

Thelonius, standing, staring at his wife's feet, nodded twice, fast. He breathed in just as deeply as he could breathe. Stress response CONSCIOUS. Stress response CONSCIOUS. Becky straightened in her seat, uncrossed her slim, white ankles, just visible below their curtain of peach-and-black satin, and dropped the *New York Times Magazine*, which landed on the floor with a light slap. She was scanning him, making sure there was movement in the midsection beneath his grey T-shirt and jeans: the diaphragm rising and falling, from long practice. Thelonius refused to meet her eye, but he was breathing deeply, sending her a sign of his intent to cope. Stress response CONSCIOUS. Let the breath in and let the breath out. Thelonius closed his eyes, saw his father holding a bloody knife.

---

xxx. Let the breath in and let the breath out.

A message of encouragement from four friends. See notes xxviii and xl.

---

xxxi. his father

A pompous windbag, from all I could ever gather. Interviews with him would have yielded nothing actionable. Died in prison 1980.

A volcano rumbled.

He shook himself, opened his eyes, meant to walk toward her.

She's a machine, kid. Take her out.

But his knee flinched, and wouldn't take the weight.

That damned limp. He sat again.

Stress breath CONSCIOUS.

Look at the puddle breathing on the floor.

11 In Which Liddell Continues a Pattern of Deliberate Obfuscation

The dead guy telling this story has decided not to give titles to these chapters.

That will be Becky's job, he predicts – aware, as he is, that each of those blanks at the beginning of a chapter will leave an opening, a gap of intention, and counting on Becky, as he does now, to fill those gaps. She fills in all the blanks as she sees fit now. And she leaves blank whatever she concludes does not or should not exist.

The dead guy telling this story wants to make sure Becky knows why he is writing this in the way he is: illuminating people and events and thoughts by impersonating them, experiencing them, thinking them through, creating and recreating them as necessary. Lying. Referring to himself in the third person, even though he's right here. Or, from time to time, in the second.

Because:

When she first took you into her arms, one of the things she did for you was lie to you and tell you stories. You knew they were lies, the things she told you to get you out of your funks, but you let her tell them anyway. She made you feel better that way. Made you feel that there could be a home for you.

She took care of you.

She made you feel whole for a while. You thought she made you survive. Here in the Beige Motel, you decided, it was the stories that did that. So you concluded you would take yourself into your own arms and tell yourself your own lies. Live your own stories, on paper. And maybe, just maybe, use those stories to resolve your own debts.

THWOCK. PLOOF. KA-THOK.

This page is full now. Maybe you wrote those sound effects too big. On to the next.

Sometimes when you stare at a new, empty rectangle of paper you see yourself entering the gold dawn of the high-mounted window in the Yard.

Sometimes, when you are writing, you find yourself floating there. Sometimes you feel like you are on your way home.

⊠⊠⊠

Fatima wore a gold headscarf her first day on the job. Her new boss subjected her to an hour-long 'orientation session'. A short, plump, mustachioed, disagreeable-looking fellow, he went by the name of Murad Murad. Thanks to family connections, he had obtained a rumpled military uniform he had no right to wear, and whenever he made the 'I'm important' face this attire seemed to him to demand, he looked as though he had just eaten something indigestible. He told Fatima she was to think of him from this point forward as her father. She spent much of her first day trying not to.

After Murad Murad had led her one-on-one 'orientation session' – sixty-four minutes of telling Fatima how to find people she already knew how to find, how to turn on a computer she already knew how to turn on – he circled past her cubicle every forty minutes or so to ask how she was settling in.

She told him she was settling in fine.

⊠⊠⊠

Becky had earned her Master's degree in psychology at the age of nineteen.

She considered that the least of her achievements, though. She took greatest pride in her status as the youngest credentialed psychologist ever to be employed by the Directorate. This came about, in part, because of her insistence on prominence in any arena in which she competed, a trait she shared with Thelonius. As she admitted to anyone who asked, the distinctions she earned also had a great deal to do with family connections. Her family tree, she liked to boast, had 'deep and twisted roots'.

The Sharps, her mother's family, had been wealthy segregationists on one side and founding John Birchers on the other. The Firestones, on the other hand, had been academics and diplomats and spies and heavy drinkers, sometimes all in one person.

At her father's personal request, and such requests from Dad were in fact orders, Becky manned, against her will, the Career Day table for the Directorate at Mt. Sinai University. She had told her father on several occasions, as Career Day approached, that she considered such an assignment beneath her.

'That,' said Dad, 'is the problem.'

Becky arrived early, fulfilling her father's request (read: order) on a grey, snowy April morning in 1992. That was how she met Thelonius, who was studying international relations at Mt. Sinai. The shivering and sole Directorate representative at a recruitment table she knew herself to be surrealistically overqualified to occupy, she spotted him eyeing her, then pretending to inspect a brochure. He left the table, skittish for some reason. He pushed his way through the big glass door. She got up and followed him out, onto a little terrace, where the flurries had picked up a dense, abrupt momentum. She recruited Thelonius in a blizzard she had no business being out in.

'I'm Becky Firestone. And you are?'

A Green Beret in a hurry, working on his Master's degree in international relations. Eyes that drilled through you. Family problems he didn't feel like discussing, beyond mentioning that his mother had died early. (Hers had, too, but she opted to say nothing of that today.) Tough. Intense. Disciplined. Loved George Bush, the first George Bush, and all he stood for, loved how he had brought the wall down, loved what he had done in Iraq. Hated Communists with a passion. Hated Saddam with a passion. Hated many things with a passion.

They came back indoors and brushed off the snow, careful not to touch each other yet. Becky resumed her spot at the table.

He filled out the form.

Thelonius watched her read his life philosophy over a second time, laugh a second time, look him in the eye.

Becky told him she thought he might like intelligence work. Even in that moment, and for reasons that he would not understand for years to come, part of Thelonius had been tempted to find some way to tell her directly, then and there, that he was not a normal person. That he had every reason to believe he was a difficult man on a difficult trajectory, a glide path that could only disrupt, in painful ways, the orbits it happened to intersect. But she held his gaze and said, right out loud:

'I'm here to help.'

So he said nothing, in those earliest days, about his being difficult, guided by the twin theories that she had somehow already figured it out – which she had – and that she must surely have known what she was doing.

'Makes a person think about things like destiny,' she said from behind the desk, still fixing him with those wide, green eyes.

xxxii. destiny

Who can recall the details of such ancient discussions? Pointless anyway. We create our own fate.

'What does?'

'Your philosophy. The eating thing.' She arched an eyebrow, as though she wanted him to repeat some part of it out loud.

He looked away.

'Simple,' she said, the echoes of a faint smile shading her voice. The voice went higher when she was interested in you. 'Maybe a little rude and obvious. Some people are afraid of that. Not me. I believe America's great moments have always come when we offered simple solutions and then delivered them. That's our destiny in this country. Simplicity. That's why Communism fell, you know. Simple ideas we proposed and then stuck to. Lines we drew and then defended. No delays, no concessions, no procrastination. It will be you next time. Defending us. I can tell. Making that kind of contribution. Drawing that kind of line. It's *meant* to be you.'

Her certainty caught him by surprise. He checked again: the green eyes were still trained on him. He was supposed to say something, but nothing came.

'You want to know why we won the Cold War?'

'Sure,' Thelonius said.

'Because our system is better. Fairer. Theirs was neither just nor perceived as just. That's why it collapsed. That's why we buried them. That's why the next century is going to be the American century. Because perceptions of justice always depend on big, shared ideas that everyone can eventually come to accept as foundational for both themselves and the community. Like enterprise and personal initiative. As you suggest.'

He nodded as though he understood.

'Personally, I think Washington is a swamp,' she said, 'and Langley, too, and yes, I do feel sorry for anyone who has to clear that swamp. You mention Bush. Bush is a good man, maybe a great man, but I do hope the swamp doesn't drag him and his family down. Langley eats people, you know. It eats them alive.'

'I've heard that, yes.'

'But maybe it's worth it – if you are *meant* to make a contribution, that is. For the country, I mean. Bush, by the way, will be re-elected. That's meant to be, too.'

'How do you know so much about what's meant to be?'

'It's our job,' she said, 'to know what happens next.'

He rushed things. She slept with him quite early on, and against her better judgement, she said, but only after assuring him that the next person she went to bed with would, according to her own personal sense of destiny, become her husband. He nodded. But he was not sure what it meant to agree to such a thing.

Nowadays, Becky does not believe in destiny.

⊠⊠⊠

All the years they were together, Becky never formally diagnosed Thelonius – no one ever did – and she never wrote any prescriptions for him, either. But she had fallen in love with him during Career Day. That was the problem.

As a result, she pulled strings for him within the Company, got him on the fast track he craved, helped him to talk things through, usually in bed. She pointed him toward the right articles in the right journals. She also begged him to get therapy, and his stubborn refusal to do so drew her closer to him. She knew he needed help. Needed taking care of.

⊠⊠⊠

Nine months into the relationship, six months into his career at the Directorate, he went silent for three brutal days of what was supposed to be their vacation, refusing to speak to her, or look at her, or touch her, sleeping in a separate room of the cottage they'd rented on the Cape. He locked her out of his room and played her mix tapes at top volume.

When he finally emerged, on the morning of the fourth day, he begged her to forgive him for the terrible things he'd said behind the door. She hadn't heard any of them, whatever they were, and she wondered whether he had said anything terrible at all. Regardless, he obviously regretted *something*. So she forgave him.

She was always forgiving Thelonius.

xxxiii. always forgiving

Given the element of surprise, I can kill a man with my right thumb. Where the hell is Clive with my dinner?

⊠⊠⊠

The little man seemed to believe Fatima incapable of error. He pronounced her first day excellent, mentioning the excellence of her first day at several points during his five-thirty wrap-up meeting with all his subordinates.

At this meeting, people were supposed to review what they had accomplished over the course of the day. Fatima's work had involved listening to recordings of conversations that American military and intelligence officials believed to be private, but weren't. She took typed notes summarizing these conversations, then forwarded the notes to Murad Murad for review. As instructed, she was careful to transcribe with total accuracy any details identifying individuals operating within the American network of informants.

xxxiv. believed to be private, but weren't

I dedicate this note to those – there are some – who doubt my objectivity in analyzing the more sensational aspects of this case. For their benefit, and for our nation's, I here openly acknowledge that not every line penned in Liddell's cell is demonstrably lethal to the security interests of this country. I know for a fact, for instance, that this alarming passage of *Jihadi* has already led to a top-to-bottom review of security protocols within the Islamic Republic and elsewhere. We may thus credit Thelonius, at least in part, with the (wholly unintentional) identification of hundreds of listening devices in dozens of outposts, with a complete overhaul of our security procedures there, and with the formal, confirmed, post-mortem identification of at least one mole under the simultaneous employ of the BII, ourselves, and Al Qaeda. That this identification took place after the mole's destruction of both himself and much of our embassy is of course regrettable, and I will let the chorus of my detractors complete the lyrics of the rest of that forgettable little 45, which they are sure to do anyway. I have another album I would much rather listen to. It gleams in the player like the holy thing it is.

That was not what Murad Murad wanted to discuss, though.

Murad Murad complimented Fatima's typing skills. He noted that her speed and accuracy were the result of her good posture while seated, which he felt was almost as remarkable as her posture while standing. Fatima was the only female in the department, which employed a total of eighteen people. She didn't see what her posture had to do with anything, but she kept that to herself. She sighed in relief, too audibly perhaps, when six o'clock came.

It was an accomplishment to exit that huge grey monstrosity of a building.

As she was walking home – she, her mother, and her sister lived a quarter of an hour's brisk walk away – Fatima heard a woman's unfamiliar voice. It said, from right behind her and in the native tongue, 'Follow me, please. We are expected.'

She didn't turn to see who it was. That would show weakness. Weakness acknowledged the importance of all interruptions. Let whoever was speaking say whatever needed to be said again.

xxxv. interruptions

That dreary Brazilian Polonius-by-the-Pool: interruption personified. Cigar. Alone. Singing. If one can call it that. Will no other guest complain? His penchant for archaic sub-disco irritates you. I can tell by your sudden kicking. My internet is out yet again. Damn Clive. Damn this place.

12 In Which the White Album Cues Itself Up

Perhaps it would be better (Thelonius suggested to Becky after they had made love in the little cottage) if they spent some time apart.

That (Becky pointed out) could create more problems than it solved.

A week later, they were married. Thelonius was never quite sure how it happened. The guilty dead guy he became reconstructs one possible scenario below.

Becky was all about solving problems. She fell in love with him knowing love was a potentially serious career mistake, knowing that, having recruited him and concealed his problems, she was, technically at least, putting herself at risk of a five-to-ten-year term in a federal penitentiary. But all that penitentiary business was only if anything ever went wrong, so really, what was quite important was that nothing go wrong, and perhaps they were stuck with each other already. Perhaps marriage really was the best option, in terms of both love and damage control, so they agreed nothing would go wrong. Remarkably, nothing did, for the longest time.

In 2005, though, in Salem, at Thelonius's dining-room table, Sergeant USA said:

Kid. She's not a woman. She's an android. Cut her head off. You'll see.

And the trouble was, he really felt like listening to that voice.

'Keep looking at my feet, T, and keep breathing from your diaphragm.'

He did. Puddles of milk near her feet breathed, too.

'Tell me who I am, T.'

She stood, slid off the peach-and-black bathrobe and let it fall to the hardwood floor.

The feet disappeared. Two gentle steps and they returned, with the graceful long Toes. He always capitalized them in correspondence to her. He shut his eyes now. She was standing nude for him, her first-line prescription for calm during periods of black rage. It had worked many times. But he could not bring himself to look at her, not with that cat crated somewhere, writhing in its own filth.

'Who am I?' she demanded again, in the familiar, insistent tone, concerned for him and for the world. 'Am I a machine or am I a woman?'

Machine, kid.

---

xxxvi. *Machine, kid.*

I am not yet convinced that T actually had this specific, pseudopropagandistic hallucination. It seems unthinkable that he could have concealed such aberrations from me. That portable silver boom box emits its squalid poolside dance music. It squawks and bleats far too loud for safety. It affects you. It *affects* you. Unendurable. Gloves on.

He was afraid to look away from the white puddle.

'I don't want to answer that question,' Thelonius hissed, his eyes tight, his words black with sarcasm. 'Put that robe back on. Hurry.'

'Okay, T.'

She did.

Sergeant USA, unseen, said *Machine. Machine. Machine.*

Have to get out now.

'Okay. Robe on, T. Keep breathing.'

He opened his eyes, looked for hers, found them.

Machine. Take it out of operation.

Get Child back. Don't lose the thread again.

He stood, stepped forward, came to terms with the angry wave that overtook his left knee (the room faded a bit with it), limped toward the kitchen door despite that long ache, grabbed the keys. Grey skies, but at least the cold rain had cleared. The leg got better if you moved it.

Just Get Started.

⊠⊠⊠

'I repeat: The imam wishes to speak with both of us. He wishes to discuss what we saw at the embassy. He is waiting for us at his home.'

Fatima refused to stop walking, refused to turn toward the source of the words, spoken far louder than necessary. The familiar figure caught her up, stepped in front of her.

'Now.'

It was, as she had already concluded, the heavyset woman. She had a harsh voice, piercing: a voice perfect, Fatima thought, for calling out orders at a busy restaurant, or shouting the names of errant schoolchildren in a playground. The voice of someone who needs to be recognized as the most important participant in any conversation she chooses to enter. A voice one wishes immediately, upon first hearing, that one had not heard.

⊠⊠⊠

Thelonius gunned the minivan to life, hit the accelerator with his good leg, ground the gravel of his driveway, spun his way onto Essex, and watched as the first of twenty-one intersections between his mailbox and the Salem Abandoned Animals Facility got out of his way. The faster the car went, the more stable time became and the further away the insistent voice of Sergeant USA.

There were two problems.

The first problem was Becky's clinical inability to shut up about the whole baby thing. He had made clear from the get-go that this point would be a deal breaker in the relationship, but she had conveniently forgotten that discussion.

xxxvii. the whole baby thing

Poolside noise problem solved. Gloves off now.

Pulled the curtains. You are safe and undisturbed. A fitting moment to address the 'whole baby thing'. An eventual reversal of Thelonius's vasectomy was implied in our marriage vows, which I shall not embarrass my readers by reproducing here. His lack of personal initiative on this subject demands close examination, as it illuminates many of the deeper strategic issues of the case. By the time he converted to Islam, Liddell had forgotten — though I swear he knew, he knew, he knew when we married! – that American citizenship carries with it both rights and responsibilities. I submit here that defaulting on the responsibilities of citizenship revokes the rights of citizenship. Despite the claims of the religionists, history has identified a citizen's chief responsibility to this country. It is the great personal obligation of the pioneers, the astronauts, the entrepreneurs, the spies who built America: self-reliance in all circumstances. Self-reliance (that which Islam rejects, that in which track one instructs us so eloquently) trumps destiny.

Absolutely famished. Civilian casualties and occasional cases of mistaken identity regrettable, inevitable, always part of warfare, etc. Never eliminate, only minimize. Like fighting traffic accidents. Those saved never aware. Come back and fill this in.

Becky forgot most discussions in which she disagreed with Thelonius and didn't get her way. The more intense the conversation, the more likely she was to forget he had won the argument. Well, that stopped now.

So: This was something she felt strongly about. Fine. So: There were biological components to this. Fine. The cat could have served as a kind of constructive distraction for her. A perfectly legitimate channel for those parental feelings. They both had them. So why not express them? Pet the damn cat. And by the way, he had absolutely no doubt that Becky did have maternal feelings for Child. She fought them, was all. Why? Because she could not stand losing an argument. Guess what? This one she was losing. Whether she knew it or not. No baby.

He had never promised this. Ever. But she pretended he had. Witness the minivan he was driving at this very moment. Becky had planned all the discussion points ahead of time, come into battle armed with fifteen different printouts from fifteen different consumer sites. Air bags, via *Consumer Reports*. Fuel economy, via *Auto World*. Retention of value, via some incomprehensible actuarial thing she had tracked down, printed out, and highlighted with two green, perfectly executed horizontal stripes. And an annotation, in her loose, unruly scrawl near 'toddler seat restraint':

Relevant to whatever we eventually do decide to pursue with our family.

What was that supposed to mean? What the hell did they even need a minivan for? Whatever there was to 'pursue with our family', here they were, already pursuing it. They had groceries delivered to the house. She avoided any and all Ryan Firestone gatherings. Guess what? There were two people in this family. Two. The Siena seated eight.

What was this green monstrosity he was driving if not a daily message from her to him: 'I want a baby in a car seat to buckle into this vehicle'?

Guess what. No.

If anyone knew about him, she did. So she *knew* this. Going *in*. If he felt in his gut that he was not suited to win at something, then it just didn't make any sense for him to commit to it. How many dozens of times had he told her: Not A Dad, Okay? The subject was closed.

Thelonius punched it, and made the light.

Leave aside his short fuse and his tiny attention span and his impatience with people not knowing how he operated. Leave all that aside. Assume him to be a perfectly well-intentioned father, with something resembling the toolbox necessary to do that job. There was still the Plum to be considered. The kid had a thirteen percent chance of inheriting The Condition. But she couldn't be told that. On Dad's orders.

---

xxxviii. The Condition

Clive brought two turkey subs, unsliced. He had to drive across town. Pizza joint had closed early. I made him fetch a knife (grey-handled, serrated, comfortable in my hand) and used it to divide mine in a civilized manner. Ordered him to eat his out of my presence. Sad Clive. Once he was gone, I wolfed mine down. Inserting the *White Album* CD, a necessary distraction and our guide. Cue it to track one. Just in case. Feel a migraine coming. I may lose that sandwich.

Thelonius felt a tightness in his chest.

Well. Nothing to be done about that.

If she was unhappy, it was her own damn fault.

---

xxxix. If she was unhappy

A veiled reference to his infidelity during that damnable trip. Good gravy. Barely made it to the commode in time. Can't seem to keep food down now. My head a basketball left too long in the rain. Just a terrific peeling and throbbing. Time to bring out the heavy artillery. I shall press play and put track one on repeat.

Right-turn here. Some sound. Sorry, civilians.

Thelonius drummed the dashboard with the fingers of his right hand and merged onto West Essex, occupying a lane and a half for a few exhilarating seconds.

Of *course* he was capable of compromise. Of course he was. Hadn't he agreed to stay here, where she had this creepy goddamn we-mustn't-abandon-Tara thing going via Dead Mother, instead of moving to Langley, as he'd wanted to? Of *course* he could compromise. What about *her*? Could *she* compromise? Not in regard to the whole baby thing, apparently. Guess what? That changed today. *Right* now.

The second problem, of course, was Dick Unferth.

Thelonius hit the gas.

A stop sign hurtled past. Thelonius heard the ascending howl of an auto horn from what felt like three o'clock, but couldn't have been, could it? Just in case, his right foot stomped the brake, and his left hand eased the steering wheel sufficiently leftwards to ensure complete safety. A red Fiat swerved around the front end of the Siena with several happy inches to spare.

That idiot could have seen Thelonius coming earlier.

He stomped the Siena to a full halt. Little screech. The Fiat, still righting itself, regained the centre of its lane and sped off. There was a long and troubled descending note as the red blur proceeded westward.

He was within a block of the Abandoned Animals Facility. Actually a good thing he had run the stop sign. Might have driven right by without this emergency stop.

Dick *Unferth*. Of all people.

He saw, in his mind's eye, a little girl's hand in a spreading pool of blood.

Stress breath CONSCIOUS.

No driveway, this is it.

xl. No driveway

My husband's all-too-brief homecoming is referenced here, as is, in hindsight, the familiar gravel strip from which he abandoned our beloved Salem foursquare.

Which brings us to Paul McCartney.

This masterpiece of masterpieces, track one of the *White Album*, this airborne allegory of espionage and self-sufficiency, this last great up-tempo offering from the world's last great band, celebrates McCartney's own great escape. It also celebrates an archetypal homecoming of deep relevance to our purposes.

In 1968, as the world burned around them, they came home to London, abandoning their misguided odyssey to the foothills of the Himalayas: Messrs. McCartney, Lennon, Harrison and Starr. If they'd started their journey in search of redemption (and the evidence suggests that they had) then they concluded it by proclaiming, with this song, their insistence that redemption was not to be found at the feet of a guru, but rather in their own craft as rock-and-rollers. Again: self-reliance as homecoming.

Let us address, then, the most obvious issue first. Their seemingly pointless sojourn to the ashram of Maharishi Mahesh Yogi – in reality, a trip demanded by the *White Album* itself, as most of the album's thirty songs were composed there – foretells a similarly bankrupt, similarly pointless pilgrimage of a certain late spouse of mine! Unlike them, however, he never truly returned.

As the members of the band laid down take after take of this exquisite, multilayered, satirical, and, yes, psychically prescient composition, they were indeed home at last: back in the UK, back in the studio, back where they belonged. Most importantly (and this is the foundation stone of the song's central conceptual joke): they were back in the West, title or no title, rocking out. My husband, Thelonius Liddell – hereafter simply T, as he is no longer my husband or anyone else's – rejected such a return to Western values the moment he spun out of our driveway.

He could so easily have embraced fatherhood. For his mistress and his twisted sleeper-cell followers, however, that was not an option. There was another, more seductive, more deadly path to pursue. This was Islam, the barren course he chose to follow as an explicit insult to me, to his Nation, and to all of Western civilization. In 1968, that tragic journey of T's was prophesied in this song's refrain. He had no idea how damned lucky he was.

Of course, I do not mean to suggest here that T consciously invoked the Fabs in this manuscript. Nor do I maintain that he chose to echo the themes of self-reliance and return that propel the fierce, incomparable rhythms of track one. I only note that this song, like the twenty-nine cunningly sequenced compositions that follow it, happens to illuminate, to anticipate with extraordinary depth and clarity, key aspects of Liddell's blind wanderings into Islam . . . as well as certain critical insights on the West's looming, inevitable confrontation with the Forces of Darkness.

Ladies and gentlemen of the jury, my father, whom T murdered, raised me to believe that there is no such thing as coincidence. My father, whom T murdered, was correct in that! If he were with us today, my father might well join me in acknowledging that the *White Album* itself is the key, not only to understanding this man, treacherous as memory, but also to securing control of the global conversation that is the great struggle of our era. Control of the conversation is a necessary prerequisite of victory.

The *White Album* is warning us and guiding us. It has been warning us and guiding us for decades.

It begins with a set of lyrics that left even the Reds speechless, which was, of course, the point. Who is to say what role this magnificent, icon-busting composition played in bringing down the Wall?

Listen, my sceptical and distracted colleagues, listen to this anthem of self-reliance. Listen. Listen to it as you have never listened to it, listen with an open mind. Hear that awakening tangle of tough guitars, watch that plane passing overhead. Feel the joyous fury of its inextinguishable engine, its nameless passenger's energizing series of commands. Follow the homeward path of that great aircraft, Freedom, a path set out for us by our Founding Fathers, a path that Paul McCartney knew, at some mysterious, semi-conscious level, T would choose to reject. Listen.

Also please skip to the end of this chapter. I did.

Still on repeat. Head much better.

A parking place.

Okay: Child.

The dead guy telling this story notes that Thelonius's wife, Becky, had (and has) significant experience as both a therapist and an interrogator. She rose through the ranks with speed, not just because she had a famous last name and was ambitious, but also because she was committed with deep ferocity to the national interest.

Rebecca Firestone was able to combine her two worlds, the worlds of psychotherapy and interrogation, on behalf of the United States of America. She became, for a time, hot – in the professional sense – for doing that.

She instituted widely praised protocols for detecting the early signs of mental illness in field agents. After 9/11, on the strength of distinctive interviewing skills, she won a reputation as one of the Directorate's most effective and sought-after inquisitors of captive terrorists. She produced leads that seemed promising.

Her record as an analyst of intelligence, and as a strategic thinker, was regarded as rather thin.

Becky built her career plan on huge aspirations, on ferocity and on the celebrated Firestone name, but all this was a precarious foundation. On one of his rare, awkward, seemingly purposeless visits to Salem, Dad said spontaneously, over a dense, garlicky ratatouille he himself had prepared, that, in order to get into the upper tier, she would probably need to develop either a more rigorous set of analytical tools, or a deeper mastery of the chess game of long-range planning. Having pronounced this opinion, Dad wouldn't look Thelonius in the eye for the rest of the night.

She was incapable of developing either skill set. It became apparent, in the weeks that followed, that Dad had not only felt certain about this for some time, but had helped her competitors to figure it out.

The ferocity, the need to set the plan, remained.

That was the last family dinner at Salem. Over a third glass of wine, after Dad left, Becky swore that he would not be permitted to return until he 'got on the team', and that any failure on Dad's part to get on the team would lead to 'serious consequences'. These remarks Thelonius reported, via a secure line, the next day, per his agreement to share with Dad any extremes of emotion or provocative behaviour.

Dad sent her an email: 'People must do what they're good at doing.'

What Becky was good at, it turned out, was looking after you in a way that disguised the fact that she was actually interrogating you. She could also, when the need arose, administer compliance blows in an unexpected, psychologically disorienting way. But that, it turned out, was not enough to get her where she wanted to be. Where she wanted, devoutly, to be, was in leadership.

In bed, mapping out her revised career plan on a helpless, battered legal pad, she told Thelonius that she refused to spend thirty years interviewing people and making notes, even though she was very good at that.

She wanted to set the vision. She wanted to be in control of the planning.

A consensus arose within the Directorate that, despite her brilliance, despite her overseas experience, she was never going to be in her father's league, either as a strategic thinker or as a builder of internal coalitions. Some of her ruder rivals claimed she couldn't assess, or even accept the existence of, data that challenged her own assumptions.

Becky denied all of this too loudly and too often, which, her rivals suggested, only proved the point. Jealous of her name, wary of her ambitions, secure at last in the knowledge that Dad was not out to establish a genetic dynasty, they did their best to reinforce existing negative perceptions of her and added to their list of Troubling Things a growing concern about her own potential for personal imbalance.

Her career plateaued. She responded to Dad's discreet efforts to find her work elsewhere in government with a series of startlingly obscene, unanswered emails, all of which she showed Thelonius. Whose star was rising.

She became the subject of many jokes, some cruel. Among these was the nickname 'Cleopatra', which started out somewhere in the upper regions of the Directorate and worked its way down to the support staff. One beaming, oblivious receptionist made the mistake of saying 'Cleopatra' to her face, while Becky was issuing instructions to a subordinate. The next morning, the receptionist had vanished. Thelonius thought he spotted her working at a LensCrafters.

That receptionist probably thought she was paying Becky a compliment. A lot of people thought that at first. But the people at the very top of the Directorate called Becky 'Cleopatra' not because she remained quite beautiful, but because they liked implying the phrase 'Queen of Denial' without actually coming out and saying it.

T said 'Cleopatra' in this context just once in conversation, during a particularly boring meeting that needed livening up. He felt instant shame at his enjoyment of that word, spoken loud and in

Becky's absence, and deeper shame at the laughter it produced around the table.

Dick Unferth didn't laugh.

She believed in herself. Should Thelonius mock that with the others?

Although he could not agree with the decision, he did respect her efforts to stay on at the Directorate, her resolving to ride out the storm, and he said so. One night, he suggested she begin exploring career opportunities with local or federal law enforcement. She snorted in disgust. Then, perhaps ten seconds later, made a brief *hmm* sound, as though she were considering the idea. She wrote something on that disintegrating yellow legal pad she always kept by the bed. Thelonius pretended to be asleep, that being one of the best ways to ensure that a point raised with Becky remained raised. The next morning, while she was in the shower, he read the top sheet on the pad.

It said, in huge letters: 'CONTROL = RESPECT'.

13 Does the 9/11 Thing Go Here?

The dead guy relating this story suggests that the imam – a man of intimidating calmness who looked to be in his late twenties but was approaching thirty-nine – sat on a cushion on the carpeted living-room floor in front of a small pot of tea set in the centre of a clean straw mat. The imam gave his salaams, received salaams in return, and gestured to the two women to take a seat before him. Each had been assigned a cushion. Fatima took the gold one, her opponent took the grey one.

On the wall was a piece of intricate calligraphy, inscribed: *Be useful in all things.*

xli. *Be useful in all things*

An unlikely motto for an Islamic scholar, attributable as it is to the Japanese swordsman and tactician Miyamoto Musashi. Track one, McCartney's ironic Cold War parody (it courses now through my brainpan, it soothes the throbbing), must not be taken as a literal rejection of American values – since those values manifestly include independence, freedom, personal mobility, homecoming, and self-sufficiency. The very subjects of the song, the very principles T rejected! Patrol car lights flashing outside. They have pulled the Brazilian from the pool.

Five rows of bookshelves, home to five well-ordered rows of scholarly volumes, lined one wall. A Koran sat open in its little wooden stand in the corner.

Other than that, the room was bare.

The imam's wife, or perhaps his daughter, in any event a small young woman, veiled and light on her feet, floated in with a plate of small pastries. She set it down on the mat, next to the teapot, and floated away again. Nobody touched the tea or the pastries.

'It is my understanding,' the imam said in the native tongue, 'that something unusual occurred beyond the range of vision of most protesters during yesterday's gathering at the embassy, but not beyond your range of vision. I should like very much to know what that was.'

⊠⊠⊠

Thelonius looked out the Siena's window, toward the Salem Abandoned Animals Facility. He didn't like the look of the place. From street level, you had to descend a staircase if you wanted to enter, and he wasn't fond of basements anymore.

He peered down at his bad left leg. Near the accelerator pedal, in the corner, beneath his good right leg, lay a white Walgreen's receipt he had not noticed. He leaned over, picked it up, and examined it.

Becky had bought a jug of antifreeze.

He crumpled the receipt, dropped it, and opened the door of the Siena.

xlii. door

From the CD player: The double agent's plane roars into the endless doorway of an airborne sunset, similar, I suspect, to the exquisite one I witnessed on my way out of Bucharest. Our retreat to the Bottomless Pit. I hear knocking.

⊠⊠⊠

In Fatima's version of the event, the marine had urinated directly on something, perhaps the pavement, while his back was turned to the two women peering at him through the bars of the embassy gate. He had never shown any awareness that he was being observed. He had simply walked away, in an odd and highly aggressive manner, when finished.

The imam asked her whether she could recall seeing a Holy Koran. Fatima thought for a moment. She replied that she could not recall that.

In the heavyset woman's version of the event, the American had entered the courtyard carrying a large Koran, flung the Koran to the concrete, kicked it open, spat upon it, unhitched his trousers, turned, exposed his genitalia in a most shameful manner to the two young women, making a point to establish eye contact with each in turn as he did so, turned again, and urinated upon the holy book, all the while laughing at the nature of his despicable act.

He had then expectorated upon the Holy Koran a second time, and attempted to set it aflame with a personal lighter he had brought along, presumably for this express purpose. Failing in this, he had sinfully picked up the defiled book with both filthy hands, cursed it in the vilest terms imaginable, referring to it in vulgar phrases as the work of a devil who had written every word. Finally, he had heaved it into the dumpster. And if the young lady now seated to her right had not observed any of this, how did it happen that at the time, she had begged so eagerly that they not mention the matter to the imam, as was their clear duty?

xliii. their clear duty

An obligation to slaughter disbelievers is the primary duty incumbent upon all true practitioners of this 'faith'. Fatima fulfilled that duty. The officer was polite and apologized for troubling us.

⊠⊠⊠

The dark stairs leading down to the basement were tough to navigate, and Thelonius's bad left leg throbbed its worst yet as he came to the bottom. He kept walking through the pain, a man in search of any face behind a desk, until the television show playing in the waiting area of the Salem Abandoned Animals Facility stopped him cold, right in the middle of the room. It was *One Life to Live*, a daytime drama that had been on the air since the summer of 1965.

One Life to Live was about people who lived in Llanview, Pennsylvania. A lot had changed in Llanview since 1965, but a lot had stayed the same, too. Despite the opening theme's musical promise of renewal and fresh beginnings, nothing much ever happened in Llanview, and it happened for days on end.

Thelonius's mother Irene had watched the very first episode, and Thelonius, all of four years old, had watched it with her. Thelonius checked in on the show from time to time. He had watched *One Life to Live* for decades now. People in Llanview still had to deal with mysterious kidnappings, and they still had a lot of affairs. These days, the show was mostly about Victoria Lord, Llanview's wealthy matriarch. Victoria had a problem with split personality disorder. Her husband Clint, an oil tycoon, had bloated a little since Thelonius had seen him last. Clint was confused and uncertain about whether Victoria had ever really loved him.

Victoria and Clint's marriage had endured many challenges. This was a running theme of *One Life to Live*.

xliv. *One Life to Live*

I have no idea whether T's late mother actually watched this programme. I do know that he did not watch it as an adult in my presence, that the plot details offered here are glaringly at odds with the summaries appearing on the 'authorized' tribute website, and that its title, in the present context, is a slur upon those who believe, as I do, in reincarnation, as foretold and sanctioned by the ninth chapter of the Book of Revelation.

Thelonius shook himself free of *One Life to Live*, found a pair of eyes not trained on him and shouted 'I need some help!' at the prim, fiftyish, elfin-looking crossword-puzzle-peruser who was stationed behind a thick glass wall. That wall bothered him. It made the place look more like the reception area of a cramped mental institution than an animal shelter.

On the puzzle-peruser's desk, beyond the green-tinted barrier, was a small television. Like the big television in the waiting room, it was tuned to *One Life to Live*.

'I'm here for my cat,' he said, louder still, having failed to rouse her. 'Charcoal. Fluffy. Probably confused.'

The woman behind the glass, her grey hair wound tight, looked up from her puzzle, creased her page corner, and sized up Thelonius. She made a little, noiseless exhalation as she straightened in her seat, placed her magazine in the topmost desk drawer without the aid of her eyes and stowed a well-sharpened pencil above her left ear. Then nothing happened.

Glass Woman seemed in no discernible hurry to do anything.

'My wife,' Thelonius explained, 'brought him in here by mistake. She believed we did not want him in the house. In fact we do. The last name is Liddell, L-I-D-D-E-L-L. Could I ask you to look him up for me, please, and bring him out? I'm a little worried about him.'

Her nameplate read, 'MELANIE DEL REY, ASSISTANT DI-RECTOR, SALEM ABANDONED ANIMALS FACILITY'. She leaned forward, toward a circular opening with a dark-green rim.

'Did you just kill that cat?'

Thelonius's heart stalled. Anyway something in his chest fluttered, and his mouth ran dry. Things were not going at all according to plan today.

Stress breath.

And again.

'Would you mind repeating that?'

'Your wife. Did she just call about the cat?'

'Did my wife. Just call about…?'

'A Becky Liddell called us about five minutes ago. Your wife, I am assuming? She didn't state any family relationship.'

'Yes. My wife.'

'I see. So you would want Child?'

'Yes, please.'

She sniffed, rubbed her nose.

'I see. Not doing very well, I am afraid,' she said, biting the side of her lower lip. 'Is Becky aware of the Plum?'

It became difficult to breathe.

'I beg your pardon?'

'Has Becky shared the problem?'

'The problem?'

Melanie Del Rey pursed her lips, knitted her fine dark eyebrows, and cast a sad gaze. 'I see. May I ask a personal question?'

Thelonius had no response, which must have counted as a yes, because Melanie Del Rey continued: 'Is a domestic dispute currently under way within your home?'

'I beg your pardon?'

'I see.'

'I beg your pardon?'

'You and your wife were in the midst of a disagreement about Child, correct? I mean, there was a conflict, correct? Please don't beg my pardon again.'

For a long moment, Thelonius stared at her through the glass from a broad expanse of bewilderment that pervaded space and time.

'These are simple questions,' she continued. 'Let's try a different one. Does? She? Want? You? Here?'

A deep silence. Within it, Thelonius gathered his resources, resolved to speak, and did. 'You don't have to try to make this difficult, and I hardly see what my wife has to do with this discussion. I had a feeling I needed to come here and get my cat. That's all.'

'I see. You had a feeling.'

She was not challenging him, merely repeating in an encouraging way, as though eager for him to continue.

No matter what he did, it seemed to be his turn to talk.

'I did *not* want him brought here.'

She appeared unpersuaded.

'And you two discussed that before sending him?'

'No. I recently got back from overseas.'

'I see.'

'Why do you keep repeating that? It's rude, you know.'

'Back from overseas. I see,' she mused, exactly as though the last remark had not been made. 'Complicated world we live in. Are you by any chance … a religious person? Some are. Some aren't.'

The dryness in his mouth reached the back of Thelonius's throat, where it suggested that it might want to be an ache.

He looked down and scanned the office floor behind the thick pane of glass. She was, impossibly, barefoot. Black pumps stood guard nearby. Her long, graceful toes, not unlike Becky's, but not the Toes, calmed him a bit.

'I don't know,' Thelonius said.

'I see. Well. You should probably know this: We were just about to put him down.'

The throat went forward, on its own authority, to a complete ache, culminating in a little choke that Thelonius couldn't quite contain, and the room began to spin. The counter was graspable, barely, and Thelonius was able to use it to slow the rotation down.

His eyes closed without him meaning them to. He opened them and leaned toward the spot where he had last presumed her to be. She was still there behind the glass. She was consulting a chart.

'We did run tests. We do prefer not to put the animals down. Some people do feel quite strongly that there is a plan. Some people don't. People do have beliefs about these things.'

---

xlv. that there is a plan

Among the more irritating elements of the religion my husband assumed at the cost of his marriage and his nation: its insistence on predestination. This is the polar opposite of the American ideal of self-reliance: to craft one's own plan.

, and the drums alone are worth the price of admission. Those five insistent, stuttering thuds at 2:15, from the sticks of the unaided, ever-goal-oriented McCartney, instantly commandeering the drum kit following Starr's petulant departure from the studio, propel the song's massive jet through the grey snow clouds – and toward disaster. This stunning opening track of the *White Album* thus predicts the 2001 attack upon the World Trade Center. When properly understood. None of the terrorists on either of the fatal flights that destroyed the Twin Towers had slept for at least forty-eight hours before undertaking their final mission. Recall that the song's protagonist complains of insomnia! With this much foretold with such chilling accuracy, how dare we ignore the other great Lesson of this aptly named album? That the white race itself is under attack? *What was the deleted transition above? An earlier reference to note xlv suggests that this does in fact belong here.*

Thelonius's nose was touching the glass. He shouted: 'What the hell is wrong with him?'

Melanie Del Rey looked up, calm, and eased her chair back a few inches, away from the barrier that stood between them, which somehow made Thelonius feel closer to her.

On *One Life to Live*, still playing in the next room and on the little TV screen in Melanie's workspace, Victoria berated her bitter rival, Dorian Cramer. Victoria was defending her daughter, Jessica. Shouting something about revenge. Jessica, like her mother, had a split personality problem. Both of her daughter's identities, Dorian whispered, had been born for trouble.

Thelonius grasped his head with both hands.

Some people (the dead guy telling this story among them) do feel quite strongly that there is a plan.

'Well, whatever your beliefs, I don't think it would be prudent of me to speculate about the cause of Child's problems,' Melanie Del Rey said with exquisite politeness. 'Now back away from the glass, please.'

xlvi. prudent

With an equally accurate, equally awe-inspiring foretelling of T's manuscript, the *White Album*'s second track emerges, its gentle acoustic guitar cycles chiming seamlessly, surrealistically, from the fading roar of jet engines. Cue track two.

Thelonius did move away from the glass, but he also took his hands away from his head and made them into fists, which did not sit well with seated Melanie Del Rey.

14 **In Which Liddell Fabricates an Interview**

The youthful imam set down his teacup. He looked toward Fatima, then toward the heavyset woman, and back toward Fatima again.

He thanked Fatima once again for accepting his invitation, as though beginning the conversation afresh. He had been so bold as to conduct a minimal amount of research in order to make a responsible decision about the present matter. Her name, place of employment, that kind of thing. He hoped she would not take offence at this. Fatima assured the imam that she took none.

The imam understood that she had recently lost a relative in the attack that had spurred the protest at the embassy. He extended his condolences. He understood also that she had been hired by the BII, and suspected she wished to keep her position for the sake of her mother and sister, an aim he considered praiseworthy. He appreciated the desire to avoid controversy. He wished to inform Fatima, however, that the matter under discussion was extremely serious, serious enough for him to cancel a meeting he had scheduled today at the refugee camp where he served as a member of the board of directors.

Quite important, their discussion today, he repeated. A great deal depended upon the question of whether or not both of them had witnessed the same behaviour from the same man. Her accounting of events, he insisted, was critical, for her, for her family, and perhaps for the country as a whole. He wished to be sure she grasped this.

Fatima assured the imam that she did.

He inquired as to whether Fatima was absolutely certain that the uniformed American she had observed inside the compound was the same man her friend had observed.

Fatima supposed he was. (She suppressed the instinct to correct the imam by pointing out that the heavyset woman was far from being a friend, and that she, Fatima, did not even know her name.)

The imam was curious as to whether Fatima was certain the man had actually been urinating.

Fatima was not. It was possible he had been pouring some substance or other on the ground from a container that she had not seen and that he then hid away.

The imam wished to know if she had seen the man's face at any time.

Fatima had not.

The imam asked whether she had noticed anything about the man's height. Was he particularly short or tall?

Fatima had not recalled anything in particular about this. She supposed him to be of average height.

His race?

Fatima was certain he was a white man. She remembered his hands. They were white.

The imam wondered if perhaps she had noticed any identifying characteristics on the man's hands or forearms. Tattoos, for instance. Many Americans were fond of those.

Fatima had not.

The imam was curious as to how Fatima explained the differences between her recollection of the event and that of her companion.

Fatima declined to speculate about this. The heavyset woman looked at her scornfully.

Would Fatima permit the imam to remain in contact with her if he made a commitment to her to keep all of their communications confidential?

She would.

Would she be willing to give the imam her family's phone number? He knew she did not want this issue discussed at her place of work.

She would, and she thanked the imam for his understanding. She wrote her mobile number on the slip of paper he provided, using the fine pen he lent her for the purpose. She folded the paper in a way that prevented the heavyset woman seeing the number, and returned both the pen and the sheet to the imam.

Did she have any questions for the imam or for her friend?

Fatima had one.

And what was that?

Fatima asked the imam to inquire of the heavyset woman whether she spoke any English. He glanced over at the other woman, who curtly informed him that she did not speak English.

Fatima asked whether the heavyset woman had heard the American soldier speaking in their own native tongue.

She had not.

How then, Fatima asked the imam calmly, had the heavyset woman understood the nature of the curse that she said she heard the man utter against the Koran? In what language had he expressed his opinion that it was authored by a devil?

xlvii. nature

Track two. The second composition in the *White Album*'s immortal sequence – Lennon's masterpiece this time – culminates in an unforgettable appeal to nature, to reviving grace, and to my MotherDaughter. Dawn up, blue skies strengthened, beauty everywhere in the firmament.

⊠⊠⊠

In 1966, when you were five years old, a campaign took hold in the southeastern United States to declare a certain British rock band's recordings to be the work of Satan.

Records were burned. Death threats were issued. Opinions were shaped. In August of the same year, with George and Irene on the outs, Wiley Clare, a lanky, itinerant North Carolina advertising man visiting San Francisco on business, encountered Irene in the bohemian restaurant where she earned a meagre income as a waitress. Was she one of those hippies? Had she ever seen those English boys with the long hair? Was she a fan? Did she know that one of them had said he was more important than Jesus? Did she believe that? Would she like two tickets to their concert, tickets that he had gotten straight from the record company and couldn't dream of using, since he had promised his wife he wouldn't, after what that boy had said about Jesus?

(So the guilty dead guy writing this book reconstructs the event, which he did not witness.)

That afternoon, with you still at the babysitter's, your mother began an affair with Clare. She accepted his tickets, visited his motel room, and took his seed, which struck home.

(Nor that event, of course.)

She attended the Candlestick Park concert, with you in tow. Swore you to silence about the trip. Introduced you to Wiley, who, having somehow materialized in the parking lot after the performance, tried and failed to make you laugh. He smelled of too much cologne. On the way back, in his car, he kept talking to you and you kept on not answering. Irene turned to you from the front seat and insisted you make an effort to be nice to Mr. Clare. Which made you say a coarse word or two about his history of maternal incest, right out loud, with him right there in the driver's seat.

xlviii. the Candlestick Park concert

As it turned out, the band's final gig before paying customers.

She turned away from you.

It could not possibly have been your last discussion with your mother, but it is the last one you remember.

⊠⊠⊠

'It wouldn't be *prudent* to tell me how my cat got sick?'

'Mr. Liddell, I have been directing traffic here at the shelter for some time. Long before this incident.'

'I beg your pardon? It's not an *incident*.'

She scowled.

'Nineteen years,' Melanie Del Rey went on, 'and in that time I have learned never to involve myself in domestic disputes. This being a litigious community.' She raised her eyebrows meaningfully.

'That means people sue each other around here over these incidents.'

'I know what litigious means.'

'I see. Then tell your wife the law is not on her side. One more such encounter as we are having today, and she might find herself dealing with a visit from Animal Protection. Nobody wants that. Such cases are sad for all involved. Couples may be prosecuted for animal abuse as a single legal entity in Massachusetts, you know. Do you want her to go to jail?'

Here she left a meaningful hole in the conversation, one that he could not fill. The pain in his throat returned with special vigour.

'Take a seat.' Thelonius did not move. 'I will check to see how Child is for you. Touch and go, frankly. There is going to have to be a regimen of medication, if he pulls through. And as I say, no one knows for sure what happened to this cat.'

xlix. what happened to this cat

In my defence, I quote from the Centers for Disease Control a passage outlining the wholly unacceptable risks I faced at this point: 'Cats do play a role in the spread of toxoplasmosis to humans, and are a cause for concern among pregnant women. For women newly infected with the toxoplasmosa parasite during the early months of pregnancy, consequences include miscarriage, stillbirth, and fetal deformity.'

l. parasite

The ambulance bearing it has gone, and that gauche squad car has at last ceased its flashing. A long day. Time for a lie down.

There was a faint but unmistakable accusation in her tone. Thelonius put his fists on the glass.

'Hold it. Are you, what? Are you saying my *wife* poisoned our cat?'

Melanie Del Rey said nothing.

'Are you calling us *murderers?*'

He didn't get an answer for the longest time and soon found himself staring at a different place. He kept waiting for the reply, but Thelonius, who had only killed people when specifically instructed to do so by the United States of America, did not see Melanie Del Rey anymore. He saw two bodies, one grown and one small, lying face-down in the street of the Kareem, a business district of Islamic City.

li. a different place

And back. Settled the account for this month with talkative Clive, who has arranged for a significant, and fortuitous, discount. As I calculate it, we have enough cash on hand to pay for this place until at least the end of September if it comes to that. But it need not. We are on the comeback trail! I do aim to finish all the annotations, submit this via a secure, anonymous server, and thereby restore the honour of this House, before you arrive. But that imposing stack of index cards! We must accelerate.

The street is called Malaika Street. Malaika means 'Angels'. Each of the bodies had been struck in the head. Cars weaved carefully around their pool of mingled blood. Collateral damage.

'We are not *murderers*, you know,' Thelonius persisted.

lii. not murderers

Clive asks with a practised gasp whether or not I heard about the murder last night in the pool area. No! 'Well. Apparently . . .' No! 'Yes!' No! Fifteen unreclaimable minutes of mutual clucking and sighing. I only tolerate such distractions because he has promised, persuasively and on multiple occasions, to protect my privacy.

⊠⊠⊠

Although she did want to save her job, this desire was not what kept Fatima from disclosing all she had seen inside the gates of the embassy compound. She also had a sense – sudden, impossible to overlook – that something ugly, beastly, rough and relentless would find its way through to her if the marine's actions were to become widely known.

Fatima did not have a name for whatever it was that wanted to be born, and she did not know of any way to stop it wanting that. Perhaps it was built into the city and impossible to stop. Perhaps it was going to be born anyway. She only knew she did not want this thing to be born on account of something she had done, or failed to do.

She had not, from a formal point of view, lied to the imam. He had asked her whether she could recall certain details. She had replied that she could not recall them. She believed recalling them to be dangerous to herself and others. So she could not.

Walking back home, Fatima pondered the imam's delicate situation. The heavyset woman had no doubt told many other people what she had seen, which meant the imam would likely be under pressure to do something, issue a fatwa perhaps. Yet how could he? When two women cannot come to agreement about a key fact, their testimony cannot be admitted. And the two of them stood as the only witnesses.

Fatima watched the beginnings of darkness seeping into the city. She stopped at a park where Wafa had often brought her and Noura, saw Wafa's familiar trees illuminated, saw the gilded cityscape less unsightly now in the approach of sunset. Fatima found a point in the sky that was secure and beyond human structure. She felt brave.

The memory of playing here, sparked by the movement of the upper limbs of those trees, settled her. She enjoyed the memory of climbing them. Of Wafa saying when to stop climbing. Of obeying Wafa.

She stared up at the trees.

Fatima had a habit, one that Wafa had remarked upon and often parodied, of looking upwards when she was deep in thought. She might be studying for an exam, trying to compose herself, avoiding an unpleasant consequence. At the dinner table, Wafa imitated Fatima pondering how best to tell her mother that she had forgotten something, some essential item during a trip to the market, say (a common occurrence). Wafa stared up towards the ceiling, counting the cracks, her eyes crossed, mumbling.

'Whenever she has to think, she looks towards heaven,' Wafa said.

Before Wafa died, a family joke cast Fatima as the daydreamer. It had brought the four of them closer somehow, that joke, despite the feigned anger of her denials. Now neither her mother nor her sister joked about that.

She had meant to be home before sunset. This was the ruling: Women were not to walk alone after dark. Fatima looked down again, stared at the pavement for a moment, then resumed her walk home. The city was descending into shadow, so she quickened her pace.

On the walk back home, Fatima wept for Wafa behind her veil. She wept in a way visible and audible to no one, her steps slow again, despite the steep decline of the sun. She remembered a story Wafa had read to her: a story about birds who said poo-tee-weet? Her sister had used this book to make time pass on the long airplane flight to America.

What kind of man, really, could pull the trigger, launch those projectiles. Or do such a thing to the Holy Koran. She saw the urine splashing upon the Word of God. Her insides churned.

Fatima wondered how those people could look into their mirrors each morning.

She entered her apartment building with four minutes to spare, and said Bismillah, which means 'With the name of God'. Time to pray soon.

Fatima ended up killing Mike Mazzoni. It wasn't murder, though.

Iii. Mike Mazzoni

A patriot and distinguished staff sergeant who served with honour in the United States Marine Corps – until Terrorist Bitch murdered him out of religious furor and a pathological hatred of our nation. A hero, he was subjected after death to a shameful torrent of anti-American rhetoric, much of it within these pages. His brother was the victim of a suicide bomber.

15 **In Which Liddell Has a Nervous Breakdown**

Thelonius said: 'Don't you dare call us murderers. *You're* the murderer.'

The little girl's hand. The pool of blood. The sound of a woman clearing her throat.

'Mr. Liddell,' she said, loud enough to make him see her, 'some of us have been down this road before, and some of us have not.'

'"Put him down". Jesus. What bullshit. Why don't you *say* it. You want to *kill* him. Murderer!'

Melanie Del Rey rose slowly, like Justice roused, behind green-tinted glass. Her eyes narrowed.

'Some of us, Mr. Liddell, are familiar with the relevant symptoms. Some of us have been called as witnesses in divorce proceedings and sued for slander and defamation of character, on the theory that a lawsuit along those lines might somehow rescue a relationship doomed and broken beyond all possibility of repair. Some of us have heard tell that pools of antifreeze sometimes form beneath automobiles, entirely by accident. Cats, some of us have learned from experience, have a taste for the stuff. Just a day or so of lapping at it can kill them. And some of us have heard it reliably reported that infidelities do occasionally take place, down here on Earth I mean.'

Icy hailpricks inside him again.

'Antifreeze kills cats. So we have heard. Sometimes, we have heard, people actually pour pools of antifreeze onto the pavement, beneath their radiators, just to be rid of a cat that a spouse loves, but they, perhaps, do not.'

Stress breath CONSCIOUS.

'My wife did *not* feed *antifreeze* to our cat.'

'I never said she did.'

'Hold it. I saw a green puddle in the garage. That must have been it. There must be a slow leak in my radiator.'

'Yes. An accident. That is the best explanation. Now take a seat.'

Something in Thelonius's chest gave way. He was breathing too hard.

'Don't "best explanation" me, bitch. Don't "accident" me. You will go to *hell*. You will *burn* there. It was *you*. What did you *do* to him?'

Melanie Del Rey grimaced, apparently intending her expression to pass as a smile, and disappeared.

Thelonius, his chest heaving, made his way to the waiting room, avoiding the row of orange plastic seats near the dormant Keurig coffee dispenser. *One Life to Live* was still playing on the television mounted high for the benefit of abandoned animals or people.

Thelonius was the only one in the place.

His late mother's favourite show spoke to him from a spot six feet or so above the floor, its dense colours playing around the glass rectangle, forming faces and voices that called him home to Llanview. Victoria Lord was in a restaurant, waiting for her oil tycoon husband Clint to arrive. Clint was late, as usual. The phone in Thelonius's jacket pocket vibrated. Both Thelonius and Victoria flinched.

Do not bring that animal 2 the house, Becky's text message read.

Thelonius brought a shaky right hand to his forehead, felt time stop and pucker.

He shook himself free, then saw his left hand fling the phone hard onto the carpeted floor. It didn't shatter. The text message was still visible.

> **liv. text message**
>
> And yet he did bring it into the house! Then buried the filthy thing in the backyard! Fortunately, no danger of infection post-mortem, given a six-hour window. Which there was.

⊠⊠⊠

On the evening following Fatima's first day on the job as a translator, the corpse relating this tale insists, her sister Noura made dinner.

Noura was thirteen and too eager to be fourteen: young enough to be excited about the prospect of cooking a real meal at the end of her sister's first full day at her new job; old enough to mind adult interference. Fatima, who had been doing the cooking for years, was glad to be rid of the responsibility and the maternal culinary lectures that always came with it.

Noura ignored her mother's counsel and, from time to time, said unusual things: 'I hear people screaming in the bathroom.' 'There's someone out there shouting about razors. I think it's Nine.' 'That baby has a stench.'

In fact, there was no shouting, no razor, no baby. There was only chicken. Ummi continued her running commentary on Noura's various procedural errors. Fatima just watched. That was the Plan for Coping: Ignore all references to Nine or any of Noura's other Intimate Companions.

Intimate Companions: Fatima's euphemism for the ever-expanding roster of hallucinatory figures influencing her sister's social life. The Companions had made themselves known back in the States, emerging with Noura's first spoken words: 'Uh-oh!' (To some unseen friend.) And a few days later, this shout: 'It's a trap!'

The Islamic City psychologists had been useless. Eight expensive, pointless sessions that only made things worse. The Plan for Coping had been Fatima's idea, an innovation – of five or six years' standing now – that worked more often than not, if working meant fewer angry episodes, fewer crying jags. The Plan for Coping had only one rule: no debates. That meant no arguments about whether there really were invisible people in (for instance) the bathroom. No disputes about reality. One moved on.

'At least Nine *looks* at people while they're *here* at the *table*, Fatima,' Noura shouted without warning. 'At least Nine asks people how their *day* went!'

Ummi reached out and smoothed her daughter's hair, but Noura's eyes brimmed with tears.

Noura's chicken curry with rice was more than passable when finally served, and it was natural Noura should yearn for Fatima's approval of it. As the three sat down to dinner, however, Fatima found herself preoccupied and disinclined to speak. Ummi, who lived to fill such conversational gaps, praised the dish in extravagant terms. Wafa, she pointed out, had always enjoyed chicken curry. Fatima only looked up at the cracked light fixture.

'Nine says they're arguing about missing diapers up there,' whispered Noura around a mouthful of her own chicken. Her eyes widened. 'The husband says the woman *stole* them, and then sold them. He says the woman made those cracks in the ceiling on *pur*pose.'

'You haven't told her how much you liked her chicken, Fatima,' Ummi observed. Her eyes said: *A compliment calms her.*

'The chicken is delicious, Noura.'

Noura swallowed, shook her head. 'You don't mean it,' she said, bitter. 'You should *mean* it.'

'Okay, it's good. Not delicious. Good.'

Noura grinned, nodded, took another bite, worked her jaws, showed them both the half-chewed food, concealed it again, nodded again. 'Crazytown says they're going to make you look at a nudie-butt.'

Ummi grimaced. Fatima stared up at the ceiling again and thought of Wafa. This time she did not cry, or even come close to it. Some kind of commotion did seem to be taking place upstairs.

---

lv. ceiling

A leitmotif for her (imagined) spiritual aspirations. Why do you torture me with this, T? Knowing full well that I would have to catalogue each of these masturbations to this poster of a saint? Because I wanted to take care of you? What the hell did you marry me for, T? If not to take care of you? *Delete this, keep saint thing somehow.*

⊠⊠⊠

On *One Life to Live,* Clint was shouting, mid-argument, in a crowded restaurant; Victoria turned away from him in disgust, told him not to make a scene.

Thelonius pocketed his cell phone, closed his eyes. When he opened them again, it was 1992 and he had just met Becky for the first time. He held in his hands the application form he'd filled out with the primary goal of impressing her, because he knew damn well she would read it in his presence, based on how well their initial chat had gone.

When would she touch him?

He scanned the sheet a final time, looked up, found a face behind a desk, a face already familiar to him, bordered with intricate locks of cayenne and flame and alive with the morning light. He handed her the sheet, and her long index finger grazed his with intention, and lingering with that touch of hers was possibility and stability and certainty. A direction home.

Here (the dead guy telling this story recalls verbatim) is what Thelonius wrote when asked, on that form, to describe his 'life philosophy'. 'Thelonius Liddell loves swimming and self-improvement. Protecting his country is important to him. He first served in the Third Ranger Battalion and eventually became a member of the Special Forces, also known as the Green Berets. He is a big admirer of President Bush and cannot even conceive of a Clinton presidency. That may not be appropriate to state on a document such as this, but hey, it says "life philosophy". He believes we only go around once in this life. One life to live. Before that, zip. After that, zip. In between, we either eat or we get eaten. No regrets and no apologies. His country eats, and so does he.'

You knew things for sure back then.

⊠⊠⊠

It was 2005 again and Thelonius was staring at Victoria Lord on the television that was playing in the Salem Abandoned Animals Facility.

What did he know for sure now?

He knew for sure his name was Thelonius.

He knew for sure the television set was on.

He knew for sure he wanted his cat back.

He knew for sure Child had to have been alive when he walked in the door of this godforsaken place, otherwise Melanie Del Rey would not have made such a fuss about getting him.

He knew for sure there was a green puddle back home in his garage. And a half-full jug of antifreeze. Did he know for sure there was a leak in the Siena? She had just *bought* that antifreeze. Well. That was why: The minivan was leaking, surely, and leaking fast. But. The instrument panel would have blinked on if the Siena was low on anything. She had made a big deal about the instrument panel and everything it blinked on for.

She wouldn't poison a cat intentionally. She wasn't pregnant or anything.

Wait. Did he know that for sure?

No. No, he didn't.

But.

He knew for sure that when he looked out at the Siena next, that asphalt beneath it, grey as a departing storm, had damn well better have antifreeze on it.

Thelonius made for the wall, took a deep stress breath, and prepared himself to scan the bottom of the narrow, grimy window that extended half a foot or so into the basement, to check the asphalt outside, to confirm the existence of a green puddle that had to be there under his green minivan. He stood on his tiptoes and looked.

The asphalt beneath the van was blank as the face of a corpse.

His insides quivered. He shut his eyes. He saw himself in the Salem house, at the dining-room table, sitting across from his wife, watching as though he were someone else. They were eating Child, both of them. Child butchered in his bloody fur and set out on two plates: they were eating him with knives and forks, weaving the silverware with care around the puddles of blood.

'My God,' Thelonius said. 'Why did I do it?'

⊠⊠⊠

On *One Life to Live*, Clint Lord stared at his wife Victoria's back, having asked her something. Victoria was always turning away from Clint.

Thelonius couldn't remember what Clint had asked Victoria, but he must have heard the question, because he'd been watching the TV when the question had caused her to turn away. Whatever the question was, Victoria answered it by saying she'd had enough.

Not a drop of antifreeze on that asphalt.

Thelonius rubbed the back of his neck, looked away from the TV set, stood on tiptoe again and stared through the sliver of window available to him, just to double-check. What might well have been a Monarch butterfly settled calmly onto a large, cold-looking maple leaf that had landed near him. The sun hid itself behind a weasel-shaped cloud driven by October wind.

Late in the year for butterflies. Remember what that freak in the cell said about butterflies.

It fluttered away. The day brightened again. Beneath the front end of the minivan, there was, of course, no green pool.

Thelonius felt the raw panic rising again in his gut, tamped it down. The voice said: *Machine, kid. Machine. Machine. It poisoned Child. Disable it. Disable it now. Otherwise it will come after you. PLOOF. THWOCK. KA-THOK.*

And still no green pool.

Stress response CONSCIOUS. Stress response CONSCIOUS. BREATHE, DAMMIT.

Ivi. BREATHE

Here, the Fabs foresee a certain ill-groomed hotel manager's inappropriate proximity and halitosis. Clive imagined I am lonely here. He imagined I must have more index cards than anyone he ever saw. He imagined there must be a lot of family who will be visiting me. He imagined I must have learned to type fast like that in high school. He imagined I know my hands sure are pretty. He imagined he would let me get back to work. Then he did just that, leaving me to ponder legislation banning all vain imaginings. I find I don't like people around anymore unless they serve a purpose. Track two, which had been on pause, resumes. In a certain sense, it plays eternally.

Thelonius stood, shouted at the top of his lungs: 'IF IT ISN'T TOO MUCH *GODDAMN* TROUBLE, CAN I SEE MY *GOD-DAMN* CAT NOW, *GODDAMMIT*?'

No answer.

The voice in his head, not his own, continued: *Machine. Not your wife. Go back. Kill it.*

'I WANT TO SEE CHILD,' he bellowed, then collapsed, arms wide, legs stiff, hyperventilating, onto an orange plastic chair.

On *One Life to Live,* Clint had just noticed that he was all alone in the restaurant. He had been lost in some rant, had turned to confront her, found only her empty place at the table. Clint closed his eyes. Thelonius closed his eyes, too. Melanie Del Rey's slim hand cupped his shoulder from behind.

'Did you kill a child?'

'I beg your pardon?'

'Don't beg, please. Dogs beg. Did you love Child?'

He nodded his head Yes.

Melanie Del Rey pursed her lips and nodded with great compassion, as though agreeing with something he had yet to say.

'I see. Poor boy. Poor boy.'

Her hand was on his cheek.

'Poor boy. His kidneys were hard as stones. I am sorry. Preparing the remains for you.'

The feeling of her hand withdrawing. The sound of the television beginning to vibrate against its fastenings. Smooth orange plastic beneath him.

Thelonius stood and approached *One Life to Live.*

Even Clint, lost and all alone in the restaurant, noticed Thelonius's approach. He tensed, stared out from behind the glass. By now, Clint's restaurant table was shaking, and the condiments upon it had tumbled to the floor.

The table within the television writhed and stuttered like a patient in electroshock. It fell over on its side, forcing Clint to back away in alarm and revealing a familiar geometric pattern. On the high-mounted screen, expanding along the restaurant floor against the surface of a hideous orange-and-black carpet, that spreading puddle of blood outlined what remained of the little dead-eyed girl.

Thelonius sat back down against the smooth orange plastic of the chair, buried his face in his hands, wept his face wet. His mother loved him very much. His grandmother promised him that.

The voice that was not Thelonius's own said: *You know why it did not want that cat in the house, kid. Go back. Cut its head off. You know.*

The problem was: Thelonius did know. Toxoplasmosis.

'Christ,' Thelonius said.

Collateral damage, kid. Couldn't be helped.

'Christ help me.'

Clint, trembling within the trembling television, wheeled, pointed at Thelonius and shouted: DO NOT CALL ON ANOTHER GOD THAN GOD!

Thelonius was on his feet again, seizing the sides of the boxy TV set with both of his hands, hoping to rip it from the wall, but instead he began to vibrate with it. Shaking, almost gone, he turned his head to look for Melanie Del Rey to alert her to the problem, but she was nowhere to be found.

---

lvii. she was nowhere to be found

Yet another vanishing woman. This obsession with familiar life narratives creates a self-fulfilling prophecy, and the patient's pathology only tightens its grip. Time for a lie down.

⊠⊠⊠

Fatima was considering a problem.

This problem kept her from making a bigger fuss about Noura's cooking, or honouring Ummi's various spoken and silent cues. Ummi had moved on to the topic of seasonings. Fatima stared up at the plaster of the tiny, cramped second-floor apartment the three of them shared. There were indeed cracks in that ceiling. Insects occasionally emerged from those cracks. An argument between the man and wife who lived upstairs, its words occasionally audible, had taken an ugly turn. It was something about vinegar.

lviii. the man

And he's back. More delays, more inanity, but at least they are served with respect.

As Ummi went into a lengthy overview of the dozen or two best ways to ensure that rice was cooked to the proper consistency – not too sticky, not undercooked, either – Fatima considered her problem: She needed the phone not to ring.

The challenge of somehow keeping her mobile phone from going off, without actually turning it off or silencing it, kept returning to the upper regions of Fatima's mind. This dilemma crowded all other goals off the stage. The desire to locate – to afford! – a better place to live; the desire to tell Ummi she could quit her job at the shop; the desire to look, at least, as though she were paying attention to that lecture about rice. All that receded into the background. Only the problem of the phone stood in the spotlight.

A few dozen friends and relatives constituted the universe of possible familiar numbers. They would be calling to console themselves about Wafa's passing, but that was an etiquette matter, easy enough to manage by ignoring recognizable callers. The larger challenge lay in the unfamiliar and blocked numbers.

Her new boss, Murad Murad, had made frequent mention of his loathing of voicemail, had warned Fatima to be ready to receive phone calls after hours in the event of an 'interrogation emergency'. This sounded like an improvisation intended to impress her, and she doubted there was any such thing as an interrogation emergency. Murad Murad might well be the kind of supervisor, however, who would call her on her first evening home after work, supposedly in order to confirm that she was following his instructions about availability, but actually to attempt, pathetically, to flirt with her again.

Although such a call turned her stomach, taking it connected to the successful completion of her first week on the job, and to the collection of her first paycheque – half the amount necessary to pay the back-rent due on Wafa's place in D—. The husband and his mother, with whom they were not close, had abandoned the house. It was large and well outside of the city. The landlord had agreed to hold it for a month ... if and only if the debt were paid this week. So calls from Murad Murad had to be taken. Yet how was she to be certain, when the unfamiliar number rang through on her cell phone, that the voice of the imam would not greet her?

She had no idea what number the imam would be calling from, either. Further discussion with him seemed unwise.

So. If the phone were to ring, and if it were not some identifiable aunt or uncle eager to hear her sob, if she should receive a call from a blocked number or one she did not recognize, should she ignore the call, or press 'answer'? If she ignored it, she placed her new job in jeopardy. If she took it, she ran the risk of becoming entangled again in the question of what she had or had not witnessed at the embassy.

The matter was out of her hands now.

Silently, Fatima sought protection from God against the telephone ringing.

Following this silent prayer, there was the familiar sound of Ummi weeping, and the unlikely sight of Noura's comforting arm around Ummi, whose head sagged and whose shoulders shook.

Noura made a cartoon face of exaggerated disbelief for Fatima's benefit.

'You didn't even *lis*ten to her,' Noura said.

lix. You didn't even *lis*ten

A frequent refrain in our household. T often maintained (for instance, during discussions about family planning) that he was not being listened to, when in fact he was not being agreed with. Men are such control freaks.

'I beg your pardon?'

'You don't *lis*ten. She wants you to promise you had nothing to do with that business at the *em*bassy. And she's not the only one, Fatima. *Ev*erybody wants you to promise.'

'Everybody.' Fatima drew a deep breath. The Intimate Companions again.

'Mother, do you really imagine I would …?'

Before Fatima could continue, however, the cell phone chimed. It was an unfamiliar number.

The guilty dead guy writing this finds himself wishing she had never taken that call, but that was not the Plan.

⊠⊠⊠

Melanie Del Rey, secure now in the conviction she had seen and heard it all, more wary than ever of displays of emotion likely to disrupt the order of her Facility, stood in the waiting room, arms akimbo, staring at Thelonius.

He had perched himself on an orange plastic chair, which he had removed from its row and placed in an unauthorized spot. He was attempting to bear-hug the television on the wall. He wept and shivered. He kept repeating the words 'Not a machine'.

She called the police.

lx. She called the police

This much, at least, is beyond dispute. She did: Salem Police Department log number 2005A2096399.

⊠⊠⊠

Far more calm and confident than she had anticipated, Fatima answered the phone. Murad Murad's voice greeted her. There was an interrogation emergency. She was to report to work immediately. Not without some relief, she stood, apologized to her mother and sister for breaking off the discussion, put on her gold headscarf – the same one she had worn earlier that day – and called a cab. It was nine fifteen by the time she made it to the BII compound, which was windowless and made of concrete.

lxi. the BII compound

A combination prison and command centre, modelled after one of our own facilities.

⊠⊠⊠

A policeman came and produced silver handcuffs. They were meant for Thelonius.

'Arms in front, okay?'

The policeman's partner watched as Thelonius extended both wrists, his fingers trembling. There was no struggle. Limping Thelonius followed them out of the shelter and up the stairs to the street. The air was cold and grey.

One of the officers, the one who had cuffed him and led him by the arm, said something about Thelonius's leg and asked if he was okay. Thelonius said he wasn't sure.

He stood on the sidewalk near the cruiser, glad to be in a new space, and so obedient that the officer holding his arm said he probably just needed a change of scenery. Thelonius agreed and nodded. He waited for the rear door of the squad car to open, then got in. He did not believe, at first, that he had had a nervous breakdown at the Salem Abandoned Animals Facility. Then he figured maybe he had. Then he decided that he didn't know. He watched the scenery change from the back of the police car.

He wondered how long he would go on like this.

He wondered whether he would always have a beast inside of him, whether he would always be running to escape it.

He wondered whether Mike Mazzoni, that marine who took a leak on the Koran and then chucked it into the dumpster, wondered about such things.

He wondered whether he would ever file a report about Mike Mazzoni. He looked out the window, then leaned his head on it.

He felt bad about leaving the Republic before he could get Mike Mazzoni thrown out of the Marine Corps. He felt bad about having married the wrong person. For having been the wrong person some-one married. He felt bad about lying to Becky about the Plum. He felt bad about letting everyone down. He felt bad for that little girl and her dad.

He started weeping again, but made no sound this time.

In the back seat of the cruiser, headed toward a bridge, Thelo-nius got his bearings. That bridge led over the Danvers River. It was called the Veterans Memorial Bridge, and it took you out of Salem. Which meant they were taking him not to the jail, but in the op-posite direction.

Thelonius leaned forward as far as he could. Through the thick bulletproof glass, he asked the glum police officer who was driving whether he, Thelonius, was going to the station. No answer. Then he asked whether he would be able to phone someone when he got to the station. Nothing came back then, either. He asked the police officer's partner, the one who had cuffed him, the same questions, but he had stopped talking, too.

At least the car was moving. At least he could hear the motor whine. At least they were approaching the bridge.

Just Get Started.

Thelonius twisted his hands, reached into the front pocket of his jeans, extracted his phone. From memory, he tapped in Ryan Fire-stone's speed-dial code, hit the green 'phone' button, put the call on speaker.

As though surrounded by bees, Dad said from a great distance: 'T?'

'I'm divorcing her,' T shouted toward the phone. 'I don't want any part of this anymore.'

They were on Veterans Memorial Bridge now.

Thelonius hung up, tried to edge the phone back into his pock-et. Failed. Then the car hit a seam where some new bridge asphalt began, and the phone flew out of his hands and dropped to the floor. If either policeman noticed what he had done, neither was admitting it. The car was over the bridge. They were out of Salem.

'Am I under arrest?' Thelonius asked, way loud enough, but neither policeman turned his head.

'Am I under arrest?' he asked again.

From his cell, the dead guy telling this story says 'Hi' to Becky, recalls her reciting *The Tempest* to him and stroking his hair in front of their window of night stars, peers at that memory before this chapter ends. Space enough have I in such a prison.

lxii. 'Hi' to Becky

What a queer sociopathic tic, this recurrent *homage à nous*.

Absurd that I should actually *miss* you, having read it.

My insides roil. Breath shallow and achy and ungovernable. Asked Clive for some onion soup. He is gone to fetch it. Who knows. Might settle this.

Sullivan Hand had dreams, you know,
Of you above, of him below.
Sullivan Hand, whose knees were sound,
Whose back was strong,
whose heart was brown,
Sullivan Hand adored red hair.
He worked in the dark when no one was there.
Sullivan Hand sought a secret untellable,
But only wound up, in the end, with …

16 In Which the Bitch First Encounters Liddell

'AMERICA UNDER ARREST NOW,' one of the Islamic City police officers shouted in Thelonius's ear, slamming the side of his face
into the hood of someone's Lincoln Town Car, snapping off the little
cross-but-not-a-cross ornament. The rectangled lower-case T skittered onto the pavement, into the pool of spreading blood.

That stylized four-pointed star, just a few seconds earlier, had
projected wealth, power, prestige, thoughtful engineering and, just
perhaps, the desire of the Ford Motor Company's design team to
allude to the NATO seal's compass rose. A few seconds earlier, the
four-pointed star of the Lincoln Town Car spoke to stability, to certainty, to safety and to Freedom in the north, south, east and west,
to the possibility of a direction home. Now the metal emblem, shiny
in a puddle of mingled blood, projected nothing but failure.

Intelligence failure. Design failure. Mission failure. Execution
failure. Every imaginable variety of failure.

The little girl's opened head released a raw, mottled mushroom,
streaked with crimson. Her hand lay near the ornament.

She had not wanted to leave her father.

'UNDER ARREST,' the policeman shouted again, pulling Thelonius's right hand behind his back. The handcuff snapped into place
around his wrist.

From the hood of the Town Car, Thelonius took in the scene at
an angle – the cool sideways-slanting daytime light of late afternoon,
the upended city aligning itself along the black street, the shops open
and active, their gravity-defying customers still and curious and cautious at the windows. A group of covered, chittering women scurried
toward a misplaced horizon. Away from him. He closed his eyes.
The metal of the Lincoln was cold. The officer pulled Thelonius's left
hand smartly into place and handcuffed that wrist too.

⊠⊠⊠

Alone with Fatima in his first-floor office, Murad Murad began his 'private briefing'. A high-value American had been detained that afternoon.

He had shot a father and daughter on a busy street, in front of dozens of witnesses, within a few hundred yards of the lamp-lit street scene now visible to Fatima through Murad Murad's window. Both the father and daughter had died. The Justice Ministry had assumed authority over the case. The father's suitcase had contained nothing untoward, despite the American's fixation upon it.

Before them were the American's possessions. Fatima, seated in a high-backed chair that had, for some unfathomable reason, been bolted to the floor, looked at the crowded surface of Murad Murad's large desk. On the desk were the following items:

A backpack, emptied.

A Glock handgun.

Bullets for same.

An infrared light.

A portable telescope.

A U.S. passport, held open with a plastic clip.

ID cards – a driver's licence, an employee pass – at odds with each other and with the passport.

lxiii. ID cards

The *White Album* here notes T's fixation on shifting identities, viewpoints and epistemologies by choosing this point to unveil track three, which I now place on repeat in the hope of sailing over a few of the manuscript's more nauseating passages. Feeling queasy and restless. That blue, unhappy heart.

A wallet.

Currency in large denominations, presumably extracted from the wallet.

A small camera. Murad Murad assured her it contained pictures of prohibited areas, installations along the border. This appeared to be precisely the kind of surveillance that regional enemies of the Republic might conduct.

A comic book, *SERGEANT USA #109*. Its purchase price was listed as twelve cents. Pristine condition, secured within a transparent plastic sleeve. Fatima picked this up, extracted the issue, made a brief examination of its fragile pages. She closed it, surveyed the troubled, resigned rear-cover visage of Norman Rockwell ('We're looking for people who like to draw'), and slipped it with care back into its sleeve, face-up.

At the time of his arrest, Murad went on, this individual had been attempting to steal the suitcase found near his two victims. Why? What did he believe it contained? How had he come to make obtaining it a priority worth two lives and possibly his own? Certain prominent persons had taken a deep interest in the case. Certain figures, certain military figures (here he paused to let the words sink in) had demanded the postponement of the diplomatic discussions the American embassy was now pressing. It was, some felt, long past time to let the Americans know they did not have a free hand in this Republic.

Trails such as these tended to grow cold with alarming speed. He had been instructed to take aggressive action, to use his own best judgement. They were to learn, ideally tonight, what they were dealing with. Who the man was, to whom he reported within the American intelligence network, what potential threats to national security he had uncovered and so forth. The Americans were always busy concealing a great deal. Any marriage incorporates certain evasions.

The prisoner's photography had been reviewed closely by people at the very highest levels of the government. Certain long-standing assumptions about their relationship with the Americans now appeared less reliable than before. It had been concluded, within the hour, that this man would not leave the country at the present time.

No other translator had been available for the interrogation. He was glad of that, though. He knew he could count upon Fatima. She would of course be compensated at double her pro-rated hourly rate. This was a significant career opportunity for her, and he wanted to be sure she understood that.

Fatima understood.

The prisoner was now being processed. There was a certain strategic advantage in allowing him to ponder his situation. Questioning was scheduled to commence thirty minutes from now. Her security clearance had been upgraded, yet another opportunity for her. Could he count on her discretion once the interrogation began?

Fatima would be discreet.

Murad Murad smiled that indigestion smile of his.

He was proud of her now. Confident she would help him to do the right thing for the country. He felt a certain protective instinct toward her, hard to describe, but perhaps she would respect it. While they waited, might she allow him to view her hair, as a father views his daughter's hair?

Fatima's jaw clenched.

He assured her that they were alone, that the door was closed, that no one would know and that it was all he would request of her on a personal level this evening.

Fatima stared at the plump little man in the uniform. Whispering, she informed Murad that she wished him to understand two things. First, there was a witness to his actions, and that witness was Allah. Second, she was capable of screaming quite loudly. She would do so the moment he attempted to prevent her from exiting the room and taking up quarters in the employee lounge. She preferred to wait there until the interrogation began. That would be all.

She stood and made her way out of the office.

⊠⊠⊠

Becky's mom died on May 2, 1972.

She succumbed to wounds she received on a trip she and her family had made to Venezuela back in 1968. Some Communists killed her.

Becky's mom's real name was Prudence. Of course, Becky never called her that. Becky called her Mother. So that's what the dead guy telling this story will call her.

The Communists threw a bomb into a beach cottage Mother and her family had rented. Mother had been reading A.C. Bradley's *Shakespearean Tragedy*. She was lying on her side, re-engaging with one of the passages on Desdemona, when the explosion went off beneath her bed. It shredded the iron frame of her bed into fragments, lodged shrapnel at the base of her nose, destroyed both her eyes and disabled certain important parts of her brain. The attack left the set of Mother's mouth off, too. For nearly four years, though capable of intermittent speech, she usually looked half-aware, determined to sleep her way through a special kind of hangover.

The Communists hadn't meant to kill Mother – or, to put it more accurately, they hadn't cared much about whether they killed her or not. The Communists had meant to kill Becky's father, Ryan Firestone, known familiarly to those who reported to him as 'Dad'.

Dad had been out golfing at the time the bomb detonated. Becky had been golfing with him. Her long hours of practice were paying off. She was beating Dad fair and square for the very first time, though it was still quite early in the round. They were beginning the fifth hole. Becky was leading, but furious.

Dad was, in the adult Becky's words, a 'control freak'. She insisted that, after the third hole, Dad had broken his promise of not trying to lose to her. He couldn't handle losing to her fair and square.

Dad had indeed broken any number of promises.

A running man emerged, agitated, from the distant pro shop. Something had happened at the cottage. Becky and Dad never finished that fifth hole.

Prudence Firestone, née Sharp, aka Mother (1931–1972) grew up in the same Salem, Massachusetts foursquare that she later shared with Ryan Firestone, and that Becky would later share with Thelonius. Too late, and only in hindsight, long after he left that house, Thelonius came to see Becky's insistence on living in this particular home and no other, ever, under any circumstances, as a signal of something being not quite right within the family.

---

lxiv. Prudence ... Thelonius

I have skipped over some pages, having read quite enough already. We endure from T in these passages, have endured, continue to endure, considerable provocation. All such travesties, insensitivities, and treasons appearing in *Jihadi* are preemptively identified in track three as libellous. None of it is real.

⊠⊠⊠

'You are a guest of the Islamic Republic,' said a teenaged girl, wearing a white robe and a gold headscarf, who appeared to be staring at Heaven. 'Please permit me to apologize in advance for any discomfort or inconvenience.' Her voice awoke Thelonius as from a dream.

---

lxv. Her voice

Enter the Bitch.

Clive (rapt, obedient, seated) has procured a bowl of onion soup, a traditional Sharp Compound delicacy, and placed it nearby. Through my headset, Lennon answers (stoic, synchronistic): *Oh, yeah*. Pressing pause.

17 **In Which Liddell First Covets Her**

Fastened by his wrists and ankles with transparent plastic cord to a pair of large, crossed planks, a human X on a low, grey slab, Thelonius found himself pinned, a butterfly on an examining-board. His cat had not yet been poisoned by antifreeze. He had not yet become a trophy to be displayed at the Freedom Banquet. He did not yet have a limp. Back in the Republic now, back in that close, stinking, windowless basement, under interrogation and naked (which explained, he reminded himself, the translator's refusal to meet his eye), he didn't yet know the girl's name was Fatima. He didn't know anything about her.

Thelonius must have been quite a catch for the intelligence arm of the Islamic Republic. From the stuff they found in his backpack, they probably deduced two things right away. First, that he was someone involved at a high level in the exciting world of American espionage. Second, that he was taking photographs of military facilities the Americans weren't supposed to see close up.

Thelonius took those pictures because people in Washington wanted to be sure no one in the Islamic Republic was building a nuclear weapon or giving nuclear materials to terrorists. They weren't. Perhaps they are now.

The plump, dark-eyed little man standing in front of him gabbled something to the girl. He scowled at Thelonius.

'Who are you?' the girl translated. There was something odd about her voice.

'I pass,' Thelonius said. 'The embassy will lodge a protest, you know. I'm an employee. You have no right to hold me here.'

The girl translated. The dark-eyed man chuckled, then said something in a high-pitched, contemptuous tone that rose to a peak at the end. 'That is a debatable point,' the girl pronounced carefully.

Now Thelonius knew what had struck him as strange about her

cadence and inflections. They were American: a miraculously clear, upper-tier, New England-accented tongue, set off with only the vaguest hint of the Republic. She appeared to be eighteen or nineteen. She was still staring at the ceiling.

'I am a contractor who works on air-conditioning projects for the U.S. embassy here,' Thelonius said. 'And I want my passport back.' That part was true.

The plump little dark-eyed man nodded to someone almost out of Thelonius's field of vision, a uniform standing in an obscure corner of that large, dank, concrete-and-vomit-scented room. Thelonius heard the uniform retrieve something from a rack of some kind, heard him carry it across the room using brisk steps. He looked at the little man, who was staring back at him as one would stare at a trapped animal. Thelonius's eyes returned to the dark, gold-framed face of the teenage girl transfixed by a point somewhere near the dead ceiling fan above him.

A wall of water slammed into his face, roared at him. An instant later, someone's fist in his solar plexus. Then an exquisitely targeted, rapid blow to his right knee, no seeing it coming or going. It might have been a crowbar or a baseball bat. The girl gasped.

Despite his training, Thelonius had been distracted. Caught unawares, seized deep in the throat and nose by a burning, tentacled wave of pain now working its way through his sinuses, assaulted by simultaneous missiles howling through his abdomen and the angle of his newly dead right leg, he still did not regret looking at her face.

He hadn't protected anything. He spent a few long moments reassembling himself, hacking, coughing up blood and water and straining with his bound hands, in vain, for his howling knee. She was staring upward again, or still, at any rate staring away from him.

lxvi. away

Breathing normally again. Tedious Clive still thinks my hands are pretty. That thin, unpersuasive, warmed-over onion beverage of his was not in the least soul-restoring. Not at all track three, which spins and beckons from its hibernative pause. Do I want to talk about where things went wrong with my husband? I do not.

The little man, who wore a gold ring, jabbered for some time. He had a high-pitched voice, much higher than the girl's, and he seemed to speak too rapidly for any language.

'Oddly,' the olive-skinned girl continued impassively, 'the senior representatives of the State Department disagree with you. I might add that they also disagree with your passport, which, of course, the State Department issued. They are apparently under the impression that you are a diplomat. Yet your passport makes no mention of this.'

The tiny dark-eyed man paused, then posed, in that unique, irritating upper-register intonation of his, what must have been another question. 'It is a bizarre discontinuity,' the girl pronounced flatly, 'your having no prior knowledge that you are a State Department official rather than an air-conditioning repairman. Wouldn't you agree?'

'Tell him I want my passport back,' Thelonius said, staring straight at the girl, who would not look at him. He coughed and spat water and snot, then laughed. 'Tell him I'll fix the air conditioning in this place if he does.'

lxvii. air conditioning

T's cover had indeed been that of a facilities repairman. The first argument put forward by the President to resolve the crisis and secure T's release went to our primary diplomatic contacts, intelligence backchannels having, overnight, grown cold and unresponsive. His appeal incorporated the quiet revision of T's cover to include diplomatic duties. Diplomats, my father assured the President in a private, late-night call, could not legally be held by a foreign power. Of course, there was no way for T to have known of this gambit in the early hours of his captivity. It failed. An altogether different solution was in order.

The little man bleated something in reply, but Thelonius understood only his own cover name, Davis Raymonds.

'Shall we go for another swim, Davis Raymonds?'

She didn't mean it. Her voice still soft, incongruous. Her eyes still inaccessible, trained upward. His leg still shrieking and throbbing.

Thelonius's real name was Thelonius Liddell, of course, but he wasn't supposed to tell that to anyone. Davis Raymonds: He wasn't sure why the handlers always chose such implausibly normal-sounding names as false identities for the people doing covert operations. The generic names sounded instantly fake to anyone with American connections and only made life more difficult. (By the time he got to the Beige Motel, the dead guy recalls, he didn't have a name anymore.)

'Tell him my name,' Thelonius said, 'is Chad Reese.'

lxviii. Chad Reese

I met this fellow during a trip to Oregon with T right after we were married. He tried, for days on end, to get both of us to do the Landmark Forum training. No thanks. Men are such control freaks. Clive asleep on the little couch. Possibilities there.

This was another lie. Chad Reese was an old friend of Thelonius's from high school. He was a drama geek with long, dirty-blond hair, who had tried in vain to get Thelonius to smoke marijuana in his dank basement, which, as it happened, vaguely resembled this basement. Thelonius, who had refused any and every mind-altering substance offered to him since The Accident, had insisted that Chad not smoke pot around him because of the danger of a contact high.

The little fat man barked. 'Spell it,' the girl instructed, in a calm voice, on the little fat man's behalf.

'C-H-A-D space R-E-E-S-E.'

The interrogator shook his head warily. Something about the way Thelonius had spelled the name did not appear to agree with him. He chattered at length.

'You find yourself in a deeper difficulty still,' the girl translated over the chattering. 'You do not lie well. And I have been trained in the detection of lies. Which makes me a good liar, too. A good liar spots a poor liar every time. Odd for a man in your position to be a poor liar. It will not go easily for you here. Recall. You have murdered two people on a city street. One of them a small girl. There are dozens of witnesses.'

There were, too. That had been the problem. Witnesses studying him closely when he was supposed to be gone. A van sent out to pick up Thelonius showed up two blocks too far south and found itself unable to navigate through the crowd. The van's driver had gotten out of the vehicle, obtained a visual on Thelonius from perhaps nine hundred feet away, re-entered the van, and attempted to create an alternate route by utilizing a one-way street in unorthodox fashion. That improvisation failed: A stray motorcyclist struck the speeding van, incapacitating it and leaving Thelonius to deal with local law enforcement. So many failures. Someone, somewhere, would analyze all the flaws in the process and correct them in due course. Becky, perhaps.

'You are lying and you are guilty,' she said, emotionless, as the chattering stopped. 'You will face Islamic law.'

Afterwards, in the father's briefcase, nothing but a Koran.

'Tell him he has no right to hold me here,' Thelonius said, 'because I work for the American embassy. Tell him I have places I have to be. People I have to see. And while you're at it, remind him your religion forbids the mistreatment of suspects, even sceptics. Tell him I have my rights. Tell him Allah has all prior knowledge, and even though Allah has seen fit to make me a sceptic of Islam, I respect His will in the matter.'

For the first time, she met his gaze. Her eyes flashed.

It was not anger, exactly, or even disappointment. It was the expression of one who is no longer avoiding a situation, but choosing it and present to it. When she resumed her task, she translated Thelonius's words while staring straight into his eyes.

No fear.

When she was done she looked back up at the ceiling.

The little man paused, then gabbled again. What he said appeared to disorient the girl, who shook her gold head briskly after he was done speaking, as if to disentangle herself from what she had heard. There was a silence, followed by a single sharp, incomprehensible word from the little dark-eyed man with the moustache.

The girl drew in a deep breath, held it for a beat, and shouted something at the little uniformed man, who looked at her with disgust, stepped toward her, and struck her sharply across the face with the back of his hand.

She swayed with the impact, regained equilibrium, did not flinch. Her eyes narrowed and glowed. A long, red welt began to form across her cheek and onto the bridge of her nose, a thin trail of blood at its edge.

The interrogator resumed his position, gabbled once again, pronouncing the name 'Davis Raymonds' as though it were a beloved obscenity. Then he shouted his final word. He looked back at the girl.

'The religion per se is not at issue here,' the girl said, her voice devoid of all emotion. 'If the religion were our subject, I should not have permitted Fatima to accompany me into interrogation today, so that she might have the pleasure of inspecting you, Davis Raymonds.'

The little man glared at her again. He shouted, in English, the word 'prick'. Apparently he knew just enough English to confirm the absence of the word he was waiting for.

The girl set her mouth into a grimace, breathed deep, fixed her attention on the ceiling, and spoke: 'So that she might have the pleasure of inspecting your prick, Davis Raymonds.' Dark blood flowed now from her right nostril. She was weeping, but she made no sound.

lxix. prick

Too obvious for its own good, this tender episode purports to establish Fatima's supposedly hard-wired modesty. Chastely glancing forever heavenward? She *fucked* him. Sharia or no sharia. She *fucked* him, hard, and she destroyed our home.

'I am so, so sorry,' Thelonius whispered to her.

She closed her soft wet eyes.

⊠⊠⊠

Indelible was sometimes mistaken for a child.

Tiny, bug-eyed, barely five feet of him, with spidery little limbs: not the best profile, perhaps, for a doctor who treats adults, but serviceable, and even an advantage, for one whose aspiration is to heal children. His physique and his face sent a silent message of compassion: 'I understand what it is to look overmatched.'

Indelible was logging onto his computer, having satisfied himself that his wife and son were asleep. He checked his email and saw this message: *Leave Islamic City immediately and take your family.*

Indelible sniffed twice, took a long sip of Darjeeling tea. After he had swallowed, he said, 'Allahu Akbar.'

He checked his next email, which came from an account whose address he did not recognize, and he noted the heading, in English: *Who are you?*

He put down his tea, clicked on the message, and saw that the body was empty.

He clicked 'reply' and wrote, in English, *Who cares?*

Before Indelible could hit 'send', his front door collapsed, and armed men in black surrounded him, their faces all curved black Plexiglas. He counted seven of them, each pointing a black assault rifle toward him.

'I surrender,' said Indelible.

---

lxx. 'I surrender,' said Indelible

The introduction of this libellous thread of the narrative constitutes a sustained personal and professional insult to which I reserve, indefinitely, the right not to respond. My head is pounding again. Need another lie down. Turned off track three. Clive – awake with my groaning – says he will escort me to bed. I decline the offer, lock the door behind him. Time for a lie down.

⊠⊠⊠

A phase of calm, easy to maintain for Noura's sake, had given way to worry once Noura had gone to bed. Worry had given way to something else, something hard to name.

Fatima had estimated her return at eleven p.m. It was nearly two hours later, and no way of determining anything. Ummi paced.

This cursed night. Well. Her Baba had said she should work if she wished. Gone. And Wafa gone. Well. Do people think that they shall be left at ease only on their saying 'we believe', without being put to any test? And Wafa so close to delivery. Butchers. And Wafa laid out like that. Making a mother identify that. Well. Fury at the heart. Not how one lives. Life a parting, she knew. But this cursed night. We shall test you with a bit of fear and hunger, plus a shortage of wealth and souls and produce. Announce such to patient people, who say, whenever some misfortune strikes them: 'We belong to God, and are returning to Him!' Well.

Ummi checked the window again. No one.

She heard her own breath. The whole week swept through her, dark and cold. To fend it off, she recited aloud: *Oh, God, forgive me, eliminate my anger, and protect me from Satan.* She recited for some minutes. When the fit passed, she opened her hands, saw that the nails had bitten into the flesh of her palms, stood, and went to the window. It was most likely that Fatima would return in a vehicle of some kind. She could not imagine they would send her into the dark to walk home alone through those streets.

lxxi. vehicle

And back. Track four and its barrow, rich with symbolic import, await the play command. A barrow: a vehicle. Control the vehicle of communication, the Fabs advise, and you control the narrative. Control the narrative and you control the conflict.

lxxii. the dark

TERROR ATTACK ON SYNAGOGUE, SHOPPING MALL AVERTED

(Special to the Post*)*

Three self-styled jihadists from Oldburgh hoped to shock America by firebombing a synagogue, shooting down a plane, and gunning down holiday shoppers — all in a carefully coordinated wave of attacks. The plan was conceived to avenge the deaths of Muslims abroad, federal and state law enforcement officials said today.

The three men, who allegedly referred to themselves online as the 'Oldburgh Jihadi Ensemble', meant to carry out the attacks Tuesday morning, planting what they believed to be car bombs outside an Oldburgh synagogue and preparing to detonate them at the same moment they used an anti-aircraft missile to shoot down a passenger plane. An attack on a shopping mall was intended to follow shortly afterwards. Instead of delivering carnage, the suspects were taken into custody amid a massive show of police firepower, including an armoured vehicle the size of a large cargo truck.

Oldburgh's mayor sounded a warning today that the Oldburgh arrests drew attention to the 'relentless nature' of Islamic terrorism, more than five years after the 9/11 attacks. A confidential informant, posing as a member of an Islamic extremist group, made contact with one of the men at the Oldburgh mosque and used clandestine audio and video equipment, 'sophisticated and quite expensive', in the words of a spokesperson, to record jihad-related discussions over a period of weeks.

18 **In Which a National Hero Is Slandered Yet Again**

At the same moment Ummi stared out the window in search of her eldest daughter, Staff Sergeant Mike Mazzoni was passing the night shift in an entrepreneurial frame of mind.

Miles away from Islamic City, he was reading *TIME* magazine beneath a high-mounted sodium light that glowed orange in the night. He was surrounded by a system of high, metal fences describing a rectangle a quarter of a mile in length and an eighth of a mile in width. Neither the orange-lit razorwire atop those fences, nor the steep, bleak, nearly naked, orange-lit hillside that he was supposed to be monitoring for movement, distracted him.

TIME said dogfighting, 'banned under the country's late and unlamented hard-line regime as un-Islamic', was experiencing a resurgence in certain corners of the Republic. Mazzoni, who had pulled night watch, chewed down a tough stick of jerky, wondered just how much ragheads really knew about dogfighting and wondered, too, what a sensible, experienced impresario from Atlantic City might be able to lend in the way of razzle-dazzle, in the way of upping the game, in the way of show business consultation.

He read in *TIME* how several thousand men and boys, most under twenty, gathered in 'empty fields on the outskirts of Islamic City' every Friday for some free entertainment. Betting was still prohibited.

Empty fields. No bets. Please. The whole point was for the action to take place in private, in a spot only certain privileged insiders could reach, a spot you had to know someone in order to get to. That place had to be enclosed. It had to be relatively small. To make it exciting enough to pay for, the venue had to carry at least the possibility of getting busted in a small room, had to deliver the visceral, physical sensation that the dogs might manage to tear the roof off of your life.

Mike Mazzoni, who had twenty-eight years on his back, was not, strictly speaking, supposed to be reading on duty. Or eating. He was protected by a good relationship with Captain X, a relationship that permitted him, most of the time, to float in a broad, open and improvisatory space of his own choosing whenever a manpower shortage forced him to pretend to guard a site – in this case, a supply depot.

Now he shook his head in disbelief as he read in *TIME* magazine about how the economics of the thing worked. The crowds got in for free. Nobody (he had to read it twice to make sure, but it was there in black and white) actually bet on anything. The ringmasters played for tips from the dog owners. The owners of impromptu food stands hawked fried potatoes to spectators. People crouched in that idiotic pose where their butts almost touch the ground. A judge, who worked for free, said which dog had won and which dog had lost. He screamed the results to the crowd, who applauded politely. The fights were always stopped – either with a stick or a bucket of water dumped on top of the competitors' heads – before a dog died or was injured seriously. What crap.

One dog had to die. At least.

TIME said the fighting dogs were 'massive'. Judging from the photo in the article, they looked like mastiffs. It took two men to hold one of them back, each holding a leash made from metal cable. This part impressed Mike Mazzoni. There was potential here. The dogs, at any rate, meant business.

lxxiii. article

To date, no less than four articles in respected national print publications – each hiding behind thick waves of op/ed-page smoke to conceal authorship – have taken various aspects of the Oldburgh Jihadi Ensemble operation to task. The fingerprints of a grey-haired familial adversary within the Directorate are not hard to detect.

lxxiv. business

Track four evokes, as I have noted, Desmond's barrow, a portable market-cart still deployed in London's barrow markets. I saw one during our vacation to England in 2002. T was unaware that the song's lyrics are based on an actual street vendor who conducted business there in the year of Mother's death.

But what about Bobbler?

19 **In Which a Sexual Motive Is Confirmed beyond All Reasonable Doubt**

At 1:21 a.m. by the living-room wall clock, Ummi spotted from her window a small, distant figure that could have been her daughter: a young woman, covered, illuminated by occasional white streetlight, walking alone down the long, dark alleyway that led to their apartment.

Ummi held her breath. The figure drew closer.

Her.

Having confirmed her daughter's light, steady, rapid gait, Ummi began sobbing. Fatima home. That was the important thing. The reprimand would wait. The demand for an explanation of that absurd decision to take the mobile phone, that late arrival, that shameful, reckless walk home alone, all of those discussions would wait, too. Now Fatima was home and safe and untouched, glory to God.

> **lxxv. untouched, glory to God**
>
> Fatima's chastity – a dubious proposition at best, and conceded here only as T's literary conceit – perpetuate *Jihadi*'s conjoined themes of sexuality and the promises of the afterlife. They all imagine they will receive seventy-two virgins when executed. Adolescent nonsense, deftly parodied by Molly Jones's (track four's) earthy, experienced, frankly carnal assent to intercourse.

Ummi's weeping, too loud, awakened Noura, who stood now in the middle of the dining room in her nightgown. 'Nine was right about Fatima coming back, wasn't he?'

Ummi looked up at her daughter, wiped her eyes, nodded.

'Is the nudie-butt coming in, too?'

Ummi ignored this question, choosing instead to affirm with two open, upraised palms that all was well.

The familiar rhythm of Fatima's tread up the two flights of stairs. All was well, yes? The sound of Fatima's hand on the door. And the sound of the door opening. All well, yes?

Dear God. Her face. Expressionless. Bruised and streaked with blood.

'I shall need to find a new job, Mother, if we are ever to leave this city. Which we will, Godwilling.'

⊠⊠⊠

The large cloth bag, tied behind and pulled tight around his head, had once, perhaps, held rice. The bag was wet now. Thelonius sagged upon his X.

'This,' a deep, low voice said slowly, in heavily accented English, 'is what a lapse in morale looks like.'

Thelonius sucked air from the cloth, with his mouth open wide.

'Contrary to popular belief, we are all quite interested in morale here,' the voice said, in English. 'So we now reach an intermission in the programme. He is tired?'

Bound Thelonius fought back a gag, nodded. Then a fearful blow struck his knee again, and a double-jointed fire-arc wound its way down his shin and up his spine. This new blast of pain took his breath away, and he heaved and writhed on the X.

Someone untied and removed the big wet cloth bag. The brightness wounded Thelonius, whose eyes shut tight. He took in air and strained against the wrist and ankle bindings. After a few seconds, he was able to look around. Fatima was gone. So was the little plump man. Half a dozen uniforms now stood before him.

A burly guard unbound him, stood him up briskly and walked him out of the basement room, unsteady and naked as the day he was born.

That throbbing knee refused to bear weight. Leaning against his assailant, Thelonius proceeded down a long, dark-orange-linoleum-lined hall, favouring his good leg and stumbling from time to time. The cold, inadequately fluorescent-lit corridor seemed to follow a slight upward incline, forever, and appeared to narrow as he walked – that might have been fatigue, though, or hunger.

'You will not like this place.'

The hallway turned abruptly, became a narrow wooden staircase that Thelonius mounted with agony, and eventually turned into a long row of prison cells. All that cold orange linoleum was back. Thelonius's bare feet went numb on it, and his knee ached with every step. They arrived, finally, at an unlit cell.

The big guard gave one of the bars a bang with his nightstick. From within the cell came a sudden rustle from a small, dark, blanketed figure, who sat up in shadows. Keys in the guard's burly hand unlocked the metal gate, its top-click and bottom-click sudden and not reminiscent of any kind of home. The metal gate opened into the cell.

'Yours. Until we learn who told you about that location you were photographing.'

The guard (whose bass voice Thelonius recognized as that of Morale Specialist) gestured for him to enter. Thelonius did.

'We ask the prisoner whether he would care for a Koran of his own to read, translated ably into English.' Morale Specialist produced, from a small cloth satchel slung across his shoulder, a black, leather-bound volume.

'Does it tell you to break my other knee if I refuse to read it?'

Morale Specialist pretended he had not heard.

'Put it back,' Thelonius said.

Morale Specialist, apparently incapable of displaying emotion, closed the cell door, which top-clicked and bottom-clicked again. He replaced the Koran in his satchel and began walking down the hallway. Other prisoners in other cells began talking again as Morale Specialist put distance between himself and them.

Thelonius noticed the silence, heard the whispers and shushes. Saw a wound on his wrist from the plastic handcuff.

Bleeding for this. Might as well go out big. Eat or be eaten.

'It's an abomination,' Thelonius said, loudly and carefully enough to keep slowly-walking Morale Specialist from missing a single word, 'your Koran.'

The murmurings in the cell block dropped a level.

'You speak English well enough to know what an abomination is? It's something that causes disgust. Your Koran disgusts me. It brings nausea to me when I think what it has created here. That makes me an infidel, a limping infidel. A kafir.'

At this word, Morale Specialist stopped.

'KAFIR. Yes, I speak that much Arabic, just for you. I am a KAFIR. I reject your prophet and I reject his message and I condemn him as a reprobate. That is SHARYAR. RASOOL. SHARYAR. Got that?'

The huge guard stood motionless. The corridor had become quiet.

Thelonius pounded his own chest three times. The sound of the pounding echoed through the hall. 'KAFIR. Allah made me a KAFIR. Get it?' he asked.

There was a rustling behind Thelonius. He paid it no mind.

Morale Specialist turned his head, stared back toward Thelonius, then turned away again, made his way slowly down the long, orange corridor.

'KAFIR! KAFIR!' Thelonius shouted at him again from the cell, pounding his own chest after each repetition of the word. 'KAFIR!'

lxxvi. cell

Before they could be conducted to their justly earned prison cells, the three members of the Oldburgh Jihadi Ensemble terror cell had to be identified, monitored, and apprehended. I tender profiles of these fanatical Islamist sociopaths in notes lxxvii–lxxx and lxxxii.

From the shadows came a low disapproving sound – *Ah* – made with a voice so raspy as to sound only partly human.

20 **In Which the White Album Identifies the Leader of the Oldburgh Terrorist Cell**

The silence broke only when Morale Specialist disappeared. A careful murmuring, from no single cell and from all of them at once, followed the guard's final, smartly executed left turn. From behind Thelonius, a voice roughened by smoke, a voice that cut like acid, said, 'Allah ya firullana' – 'God forgive us.'

---

lxxvii. left turn

Paul McCartney was and remains left-handed. The *White Album* here singles out the most lyrically trivial composition of his career, track five, in order to identify 'Honey Pi' Ramzan, a self-taught math geek who claimed to have identified a divine numerical code within the Koran, and who was the OJE's ringleader. (His fortuitous nickname is, I acknowledge in the interests of full disclosure, my coinage.) Ramzan is a madman. Transcripts of the relevant mosque discussions have, alas, been lost. Sullivan Hand, however, heard these exchanges personally and has testified under oath as to their lethal content. The *White Album*, foreseeing T's chapter break here, has assigned its shortest number – track five runs a mere fifty-two seconds – to the shortest chapter in T's book. *Is it in fact the shortest in the MS? Confirm.*

Great. Another fanatic. Thelonius turned, forced a hello smile in the direction of his roommate, received none in return. He held the smile, making it harsh, and nodded.

'Howdy,' nude Thelonius said, trying to sound as much like the President as possible.

21 In Which the White Album Arraigns and Convicts a Murderous Oldburgh 'Poet'

Within a week of reading that *TIME* magazine article, Mike Mazzoni had sworn Bobbler to secrecy and enlisted his help in establishing an underground dogfighting operation. He did this for at least three reasons: out of a nagging sense that cutting Bobbler out of the project would only fuck things up worse between them, because he had promised his mother he'd Take Care of Dayton, and because he needed operating capital. This kind of thing took work, though: Mike Mazzoni had to pretend, to his brother's face and at family events, that Bobbler was not the kind of person who always screwed things up. Which he was.

They decided to run it out of D— Base, where their unit had been stationed after rotating out of the embassy assignment. D— Base was near, but not in, the village of D—, where Wafa and her unborn, unnamed daughter had died.

The first dogs had cost serious money, but people paid even more serious money to watch them fight in earnest at night. People paid to place bets with the house. They paid for things to eat and drink. Usually they paid to drink beer, too. Beer was illegal and drinking it felt dangerous. Danger made everything more expensive.

The fights consumed the take-home pay of U.S. servicemen looking for a quick thrill, as well as the pocket money of aspiring local troublemakers who saw the servicemen as role models. All of them convened after midnight in a repurposed canteen that served as the venue for the show.

A dog, Wreck, died that night. Mike Mazzoni named the place the Wreck Room.

'Don't you dare screw this up on me,' he muttered, counting the first night's take, thinking that his brother couldn't hear.

The betting in the Wreck Room spun off profits in three directions. One was the owner of the winning dog; another was the local municipal official, Jamal, who spoke good English and promised to keep quiet about the matter; the third was Mike Mazzoni and his younger brother Bobbler. Roughly equal amounts of cash reached these three groups of stakeholders, every bit of it darkly illegal under Islamic law.

Everything aside from the money earned from wagers went directly to the senior partner, Mike Mazzoni.

Eleven dogs died in the Wreck Room in the first two weeks. Mike Mazzoni marked off a square of rough terrain behind the shack.

lxxviii. dogs died

The Fab Four's premonitory instincts here move to a level of specificity even the most hardened sceptic cannot refute. The reference to dead animals blatantly evokes track six, Lennon's grim parody of the Hemingwayesque, tiger-hunting bravado he encountered by chance in India. Thus the band foresees, suggests, endorses and justifies my arrest of Dr. Tarek Jannah, a pharmacist and the second member of the OJE, whose similarly bloodthirsty fantasies I detail in the next note.

'Dig the holes deep, Bobbler,' he said, handing a shovel to his smaller, gentler associate.

lxxix. holes

Track six continues its potent commentary on the OJE case via its subtle reference to bullet-holes. It was Jannah who proposed puncturing the occupants of a shopping mall with automatic gunfire. The attack was to take place on Christmas Eve.

Bobbler was Mike Mazzoni's junior partner. His real name was Dayton. Nobody knew how they came to be assigned to the same unit.

lxxx. the same unit

Before being taken into custody, Jannah wrote and posted on the internet a number of execrable 'poems' glorifying the prospect of meeting one's death at the hands of American soldiers. The verses are well known to any serious student of the case, and I refuse to reproduce them here.

Mike Mazzoni liked being the senior partner, just as he liked occupying a higher rank than his brother. He'd nicknamed his brother Bobbler because of his supposed inability to field ground balls back in Little League. There was irony here: Dayton had taken the starting shortstop's job away from his older brother that year. Yet Mike Mazzoni, a restless, unwilling second-stringer who talked a lot on the bench, had somehow made sure that the nickname stuck. A reputation for clumsiness attached itself to the boy, though his mother insisted, once it stuck, that her two sons were equally likely to spill beverages or drop glasses. Whenever you rename something, you control it.

> **lxxxi. reputation … control**
>
> After this sociopath's arrest, T tried, in vain, to turn him and his accomplices into some kind of cause célèbre within the Directorate. That was the virus talking, of course. Yet he inspired another damnable round of paternal meddling. The pair of them. The pair of them. Noses in other people's business. Need a lie down now.

Mike Mazzoni renamed his commanding officer 'Captain X', which stuck, too. He renamed the dogs he bought. He renamed just about everything he ran into in the Islamic Republic. He said it kept him from going crazy.

⊠⊠⊠

Wafa had always insisted it was their father's passing that brought on Noura's hallucinations.

This was tact. Fatima was certain Wafa had only pressed the point to comfort their mother, who did not like to imagine any influences besides grief upon Noura's state of mind. A great-grandmother on their mother's side had been institutionalized for similar problems.

Fatima recalled many early clues that there was something different about her sister. Some of these extended back to their days in New Hampshire. Noura had been staring too intently out the car window. The sun had set. Fatima could no longer tell in what direction Baba was driving. Mother and Wafa were singing. They were on the way to the mall to buy something for Noura. Fatima interrupted the song, sought a promise that, wherever they ended up, something would be bought for her. Baba said they would see. Fatima, unhappy with that response, had wished aloud that SHE had been the younger sister. Baba had reminded her – gently – that wishing for the past to have been different was sinful. He flicked on the interior light. Fatima saw his hazel eyes smile in the rear-view mirror. Fatima glared at her younger sister, then whispered a coarse word. Apparently Baba heard. Fatima heard his tisk, saw his eyes darken in the mirror.

'No dessert tonight. And nothing at the mall.'

Off went the light. But Noura hadn't heard. She was still staring out the open car window at … something.

Mother asked: 'What are you watching, Noura?'

'Devils, probably,' Fatima said in a sour voice. 'Her best friends.'

'You are a better girl than that, Fatima,' Baba said, sad.

Silence. Mother turned on the radio. A newscast played.

Noura leaned over. 'I do see them,' the three-year-old whispered to Fatima, as though imparting a deadly secret. 'And hear them, too. Devils.'

Now, ten years on, there were, for Noura, no more secrets to keep. This morning, she entered with groceries and announced loudly that a red-haired boy named Crazytown was outside writing out detailed instructions for blowing up their building. She insisted that his intricate bomb designs were laid out on the sidewalk in luminescent purple chalk, as was his lifelike sketch of Fatima laid out 'naked, naked, like you were coming from the shower, but also how you are right now'.

'That's none of his business,' Fatima said, opening her laptop. 'Or yours.'

'He said you'd say that.'

'Put away the groceries, please. No point standing there all day.'

'He said you'd say that, too.'

'Just put them away, Noura.'

Why was Noura as she was? Fatima had given up on that question. She no longer wasted energy determining a single cause for something. It was her experience that important circumstances usually existed in a vast, elusive cloud of correlation, rather than in a single chain of cause and effect. The will of Allah was what counted, and that was beyond appeal. She booted up her computer, saw a dark bruise on her face in the black screen's reflection, then the screen flashed blue and then mostly white and the bruise was gone. There was work to do.

'Crazytown sees you, but not like I see you,' Noura shouted out of the open window at a puzzled, matronly pedestrian. 'He sees you naked.'

Fatima rose and closed the window. 'I said put those groceries away, please.'

Crazytown had become a regular visitor. Once, Noura had ordered him out of her bedroom at three in the morning.

Noura put down the bags at last and informed Fatima that the man she had seen in the car outside had decided to wait there until he was permitted in for a cup of tea.

Fatima, back at her laptop, feigned interest, asked what the man in the car looked like and continued to search for career opportunities.

Noura humphed. 'He is *really out* there, Fatima.'

22 In Which the White Album Unmasks Another Conspirator

The refugee camp was (the government insisted) to be called Camp Rahma, but all the workers, including Indelible, called it what the residents called it, which was Camp Jahannam. Rahma means 'mercy'. Jahannum means 'Hell'.

Indelible, who worked as a paediatrician there, ended up missing four straight days of work. No one who reported to him knew why. He had warned each staff member privately that such an absence was possible, that this was in the course of things. The staff were to assume that such an unanticipated absence might last for a week. If it continued for longer than that, they were to contact Indelible's wife, face to face and voice to voice, no telephone and no email.

Among the patients Indelible had been unable to treat because of that unscheduled absence was a boy with bleeding, swollen arms, whose father carried him everywhere. The staff at Jahannum had found the pair wandering through the barren stumps of what had once been a grove of olive trees. The father repeatedly muttered a single word: 'Sorry.'

When pressed by a nurse, the man had called himself Abu Islam. That, the nurse assumed, made the son Islam. The father's eyes gleamed.

The boy he carried, dangerously dehydrated, perhaps eight years old, swung in and out of consciousness. He had dozens of puncture wounds on his arms, but none elsewhere. The wounds were from flechettes, all of which someone had extracted. Now both arms were angry, alive, weeping with infection. It took two hours for the staff to extract the boy from the man's grasp. They cleaned the wounds, administered the first rounds of medication, gave the father a handful of blister packs. The next morning, both of them had vanished.

lxxxii. weeping

And back. Unpleasant dreams I shall not recount here. Skipped tedious Fatima bit. The weeping lead guitar solos of track seven confirm my deepest initial suspicions concerning studious Henry Lowdon, the third active member of the OJE terror cell, and the loudest advocate for the (foiled) attack on the synagogue. So many mistakes. So little learned.

⊠⊠⊠

Before murdering his wife, George Liddell boasted to customers that he was not a jealous man, but, to the contrary, rather a free thinker on sexual matters.

George had moved his small family from Los Angeles up to San Francisco – this was before any 'hippie scene' emerged there – where he ran a used bookstore that became popular among aspiring beatniks, jazz freaks, poets, artists, restless businessmen in search of illegal words and images, and professional nonconformists. George was all of these.

Thelonius's first clear memory is of the helpless, unsorted cardboard boxes in the back room of this shop: the hundreds of varied book spines, the scent of decaying paper, the long wait for proper public display. Among those boxes was one containing used comic books his father had not yet sorted into subgroups (Marvel, DC, Other). Thelonius, an early reader, was five when he set up a folding chair next to this box. Without prompting, he inspected all new arrivals, instinctively treating the delicate colour masterpieces with care and respect.

The grown-up volumes in the main store were displayed mostly from the ground up, their titles reading left-to-right in vaguely accessible stacked towers, and only occasionally on shelves in boring, horizontal rows. The whole floor-to-ceiling collection was marked with thematic overhead clues. These were hand-painted in huge, fantastic letters on signs suspended, miraculously, by invisible fishing-wire: OLD LIES. FANTASY. ALLEGED HISTORY. JAZZ.

SELF-RELIGION.   BLIND-RELIGION.   EXPLOITATION.
PHYSICAL ROMANCE.

There must have been thirty or more of these huge signs hanging down, announcing the corridors of a palace: his father's domain, immeasurable, unfathomable, stuffed at every corner with gigantic ideas. A hall of miracles. But.

When Thelonius revisited the place in 1990, it was shockingly tiny. It had become a soap shop, and smelled no longer of dying paper, but of warring perfumes – lavender versus patchouli versus musk – and, beneath that, the faint, ancient stench of blood.

In the bookstore he now wandered in his memory, though, the scent was still that of books. OLD LIES was still classic fiction. Perhaps there had been another sign, NEWER LIES, for the contemporary fiction of the period. Thelonius was uncertain whether he actually remembered this sign or had concluded it into existence. There was nothing pejorative in the 'LIES' tag. George considered inspired, shameless lying a prerequisite of good storytelling, and could cite essays to support the point.

FANTASY was definitely Tolkien and Carroll and such, and those beloved comic books. When George wasn't in the office or at the counter, Thelonius spent most of his time in FANTASY. ALLEGED HISTORY was, in all likelihood, history. His father would never have raised a sign that said HISTORY. PHYSICAL ROMANCE was pornography, much of it visual and explicit. Technically, PHYSICAL ROMANCE was off limits to the boy, but George always pretended not to notice brief visits. George, unlike Irene, was inclined to let Thelonius read anything from any stack. 'Good and bad are whatever the hell you say they are,' George had told his son. 'Slap anybody who tells you that a book that he hasn't read is bad.' PHYSICAL ROMANCE must have been an important profit centre. Thelonius recalled seeing a slow parade of grim men in dark suits under this sign. He also recalled an argument there, a loud one, between his mother and father, who happened to be standing in PHYSICAL RO-MANCE when the subject of Irene's unexpected pregnancy came up.

lxxxiii. Good and bad are whatever the hell you say they are

The beatnik ethos. Reality, alas, is starker. It is one of the better-kept secrets of the Directorate – a secret even my late father and my fiercest detractors never disputed in my presence – that good and bad, right and wrong, do not exist. There is only, ever has been only, ever will be only, strategic interest.

It was well after hours. Thelonius, presumed asleep on the little mat that served as an alternate bedroom, was wide awake, having munched a handful of what he thought was some exotic dried fruit, but turned out to be hallucinogenic mushrooms. He had just been reading a comic book: *SERGEANT USA #109, THE HERO THAT WAS*.

lxxxiv. awake

The Fabs remind me here to note that Sullivan Hand, who worked endless sleepless hours undercover impersonating a newly minted Muslim addicted to offering prayers in the mosque, was essential in bonding with these solemn, bloody insomniacs. Their convictions could not have been secured without him.

lxxxv. *SERGEANT USA #109*

This comic book is now in my possession.

Thelonius, pondering an impossibly coloured butterfly that had just settled onto Sarge's troubled red-white-and-blue head, heard his father shouting the unfamiliar phrase 'knocked up', then a scuffle and a scream. He ran to investigate. He left the back room, which opened onto FANTASY.

The sudden undulation of the store's walls notwithstanding, he made up the distance between FANTASY and PHYSICAL RO-MANCE in no time, having long ago memorized the maze. There, in PHYSICAL ROMANCE, he saw his mother's opened throat spouting blood like wine.

23 **In Which the White Album's Second Side Begins**

Indelible had been brought in for questioning for one reason: He was the proprietor of a website that featured videos showing American soldiers being shot, incinerated, detonated and beheaded. Truth be told, there was only one beheading video, but it was very popular. 'Politically extreme' websites were illegal in the Republic.

---

lxxxvi. shot

This word keys the entire dreary chapter to the first song of the *White Album*'s second side, track eight. Like *Jihadi* itself, the song poses as a plea for pacifism and concludes in violence. Charles Schulz's wildly popular cartoon poster 'Happiness Is a Warm Puppy' inspired track eight. In 1968 the National Rifle Association circulated a clumsy, ineffective advertisement (which my father, a sportsman, framed and hung). It retained the familiar image of Snoopy, and replaced the word 'puppy' with 'gun'.

Asked whether he would do all Murad Murad ordered, and thus avoid a prison term, Indelible swallowed hard and replied: 'Insha Allah.' His new handler smiled.

---

lxxxvii. Insha Allah

'If God wills it'. A phrase employed to avoid assuming the personal responsibility that accompanies either 'yes' or 'no'. One never gets a straight answer out of these people.

Indelible's site would have to be shut down, of course, and it was assumed from this point forward that he accepted that. The site having existed, though, provided the perfect cover for the work he would now be doing for the BII. Something he could boast about once having created.

Murad Murad opined that there was no limit to where this might go.

Indelible insisted that there was only one online source for his videos: a foreign site he suspected was affiliated with Al Qaeda. He quickly volunteered its details, including his own login and password information, so that the BII could track down who ran it before the Americans did. Insha Allah. He shot Murad Murad a suitably servile glance, then supplied the email address of the unknown person who had advised him of the site's existence.

That address was fabricated. It ended up connecting to no one.

⊠⊠⊠

Standing naked in his cell in the Islamic Republic, Thelonius examined his surroundings.

A window, barred from the inside with iron grating, suggested vaguely either that dawn had risen or that the sun was about to set. A hole cut dead centre in the floor issued a smell that said 'toilet'. His roommate was sitting and coughing between pleas for forgiveness.

'Allah la firullana.'

Racking cough.

'Allah la firullana.'

Another racking cough, but longer.

'Allah la firullana.'

The longest racking cough yet, followed by a deep, nicotine-scarred inhale.

Thelonius shared this musty, pungent space with an old, transparent-looking being whose face was wrinkled like paper, who huddled in a gold blanket smoking two cigarettes at once, who gestured toward a cot on the other side of the cell. Another blanket, grey, and a set of yellow prison clothes lay folded there. The being exhaled a long jet of smoke. Thelonius sat on the cot, wrapped himself and shivered.

Slight brightening at the window. So sunrise.

It probably wouldn't be all that hard to get through the day. The thing would have to stop smoking eventually.

⊠⊠⊠

The usually taciturn local official whose bribes had been set at thirty-three percent was named Jamal, but Mike Mazzoni called him Jimmy, a nickname this official disliked. Whatever one called him, he got more chatty late in the evening over illegal Heinekens. While Bobbler pursued shovel duty outside, Mazzoni heard this local official announce, without warning, 'the new terms of agreement'.

He now expected, he announced in English, to be called by his actual name, preceded by the word Mister.

He expected a cut of fifty percent from Mike Mazzoni from that night forward on all earnings, including the illegal wagers.

He expected weekly written reports.

Mike Mazzoni inquired as to what the hell all this was about.

Jamal shared some income figures he could only have received from Bobbler.

Disagreement followed.

Outside digging, Dayton Mazzoni heard each man offer his own colourful metaphors and emphatic predictions as to how the conflict would be resolved. Somebody took a swing at somebody. The place was empty by the time Dayton made it back in, having buried another dog.

lxxxviii. buried another dog.

This passage evokes not only the butchered tiger of a previous song, but also the original National Rifle Association advertisement that dominated my father's study and inspired the present track.

The next morning, in the mess hall, the brothers discussed, at some length, a controversial question: what the fuck was wrong with Bobbler. It was resolved, not without acrimony, that he would stop answering questions from ragheads. It was further resolved that his primary skill set out here was keeping his mouth shut and doing what he was told and that he would continue to cultivate and expand those skill sets, inasmuch as they had kept him alive so far.

⊠⊠⊠

The loss of his eldest and youngest sons had changed him.

Before that loss Atta had (like everyone else in his family) been only intermittently religious, praying on the two major holidays and during the month of Ramadan. He now walked the streets of Islamic City in rags, reciting the Koran. He fasted three days a week. He made his ablutions in public fountains and he slept according to the model of the Prophet, peace and blessings be upon him, upon his right side with both hands placed below his head as a pillow. He ordered his sole surviving child to sleep likewise, despite the open wounds on his arms.

They slept in alleys. The boy woke often, choosing always to let his father sleep.

Before the flechette attack, Atta had worked sixty to seventy hours a week as a chemical engineer and had created a colour-coded printed schedule for the four babysitters he engaged. Now his chief, and for all anyone in his family could tell, his only obligations were religious. The Prophet said to be as an itinerant, and so Atta was no longer fond of houses.

He awoke well before dawn, in time to make both the extra prayers and the obligatory prayers. He learned to avoid police, who had a habit of preventing him from reciting and telling him to go home. His little boy, he insisted, did not want them in a house. They *were* home.

He began by giving a loud speech to his son at around the time of the midday prayer. The next day, Atta renamed himself the New Imam and called the city to prayer, proving, if nothing else, that he still had a vigorous set of lungs.

A few vagrants came to listen.

The next day, there were a few more vagrants and they stayed to pray. The next day, there were a dozen men. The day after that, there were about seventy. And the day after that, it looked like four hundred, most of them better dressed than the vagrants.

The following day, they started to dress in white because he told them all to do that. The white they used to dress themselves was as empty as a politician's promise, as empty as Becky's eyes staring him down between compliance blows, as empty as the rest of this guilty dead guy's page.

⊠⊠⊠

Having slept a dreamless morning, Thelonius awoke and regarded his shrivelled, inscrutable cellmate. Was it possible the little heap had stared at him, chain-smoking two cigarettes at a time, since sunrise?

They inspected each other. Without warning, the figure in the blanket extinguished the latest pair of cigarettes and stood in preparation for the noonday call to prayer. How it had anticipated the squawking 'Allahu Akbar' of the speaker system by ten or fifteen seconds was unclear.

lxxxix. unclear.

Not to me. Simple coincidence is often misinterpreted.

Thelonius counted twenty orange linoleum floor tiles. Some of them were fractional, though. The squares surrounded the pungent hole in the middle of the floor.

A tasteless lunch – rice and disintegrating, overcooked lamb on a metal plate – slid through the slot at the bottom of the cell door. Thelonius ate it and slid the plate back again at the barking of some foreign word or other from the guard. Time passed.

A bland chicken dinner on a similar, but not identical, metal plate slid through the slot. Thelonius ate it.

In between those meals, several dozen pairs of cigarettes had illuminated and extinguished themselves, using his roommate as a kind of bellows, and several prayers had come and gone. Not a word was spoken in the cell, beyond the occasional dull mutterings of the prayers, until Thelonious, having delivered his latest plate to the unseen barking voice, turned to his cellmate and said: 'So. Were you asking for God to forgive me, or to forgive you for being in the same room with me?'

The little wrinkled figure stared back at him from beneath the blanket, which covered everything up to the chin. The two cigarettes kept glowing in the dark and the smoke from them kept rising in twin clouds that played in synchronous, complementary pirouettes above the spindly prisoner's shaved head.

Tired of waiting for an answer, Thelonius limped across the room and checked the window. It was bolted shut. The glass was thick and shatterproof. Late evening drew itself in.

Half an hour later, night had taken over the city completely, and the sharp, insistent chord of the fluorescents hummed on and on overhead. The endless smoke was getting ridiculous.

'That's not good for you, you know,' he said. 'Sucks you dry. If you're not careful, it will make you look like a raisin. Well. More like a raisin than you already look.'

The prisoner across the room ignored the insult, or perhaps occupied a dimension where nothing had been said, and kept staring, blowing more smoke.

'Look,' Thelonius said, 'I'm a patient man.'

'Not from what I've heard.'

That raspy, acid voice again. So: it spoke English.

'Regardless,' Thelonius said. 'This window doesn't open. We're likely to be here together for a while, and I've been more than fair about the smoke so far. But if you don't lay off those cigarettes, we're going to have to have ourselves a problem. Now, do you think you can take a break so we can clear the air in here, Raisin?'

It was hard to tell with the blankets, but Thelonius guessed that the Raisin could not have weighed more than a hundred and ten pounds. Someone that size, and unarmed, would not last more than a few moments in a toe-to-toe with him. If it came to that.

Which it might. The Raisin blew a long jet of smoke, stared at Thelonius and frowned.

'I don't like repeating myself,' Thelonius said, 'but I'll do it this once. Just for you. Because you've got a lucky face. Suppose you were to put those goddamned cigarettes out for just a few minutes, chief? And spare yourself a hard time? What do you say?'

The Raisin stood, removed both mouth-bound cigarettes with a scrawny hand, held the half-smoked filters at a distance, cupping their orange embers gracefully to one side, looked the opponent over, and said: 'I had a dream about you …'

'Really. Did your dream tell you how long it would take me to clean the floor of this cell with you?'

'… and about your mother,' he continued as though Thelonius had not spoken. 'The dream was about you and your mother. You miss her a great deal now, I think.'

Wreaths of smoke rose from the two palmed cigarettes. The Raisin brought them back and began to suck on them deeply.

'In my dream, you were both in San Francisco. It was some time ago. You were a small child.'

Thelonius looked away, held himself immobile. He listened to the Raisin drawing yet more mouthfuls of smoke out of those two foul death-sticks. He listened to the expulsion of the smoke, to the purposeful sound of someone breathing uneasily, someone with a great deal of time to waste. The smoke danced upward. He took a stress breath and then looked back, with purpose, toward the figure behind the two glowing cigarette-ends.

'What about my mother?' he said, his voice more raw than he intended.

'I dreamt that you saw her die when you were a child. You watched something kill her in your presence. Your father, I think. Or a beast. Or both. There was a great deal of blood.'

More smoke. More silence.

'I dreamt that when you saw her die,' the Raisin continued, 'you began a period of trial and hardship and pain. I dreamt that delusions followed you through childhood, that you fought them off through sheer force of will. I dreamt that you convinced others that you were healed. I dreamt that your wife, alone, suspected you might not be.'

The room began to writhe.

'It was not an unpleasant dream at all,' the Raisin remarked.

xc. not an unpleasant dream

Dozed off there at my little desk. You dear dreamer, you awaken yourself to history, you kick within me now.

⊠⊠⊠

In the aftermath of his disorderly discussion in the Wreck Room with Mike Mazzoni, Jamal filed a formal written complaint with a representative of the Council of Elders. The letter set forth piously and movingly against what Jamal believed to be an illegal dogfighting and alcohol ring being operated out of D— Base.

He pleaded with the elders to take action. From such pits of corruption sprang vipers of secular influence, eager to spread their poison throughout the state. His own faith and that of his fellow believers, he warned, indeed their entire way of life, was under direct American assault.

Testimony concerning these vipers and their low desires came from Jamal and several pious associates, all of whom happened to be male members of his own family. They all swore that numerous bets had been placed, that numerous dogs had died and that much alcohol had been consumed. They all proclaimed their love for and allegiance to the Republic and all repented any past association and/ or familiarity they might have had with such vipers.

The dead guy writing this ponders the fatal mistake of defining love for country by identifying the people one hates.

⊠⊠⊠

'Yeah, the man *wait*ing out there in the car looks pretty im*por*tant,' Noura said.

'Mm hmm.'

'Pressed suit. White shirt. Dark tie. Good hair. He asked me if you lived here, and I said yes. He asked me if you got home late last night, and I said yes. He asked me if Mother had gone to work, and I said yes. He told me he wanted to have a cup of tea with you. It's fine with him if I serve as *chap*erone.'

'Mm hmm,' Fatima said, still perusing job openings on her computer. 'What kind of car? Purple, I suppose.'

'Hmph. The car is big and black, like all those limousines, and he's sitting all *alone* in the back seat. I think a driver must be in the front seat. The glass is dark. I wouldn't have seen the man in the back seat if he hadn't unrolled the window and called to me. He *said* he was from BII.'

Fatima looked up. 'What?'

'B.' (Pause.) 'I.' (Pause.) 'I.'

'Noura, are they real? The man and his driver?'

Noura's face darkened. 'You and Mother tell the entire *uni*verse,' she said, 'that everyone I meet is a halluci*na*tion, but what does that make *you*?'

Fatima scoffed, approached the window sidelong, spotted a black limousine.

'What does he want, Noura?'

xci. What does he want …?

The very question that provoked and bemused me last October. Conversation with T, already strained, was even grimmer than usual upon his return from the Islamic Republic. Eros, or the promise of it, had historically brought about denouements to such melodramas. (Yes, sex was a reliable coping tactic for each of us.) At that point, I was still willing to consume what was man of him, a favour I could not recall him ever declining. Yet he declined. The arrogance. The contempt.

'Well, how should *I* know? Nobody I ever talk to is really *there*, are they?'

⊠⊠⊠

The man who guided the little boy with the scarred arms through the streets, the man who found places for them both to sleep and pray, was no longer Atta. He was Abu Islam: the father of Islam.

He wandered Islamic City as though inspecting it prior to demolition. Often and loudly, he recited certain verses from the Koran. His father had taught him passages, years ago, and as a youth he had been praised for the accuracy of his recitation and for the strength of his voice, which one of the judges wrote was 'loud as the blows of a hammer'. He had even won a contest at the age of fourteen. He thought he'd forgotten it all. But he still knew many passages. He knew, for instance, the 'Verse of the Sword'. He now ended every day by reciting it in great, keening peals that could be heard for blocks until after dawn.

People gave them food. They took it and walked away as silent itinerants, in obedience to the Prophet. From a black-market warehouse he burgled one night, Abu Islam stole a decanter of bourbon meant for Americans. He drank it as though in a private place, yet the boy saw. Abu Islam found, in the days that followed, that the bourbon, when consumed surreptitiously, helped him identify which words, which intonations, which emphases were likeliest to draw a large crowd.

24 **In Which the Guns Continue To Warm**

When asked about 'this crap I'm hearing about dead dogs and some kind of Raghead Council', Mike Mazzoni suggested to Captain X, his commanding officer, that he might want to deny all the allegations that might be coming down the pike, because that's what he, Mazzoni, planned to do. This proposal wasn't well received.

The captain, stone-faced and fuming, was more pragmatic than he let on: He was not eager to alienate a figure the men looked up to, the elder brother of his best (and only available) sharpshooter. Even so, it was time to make a point.

Seated behind his desk, he asked Mazzoni point-blank whether all this dog business would be going away. Stared him down.

Yet Mazzoni, standing, knew that he was actually being cut slack. He held the necessary awkward silence. He inspected his boot-tops and, after half a minute or so, said, 'Yes, sir.'

By 'away' (the captain explained), he really and truly meant away. The operation that Mazzoni had been running would have to be put out of commission, at least until things cooled down. Did Mazzoni understand that?

Mazzoni nodded.

Was Mazzoni familiar with how a hammer worked? How nails penetrated certain objects? What plywood was?

Mazzoni nodded again.

'I treat you like my own boy, Mike. Maybe I shouldn't. But I do. Now go clean up your mess.'

By reveille the next night, he and Bobbler had boarded up the Wreck Room, and he had sworn with every other swing of his hammer that Jimmy would pay.

xcii. pay

I pay fifty-eight dollars a night for this place. And for what? The peremptory ineptitude of that nigger cleaning lady. Bustling in after a single knock like she owns the place.

⊠⊠⊠

Crouching in a corner, Noura watched the well-dressed man who had emerged from the limousine as though he were a film projected into the good chair near the dining-room table. He would not smile.

Ra'id, the son of the most famous man in the country, had made a point of not becoming famous. He did not enjoy being stared at, so he turned away from Noura, but he remained polite. 'What we want you to do,' Ra'id said to Fatima, putting down his teacup with practised grace, 'is keep an eye on things. Converse with people. Pay attention to them. Compliment them. Decode whether or not they're interested in overthrowing the government, and let us know, discreetly, if it appears that they are. I should be happy to double the salary that Murad is paying you. To make amends.'

'And to keep me quiet,' she said. He did not disagree, did not agree. 'Well. I know fewer people than you imagine.'

'Would you be willing to talk to individuals we pointed out to you? Virtually or otherwise?'

'I suppose.'

'Then we are in agreement? You accept the raise, you accept the assignment, you update me once a week at least, and more often as you see fit, and you agree not to speak of what happened with Murad last night?'

A bird called to Fatima from the broad, convenient tree outside her open window. She turned to look at it. Ra'id took this for a sign of assent.

This was how these people operated, how they secured agreements. They made silence mean whatever they wanted. But it was good this way. It was what *she* wanted. She allowed him to believe he had manipulated her.

'Your face,' he said, smiling at last, 'is now a state secret. To be clear: You have not spoken of last night online? Or anywhere else?'

'No,' she said. 'I told no one what happened.' That was true.

'Good. And you are willing to undergo another background check? A rather more thorough one?'

'Of course.' (This second background check never materialized, as she suspected it would not. He was testing her for compliance, as men do.)

'You may consider yourself provisionally reinstated. There is one other question. Do you happen to recall that man you saw interrogated? The American?'

Fatima was thinking of Wafa's house. Of her mother no longer having to work. Of Noura: of her safety, finally, from these unpredictable streets. Of those many secret worlds of Noura's, of their persistence, of the difficulty of keeping them unexamined by strangers here in the city. Of the possibility of political instability.

Without a pause, though, she said: 'Yes. I remember the American.'

xciii. American

Clive agreed, though not as quickly as one might like, to confiscate that nigger woman's key. Not my country when their kind can waltz, while talking on a cell phone, into a white woman's room. Left me his direct number. Said I could call any time if I ever had any problem. Wished he didn't have to go. Asked me if I believed in love at first sight. Why not?

⊠⊠⊠

There was no ambiguity in the New Imam's scholarship. His sermons centred on a single religious obligation: that of killing Americans.

xciv. killing Americans

The (apparent) disapproval of T's tone here is a trapdoor through which many an untrained analyst has fallen. Misdirection on any and every topic is to be expected from traitors who have lost their way.

'We are reclaiming the true belief system of the Muslims,' he told his little boy, who nodded.

The boy knew well enough what consequences accompanied not nodding at the appropriate moment, and how much weightier these consequences had become since the nightly bourbon sessions had begun. The boy strongly resembled his father and often reminded him of his own childhood, a circumstance not always to the boy's advantage.

Abu Islam began transporting four or five bottles of bourbon at a time in a little grey-wheeled suitcase that some admirer gave him. He kept his Koran in there, too.

Whatever Abu Islam found in that Koran that seemed to support killing Americans, he shouted in the streets. He ignored everything else. He also ignored the life, teachings, and practice of the Prophet. That particular life was full of complexities he could not manage. His own, thankfully, had become considerably simpler. Kill the Americans: That was his message and, now, his life. He called it The Point.

'We two have dedicated our lives to The Point,' the New Imam said in public, and the boy always nodded. 'We two against an empire. With Allah, that is a majority.'

Those believers who got The Point, and they were more numerous each day, began to express concern for him and for the boy, offering them living rooms and spare bedrooms to sleep in. He turned them down. They would sleep only in abandoned buildings or on the floors of mosques, he insisted. When the building was dark enough, when the mosque had emptied, he flicked on a little flashlight, jotted notes in a tiny memo pad and consumed Styrofoam cups of bourbon, an increasingly important scholarly tradition.

People began following them around the city, even quoting memorable bits of The Point. Among the earliest of these followers was a heavyset woman who told him he was too important to the Rising Nation to sleep in abandoned buildings and unlocked mosques. There were, she argued, security issues to consider.

⊠⊠⊠

Thelonius took a deep, woozy inhale of the tobacco-stained air, and the room slowed down, and then it stopped. He continued breathing in this way for some time, to keep the room steady.

Lack of food, lack of sleep. Bad breathing. That was probably why the room did that. And of course auditory hallucinations were a possibility. Which would account for …

'I studied such difficulties, you know,' the Raisin said, eyes aglow, 'difficulties arising from childhood trauma. When I took my degree in psychology.'

> **xcv. degree in psychology**
>
> I here record my considered opinion that T received nothing resembling therapy from this individual.

The Raisin mouthed both cigarettes expertly, drew one last double puff from them, removed them and crushed them on a raw open palm before depositing them in a tin can. The fluorescents shut down and the room was much darker.

And then it was later and the sun had considered rising again and the Raisin was praying again before it did. The Raisin sat and read the Koran for a long time, then prayed for a long time, then returned to bed, then slept. Then awoke and then lit up with another double glow, familiar by now to Thelonius and not as threatening as before, and then the cigarette smoke swirled in the light of the flowing dawn.

⊠⊠⊠

The Investigating Representative of the Council of Elders filed a formal demand that the Americans court-martial Staff Sergeant Michael Mazzoni. The letter was returned unopened.

With the unanimous approval of the Council, the Investigating Representative used email to appeal to various individuals in the

American command chain for guidance on the matter. These appeals were ignored as well.

The Investigating Representative made personal contact with a high-ranking, charismatic American general whose name need not be repeated here. Their unscheduled discussion occurred during a party hosted at the embassy by the Cultural Attaché.

'We will take care of this,' the general said over his Tom Collins, all business. 'I promise. You will hear from us.'

The next day, Captain X received a call from Central Command informing him that, while he did not have to press charges against Mazzoni, he did have to make a written response to the Council. There had to be a formal denial. A sworn affidavit that no betting on dogs and no consumption of alcohol had taken place would do the trick.

xcvi. affidavit

The affidavit under discussion is on file and was indeed submitted to the Council of Elders. There is no reason to doubt its authenticity or the veracity of the circumstances it describes.

⊠⊠⊠

'Who on earth is this? Tell me no lies!'

Ummi had entered, taken a look at Ra'id and been properly scandalized. The presence of an uninvited, unknown man in the home was, historically, forbidden.

'Only the son of the prime *min*ister,' Noura said, on her feet in an instant, in obedience to the uniqueness of the moment. 'Fatima pretended he didn't even ex*ist*. But he *does*.'

Ra'id stood for inspection. Noura mimicked and exaggerated his shoulders-back stance.

'Sit down, Noura,' Mother ordered. Noura did not sit. Fatima raised an eyebrow. Noura sat.

'We will be moving out of the city, Mother,' Fatima said.

Noura began meowing like a cat.

xcvii. meowing

Yet another wounded, self-indulgent reference to Child. Also, I think, a grating attempt to build sympathy for a halfwit girl who was, in all likelihood, genetically predisposed, like her older sister, to early-onset promiscuity.

⊠⊠⊠

At the heavyset woman's urging, Abu Islam began stressing the specifics of The Point in all his talks.

The killing of Americans by gunfire, explosion, hand-to-hand combat, or any means whatsoever – any American, at any time, in any situation, playing any combat role or no role at all, of any age or gender, of any mental status, while located within the Islamic Republic or in any other locality – was a binding religious obligation upon all Muslim males who had passed the stage of puberty.

He supplied no scriptural evidence for this amplification of The Point.

He pressed it anyway, and returned to it with an energy that seemed superhuman to his admirers. Here is why: One of them, the heavyset woman (to whom he had recently married himself without witnesses) procured amphetamines for him.

Ever cautious, she did some online research and warned him sternly about the dangers of mixing the pills and the bourbon. She took responsibility for his intake, ensuring at least twelve hours lapsed between the stimulant and the alcohol. She monitored his sleep patterns over four consecutive days. He averaged ninety daily minutes of slumber. Acceptable.

And he much preferred being awake, preferred spending his waking hours shouting in the streets about the necessity of killing Americans wherever they could be found. The number of his followers had grown in direct proportion to the intensity of his insistence upon this new religious obligation, The Point. Barely a week after he began preaching along this line, his Friday jumuah exceeded five hundred. He was in his element.

This destitute with no religious credentials, this wanderer toting a small boy like a pet, this roving gambler with his new wife and his grey-wheeled suitcase, beamed at the crowd.

xcviii. new wife

The gathering of mobs in the streets of Islamic City appears to have been a turning point in T's psychosis. This woman, her name still unknown, inflamed the crowds by (literally) calling for his head. The precise nature of her relationship to Fatima Adara remains obscure.

⊠⊠⊠

Another grey haze had filled the cell. After lunchtime, Thelonius asked the Raisin: 'Do you think we could discuss the smoking?'

'Certainly. We can discuss anything you like.'

'It's just that smoke makes goodwill in here more difficult.'

The Raisin smiled, exhaled a grey jet and tipped ash into that waiting can. 'A priority for you, is it? Creating and sustaining goodwill in the Islamic Republic?'

Thelonius sighed and ran a hand through his hair. 'Backtalk. Every time. You're a hard man to connect to, you know that?'

'Am I?'

The Raisin crushed the nearly full-length cigarette along the palm-ridge of a hand red and thick with calluses.

'Victory,' he said. 'Until the next skirmish, at any rate. Another victory for the Americans.'

The Raisin dropped the remnants of the smoke into the can and caught Thelonius staring at the ruined terrain of the slender hand that had consumed the ember. 'It doesn't hurt anymore when I put them out that way, you know.'

'Whatever. For your information, I didn't want a victory. I wanted a discussion.'

'Hard to tell the difference, perhaps.'

⊠⊠⊠

One bright, hot Monday morning, Mike Mazzoni and his commanding officer, Captain X, reported to Alpha Station and swore under oath that Mazzoni had been involved in no illegal or dangerous behavior involving alcohol or dogs. They also swore that rumours to the contrary were the work of local insurgents working under the influence of terrorist cells. The affidavit was submitted. The legal problems appeared to have vanished. Then the letter from Washington came.

Jamal had requested a day of personal testimony before the Council from both Mazzoni and his captain. The Council had agreed to his request and had filed an appeal with both the Adjutant General's office in Washington and the American embassy in Islamic City.

More court time. More red tape. All because some raghead wanted fifty percent that he didn't fucking deserve. All because he couldn't tell when a certain subject was closed.

'If a man ever got into an accident, it would be a shame,' said Captain X one morning, to no one, as he slowly passed the table where Mike Mazzoni was eating breakfast.

---

xcix. If … breakfast

Yet another evidence-free calumny against the memory of Staff Sgt. Michael Mazzoni. Sounds of a storm.

⊠⊠⊠

He was gone and they could all speak freely again.

Ummi had at first been hesitant to say much about the prospect of her daughter's returning to work at the BII, but the immense raise and the social status of their unexpected visitor went a long way toward overcoming her misgivings. She nodded at Fatima's recapitulation of each point she had negotiated.

Two additional weeks of vacation, making up four now. Two days to be taken immediately, for the move. Fatima would report directly to Rai'd; she would never have to enter the compound again; she would receive an advance on her first month's salary sufficient to pay off the outstanding debt on her sister Wafa's house in the village of D—. Rai'd had granted all of this without hesitation before he left, leaving Fatima wondering what more she should have requested.

Ummi asked: 'Does all this mean we can leave the city?'

There was happiness in Ummi's voice and a new vulnerability, such that the question gave Fatima a strange sensation in her stomach. Not fear exactly. The queasy feeling of something important definitely being over. It was the first time in her life her mother had openly acknowledged Fatima's role – obvious but unspoken over the past months – as head of the family.

'Yes. As soon as possible,' Fatima said, almost without missing a beat. And looked out the window at the fluttering bird that had soared away from its tree in search (she assumed) of food for its young.

Ummi supposed aloud that all the painful things likely to happen in Wafa's village must surely have already happened. She sniffed and touched the tip of her nose and then her cheek with the back of her hand. Noura stared fixedly at some Intimate Companions that had congregated in the corner of the room.

c. the room

The Album knew (though I did not) that a blackout would darken our little compartment of Motel 6, as indeed it has. No lights visible elsewhere. Writing this on battery power! Need to secure perimeter. Back soon. Storm still.

⊠⊠⊠

In the parking lot outside a mosque far too small to accommodate his purposes, Abu Islam led the late-evening prayer before perhaps seven hundred sweating people. Then, after his own remarks, which he had delivered with a bullhorn, he asked the congregation to listen to a few important words from his wife about an American she had encountered.

She took up the bullhorn and announced that she had seen an

American urinating upon the Koran, swearing vile oaths against it all the while and predicting the literal, global obliteration of the faith. Her pronouncements spread like a flame through the city.

One of her pronouncements in particular caught the public imagination and was much repeated: 'He came from nowhere, this American. Like Shaitan. And he will return like Shaitan.'

Unbidden, a restless crowd began to jostle in the darkness around the American embassy, not quite so calm or organized or patient as before. The Americans turned on the emergency lighting. Several thousand people, many of them dressed in the long white cloth favoured by Abu Islam, could be seen milling about, failing to disperse as ordered. Water cannons did not clear the street. They seemed only to draw more white robes.

The next morning, with white still surrounding the embassy, Abu Islam's heavyset wife stood on a car parked in front (a Lincoln Continental, as it happened) and used her megaphone to repeat, with previously undisclosed, thrilling details, the story of the man who had slandered the faith and urinated upon the Koran. Her account had gained potency. Its pacing had improved with every retelling and it was now as eloquent as the tail of a rattlesnake.

She had seen these events herself. She was prepared to swear it was the very man who had just been taken into custody for murdering a father and his daughter in the street in broad daylight. She had seen that crime too. And so forth.

She assured the crowd she had many sources. This infidel, she predicted, would soon be returned to America. Heads in the crowd shook. Voices shrieked 'No!' Fists shook in time with her chants of *Allahu Akbar*.

Somewhere within the tightening knot of dissatisfied citizens, a man stumbled while attempting to extract himself from the centre of the throng. Word spread that he was a recently unmasked spy eager to return to his American handlers.

In fact, he was a tow-truck driver who had been summoned, via his cell phone, to retrieve a crashed vehicle.

Someone shouted that the spy must be stopped.

Someone else repeated the order.

Soon it rang out everywhere.

Before he was a block away from the embassy gate, some faithful citizen or other pulled the man to the ground, produced a box-cutter and slit his throat.

The crowd, dense and sweaty in the morning heat, withdrew on sudden instinct from the space surrounding the prone body, like the tentacles of a sea anemone retracting when touched by a foreign object. Whoever had severed the jugular withdrew too. The man bled to death in the street, but the heavyset woman kept shouting into her megaphone. Worshippers were advised to wear white when attending the New Imam's sermon that afternoon. Brothers only, please.

The dimensions of that day's crowd of worshippers at Abu Islam's formal Friday sermon became difficult to calculate. All that could be said for certain was that people occupied all available space on all the sidewalks and all the streets for at least four square, downtrodden city blocks in the poorest, grimmest and oldest sector of the city. Maybe there were ten thousand of them – overwhelmingly male in proportion, whatever their number – waiting as the necessary acoustic adjustments were made. They remained in their ranks, rapt and silent, as Abu Islam finally gave his salaam and began outlining the moral obligation to obliterate soldiers and anyone else born in the United States, and not stop doing so until the American military presence in the Islamic Republic was broken.

A few police officers predicted an uprising that afternoon.

When the time came, eighty-five minutes later, the sea of white robes prayed toward Mecca without incident. The worshippers bowed and supplicated in straight lines that intersected disjointedly with the crooked, filthy and ancient streets they occupied. They shone in the harsh sun. They waited for instructions. They did not disperse.

Secular commentators began referring to the white-clad crowd that followed Abu Islam as 'the great White Beast'.

⊠⊠⊠

'Your Mr. Bush Two,' the Raisin said, extending a long gaze out the tiny window and over the cityscape, 'is a Bolshevik and nothing more.'

There was no smoke at the moment. They had reached a compromise: staring at the walls for what turned out to be the better part of a day. The Raisin's sudden pronouncement suspended itself in midair. Outside, visible from the window, the gathered white crowds issued well-coordinated shouts.

'How do you reckon that?' leaning, yellow-smocked Thelonius asked at last, aslant the window. The Raisin looked satisfied, as though tired of the distant noise and glad to have a replacement for it.

'Two and a half years ago,' the Raisin answered, not looking at Thelonius, 'your Mr. Bush Two ordered his armies and his bombers to dismantle this country and overthrow our leader. A bad man. A bloody man. A man to be despised. Many of us were in the streets, shouting for joy, after he was hanged. But the question remained: what, exactly, was to come next? Not the Islamists who had preceded him? Then what?'

Thelonius shrugged and looked away.

'Your Mr. Bush Two said it was more satellite dishes and more computers and more music and more women naked on the billboards. The young men scale the billboards now and rip off the images, sheet by sheet. They destroy music where they find it. They chant in the streets for the death of your Mr. Bush One and Mr. Bush Two. And, the guard says, for your death.'

At these words, Thelonius felt his insides tighten and go cold. A drumbeat took over his head. The Raisin looked him over, as though assessing a captured insect. There was more noise from the late-afternoon street.

'I still don't see how that adds up to Bolshevism,' Thelonius said, in a careful, even tone.

'The earliest Bolsheviks comprised a loosely knit gang of thugs,' the Raisin continued, more than prepared for the challenge. 'They had convinced themselves the people of Russia would rise up in righteous rage and overthrow their oppressors if only Czar Alexander II were assassinated. One morning, they stationed three men with bombs to follow the Czar as he went to observe a military roll call.

'As it started to snow, the Czar emerged from his carriage. The first thug threw his bomb. It misfired. The second thug threw his bomb. It blew the Czar's legs off.

'The Czar died that night. A third thug had been ready with a third bomb in case the first two failed.

'But the people of Russia did not do as the thugs believed they would. Even though the serfs were oppressed. Even though there was poverty and abuse of human rights. Even though there was torture of political prisoners. Even though there was oppression and had been oppression for centuries, the people declined to play their role. They did not gather in the streets and demand the abolition of the Czars. They refused to follow the script the thugs had handed them.

'The Bolsheviks served only their own theory. Not the people.

'The assassination of the Czar did not ignite any progressive revolution. It left the nation numbed, confused, humiliated, paralyzed. It produced nothing.

'If you had been there that morning, if you had looked through the falling snow at the carnage outside the Czar's carriage, you would have seen that third bomber shivering in his boots, clutching his undischarged explosive, imagining himself the agent of history. There is always some idiot Bolshevik in the crowd.

'Your Mr. Bush Two is such an idiot, such a Bolshevik. He imagines a new kind of society, or thinks he does. But he believes he can impose it by sheer force of will. He imagines history is a script he has written. And yes, there are Bolsheviks out there, in our streets, too, waiting with bombs in their hands.'

The Raisin took a pair of cigarettes from a box labelled Elite Tobacco, then stopped and put them back and said, 'Sorry. In honour of our agreement: not until sunset.' And a smile Thelonius could not manage to return. His hands were trembling.

'Are they really calling for my death?'

The Raisin listened, nodded, and waited for the sun to set.

The sound of the Raisin mustering the rough consonants of the Koran still set Thelonious's teeth on edge. He shifted back and forth uneasily on his cot. A few minutes later, the two cigarettes glowed. Then, when they were extinguished on a rough palm, Thelonius heard the Raisin gasping and wrestling onto the bed, and then, finally, he heard the Raisin snoring.

---

ci. heard

Heart still racing. I can hear it. Literally hear the noise of my heart. Twenty-seven minutes spent near our doorway in the security stance. I held that purloined grey-handled steak knife aloft the whole time, switching hands as necessary. For you, Prudence. Then the power returned, the lamps reignited. Bright again. I feared the worst. False alarm. Heavy, unseasonable desert tempest outside. Power line down somewhere, according to Clive, who checked in personally, tried to kiss me. Still a bit jittery. Not from that, though.

⊠⊠⊠

Mike Mazzoni's incident report noted that a local man, Jamal F–, also known as Jimmy F–, wandered into U.S. munitions storage facility DJL-66 late one night, presumably intoxicated. At the time of the incident, Staff Sergeant Mazzoni, the officer on duty, had issued a clear order for the individual to stop and raise his hands in the air and cease all movement. This order had been issued in the native language. The individual continued movement of a threatening nature. Staff Sergeant Mazzoni repeated his order. The individual made an approach toward Staff Sergeant Mazzoni and intimated in English that he had a firearm. The report stated that he then reached inside his clothing.

At that point, Sergeant Mazzoni discharged his weapon in self-defence.

The concealed firearm had been found in the individual's clothing. The body had been returned to the family.

cii. The body

Excuse me. There are stumblers into unauthorized areas and threateners of our men. There are regions of the world that we may set apart. We need not make martyrs of every single one of these people. They do die from time to time.

After this report was filed, the case was closed.

⊠⊠⊠

All of this grass had been soaked in blood.

Mother and Noura were shopping, which left Fatima to deal with the neglected lawn. No trace of the flechette attack was visible now, praise God, a circumstance probably due, at least in part, to the vigorous rainstorm that had cloaked the suburbs yesterday. She was glad it had rained, but the thought that the overgrown tangle beneath her feet had been fed with her sister's wounds and the wounds of others still sickened her.

ciii. rainstorm

Clive 'keeping an eye' on me 'till the storm passes'. In case I 'need help'. Something amusing about all this. We will keep an eye on each other.

She called the number her mother had given her for a gardener, heard an old man answer the phone, introduced herself and asked if he could come in and mow the place immediately. Told that he would be at least three days in arriving (he was now the only landscape man in the district, and his list of outstanding obligations was long), she thanked him, confirmed him for the following weekend and went to the shack out back. There she rummaged around.

When she came out, she had a machete in her hand.

She set to work on the wet grass beneath the spot where she had been told that Wafa had fallen. She worked her way outward in concentric circles. Within forty minutes the portion of the home visible to the winding road, at least, was presentable again. Not manicured, to be sure. But presentable. Even clean again. Her back ached and there were blisters on two of her fingers, and she had piled a great heap of grass in a corner.

civ. clean

Clive suggests I take a bath to calm down, but that damnable nigger woman did not bother to scrub out the tub. I informed him of as much. Did he relieve her of her key? He isn't sure. He might have. Oh, he makes my blood just boil. I order him out of the room.

She was glad to see it clean.

⊠⊠⊠

Nine Bearded Glarers were selected at some point as Abu Islam's bodyguards and advisers. Discreetly, they located the necessary pills and liquor to support his work, citing among themselves an obscure ruling about the demands of necessity in wartime.

No one was quite sure where they came from, but evidently the New Imam approved of them. They constituted an inner circle that gave the appearance of having been in place for months or years, surrounding their man in perpetual shifts of three and providing brisk, elaborately polite clarifications to curious members of the congregation on such issues as access to the New Imam (none was available at present), the status of the New Imam's family (they were well), and what should be said or done concerning inquisitive members of the congregation who appeared to be, and in fact were, spies (their names, whereabouts and images, if known or possessed, should be forwarded directly to the bodyguards of the New Imam). They settled disagreements in his name and forwarded all their decisions to him. Some of them he reversed. Most of them he let stand.

cv. stand

I was up and in position for far too long. That little test of the emergency response system left my hips, my knees and my turgid feet throbbing. Here they are again: my sad, bare, puffy, unworshipped feet.

⊠⊠⊠

(After his commanding officer casually mentioned the possibility of an accident befalling someone, but before the accident actually took place, Mike Mazzoni made certain remarks to Jamal. He made them while holding Jamal face-down on the ground and digging one knee into his back. Jamal, his mouth duct-taped, did not respond intelligibly at any point.)

Jimmy. Let me bring you up to date. Everything out here is legal until I say otherwise. Nothing spots what you're doing out here but me and this sky. (Here Jamal's face tilted up wildly to embrace the sky of the Islamic Republic.)

Does that sky look like it has a problem? (And plunged back down into the dust.)

Rule number one under this particular sky: Don't be the bait dog. That's a dog you draw blood from on purpose, Jimmy. You tie that dog down, pull out your pocket knife, dig a hole clean through his paw, let him start bleeding. You want that scent of blood in the air.

---

cvi. scent of blood

All of this libel against the Mazzoni family provokes rapid page-turning, sours my mood. I've read this passage dozens of times by now, and I do so want a bath. Could have asked Clive to scrub it out, and I'm in no condition to do it myself. Damn. How many niggers *are* there in Death Valley, anyway? What are the odds?

You want him bleeding all over the goddamned ring. Because that's how you train the good dogs. By rewarding them for killing the dog that's bleeding. That bait dog is going to die anyway, Jimmy. So sick and thin and scared and screwed up he won't last a week out on the street. You know it just from looking at him. And that little pussy dog knows it, too.

So you do that dog a favour. You get it over with tonight. And that dog becomes your bait. You throw a big glass jar on that bait dog's head. That way he can't defend himself and it's all over a hell of a lot quicker.

He is checking out tonight, Jimmy, and he knows it.

So you throw him into the fighting cage with a real dog, and you watch your serious fucking gladiator dog get to work on that bait dog wearing the suicide jar. You watch your gladiator tear that bait dog to shreds. Then you give your gladiator the raw steak.

Start off with two dogs in a cage, end up with one dog who knows how to win you money. That other dog died for the cause. The dog who dies for the cause is always the bait dog. Now, I may be a dog, Jimmy, but I am nobody's goddamned bait dog. I am a fighting dog, and I may or may not make it home, but I will run with the fighting dogs while I'm here. I know I will never have that jar over my fucking head. And Jimmy, you know you will.

(And Jamal saw a handgun.)

cvii. handgun

With a salute to doo-wop that verges on religious devotion, John Lennon offers an ode to self-defence, to the silent gunslinger willing to take a stand for his freedom, to the great struggle against the forces of chaos and darkness: the brilliant track eight.

cviii. track eight

We know nobody can do us harm! Lennon knew – all four of them knew, but only he had the courage to admit in words – that violence was to be a prerequisite of the ninth great revolution, the revolution on behalf of the White Race, the revolution for which, you, dearest Prudence, would be reborn.

25 **Important Reminder**

From this point onward, never more than an initial pass on these notes. Much to be redacted before submission to Directorate. Some cut-and-paste here, all of which has to be double-checked. Placing this reminder to myself prominently, at the beginning of this chapter. Just in case memory fails.

Becky Firestone refused to tolerate being at a disadvantage in any undertaking. She equated that with betrayal, with personal disrespect, with a certain unacceptable loss of control.

The dead guy telling this story knew this trait of hers first hand. He had built his career on its back.

There came a time when this non-negotiable thirst for primacy of hers was no longer necessarily operating in his favour – a time when, to the contrary, he was rather inclined to conclude that it meant he wasn't getting out of here alive. Becky had refused to remain at a disadvantage in an important conversation. She had resumed control of that conversation by drawing a line, a line that excluded him forever.

Once he knew for sure he was on the wrong side of that line, once he knew he was never, ever coming back again, he began to work on this book. He began to pray it might not be destroyed. Might repay a debt. Might get him out of here safely. Get him home.

He owed Becky so much.

cix. Becky

I have had just about enough of this. Need more coffee.

⊠⊠⊠

The blisters on her hand wept raw blood. She opened the door to the shed.

You might wonder why someone like Fatima, who had been

subjected to such degrading treatment, would agree so readily to work on behalf of the Islamic Republic's security network. Why she would help to identify subversives plotting to overthrow a government that colluded in the death of her sister. Why she didn't agitate online to dismantle certain native institutions she knew to be corrupt, or organize a group of protesters to gather in front of the BII building, where she had been attacked and verbally abused, or create a movement demanding, say, the suspension of the country's constitution.

The reason she did none of these things was this: She held firmly to the rope of the Koran and the Sunnah, the traditions and the teachings, of the Prophet of Islam. These hold that even a tyrannical government is preferable to no government. And no government whatsoever – she had sensed during that protest – was what lay ahead.

'The best scholarship,' Fatima had once written in her diary, 'has insisted for fourteen centuries that dismantling an established ruling governmental authority is a major sin unless certain clear conditions exist. These are: ejection of the Muslims from their homes; violation, destruction or shutting-down of the mosques; or a just ruling declaring a state of war from the legitimate leader of the Muslim community. These conditions do not obtain here.'

Meaning: Fatima herself was safe in a new home.

Meaning: The mosques were open to her.

Meaning: There *was* no legitimate leader of the Muslim community. The prime minister, installed by the Americans and promptly ratified by a close but vaguely plausible popular vote, was an ancient secularist. He had not, so far as anyone could tell, mentioned the Koran in public at any point in his career. Neither, for that matter, had Ra'id, his son. Whether these were the men she would have first chosen to obey, whether they had been selected by a process she would have endorsed, was irrelevant. They were the country's leaders and were accepted as such by a clear if distracted majority of its people.

So: None of the three necessary preconditions for revolution now existed within the Islamic Republic. Even on those days when its leaders did the bidding of the Americans, even when it was feckless or corrupt, even when it imprisoned and abused its opponents, the government served a purpose. It registered vehicles, prevented looting and offered occasional imitations of pension management, road maintenance, criminal justice and garbage collection. It ensured a certain essential social order. It was *regarded* as the government. That was a blessing. If the present regime had accepted too many bales of hundred-dollar bills, bought off too many imams, promoted too many incompetents, well, these were points justifying discussion and reform, not points justifying anarchy. Anarchy was, quite literally, a sin.

She had helped to organize the protest after Wafa's death because she wanted to ensure that such an attack never happened again – not because she wanted the skullcap-clad freaks who shouted bilge in the streets running the country.

And now it seemed there were dozens of them: self-proclaimed scholars with no credentials beyond their own grievances. They pronounced the necessity of the overthrow of the government and all manner of similar nonsense, as though compliance with their every shouted syllable were some religious duty.

Duty could never be so wild-eyed, so desperate, but were there so many people who imagined obeying those rantings to be a duty? That would make the place unliveable. Those grave doubts of hers about the wisdom of living in the city had only deepened since the demonstration. Now she was free of it, praise God, and in no danger, Godwilling, of ever having to return.

Barring brief trips for work, of course.

Ra'id had promised to send her a driver.

She would pass these so-called Islamic revolutionaries in the streets, then. In a limousine. Watch them through a window. Lock them out. Stay off their corners. That was where they issued their so-called rulings. In the street.

The very sight of them made her livid. For years, whenever she had been obliged to walk near them, seen their long robes and their dead eyes, heard their shouting, she had always kept a wary distance and walked a little faster. Like that heavyset woman who had tried to make such a commotion in front of the embassy.

Fatima never said so out loud, but she trusted these revolutionists even less than she trusted the fools who had launched the lethal attack on her sister's village. The revolutionists who blew themselves up, who told others to do so, who called for the dismantling of the government in the name of Islam, had no excuse for their excesses. They knew, had to know, that Islam means knowing when to stop. Such knowledge carries responsibility. These people were accountable to God to identify, uphold and model civilized behaviour. Instead, they took Islam, turned it inside out and left it on the pavement like a dead glove with its seams showing. As though Islam meant *never* knowing when to stop, as though it were nothing but a groping backwards in the darkness, naked, forever. The revolutionists were the worst.

They had a thousand schools, ten thousand grievances, a hundred thousand gory personal traumas. They claimed to pursue the same political goal – the Caliphate – but were famously incapable of finding common ground with each other. Their final, unifying theology was *dispute*. Beyond that, they agreed only on the perversions of the faith that the foreigners noticed: suicide, violence, intolerance, barbarity, hatred. They were spiritually dead. Worse than corpses in fact. Zombies.

cx. Zombies

Some marital trivia: to spite me, and to lend a note of authenticity to his mistress's implausible political posturings, T here purloins a phrase ('zombie') that I coined during an intimate dispute. I used it to describe his periods of torpor following a completed mission. He *needed* me. Clive on the way.

Fatima wanted the Americans out of her country, but she wanted the zombies out, too. She was more than content to identify troublemakers for the government, because a nation of zombies was too terrifying to consider.

In the shed, with the door left open for light, Fatima replaced the machete, examined the gleaming, green-streaked blade as it hung on its nail on the wall. Such an edge should not be allowed to become dull.

She resolved to sharpen it.

Wafa must have left a whetstone around here somewhere.

⊠⊠⊠

Jahannum: a busy place.

The conflict consumed, as its primary fuel source, the innocence of young people. On any given day during the government's ongoing campaign against the insurgents, Indelible treated between a hundred and a hundred and fifty children whose parents had been killed, maimed, imprisoned or driven insane by one side or the other. He had his own opinions as to which side bore the greatest responsibility for this sea of wounded bodies and wounded minds. Mostly, he kept those opinions to himself.

The children Indelible treated at Jahannum presented with typhus, with malnutrition, with exposure, with shock, with anaemia, with various infectious skin diseases, with wounds accumulated in crossfire, with psychological disorders of unknown nature and indefinite duration. All but the most recently admitted of the children called him by the name Doctor Indelible, which was a kind of pleasant tongue twister in the native language. It could be mastered after a few tries. Even the most dazed survivor, upon meeting him, could eventually be made to laugh while trying to pronounce it for the first time. Doctor Indelible was the only name he liked.

Although he was not present for the fitting, the dead guy sharing this story insists that, on the day Doctor Indelible returned to work, a graduate of Jahannum – an eight-year-old with severe scarring on his arms, a boy with whom the Doctor had no relationship whatsoever – was two miles away. He was being measured for a suicide vest.

> **cxi. measured for a suicide vest**
>
> In a rare foray into factuality, T here alludes to an actual security incident.

⊠⊠⊠

The next morning, Thelonius hobbled to the window hoping for a glimpse of the sun, but found only a throng of darkening clouds and an English translation of the Koran on the sill.

> **cxii. English**
>
> Paul McCartney's English sheepdog inspired track nine, which I cue. Our song. Clive knocks: 'Miss Becky?' Pause it.

'How the hell did this get here?'

The Raisin did not look up from the prayer beads. Thelonius felt his teeth grinding, stopped them with an effort.

'I will not open that book, you know. It's an abomination. Good for crowd control, though. I will say that.'

'As you say. You speak with the confidence of a scholar.'

Thelonius heard chanting from the direction of the embassy.

> **cxiii. track nine**
>
> Clive points out the hour — eleven fifteen — and asks whether I am all right, then whether I am sure I am all right.
>
> I had not realized it was so late.
>
> Has he brought coffee? 'Yes.' Is it brewed strong, as I instructed? 'Yes.' Will he scrub out the tub? 'Of course.'
>
> (He does so.) Has he withdrawn that nigger woman's key, as we discussed? 'Not yet.' Leave us alone then. 'Wait. Can I explain?' No.
>
> On my own again. I usher him out, lock and bolt the door, return to my little desk and press 'play'.
>
> Much has been made of track nine's sheepdog: Martha. She served as a kind of muse for McCartney, a guardian, a conduit to greatness. With this in mind, we each took 'Martha' as a pet name, as it were, for the other. Each other's muse. Each other's protector. Track nine echoed repeatedly during certain important lovemaking sessions, and, years later, during an interrogation. I have pulled out some index cards inscribed in Bucharest and set this important track on Repeat.

26 In Which Our Song Is Played Repeatedly, and T Spends His Days in Isolation

Dayton just wanted to relax and not think about Jamal.

'Up to this point, Bobbler,' Mike Mazzoni said while losing at cribbage, 'we've played a game with all the rules dictated by the fucking ragheads.'

His brother played a card and said nothing.

'And then,' Mike continued, 'we wonder why we keep *losing* out here. It's because we are playing by raghead rules. We have to change the *rules*. Out here, if you play defence, you die. I don't know about you, but I'm going on *offence*. You know what I'm saying?'

Dayton nodded and said, 'Offence.' Mike played a card and pegged three points on a go for which he should only have received one point. Dayton considered pointing out this error but opted, as he usually did, not to risk an escalation.

> **cxiv. escalation**
>
> We will begin with a simple physical suspension of your arms. What happens from this point forward, T, is up to you.

'Say it *louder*, dammit,' said Mike Mazzoni.

⊠⊠⊠

From her study, Wafa's old bedroom, Fatima did her work with her head down that first week, in no mood for a vacation.

Work consisted of logging on under a new username to message boards with which she was already familiar, asking questions whose answers she could usually predict, making compliments and combining a feigned ignorance of scholarship with a pronounced and quite authentic disinclination to flirt. All of that spoke powerfully, to some men, of her viability as a future Muslim wife. They opened up to her, dozens of them.

In just three days she had identified and charmed contact information out of four likely troublemakers. She left the job of confirming their physical whereabouts to the BII. She had been right about them all, though. Each turned out to be a zombie.

Fatima took pleasure in identifying zombies at a distance, and took pleasure in being paid for it, but there was something that made her uncomfortable about this job.

It was the weekly ride into Islamic City. She had agreed to frequent three of Islamic City's internet cafés on her 'city day', but she had regretted this promise on the very first day. Uneasy and skittish during this tour of spaces simultaneously public and private, she certainly hadn't uncovered any offline behaviour likely to belong to a zombie. Men's eyes were on her, veil or no veil. Her driver had been dour and morose throughout.

cxv. Uneasy

This lesson stops whenever we get the answers right. Up you go.

She couldn't imagine they weren't attracting attention when he parked outside these places, waiting for her. The trip into the city felt unnecessary, ugly and dangerous. All the way there, all through each ride within the city, and all the way back, she pressed her knees together.

⊠⊠⊠

The noun Murad Murad liked to read most was 'insurgents'.

'Insurgents based near Jahannum,' Indelible typed in the latest of his dutiful, obsequious reports, 'scuttle through mountainous and wooded areas near the border, areas that afford ample cover. The insurgents (my sources say) move in small bands and constantly shift position. The insurgents occasionally make appearances at the camp and leave stolen American supplies for the children, but I have been unable to engage them in discussion. The insurgents seem to avoid me now. The insurgents advocate (my staff members report) a return to the Khilafah system of government. The insurgents (they tell me) steadfastly refuse to disclaim that point of view. The insurgents never stay in camp long and never give me their names. They appear stealthy and resolute.'

> **cxvi. never stay**
>
> You thought you could leave everybody behind. Everybody but your Martha, motherfucker. Everybody but me. Now I need a name.

All this was plausible enough. Indelible never identified an actual insurgent for Murad Murad, though. Not one.

⊠⊠⊠

Damned if the Raisin wasn't up and about in the middle of the night, certainly before dawn, bowing and scraping again. Thelonius, shivering in the dark, passed in and out of sleep as the prayers wove their way in whispers through the cell. Presumably he was within his blanket.

He turned over in it, inside something, at any rate, trying his best to keep his back to the mutterings. Then he walked down a street, holding his father's hand, and he saw a Lincoln Continental. Then he heard a murmur very close, right behind him, a voice raspy and hoarse with recent injury, a voice full of ashes and holes:

'Run.'

But his legs would not move. His blood ran cold. He looked behind him, saw nothing, clasped his father's hand tighter. His father's hand, made of metal now, tried to withdraw. Thelonius would not let it.

Another voice, concerned, said: 'Where, then, are you going?'

His father's hand had changed; in its place, Thelonius felt a revolver.

The sound of the Raisin's rasping breath roused him.

Thelonius turned and looked. The Raisin's bed had somehow shifted, and the glowing embers now occupied a different corner of the cell. Thelonius caught an image from that dark corner: the spur of a flame. An unseen hand shook its dark matchstick, and the flame disappeared.

To get up now seemed unwise. He turned his back on the orange tip of the otherwise invisible cigarette.

The cell wall was dark and cold against his face. Footsteps. From directly above, violating the safety of the blanket, or whatever it was that had cocooned him again, Thelonius felt the near presence of the Raisin whispering.

'How you concealingly deny against One God, while you dead not existing, and This One aliving you? Then This One will give you death, then will bring you to aliving! Then unto This One your RETURN!'

Get the hell back in your bed, Thelonius said, or perhaps thought.

The desire to sleep. Then a long plain of green beneath him.

After a tense breakfast the Raisin insisted that Thelonius had memorized a verse of the Koran. And recited it to himself. In his sleep.

'That's absurd.'

'It is quite a famous verse,' the Raisin insisted. 'And may I point out: the cots are bolted to the floor. You said the bed had moved. Presumably you meant the cot. Do you mean to suggest that I un-bolted it with my bare hands and moved it around the room without waking you? Or the whole cell block? Do you imagine I then moved it back? And rebolted it?'

Thelonius cracked his knuckles. 'Don't get me after you, god-dammit. I didn't say anything from the Koran. And stop staring, will you?'

'As you say.' And the Raisin looked away.

The Raisin was hardly a person anyway. The cell was basically empty. And cold despite the dawn. Counting those damn beads. Thelonius rubbed his hands together and hugged himself.

The quiet got bad.

'Suppose you cut me some slack. I don't do well in enclosed spaces. That's all. I just want to get the hell out of here. I just want to go home. You're a lifer. Maybe you wouldn't get that. You're used to this now.' The cell got quieter still and the grey walls lightened and Thelonius wondered whether he should have even tried.

'To the believer,' the Raisin said, 'the world itself is a prison. We are both in a prison, you and I. It is the kind of prison from which escape is only possible through obedience to God unto death.'

cxvii. unto death

Don't imagine we can't kill you here. Don't flatter yourself with that. You are no American now, my dear.

Thelonius worked his tongue in and out of the side of his mouth. 'Not a believer, buddy.'

'As you say.'

⊠⊠⊠

'Well, I suppose the boys do need to blow off some steam from time to time.'

By special permission of Captain X, the Wreck Room was unboarded, on the condition that all locals would be excluded and 'this dog business' forgotten. The place was alive in the night again, glowing with movement and money and beer. A boom box thudded Mazzoni's favorite mix, which inclined to Metallica and the Ramones. No women were in attendance (there had never been any women present at any of the evening Wreck Room sessions, and never would be) and no dogs.

Mike Mazzoni watched from his table, nursing his second Heineken of the evening. Bobbler passed out the sheets. Bobbler who fucked things up for a living.

cxviii. passed out

Wake up, T. Wakey, wakey. Rise and shine. I recall you had some problem with your knee. Which is still tender, isn't it? Hey, do you like this song? Hey, did you ever call me Martha? Hey, did you promise me a child while we listened to this?

⊠⊠⊠

The phone's email alert chimed. Fatima clicked on the message.

It contained instructions to relay a certain confidential offer to the American.

Fatima was to discuss the attached confidential offer with the American in person with all due speed, and in a manner that did not intimidate him or antagonize him in any way.

The American's interrogation sessions (she read in an encrypted email) had been suspended on the direct orders of the prime minister.

That meant the religious faction had been overruled. A pragmatic rapprochement with the Americans, it had been decided, was in order, at least for the time being. Fatima was to be the American's primary point of contact from this point forward. This was as a result of her familiarity with American culture, her presumed advantages in the arena of appropriate communication between genders and her apparent ability to elicit sympathy. She had been granted visiting privileges and was advised to take advantage of them as soon as practicable.

Fatima read the offer. She requested a day to prepare.

cxix. requested

Do you want it to stop? Give me a name.

cxx. name

I gave you everything. I took care of you. I told you her name. I gave you a year. A YEAR to schedule that operation. Now you owe me a name.

⊠⊠⊠

The nine Bearded Glarers parted, scurried, scanned the streets separately, reconvened and jointly surmised that between fifty and seventy-five thousand souls had gathered for the next midday prayer to be led by the New Imam. It was not even a Friday.

The Islamic City police refused to give an estimate for public circulation. BII analysts, preparing a summary for the prime minister, put the figure at sixty-five thousand, a number described within the report as 'significant, given the city's population of three and a half million'.

The huge congregation presented logistical challenges. In service of the man with the sallow face and patchy, scraggled beard, and of the silent boy by his side, the nine Bearded Glarers recruited a hundred earnest-looking brothers and gave them all armbands. These men directed the crowds.

The New Imam's sermon that day, although amplified erratically, landed its point: the legal necessity of serving justice upon a particular American, now held by the government. He had urinated upon the Holy Koran and then murdered a father and his daughter in the street. His name was unknown. The sentence upon him was death.

⊠⊠⊠

'You recited one of the promises of God.'

The Raisin rose, went to the window, retrieved the Koran, found a certain page, then walked over and offered the book to Thelonius.

'The verse you recited.'

Thelonius swatted it to the floor. The Raisin only sniffed, smiled as an unconvinced judge smiles, retrieved the book, put it back on the windowsill, settled into the cot, turned over, and went to sleep. There was no more conversation that day.

The next morning, the Raisin asked: 'Is it possible that something went quite wrong on this mission?'

'Why do you say that?'

'Because you talk in your sleep.'

Thelonius's insides froze. 'What?'

'You said, "Why did I do it?" You repeated it several times. In your sleep.'

The cell drew itself in tight.

'You can talk about what happened, you know,' the Raisin said. 'Better for you if you do. Perhaps you lost something along the way. Better to talk about such things. I think this mission was a difficult one for you.'

'Don't think about me,' Thelonius said. And turned over to face the wall again.

⊠⊠⊠

As he handed them out, Dayton had no idea what significance the curious symbols on the sheets of grey paper were supposed to have. He thought maybe Mike had some kind of game in mind. Games calmed Mike down sometimes.

When he found out that night, as Mike sat on a crate, handed him a beer, and told him to sit his ass down so Mike could explain the grey sheets before he explained them to everyone else, Dayton kept his face expressionless.

When Mike was done talking, there was a gap between songs. Mike kept looking at him and Mike's eyes didn't look calm at all. Then the boom box played 'I Wanna Be Sedated'.

Mike said, 'Yes!' and gave the three-fingered salute to the world at large. He stood up like Dayton had agreed to something. Then Mike began to party, not in a calm way, though.

Dayton waited until he thought people weren't looking before he left the Wreck Room.

⊠⊠⊠

Up very early, Fatima wrote a letter by hand, sealed it in an envelope, and called for her driver. His lateness and gruff demeanor put her off, as usual. She had forgotten his name. From the back seat, she decided against asking him.

Within the BII compound, before all but a handful of people had arrived for work, she showed the appropriate clearances, made her way to the proper plastic bin, pulled the prisoner's file, saw to it that her letter was placed within *SERGEANT USA #109* and entrusted the plastic-sheathed comic book, with clear instructions, to Ra'id's assistant, who came in early. Fatima had been gone for over an hour by the time Murad Murad, who always checked the front-desk logs, made it to his desk.

> **cxxi. prisoner**
>
> See what you did, love? It's bleeding again. And you know how hard it is for us to get a doctor in here to attend to the guests. A name, please.

⊠ ⊠ ⊠

Thelonius concluded himself awake, then, eyes still closed, reconsidered. Things had been odd lately. It was worth double-checking.

He opened his eyes, scanned the floor, and sat up with a start. What appeared to be, but could not possibly be, his favourite comic book, *SERGEANT USA #109*, lay on the floor right next to his cot.

He looked around. No sign of the Raisin. Thelonius was all alone in the cell.

His attention returned, like iron to a magnet, to the familiar cover. His right hand twitched, as though it recognized an old friend. He picked up *SERGEANT USA #109* – yes, it was real, or at least as real as anything else in the cell – and unsheathed it. He let fall the plastic cover. It made a clicking sound as it fell to the linoleum.

Page one should have read THE HERO THAT WAS.

As indeed it did. He turned a page, convinced for the moment of the book's objective existence and of his own.

Inside the familiar bright leaves was an envelope, sealed. It fell to the linoleum, as the plastic cover had, but it made a softer, rustling sound. Thelonius picked the envelope up and read what was written on the front of it.

It said, 'READ ME'.

Eyes wide, he opened it and removed two rectangles, folded upon themselves, inscribed in the same tiny, neat hand as the words on the front. The letter read:

Thelonius Liddell:
Pardon my familiarity, but I believe you to be a military man and have no idea of your rank. You will recall me from your interrogation. I heard you say then: 'Allah has seen fit to force upon me the sin of making me a sceptic of Islam, and I respect His will in the matter.'

You are clearly aware that there is such a thing as sin. I pray that you receive the Divine guidance that is our shared human birthright, that you follow that guidance, that you deploy to your own benefit the power of choice bestowed upon you by the merciful One God, and that, if you bear any responsibility for the flechette attack upon the village of D—, for the deaths of the father and daughter on Malaika Street, or for any of the other outrages upon our nation of which you stand accused, such as the desecration of our Holy Book, you seek repentance for those crimes from the One God.

I do have an opportunity for your release I am professionally obliged to discuss with you. Admit my appeal for a visit.

Very truly yours,

Fatima A—

cxxii. yours

Whatever it is that you and I have, T, and I've never claimed to be able to describe it well, I think we would have to agree at this point that it constitutes a committed relationship. A name. Goddamn you. A name.

Thelonius felt a pounding in his ears. He read the letter from beginning to end three more times. Once he reached the end for the third time, he stopped at her name (which of course was rendered without dashes in the original) and stared at it as though it were the only island on a horizon. Then, having established the reality of the island, having confirmed it was no mirage, he worked his way back up to that sentence that spoke, however obliquely, of the possibility of a return home, and confirmed the reality of that, too:

I do have an opportunity for your release I am professionally obliged to discuss with you.

At some point, Morale Specialist must have readmitted the Raisin to the cell – when and from where, Thelonius had no idea.

'That coloured booklet came for you while you were asleep,' Morale Specialist said from the free side of the bars. 'I was instructed not to wake you. You are to read it, now that you are awake.' He strode away.

The Raisin settled in.

'I hear a person's name actually means something in this country,' Thelonius said to the Raisin. 'What does Fatima mean?'

'A person's name means something in every country,' the Raisin replied. 'It's just that Americans tend to ignore the meanings.'

'Right. What's it mean?'

'She who weans the infant,' said the Raisin.

'What does A— mean?'

cxxiii. A—

Clive trying to call my cell phone. Ignoring him. My little trip down Memory Lane has detoured, but note that the surname that T obscures and the Fabs reveal here – in fact, Bitch Hajji's actual last name, Adara – rhymes with the name 'Martha', the keyword of track nine.

'In Arabic, "virgin". In Hebrew, "fire". In Greek, "beauty".'

Thelonius studied the Raisin as a man might study a page too dense with someone else's handwriting.

'And what does my name mean?'

'That you must learn for yourself.'

cxxiv. learn for yourself

Yes, do look that up. You always told me you were named after a piano player. Some jungle bunny or other you favoured. You heartless niggerloving bastard.

27 **In Which Liddell Is Strapped Up**

As 'I Wanna Be Sedated' yielded to 'Sweet Home Alabama', Mike Mazzoni shouted 'Turn it up!' strutted, took a pull from his Heineken and showed off to all and sundry a sharp new black pentagram on the back of his left hand, in the little well between the thumb and the forefinger. Around it ran the words UNITED WE FUCKING STAND.

The tat was calculated, Bobbler had observed before starting up the ink gun, to piss off their mother, a cradle Catholic. 'No shit,' Mike had answered.

Not about going home. About getting respect while you're here. Which of course some people don't get.

That star was too damn small. Mike Mazzoni had paid Bobbler the fifty bucks anyway – no discount for blood – and advised him that he would be doing a lot more business soon.

---

cxxv. business

In our business, sleep deprivation has, the laments of the editorialists notwithstanding, a long and proud history as an intelligence tool. Those who shy away from it sell their history to the highest bidder.

It was Mike Mazzoni's experience that Captain X would grant certain enlisted men operating under his, Mazzoni's, authority, significant personal discretion in timing their return to the barracks at night. The men knew this and appreciated it. They started shouting 'Speech!'

Mike Mazzoni stepped onto the platform where the dogs had fought.

'Where the hell's my brother? I've got to keep my mom happy, guys. I promised her I would keep an eye on Bobbler. Where is that gap-toothed loser?'

No one answered, and the gathering was not much troubled by this. The meeting, fuelled by several cases of Heineken, progressed methodically through the items on its complex agenda, an agenda no human mind could have consigned to bullet points. The assembly ran louder and later than anticipated, and toward its conclusion the sun rose – which was, for a few of the attendees, a hilarious development in itself.

Mike Mazzoni strode to the centre of the crowded, noisy, odorous paradise over which he would still rule for another twenty minutes. He had saved the best for last. 'Okay, there's a rumour,' Mike Mazzoni said, 'that Allah sets the rules in this Republic, and we all know Allah has a problem with tequila. So if you guys don't mind, we'll just keep Allah out of the loop on this one.' He produced a bottle, cracked the metallic top and took a long, vigorous pull. The Wreck Room sent up cheers that resonated for half a mile.

He wiped his mouth and recapped the illegal bottle. He held it aloft and informed all assembled that once they too had downed a swig, each of them was to consider himself born again in the Church of Cuervo. The bottle made the rounds, and each man converted.

It cost forty dollars to enter the Wreck Room, twenty of which went into a pool. Two hundred and forty bucks was now up for grabs. That money, and two bottles of Cuervo, would be awarded to the lucky, born-again bastards named Heroes of the Week.

'Hey. Listen up, ladies. Listen up. Almost bedtime. Before we say goodnight, I bet you're wondering: How do you become Hero of the Week?'

cxxvi. Almost bedtime

The very phrase 'sleep deprivation' is subject to profound misinterpretation. (And this chapter's alignment with track ten's sequentially mandated theme of fatigue is too obvious for even my detractors to miss. Cue track ten.)

The obedient new converts shouted, 'How, Mike? How?'

He held the black pentagram tattoo up for all to see.

'Step one. If you're serious about your team, tattoo yourself with the logo you and your partner were assigned. My brother backed out, which makes me my own team. Fuck him. I'm the only team with one guy. The Starfuckers.'

The men howled and clapped to show their approval, presumably of the name. They were in a mood to approve of virtually anything.

'Step two for being Hero of the Week,' Mazzoni continued, waiting a couple of seconds for the various rebel yells to die down, 'step two, boys, is to submit the best photograph of yourself next to a dead raghead. Ideally,' and he had to say the word again louder to be heard over the whoop and roar, 'ideally, an insurgent.' This repeated qualifier produced raucous laughter, followed by more prolonged whooping.

'All you raghead bitches, watch out!' Mike Mazzoni screamed, his face red, his eyes set for distance like a hawk's. 'We're eating this place alive!'

He raised his arms and gave the arena-rock, pagan salute: thumb, forefinger, and little finger extended.

The loudest cheer of the night, or rather of the day, shook the puny walls of the Wreck Room. A spidery little hillside occupant, perched behind a dark boulder less than a hundred yards away, heard that cheer.

He had been stationed on the hill for nearly an hour, nursing a plastic cup of Darjeeling tea, waiting for his shot. Indelible took a final sip of tea, capped the vacuum bottle, set it aside, and pulled out a carbine from a coarse cloth sack. He took aim at the man in the centre of the window.

cxxvii. He took aim

Did he pull the trigger, didn't he, was there a mole, wasn't there, did we lose control of an operative, didn't we, does a bear say the rosary, does the Pope shit in the woods? Etc., etc. All this relentless effort to focus on that which we lost: the taproot of all anti-Americanism. The reader will recall that I have declined all comment on the Indelible affair. Our present topic (the *White Album* insists, via track ten) is sleep deprivation. During what might or might not have been our final supper together in Mother's house, I recall T's too-righteous, too-familiar insistence that Harry Truman would never have signed off on such interrogation initiatives as prolonged sleep disruption. As though Truman were now President! Time for a bath. May help me get to sleep.

⊠⊠⊠

This modest one-storey house, which they could not help calling 'Wafa's house', commanded a full acre of overgrown and weedy land, untamed except for the patch Fatima had cleared out front. It boasted an old, sturdy tree that reminded Fatima of one of those great New England oaks, but wasn't an oak. The chaotic secular community of insects, overgrown rodents, unnameable grassworms and various stray cats had apparently not bothered Wafa and her husband. A scattering of empty, filthy bowls within that jungle of a lawn: even daydreaming of untangling it all seemed too much for three longtime city dwellers.

Fatima's mother avoided the green tangle, preferring to set up the kitchen. Noura attended to her room. That left Fatima to pull out the machete again from its green cloth casing. Within a day the immediate surroundings were freed of the tall grass and the most audacious of the vermin. Now she could face the neighbours.

She refused, at first, to feed the sunset- and dawn-coloured feral cats, then had a change of heart when they mewed in chorus. She opened a large tin of Wafa's tuna, dumped it into a white ceramic bowl and set the bowl on the back porch. They wove and danced around her as though this were settled ritual. The four of them ate their fill. Unlike Wafa, she retrieved the bowl and cleaned it.

That wan, older woman next door spied on them from her window. Noura called her the Spy.

The Spy refused to converse, even after Fatima delivered a small homemade pastry and said 'Salaams, how are you today?'

Wary, the grey-haired crone accepted the gift without thanks, through a crack in the doorway that closed a second later.

Fatima heard her mutter, from behind the door: 'Not your business anyway.'

This exchange with the Spy should not have left Fatima feeling as low as it did. She knew all this by now. There were no neighbourhoods here. There were no communities. The Islamic Republic was not a republic at all, not a nation rooted in a shared conversation and a shared consent. It was bits of stray foam on the cusp of a wave.

Giving thanks to a neighbour, Fatima should have known, was a dangerous thing. The fact that Fatima and the Spy lived next to one another, that they were both women left to their own devices in a world run by men, that they had, perhaps, both suffered losses – these were interesting coincidences, but such coincidences were best overlooked.

That afternoon, two disapproving aunts presented themselves, following an invitation Ummi had failed to mention. They questioned (as though Fatima were not sitting at the table with them) the wisdom of Fatima's being driven into and out of the city by a man to whom she was not related, of her working with male colleagues, of her spending so much time in front of a computer screen. They reminded Ummi that this was not the first time this subject had been raised.

Did she really intend to permit her daughter to carry on in such a shameful manner? Was there no available suitor? Had she no sense of obligation to the family? Was the girl to become an old maid?

⊠⊠⊠

As he gave that three-fingered salute on the stage where the dogs had died, Mike Mazzoni screamed, 'On the hunt for raghead pussy!'

In his back pocket at the moment he gave that salute was a wallet. In the wallet was a little plastic window where you were supposed to put your driver's licence. Set behind that window was a tiny Sears photograph of Mike Mazzoni, age nine, seated in front of a fake forest background with his father. Each of them was trying to smile. They were dressed in identical hunting outfits.

The photo was taken a week or so before the older of the two hunters disappeared with that talkative Puerto Rican woman whose name could earn you a slap across the face if you said it out loud.

Mike Mazzoni never actually went hunting with his father, though. That was something Dad did with Dayton.

⊠⊠⊠

Noura took to wandering around in the brush. After the aunts left, she announced there was a swimming pool behind the house. Fatima laughed, but went out to confirm the report. A small pond, clear and apparently thigh-deep, lay at the outer edge of the wilderness.

Despite the rainforest one had to navigate to reach it, the pond was not as secluded as all that. An access road, not on the map, newly paved, ran near it. Fatima learned that night from an online ally, amiable and familiar with the area, but as anonymous as Fatima herself, that the Americans made steady use of that particular stretch of fresh grey asphalt, usually in the morning. They had built it recently to get supplies to their troops. For all Fatima knew, this online ally was the cold, grey woman who'd refused to thank her.

cxxviii. night ... morning

The complete *absence* of sleep over long periods is impossible in humans – brief bursts of microsleep inevitably intrude – but even a few days of generalized, varied stimuli are sufficient to ensure the absence of *prolonged* sleep. This deficit, when accompanied by the radical dislocation of the patient's sense of time, can disrupt the circadian rhythm and produce real breakthroughs in therapy. Yet there is also a kind of personal liberation in even an unproductive interrogation session, a shared sense of finally attaining due respect from life, of having at last imposed something resembling order on a chaotic world.

Noura, ordered to stay away from the pond, refused to comply.

⊠⊠⊠

The boy began spending less time with his father, due to two circumstances. The first: His arms had finally healed over, though there were still dozens of fearsome scars. The second: Abu Islam's list of responsibilities as an imam had grown, and the days were full.

The heavyset woman wanted nothing to do with motherhood. She grunted at the boy and ate meals in his presence only at Abu Islam's insistence. The boy was assigned to a quiet, sallow-faced brother who had emerged as the first among equals within the fraternity of the Bearded Glarers. His face was harsh and thin like a skull's.

In conversation, this man referred to himself as 'Your father's friend'. The boy thought of him as Skullface, though he had never spoken this nickname aloud.

During a meeting with the New Imam, Skullface made certain strategic proposals and certain suggestions concerning the content of the daily and weekly sermons. Skullface made a point of raising these issues during his one-on-one meeting, so that none of the other Bearded Glarers heard. The boy got the impression that his father was uneasy about the possibility of some of the other Bearded Glarers objecting to these proposals. He heard his father promise Skullface that he, Skullface, would have an answer to relay within twenty-four hours.

Skullface warned the boy to say nothing of what he had heard. The boy nodded.

The next day, Abu Islam confirmed everything that had been discussed the previous evening, and instructed Skullface to fit the boy for a vest.

cxxix. day … evening

For internal posterity, and in keeping with our continuing duty to record best practices: The patient's feet should be bound closely together and then shackled to an eyebolt in the floor and/or wall for a period of between thirty and fifty consecutive hours, with the arms upraised, as noted earlier. This places weight on just one or two muscles, creating an immense, and ultimately unsustainable, amount of pressure in the legs, and a persistent internal question (for the patient, that is) of survivability. Clive is calling for the third time. Will I answer?

⊠⊠⊠

Her evening prayer not yet made, Noura was missing again.

Fatima, having noticed Noura's absence after making her own sunnah prayers – her little sister excelled now at sneaking off while one was praying – gave thanks Mother was napping. She wrapped a good shawl around her shoulders, flicked on her key light, made her way outside, into the deepening brush. And spotted her.

By the weak light of the keychain's tiny bulb, Noura's angled body twisted and danced in the water of the pond. Fatima hissed Noura's name, saw the silhouette crouch and freeze. She hissed the name again.

Nothing came back.

Then her sister's eyes gleamed for a recognizable instant through the mist, and beneath them, no doubt, the smile that Noura used when negotiating terms of surrender. Fatima ordered her to remain still. Noura meowed. Fatima advanced her tiny light. The fool had no clothes on.

In the house, her hair damp and awry, a flower within the big shawl, Noura said she found the water quite calm. 'The whole world reflects back. The pond knows that everyone but me who's a person is sleeping.'

'Well, I wasn't sleeping. There could be vehicles going by on that road, you know.'

As Fatima ran a towel over her dark, unruly hair, Noura explained that there were numerals in the water who swam with her. The numerals, Nine for instance, watched over her, and would alert her to any danger. Fatima scoffed at that, quiet but firm. She glared to signal that this was serious.

There were times she wished she could hit Nine and Crazytown and all the rest of them. Noura too. Noura most of all, actually. Perhaps she should slap Noura now.

Fatima did not slap her sister. Instead, she stood and said it was time to get dressed and pray. Noura, wrapped in the big shawl, remained seated, counted her fingers.

'I know what I'm going to be when I grow up. A cat. Then I could swim whenever I want. There are cats who swim in that pool, Fatima. Grey ones, gold ones, little kittens. Eight or ten of them.'

Fatima assured Noura that the place she had been splashing around in like a lunatic was not a pool. That cats did not swim.

'These do.'

Fatima stood Noura up and reminded her that, whether cats could swim or not, she was not to go outside without permission. They had discussed this. Did Noura remember her promise, the promise she had made with hands held? When they'd left the city? To do as she was told? To be a good girl?

Noura sat down again in a heap and said nothing.

'I'm disappointed in you. Don't go to that pond again. I'll know if you do. It would be different if the road weren't there, but it is. Next time, Mother will hear of it.' Fatima meant it, too, or thought she did.

'Tell her. I don't care.'

Again, the urge to slap her. As though her sister were daring her to strike.

'It's time to pray now.'

But Noura only sat there, counting again. Fatima placed her cupped hands in front of her eyes and prayed the day would end.

'I bled between the legs today,' Noura said finally. 'I only *went* to the pool to wash myself.'

Mother had awoken, and was making sounds in the bathroom. Noura would not be praying. That would be interesting to explain.

Later that night, Mother was talking on the phone to relatives about Noura's cooking skills, and about other matters pertaining to Noura. Noura was sleeping. Fatima walked, alone, toward the pond.

When she reached the pond, this time with a proper flashlight, she saw a few grey flashes in the brush. Cats. Who was to say whether or not they swam? She made her way up the embankment to check the road. She wanted another good look at it.

It was just too close. The road came in grey and empty and severe, and too straight. It cut in too far, too unnaturally toward the natural border of the pond and its surrounding green. Had obviously disturbed that border. The road made her insides constrict. As she turned to make her way back home, the beam of her flashlight settled on a tiny wide mouth by the shoulder: the intact corpse of a grey kitten, perhaps struck by a car.

What on earth had she been thinking?

'I feel safe there,' naked Noura had told Fatima as they'd walked back toward the house in double-time, Fatima holding the shawl secure around her. Noura turned her head for a moment and stared back toward the pathway she and Fatima blazed through the wet grass. 'I like it.'

'I know you do,' Fatima answered, pressing her forward.

'Crazytown says the ripper is either a bad man or a bad smell. Nine says it's definitely a man. Here comes a blanket to put him to bed, Nine says, and also a chopper to chop off his head. I'll never pray again, Nine says.'

28 In Which the White Album Indicates a Necessity

Thelonius was lost in thought, considering the meaning and deriva-
tion of his own first name, when the Raisin told him, with what
appeared to be subdued satisfaction, that an American had been
killed outside the embassy.

The man in question – a grey-haired public relations liaison, according to the Raisin's sources – had been standing on a car, trying
to say something to a crowd while using a megaphone. Thelonius
was pretty sure he had known this man.

If he was the liaison Thelonius was thinking of, he had started
working in the embassy about three months ago. He was a Directorate man who came from Massachusetts. Thelonius had gone bowling
with him back in the States. As part of his job in the embassy, he
had written press releases, composed social media messages, crafted
radio and television talking points about the American commitment
to democracy and justice and human rights and so forth. He had
loved the Red Sox and rejoiced in 2004, as Thelonius had. With
Thelonius, in fact. He had been a friend. Now, if he was the man
Thelonius remembered, he was dead.

cxxx. job

Clive apologizes telephonically. Claims to have withdrawn my room key from that nigger woman.
Surely she still has a master key? He has withdrawn that as well. That's what he meant. Really!
A lie.
Will he fire her if she intrudes again, or attempts to? He says he will. Another lie.
He's having trouble sleeping. Can he drop by? Not yet, please.

The capital had leaked away almost all of its visible light. Through
the little window in the far wall, Thelonius watched Islamic City
erase its own outlines, until it seemed to deny all existence.

Whatever home was, Thelonius was now in the opposite of that. There was not even a direction home in Islamic City. If it ever found him, this anti-city, it was all over.

Long after lights-out, in the well-darkened cell he shared with the Raisin, Thelonius saw, without meaning to see, the darting, rat-like eyes of Dick Unferth.

> **cxxxi. rat-like eyes**
> Oh grow up. I did not invent realpolitik.

⊠⊠⊠

Dick Unferth was, and doubtless still is, a senior American intelligence official whose career was dedicated to the proposition that everything is very, very simple.

Becky Firestone's last remaining ally in the Directorate, he began an affair with her at some point during July, 2004. This fact remained, in September of the following year, a kind of crisis in suspension for Thelonius. Once, during a hot, late-summer evening right before the collapsing point, during the last phase of a long period of distance, of evasion, of overreliance on to-do lists and ritualized humour, Becky called Thelonius by the wrong name while they were making love. She called him 'Richard'.

With the escape of that word from her lips, Thelonius felt everything in him still and go cold. What he had suspected. What he had feared. Thelonius's soul shrivelled, his erection died. A sob caught in his throat. Above him, Becky sniffed, shook her head as though activating some kind of mental rewind button, tensed and slid what was left of him out of her. She strode out of the bedroom, made noises in the bathroom next door and peed or pretended to pee. He thought the sound came from her pouring a paper cup full of water into the toilet and then flushing.

She returned, and he pressed the matter, demanding to know when he had first disappointed her. She met this challenge with silence. When he persisted, he heard a stony 'For both of our sakes, T, I don't want to answer that question.'

He got up, showered, dressed, grabbed his phone, left the house, and peeled out of the driveway in the middle of the night, opting to take consecutive personal days and sleep in the Siena.

This prolonged absence got Becky's attention. It also appears to have coincided with an expansion of the Plum.

No direction home.

⊠⊠⊠

Thelonius awoke, to his surprise, alert and refreshed. Perhaps he had slept a full day through. It seemed just as dark in the cell as it had been, but nothing hurt.

If he continued to lie immobile on the cot, that knee might feel better when he finally decided to move it. The possibility of approaching the world with sufficient rest settled over him like a long embrace. He held his breath and listened. There was no noise of crowds outside.

The Raisin, lively as a robin in springtime, sat chanting on the opposite cot. Not a problem. That could be tuned out.

He lay still. It was sunset: a dying glare visible through the window. Thelonius recalled his first encounter with rat-eyed Dick Unferth. It was during a meeting Dad had put together. A similar dying glare had draped grey Langley as Thelonius stared out the broad window of the conference room.

During that brainstorming meeting, newly hired Dick Unferth had said: 'America as a whole does not do messaging well. As a result, we are getting crushed, shut out, stomped on in the marketplace. Our anti-Americanism problem abroad has nothing to do with our behaviour. Nothing. Quote me on that. Our messaging is the issue. And we can actually control that.'

To make the memory of this discussion go away, Thelonius began reading. When the glare died and the fluorescents snapped off, he read in the total darkness of lights-out.

Thelonius could read by smell alone, without the help of the fluorescent hallway tubes that pretended to illuminate his cell from time to time, because his reading material was *SERGEANT USA #109*.

The cover, he knew, read as follows: THE ORIGIN OF SERGEANT USA! It featured Sarge bursting through the front page of a newspaper. Twelve cents. 109. Jan. Marvel Comics Group.

The cover had a distinctive welcoming smell, predictive of, but not identical to, that of the pulpy sheets inside. He had, by now, read this story at least a dozen times in his cell, several thousand times over the course of his life. He could easily have recited it from memory, word for word, or at least the twenty illustrated pages of it that had no advertisements. He knew the sequence of pages as he knew the alphabet, knew the details of the bright panels on each page as well as he knew how to spell 'Thelonius'. The act of turning pages and inhaling faint, decades-old inks brought an ancient, familiar comfort. The narrative – frail, scrawny Roger Stevens is transformed by a 1940s brain trust into an all-American superwarrior – was so deeply worn into his mental grooves, in both word and image, that Thelonius usually finished reading without meaning to.

I've got a secret, kid. Everybody's got a secret.

When the sun rose, he promised himself, he would move on to the material he had not yet memorized: the ads with their tiny print, which he now considered, a little guiltily, the most rewarding part of the volume.

In the dark, Thelonius could recall the details of only one ad: page four; STAMP COLLECTING OUTFIT; a packet of worldwide stamps, nine triangles, two diamonds; L. W. Brown, Department Something, Something, Michigan, a zip code beginning with the number four. With his mother's help, he had sent away for it. Never received it.

To be fair, that might have been because of the sudden move to his grandparents' following her death. In Oregon, he read and reread the ad. Imagined he longed for his stamps. All he really longed for, though, was to go home.

This must be page four. The scent of old paper said to Thelonius, 'On the opposite page, there is a full-page drawing of Roger Stevens a few seconds before he became Sergeant USA.' Zapped by a gleaming, just-invented machine, Roger looked as though he were being burned alive. Or, having accidentally detonated something in his heart, was in the process of exploding.

That was Roger's secret. He had had to catch fire in order to turn into Sergeant USA.

Thelonius had read this story over and over again for nearly forty years, had memorized all details of that odd image of Roger Stevens, and every word connected to it. More than memorized: That picture of a man aflame was part of him now.

The pictures in the old ads were part of him, too. And so was the scent of decaying newsprint. Something was getting in the way of that smell, though. What the hell was that? Chlorine?

Some cleaning agent sloshed around in some bucket down the hall. Thelonius clenched his fists. Unclenched them. Took a stress breath.

Chlorine had confirmed the existence of the first demonstrable line of bullshit he'd received about Dick Unferth. Long before Becky had said 'I don't want to answer that question', Thelonius had a funny feeling about this guy. One afternoon, from the upstairs bathroom, she shouted that he should answer her phone if Langley rang. She was expecting a call. She'd be in the shower. Langley needed to talk about a legal memo Justice was preparing. Her phone was in her purse.

The water drowned out the rest.

Becky's phone sang the first few seconds of 'Respect'. Thelonius opened the purse and grabbed the phone.

The display said, 'Richard'.

Thelonius let it ring through. A text message from Unferth materialized: *Swimming, etc. here = yes.*

Only 30 min. A photo of his upper torso.

Dozens of messages from that number.

Thelonius put the phone back.

Becky swept downstairs, checked her phone. Said she had to go shopping. Vanished.

A voice said, *I've been telling you to take her out for years, kid.*

At dinner that evening, having smelled chlorine on her when she gave his cheek her usual welcoming peck, Thelonius recited the message, knocked a pitcher of ice water to the floor, and called Becky a liar to her face for the very first time.

'People lie,' Becky said. 'Welcome to grown-up world. So I went swimming. Sorry.'

And went on eating.

Thelonius began to think about killing Dick Unferth.

'Boy, I wish I was Sergeant USA. I wonder if we'll ever learn who he really is?'

'Not as long as he keeps winning,' said cagey Roger Stevens on page nineteen.

⊠⊠⊠

After she called him Richard during sex, after he left the house, Becky phoned him again and again. Thelonius did not answer. He kept the phone in his overnight bag and shut the ringer off.

He realized he could not recall a time, in the entire history of their relationship, when she'd had no idea of his whereabouts. She'd always been responsible for placing him in various positions on the chessboard – in a meeting, or at a dinner party, or overseas, or off to Langley for a day, or down in the study – and then placing him somewhere else. As though there were no other way for either of them to live: Thelonius being moved around on the squares.

She had gotten him into the Directorate that way. Placing him on the correct squares. In the correct rooms. With the correct people. And she had always gotten him out again safely. He had to give her that. For as long as he could remember, he'd been able to count on her getting him out of trouble and pointing him homeward.

Until Dick Unferth came along.

cxxxii. Until Dick Unferth came along

As though he never had his own dalliances. Cue track eleven. Skipping past this whinefest, and past the next few utterly irrelevant pages about sin and speed limits and headwinds and whatever other madness they managed to pump into him over there.

⊠⊠⊠

'The prisoner is respectfully requested to stand for an important announcement concerning his schedule.'

Morale Specialist, arrogant and impatient and free on the other side of the bars, waited for Thelonius to stand, which took a while. He announced in low tones that Thelonius was to prepare for a visitor. The visitor was scheduled to arrive at nine the next morning.

Thelonius had no idea who that visitor might be. Then he did.

29 **In Which I Make No Notes**

Mike Mazzoni bowed his head in triumph before his audience of dawn-worshippers.

The bullet whistled past, four inches or so above his head, and embedded itself in a wall, where it became evidence.

Indelible fired again, and missed again. More evidence. Everyone had hit the deck. He was on duty at Jahannum within forty minutes of the gunshots.

Mike Mazzoni's day was eventful. He found himself an even larger celebrity on the base. He was already the guy who got away with running the dog ring, had maybe gotten away with more than that. Now he gave the impression of living a totally charmed life, of being the hunter who could not be hunted.

Mazzoni spoke quite fast all that day. He concluded, for reasons known only to himself, that he had seen a woman take a shot at him while he took that bow in the Wreck Room. The men ate and listened.

Usually, he explained, they're concealed in some kind of urban cover, snipers are. Usually they're waiting for you to pass by some neutral spot, like when you're out on patrol. Usually they don't leave the city, but this hajji bitch had followed him all the way out here and waited for him. Whoever she was, he would find her. That, he could promise.

⊠⊠⊠

Fatima wondered aloud what the speed limit was. The sullen driver of her unmarked car pretended not to hear, only grunted as they coursed past some of the most obscure alleys Islamic City had to offer. Fatima saw a gathering, spotted a familiar face and said, 'Pull over, please. Right here.'

Fatima pushed the metal button that unrolled the window, listened to the faceless, expanding crowd. The window lowered with a hum in the same key as the hum from the people.

Was it her?

A woman with a megaphone was bellowing over both of the hums.

The woman, who appeared not to notice Fatima's car or its driver, had fixated on the growing throng before her, become intoxicated by it, drawn energy from it. She shouted at it. She informed it that her husband, Abu Islam, was the Khalifah, the global leader of the Muslim true believers, that Islamic City had been formally designated as the capital of his administration, that her husband had declared the present government of the Islamic Republic illegitimate, in large part because of its failure to deliver up to holy and immediate execution the American Satan who had urinated on the Holy Koran in her presence. She had seen him perform this abomination herself, while separated by iron bars that prevented her from taking action to defend her honour, her religion and her nation. He had then murdered two people in the street. She had seen that, too.

The woman with the megaphone confirmed that the geographical borders of the Khilafah her husband administered extended across seven countries, which she named. Her husband had also ruled – and here she confirmed only what she prayed to Allah was already the heart's desire of every true Muslim present – that Americans were subject to immediate death in all of those lands. Paradise, and the full remission of all sins, awaited any Muslim who fulfilled this ruling.

In the time Fatima had been watching, the crowd had grown by several dozen people. All the new arrivals were dressed in white.

'The White Beast,' the driver said. 'In person. What do you make of it?'

His tone was difficult to read. It might have indicated sarcasm. Not admiration, surely?

'Yes. The White Beast. Get us out, please.'

The window hummed shut without her pushing anything, and still the crowd grew. Some of the men blocked their path now. The driver struck the horn, unnecessarily long in Fatima's estimation, then eased around them.

A river of nationalist sewage, disguised as religious worship, seeped through countless unseen compartments beneath the surface of Islamic City, threatening to flood the streets. Threatening to engulf them all in shit.

'You are not ready for Khilafah,' Fatima said out loud to the woman shouting into the megaphone. She spoke the words knowing they could not be heard. The car found its way past the throng, picked up momentum and sped through another back street. 'You have not earned it.'

The driver caught her eye in the rear-view mirror.

⊠⊠⊠

'Have you ever piloted an aeroplane, Thelonius?'

'A what?'

'An aeroplane.' The Raisin regarded him with one eye open slightly wider than the other.

'Who calls it that now?'

'Those of us colonized by the British.'

'I know some British people. I think they say "airplane" now.'

'That's because they, in turn, have been colonized by the Americans.'

The moment passed in two smiles.

'I've never flown one, no.'

The Raisin lit two new cigarettes, and said, 'An aeroplane, Thelonius, flying into a headwind, and wishing to reach a target that is due east, must fly, not in an *easterly* direction, but in a *northeasterly* direction. Ask me why.'

'Why?'

'To account for the stiff headwinds. The headwinds of Satan, the reigning power on earth. They have been blowing for centuries. They will never blow themselves out. This is Islam: idealism in the face of Satan's headwinds. To fly northeast when you wish to go east. Knowing this is the true religion.'

Thelonius heard something, sat up, checked the window, saw the outlines of the city re-established, started toward the sound, caught sight of the open Koran on the sill, then returned and lay back down.

'No point bowing and making ablutions and fasting and visiting the Kaaba if that much is not understood.'

'Islam is about flying, is it?'

'Islam is about intention, which means it is about aspiration. Purpose. Moderation. Worshipping the Creator in every act, and never the creation. Islam is about changing direction. This is from our Prophet, peace be upon him. He would order the pilot to live his life northeast. This is from our revelation. That book you refuse to read asks, "Where, then, are you going?"'

Thelonius began to answer, but stopped, pressing his teeth against his tongue to keep the breath of the word inside.

'This question is from God. It is from all the great prophets and all the great minds. It is from Moses. It is from Jesus Christ, may the peace and blessings of our Lord be upon him. It is from Goethe, Rumi, Frankl. Without this question, without this search for a purpose that is higher than ourselves, without this search for who we are meant to be, all struggle is in vain, all religion is blasphemy. We must find our best selves while there is time to do so.'

Outside, the chanting from the streets strengthened.

Thelonius felt a sour tang in his mouth.

'One either steers northeast or east. One either believes one has an obligation to become a better person or one does not. There is no middle ground.'

Thelonius nodded. 'Yes,' he said, his voice clear. 'I do believe that.'

'Then you are a Muslim. You are my countryman. More than those fools outside who think they are protecting the Koran by keeping it from being pissed on. They piss on their own hearts.'

Morale Specialist came, said something impossible to understand and led Thelonius away.

Presently he found himself in a brightly lit room.

A long concrete slab divided it from floor to ceiling. Within the slab lay a series of small window frames filled with double layers of glass, and before each window, on each side, was a small table and a chair. Thelonius approached the furthest window, as directed, and took his seat. On the other side of the bulletproof Plexiglas sat, not a State Department official, not a representative of the Directorate, but Fatima A—.

A headscarf and a facial veil obscured everything above and below her eyes. But those large eyes (really, that blue?) spoke in a familiar, cautious tone he recognized. 'Here we are again,' they said.

'Here we are,' Thelonius's eyes said back.

Thelonius said hello out loud first. She returned a cautious, identical hello. Morale Specialist had somehow disappeared from Thelonius's side of the glass and reappeared, standing at a discreet distance, behind Fatima.

Their hellos had been comfortable enough, electrically amplified, so there was no need to hold a receiver when you wanted to speak. They were being recorded, no doubt.

What was there to say?

She sat up straight, her two, cloth-covered forearms resting on the table. Her fingers were interleaved. Two thicknesses of Plexiglas separated her from Thelonius, but neither of them worried about that.

The wrists suggested that they led to slim forearms, but somehow he managed to put that aside and focus only on her eyes. They had varying depths and colours, but all inclining to that blue. She looked into his eyes head-on, not approving, not disapproving, capable of stopping him with nothing but attention. It occurred to him again that she really had no fear of anything whatsoever.

They inspected each other.

'You will have received my letter, then.'

'Yes. Thank you for returning *SERGEANT USA*.'

She gave a little smile. 'I tried to secure a medical visit for you. They say it's mandatory, but won't set a date.'

He nodded. Then, filling the space, she said: 'Certain elements of your government may have created an opportunity for you. I have inherited the responsibility of transmitting the details of this opportunity. Before I do that, I want to know whether you agree to tell me the truth.'

She had found a way to irritate him already.

'Do you mind my asking why you sound … American?'

'No. I don't mind that. I was born in Canterbury, New Hampshire. My father was from there. My mother's family is from here. Now. Will you agree to tell me the truth, the complete truth, about anything I might ask you?'

'What happened to that animal who hit you?'

She shook her head very fast, as though she were shaking off a fly. 'I was asked to introduce a diplomatic resolution to you. In person.'

'Because I might trust you.'

She shrugged. 'Who can say. Now. Can I count on your honesty?'

He laughed. The laugh had an edge that he regretted right away. He decided to talk through it. 'Look. I know we've botched everything very badly here. We're sorry. Okay? You've got our attention. We're sorry. Tell whoever you have to tell that we're sorry. Now, I need to know what they've come up with at Langley.'

Fatima considered this, then shook her clothed head again, slowly this time. She peered at him through the borders of another world, through the narrow slit, through the two walls of bulletproof transparency. 'Not there yet. Let's review. You are in jail, awaiting trial for murder. This country finds itself hostile to Americans at the moment. And to spies in particular.' She pursed her lips, impatient. 'Yes?'

'Yes.'

'I am here to get you out of this mess.'

'Yes.'

'I have a precondition. You tell me the truth about everything.'

He took a deep breath. 'I could go to prison for that.'

'You are already in prison, fool. Would you rather take your chances in this prison, where you will die, probably before Ramadan, or the prison the Feds might send you to?'

Thelonius stared at his hands.

'Did you kill that girl and her father?'

He could hear the ceiling fan above him, on his side of the glass, turning and creaking. Thelonius dove, on faith, into those endless eyes and heard himself say, 'Yes.'

The light cloth rippled as she inhaled air through the nostrils. And rippled outward as she exhaled through her mouth.

'How do you feel about that?'

The sound of the fan whirling overhead grew louder.

'Like somebody I don't know.'

Another inhale, slower, and another exhale, slower still. 'Then perhaps I can help you.'

'Not likely, lady,' said a voice.

Sergeant USA, his red-white-and-blue mask gleaming in the morning sun, struck a fists-on-hips pose for Fatima's benefit, then took up a seated position next to Thelonius. He sat with his chest out and his chin raised, as though he were a politician or an attorney. He whispered, 'Don't listen to her, kid.'

'Under Islamic law,' Fatima continued, 'someone who kills without just cause has the opportunity to make reparation to the family deprived of a relative. The murderer does this by paying the relatives blood money. It sounds like a bribe to be quiet, but it's actually a form of repentance, even a form of worship. Given the right intention.'

'"Without just cause",' Sergeant USA muttered, his voice low. '"Repentance. Worship". What bullshit. They don't cremate, you know. Worth a call to Langley. The bodies might need to be retrieved and burned, is all I'm saying. We should check on that.'

Thelonius closed his eyes.

'The family of the father and daughter you shot have agreed to such an arrangement, and so has the family of the civilian who was struck by the van trying to pick you up. The total amount in question is 1.8 million dollars. The State Department has arranged to make the payment from a special discretionary fund. Both families are adamant, however, on the point of true personal repentance.'

'The hell with that,' Sergeant USA shouted. Fatima made no reply.

'So the man on the motorcycle died?' Thelonius said, wrenching his eyes shut tighter.

'Yes. In any event, none of this can happen unless you draft letters of remorse.' Fatima's voice was calm beneath her veil.

'Open your *eyes*,' Sergeant USA shouted. 'This is *Western civilization* we're fighting for, T! "Remorse"! Tell her where to go!'

Thelonius opened his eyes. 'I'm working here, Sarge,' he said, his voice curt.

'What?'

'Nothing. Sorry. You were saying something about remorse.'

'Yes. Two letters at least. You must write to each of the families and explain to them the depth of your regret for your sin.'

'My...?'

'Oh, Jesus Christ in a Humvee. "*Sin*"?' Sergeant USA raised his gloved hands and leaped upward, did a barrel roll in midair, and perched himself, with perfect balance, on the rotating ceiling fan. He stared down at Fatima, withdrew his Expand-A-Shield, and tensed himself as though he intended to breach the Plexiglas barrier in the very next panel. Thelonius gestured for him to cool it.

'What are you looking at?' Her eyes said: *Strike one.*

'Forget it. Do I have to use the word "sin"?'

She looked upward. Then down again.

'Use whatever words you want. I will return for these letters at ten o'clock tomorrow morning, Godwilling. Give them to the guard before our visit. The key principle here is repentance, Thelonius.'

'Like we're, what, like we're in *detention*?' Sergeant USA shouted from the spinning fan. 'In the *Principal's* office or something? What the hell are we even *doing* here, sister? And by the way, who put you on a first-name basis with us?'

Thelonius said: 'Are we done?'

'No. You may wish to address in either letter, or in both, other topics of relevance. For instance, any desecration or genocide you may have ordered or countenanced or committed recently.'

She stared at him. Sergeant USA levelled an icy glance her way every time he spun past.

Amazed as any man struck by an unexpected bullet, Thelonius said: 'Desecration or genocide?'

'Yes. The desecration of the Koran. That's what all the shouting's about out there. In case you didn't know. They're saying you did that.'

'My God.'

'And that attack in which … in which my sister died. The attack on the village of D——. If you had anything whatsoever to do with either of those events. I think—' Her voice caught a rough note. She took a deep breath. 'I think you'd better write about them as well. Agreed?'

Sergeant USA was a whirling blur now.

Her eyes – an even colder blue – flashed again: *Here we are.*

The fan kept spinning, kept reverberating into his chest some-how. Like bees buzzing in there. She wouldn't look away.

There was a little pop from above, as though someone had thrown an unseen switch. As Thelonius looked up, the ceiling fan stopped spinning. Sergeant USA reached one arm back and removed a revolver from his backpack.

'She's an android. Cut her head off after I take her down. You'll see.'

'No!'

She glared at him. The eyes seemed to say: *Strike two.*

'I swear to you,' Fatima A— said, 'it is the only way out of here.'

'T,' said the unseen voice, sharp as the crack of a pistol. 'Don't *do* it, T. Don't take this deal.'

There was a rustling of cloth. A whistling sound. He looked around. Sergeant USA had vanished.

'I'm waiting, Thelonius.'

Answer her, at least.

'Look. I can't write those letters.'

Strike three.

She stood, turned, and made for the door. Morale Specialist began to follow her out. The buzzing in Thelonius's chest broadened and deepened. She would be gone if she made that door.

'I don't mean I can't as in I *won't*,' he shouted. He was standing. 'I mean I *can't*. I mean I need help. I mean I want to do it. I should do it. I know that. I just ... I don't know how. I can't do it on my own. I'm not good at talking about things like this. I guess I need some help.'

She kept her back to him.

'You will tell me the truth.'

'Sure. I mean yes. Yes, if we can meet in private. With the mike off. I will tell you the truth.'

A glance backward. Evaluating him. His hands began to shake.

'I'll arrange it.'

She was gone.

⊠⊠⊠

That night, in his cot, Thelonius had a nightmare from which he couldn't awaken. A grey, foreign city. Its streets empty and sunless. Forced to wander them forever, in search of a brother he didn't have.

30 **In Which Liddell Is Force-Fed**

As was her right under contract, Fatima spent no more time in the BII compound than absolutely necessary.

After the interview with Thelonius, she sped homeward again in the same unmarked car, but instructed her taciturn driver to take a different, longer route back. She wanted to monitor new streets and wanted time to update Ra'id via her mobile.

Ra'id took the call right away, a rarity.

Having no idea of the heavyset woman's name, Fatima contented herself with outlining her rhetoric in broad strokes for Ra'id. She admitted having seen her before, but said nothing about the still-unidentified man she had seen urinating on the Koran. Fortunately, Ra'id did not ask.

---

cxxxiii. rhetoric

I understand the Fabs here to echo Churchill's remark that the era of talk, delay and compromise has passed, and yielded to the era of action and consequences. The decision having been made to bring justice to the evildoers, there could be no more natural course than to act with all deliberate speed to separate them from the common run of conventional military adversaries. The Geneva Conventions were written in and for another century. Some of my adversaries dispute this. These cowards can never bring themselves to complete this sentence: 'If Khalid Sheikh were in my custody, I would . . .'

Midnight. Which makes it August 8. Clive texts for the third time in five minutes, begs an audience. I assent.

The call complete, Fatima watched the city pass. Almost every corner featured a group of three or four men in white. It seemed the females had all been banished from the movement and from all public gatherings, the heavyset woman and her megaphone notwithstanding. These white-clad thousands who gathered in the street daily now, all of them men, men who screamed for justice until hoarse: What had finally united them? Certainty. Not the ally of justice. The enemy of justice.

'Abu Islam would let his own yellow stream flow onto the Koran if he knew it would help to draw a bigger crowd,' she muttered.

The driver examined her once again in the rear-view mirror. Fatima only noticed now that he had a mismatched eye that looked out at a strange angle. He seemed to turn his attention back to the road and pursue it with a dark scowl, but she was not entirely certain he had stopped looking at her.

⊠⊠⊠

They all prayed, and dawn came, and Father left, and the boy found his new caretaker in the masjid.

Sitting in the prescribed fashion, knees folded and tucked beneath him, facing Mecca, Skullface withdrew a gold container from his vest. He opened it, extracted a white pill, crushed it in his mouth as though it were a piece of candy and swallowed. Then he replaced the container and lay down on his side in the prayer area of the masjid, cushioning his head with both of his hands.

'That is for my heart,' he said, concerned that the boy might misunderstand. 'We have prayed and we should sleep if we are tired, yes?'

The boy nodded.

'It was in this fashion,' Skullface said, 'that the Prophet used to sleep, sleep being a kind of death. You should sleep too.'

But the boy (who knew as well as Skullface the proper way to sleep) did not lie down. Soon, Skullface was snoring.

cxxxiv. sleep being a kind of death

As usual, the Fabs have the last word in the discussion. Let those who doubt the necessity of my mission, of my life's work, explain the presence of this particular line, in this precise spot, so clearly evocative of tracks ten and eleven! Clive knocking at my door. Is he prepared to sit in silence while I work? He is. I let him in.

⊠⊠⊠

Half the day in the mosque. The dhuhr prayer complete. Skullface had to post some letters.

The sun was too bright for the boy at first. The stench of garbage nearby. Gnats everywhere, men in white everywhere. Skullface took his hand, led him through the crowd.

A youthful-looking man followed them, but Skullface did not notice.

They took a sharp turn at a fruit stand. The boy looked back. The man took the turn, too and maintained half a block's distance. Then, right after Skullface had posted his letter, the man caught them up and acted as though he had been talking the whole time. He said:

'Who is your second witness?'

cxxxv. witness

No witness was required during my interrogation of T, despite the whinging of my detractors. Following the 9/11 attacks, a long-overdue sense of pragmatism carried the day. This led to a comprehensive review of certain archaic legal standards governing the interrogation of prisoners, and to breakthroughs in research. Reverse engineering, initiated through the SERE programme, revealed to us precisely how the Chinese and the North Koreans extracted so much valuable intelligence from our own servicemen in the fifties and sixties. Thus track eleven, McCartney's lovely ballad serenading Blackbyrd Systems – the private consulting firm that all but single-handedly unlocked the SERE riddle and developed a comprehensive American psychological interrogation model – marks the turning point of the album. And, I might add, of our Directorate's history. Clive, following instructions, has made me a cup of tea, and now waits to be questioned.

Skullface swept a gnat away and turned.

'I interviewed that megaphone woman, you know. I found her unpersuasive. There is another witness, a young woman, but their testimony did not cohere. You cannot put a man to death on such evidence. If you don't have another witness, you must stop the woman with the megaphone from calling for this man's death. Unless you produce a second witness.'

They regarded one another, Skullface and the man who had followed them, two birds twisting the sky, circling each other above a plain.

cxxxvi. twisting

I still recall Liddell twisting like a flame, suspended from the ceiling, as I tucked chunks of pork between his lips and forced them, with a kind of wooden dowel, through his gullet. There was some choking. This from his second and final period of interrogation. The song to which the *White Album* draws attention here, track twelve, is Harrison's. Some traitors do need whacking. This choking incident, important enough to be foretold explicitly by the *White Album* in our defence, is referenced within the song at 1:39–1:41.

The interrogation technique referenced here is known within the Directorate as the Graner Maneuver: standard operating procedure, though of course I added my own refinements. Time to interrogate patient Clive. The question with Clive, as with all men, is whether he can be taught a lesson about respect. This remains to be seen.

'You have raised an excellent point. I shall mention it to Abu Islam. Perhaps the two of you should discuss the matter. Where can he reach you?'

31 **In Which Material Related to National Security Does Not Appear, the Manuscript Becomes Quite Tedious Indeed, and the Time and Attention of My Colleagues Is Better Invested Elsewhere**

Thelonius woke and started the conversation before the Raisin could.

'Did you hear me say anything as I slept?'

'Yes. You said, "Why did I do it?" Over and over.'

A dangerous habit, one he did not know how to reverse. Best to focus on lunch – greasy rice, what appeared to be chunks of lamb and a little carton of milk. The fading glow from the window bothered him. The Raisin's eyes were down, their owner eating, as usual, with the thin fingers of the right hand.

'Did you ever hear of a fork?' The instant the words left his mouth, he loathed them.

'This is how the Prophet, peace be upon him, used to eat.'

Thelonius nodded. 'I didn't mean to insult you.'

'You didn't.'

'It's just – fingers…'

A little grimace from the Raisin. And that was all. Who knew what it was thinking.

How to talk to someone like there were actually two people in the room. How to sew something back up when it ripped. That had always eluded him.

Thelonius got to thinking of the many times in his life when he had tried to reconnect after things had gotten weird. Usually, that kind of discussion had not gone well. He would start out thinking he was improving matters and end up being part of something darker, something he hadn't intended. The kid he ran down and elbowed in that race – Thelonius knew he should apologize, and thought he was about to, but he taunted the boy, called him out for being an android while he was prone and gasping.

Also Becky, back in Salem, right after he learned about her and Dick Unferth and then bolted for three days. He'd had every intention of being mature.

After those three days away from her, with the volcano in the centre of his chest pulsing out new rivers of molten rage at unpredictable intervals, Thelonius had reached only one firm conclusion: that he should, somehow, at some point, find some place to stand that was lava-free. Find some way to act like an adult about all this. That would be essential if they were going to get anywhere.

At one point, he awoke from the reclined driver's seat of the Siena at about two in the morning and thought: What the hell do we do now? As though there *were* a we. He didn't know about that anymore. *Was* there a we? Could there be a we? Should there?

Had he ended it already? A better husband would have shared what he knew about her medical issues, no matter what Dad had had to say about it. Did he owe her an apology, some sort of full accounting of all his mistakes? He imagined he did, but every time he set about connecting any one part of that apology (what might be said to her) to any other part (where and when it might be said), the unstable mountain had taken over, and his heart had rumbled and spattered fresh waves of lava.

Dick Unferth. That bullshit artist. Of all people. Dick *Unferth*.

Even thinking his name, even picturing his rat-like eyes and pockmarked face, set the mountain's insides churning.

On the morning of his third straight brunch at Starbucks, an unwelcome thought presented itself to Thelonius: The affair was utterly unlike Becky.

At least (and this was the disturbing part) it was unlike the Becky he had been led to believe was still on duty: the careful organizer of notes, projects and agendas, the collector and resuscitator of couple-related anecdotes, the supplier of knowing glances and mock-serious scoldings. The cautious chess player. The avoider of sudden moves. The one who knew what to do and what not to do. The therapist.

Someone far angrier, far less certain about the terrain, now lived in her. He had seen that furious, reckless, lost person surface when she bore down on him and set free that indiscreet word 'Richard'. Even replaying that moment for a fraction of a second made the lava of Mount Richard stir, flow and burn in him.

He leaped over the lava, landed on a safe place, found his balance, caught his breath.

He asked himself whether this enraged, misplaced person he had seen could have taken up residence within Becky overnight … or whether she had *always* been hiding inside Becky. Perhaps what had changed was that the Plum had grown enough to create a crack through which this person was now visible.

What would he do if the crack continued to widen?

After years of being the one whose behaviour had to be moni-tored with care, Thelonius found himself locked in a minivan, in the middle of the night, face-to-face, not just with insomnia, not just with betrayal, but with a role reversal. He had to address the possi-bility that *Becky* might be the one in need of close watching. That *he* might need to do the watching. That her behaviour was likely to get worse, more impossible to ignore, perhaps more dangerous as time passed. That they had reached the endgame, the point of sudden shift or collapse, much faster than he had anticipated. He had done nothing to prepare her for it. Nothing. Why?

Dad. Obeying Dad.

Things had gone wrong now. Thelonius had been part of the wrongdoing. He knew that. Once the lava had cooled, he would be forced to admit that much, after her years of care and patience and support. He certainly owed her *something*.

She had a right to know everything. She had had a right to know years ago. He had kept too much from Becky for too long.

This realization changed him.

He would tell Becky of the Plum spreading within the confines of her skull. He would tell her that face-to-face. She was sick. Whatever their differences, whatever they decided or didn't decide, whatever Dad might later have to say about it, he owed her that information. Now. And he owed her an apology for obeying Dad, for deleting and shredding all the documents that told him what her prognosis was. He owed her for his silence. He wasn't sure what would happen next in their world. But he was sure he had let her down. Maybe it was best to begin with that. Maybe he could start by making amends.

Mount Richard rumbled, though.

From his self-imposed exile in what had become 'his' Starbucks, he'd sent her a text, arranged to meet her for lunch at The Campaign, a quiet upscale Salem restaurant they once favoured, and an important early mutual staring venue in the first year of their relationship. She'd texted she would take a cab. It was to be the first time they had seen each other since he'd bolted out of the house in the middle of the night.

He'd shown up twenty minutes after the appointed time.

'Sorry to be late,' Thelonius lied. And when she looked him over, he felt it rumble, felt the lava glow, unglue itself, break through, and begin flowing down the sides of the mountain.

She waited for him to take a seat.

Just Get Started.

He sat.

She flipped on, without warning, an odd half-smile he had never seen before.

'Every one of us knows,' Becky said calmly, all in peach, dark eyes clear, firing the first round, 'that as time goes on we get a little older – tick tock, tick tock – and a little slower, too. Tick tock.'

Something had changed. She knew all about the Plum.

How she'd found out, Thelonius couldn't say, but there was no doubt that she knew. For a split second he considered leaving, because he had no plan in place now, a perilous situation. But he had been in quarrels with Becky before. Walking away would only make things worse. Better to ride it out.

He considered asking her outright, nailing down when and how she'd found out, whether Dad had had anything to do with it, but after looking into those eyes, malevolent and clear and quiet and terrified, the resolution he saw there led him only to crevices and unstable hot ground.

Stress breath.

Calm her down.

'You look nice.'

'Don't I, though. Richard thought so.' A false wink. She was beyond herself, well beyond.

Wait. Had Dick Unferth had her since Thelonius had last seen her? The mountain churned and glowed. Deep seduction in her eyes now, but the kind that only gleamed with toxins.

The waitress came, thank God. Early twenties. Short, blonde, ponytail, radiant, clear skin, well-balanced features, loose white blouse with the sleeves rolled up, jeans too tight, Celtic tattoo on her forearm. Smiling with them as though she had been part of the conversation she'd interrupted. About to introduce herself. On the cusp, the inhalation point, of some word beginning with H.

'Take away these flowers,' Becky ordered.

'Sure,' said the waitress, puzzled only for the briefest instant. Beaming grin. Both she and the vase of wildflowers disappeared.

'Have a drink?' Becky asked, too bright and too sudden. 'She'll be back soon, you know. You can ask her for anything.'

'No, thanks.'

'To our new life.' She toasted him with what appeared to be a shot of tequila. She downed it. Her cheeks flexed in parody of an instantaneous grin, which then collapsed. She held the shot glass toward the stained-glass lampshade above them. 'To it. However badly it may suck.'

'Is that your first shot of the day?'

'No.'

'Not safe for the drive home.'

Becky always drove whenever the two of them travelled. It had become a habit of over a decade's standing. Never challenged, never discussed. Like which side of the road one used.

'Oh, it's perfectly safe, perfectly legal.' She set the shot glass down in front of him. 'Or. *Or – you'll* be driving home. That's better. Such a big boy, now. And you're well below the legal limit. Come on. Have one. Bet you can't catch up. I got here early.'

Thelonius took up the shot glass and sniffed it. Tequila.

'Not my brand. Sorry. So. How are you?'

'Don't be sorry, T. *Please* don't be sorry about anything, ever. How. Am. I. Well. How should I be? Really, how *am* I? You and Dad would know better than I would.'

He set the glass down in front of her.

'You put on quite a show the other night,' she said.

'I needed some time to think.' And *he* faked a grin.

'And? What did you think up? After all that time thinking?'

'Becky, I came here to tell you something it looks like you already know,' Thelonius said.

'*Do* I?' Becky asked, perilously cheerful.

'I think it's time for us to talk about finding a way for you to be better taken care of.'

'*Do* you?' Becky demanded. '*Do* you think that? Have you been studying up on the Massachusetts spousal commitment statutes, T? Is that what you've been busy with?'

'What? No.'

'No? You sure?'

The waitress returned and resumed her assault on the conversation with the same battle-tested initial consonant: 'Hey there, guys.' Imperturbable. Professionally upbeat. As though the flower thing had never happened. 'I'm Sally and I'll be your waitress tonight.'

Becky sniffed, pursed her lips, and spewed a gob of greenish spit at the waitress.

She missed. Not by much. It flew past a white-clad, cotton-covered shoulder, landed on the garish, geometric orange-and-black carpet beyond.

'You know, I'm really not a political person,' Becky announced
to the world at large, far too loud, while fixing the waitress in her
crosshairs. 'But someone like *you* looks to someone like *me* to be
socially active, if you know what I mean, Sally. One of the Young
Reformers, capital Y, capital R, and leading, shrewdly, with those
ominous breast implants and that tightly clad groin. Yes? That's you?
Social revolutionary? So quiet all of a sudden. Where's the perky?
You do get paid for perky, right? I mean, the tips do correlate with
that, over time, yes?'

Sally, frozen, made a tight 'O' with her mouth. Thelonius guessed
she was now attempting to leave and not succeeding. Perhaps something had happened to her once.

Things were always happening to people.

'So, Sally, Sally, clarify, please. *Are* you one of those serially poly-
gamous, personal-relationship reformer types? What I mean to ask
is, *are* you out to change the world for the better now, like my husband here? Get to the bottom of everything? He's got a conscience
now, it turns out. Harry Truman, sleep deprivation, unconstitution-
al, *et cetera*. What the hell did he marry *me* for, you might wonder?
Anyway. You. Sally. The moment I saw you, I wanted to ask you:
Do you suppose that maybe if you screwed my husband in that
storeroom back there, he and I could even things out and then perhaps pick up from where we left off? Wouldn't take you two but five
minutes or so. I said screw. Apologies. I presume upon your virtue.
You could stay upstairs with him if you like, for all I care. No, no,
I know there is no *architectural* upstairs here. Stay fully clothed, I
mean, if that's important to you. He doesn't have to go downstairs,
this one. He's quite happy with upstairs. You'd be striking a blow, as
it were, for liberty or self-determination or autonomy or the ability
to sleep or whatever it is you people post all your messages about.
Watch out, though. No straps, no blindfolds. This one will go on
at length about Harry Truman, about civil *liberties*. About having
a *conscience*.'

She sniffed, spat again. Hit Sally square in the face. Shaken out of her trance, Sally screamed, dropped her menus, and ran off in a kind of crouch.

A short, bald manager, and what appeared to be the entire wait staff, stood in front of the bar, rapt. The manager received a whisper from a tall man behind the bar. The tall man, who sported a crew cut forty years behind the times, produced a telephone and began to dial it.

'He *knew* I was sick, by the way.' She was standing and shouting now, full voice. To everyone and no one. To Sally, now weeping and cowering in the storeroom.

'He *knew* it. But I have to get checked up for everything, everything now, whether or not Dad knows about the appointment. That's what they forgot. And my husband *knew* I was sick, Sally. Kept that to himself. Not sick venereally, though; you two don't have to worry about that. But sick in the head. *That's* why I cheated on him. Just so we can all know what he came here to find out. That's why I did it. Get him back. For not fucking telling me I'm sick in the head. Still working on how to get Dad back. Can you ever really get Dad back? Anyway, *Sally. Sally.* What's your *answer?* If you two were to start right now, back there in that storeroom, do you think I would get *this* guy back by the time we got our appetizers?'

The man behind the bar punched a button, nodded to the manager, and put the phone away. Then: nothing. An awful silence descended upon the whole restaurant.

Only Thelonius heard the volcano's low rumble. It forced his eyes shut, made him think of what it would be like to shoot rat-eyed Dick Unferth through the head. Who ought to have known better, for Christ's sake. Who at least ought to have come to him.

'Look at me, you sick bastard,' Becky screamed. 'You had this *coming.* You *both* did. I have been double-crossed for the last time. You hear? I will not let either of you, or any other man, get the jump on me, ever again. I will *not* be infantilized. I am taking up management of R. L. Firestone, Incorporated for the foreseeable future, and

I will control our messaging as I see fit, by whatever *means* I see fit, and I will pursue *whatever* kind of alliance with Dick Unferth that I decide makes the most sense for you and me strategically.'

Thelonius, who had been trying to make the scene go away, stood, opened his eyes.

The volcano blew.

He flipped the table. Silver clattered. Glass shattered.

'Choose. Him or me. By the time I get back from this mission. You hear?'

Becky turned away from him.

She headed toward the door without a word and was gone. The restaurant went still as a corpse. Thelonius stood in the middle of that stillness for a long time.

'He could have warned me,' Thelonius shouted. 'He knew before I did. It was *his* damn fault things got out of hand. That bastard could have told me.'

'Told you what?' asked the Raisin.

The cell again. The window again and the city at nightfall outside again. The book again on the windowsill. All of it waiting for him. Had he wanted this discussion? Was it even worth avoiding?

'That my wife was over the goddamned edge. That she wanted him, wanted his body, I mean, but only to prove a point.'

The Raisin turned away. Negotiated a new pack of cigarettes that needed opening.

'A private matter,' the Raisin said.

Another emptiness. Just like Becky turning away when he flipped the table.

Damn it.

'Don't you dare tune me out. Listen, I try to fix things when they go wrong. I do *try*. Your eating with a fork or with your fingers. It's none of my business. I know that. I try. Sometimes the words just come out wrong. But when they do, it's just *words,* goddammit. It's just *words* we say. We're not murderers, you know. Listen to me. Hey. Look me in the *eye* when I'm talking to you.'

He had, without quite realizing it, advanced upon the tiny grey figure. He had come to within an inch of it, and was hissing into its face.

32 **In Which I Interrogate Clive**

'So. America is in a rage,' the Raisin hissed right back, closing in to within an inch of Thelonius.

'America is about to strike. And it is always the women and the children who end up suffering whenever you resolve to make one of your points, whenever you decide to say something no one can ignore, whenever you choose to destroy something you think needs destroying.'

The 's' sounds caused little drops of spittle to land on Thelonius's face. The Raisin's cigarette breath was raw and open.

Thelonius began backing away. He had not meant to go nose to nose, had not meant that at all.

On the floor, the little milk carton on his lunch tray began to vibrate.

'I am an old woman now,' the Raisin pronounced carefully, but with a lower, deeper, angrier rasp than before, a rasp that cut right into him. 'I may seem an easy target. I am fifty, but seventy to the eye, I know, and likely enough to die soon. Two years in here, America. And twenty-four on your American cigarettes. Haram. I shall die here. I have lost a husband and two sons. The husband to the BII, one son to disease, another to murder. All I had. Never a grandchild. Because of *you,* America. And I have something *left* in me.' The word 'left' growled with a ferocity that unsettled him.

Thelonius, stepping and stepping and stepping his way backward, hit the cot, stumbled, flopped upon it without meaning to, and stood again. He took up a position to the side of it, with his back against the wall, as far away from the diatribe as possible. His heart beating hard. The little carton of milk on his tray vibrating still.

'Are you listening, America?'

cxxxvii. America

I shall grasp and then conceal the grey-handled steak knife with which I sliced the turkey sandwich that Clive brought me the other night. My lie detector.

An old woman?

'Two sons from my womb, do you understand?' The rasp. The blanket. The eyes, yes, no, wait. Wait.

'Stop *messing* with me,' Thelonius shouted, 'I just want *out* of here. Stop *shaking* things. Stop shaking the milk, goddammit. How the hell do you do that? Whatever you're doing, man. Just stop. What do you mean, you're an old woman? *Woman?* What is *wrong* with you people? How stupid do you think we *are?* What is with that *shaking?*'

And still the little milk carton shook.

The Raisin scowled, gathered the blanket up shoulder-tight, and rushed at Thelonius like a skittering insect, unpredictable, immediate, inevitable, across the length of the cell in an instant.

She slapped him across the face with surprising force. She grabbed his right wrist.

'We *all* want out,' came the sharp, lethal rasp again, and she placed Thelonius's hand at the fold of the blanket covering her chest. 'Feel this. Feel it.'

Thelonius did. Her cold hand clasped upon his. He felt her heart beat through the blanket. It paralyzed him.

'Do you feel this? Do you, America? This is the breast of a woman who nursed two baby boys gone. One from the typhus. When you took out the power grid and the water in 1991. One from a BII sniper, 2001. Both of them dead. All my milk for nothing. You understand?'

Thelonius shook his head. He did not understand.

'You in your national rage. Making your points to the world. 1991. 2001. 2002. 2003. Your oceans of rage, your flames and your press conferences, your shock and your awe. And always the women and the children cut and howled at and killed in your rage. I will thank you to stay on your own side of the room henceforward, sir.

Thanks to you, they came for me. For *me*. Because I dared to say out loud that the government you installed should be taken down. Concerned I might elicit sympathy, might organize the female inmates. Stuck me here. You want *out*? You have the State Department to talk to. They will get you out. I will *die* here, America. With the men. On your cigarettes. And with all my milk spent for nothing. For America. For you. For your rage. For you to blame your mistakes on others. For you to pretend only other nations go insane. You will stay on this side of the cell, *Murderer*. Do we have an understanding *now*?'

He nodded.

From the corner of his eye, Thelonius saw Sergeant USA crouching at the edge of the cell, his red-white-and-blue mask ablaze in the remnants of the midday sun, levelling a revolver at the wrinkled old woman.

'No, Sarge. Don't. Don't do it.'

She unlocked his hand, surveyed the cell and regarded him with a familiar, professional tolerance. She withdrew slowly, stepping away, her eyes trained on him. When she reached her cot, she averted her gaze again like a cat that knows it is out of attack range.

She just sat there for the longest time.

'Do us both a favour and avoid telling me how sorry you are,' she said. 'Sorry compounds the problem at this stage.'

She picked up her pack of cigarettes, stared at it, discarded it, picked up the prayer beads instead and began to mumble. Sergeant USA holstered his revolver and slipped noiselessly under the cot.

That left Thelonius to sit mute, listening to the mumbling and the humming of the milk carton, which combined for strange harmony. He couldn't look at the carton for more than a second at a time. So he stared at the ceiling, or at the floor, or at her watching him.

After five minutes or so of moving her beads, she stopped and said, 'Whenever something vibrates, America, slow down. You should learn how to look at it. Vibrating means change. It means Allah wants you to notice something. And grow. Allah says, "You see the earth barren and desolate, but when we send down rain to it, it vibrates, and its yields increase. Truly, He who gives life to the earth can give life to those who are dead." Vibration is life. Change. Growth. If it bothers you at first, look at whatever is shaking for a while and then look again, longer next time, so as to slow down. Keep looking until things *slow down.*'

Thelonius was glad when the guard, oblivious, came to collect the trays.

He stayed on his side of the cell.

cxxxviii. his side

Clive tried, alas, to change the subject. Asked for a shoulder rub. Disrespectfully.

That grey-handled knife's gleaming, serrated edge raised itself to the lower hollow of seated Clive's unguarded throat. His halitosis and his sudden sweat stank. Did he in fact remove all key cards, individualized or generic, from the possession of that nigger maid whose name I cannot now recall? A simple question, deeply relevant to my privacy, meriting a simple yes-or-no answer. In the long silence that followed, I had my response.

cxxxix. cell

Reference, indirect but indisputable, is made in track thirteen to your biological father, a rising member of the Directorate who was instrumental in eradicating the OJE terror cell. This man, whom I trained in the SERE techniques, is analogous to 'Daniel' in his triumph over that song's doomed protagonist, who is in turn analogous to T. Raccoon = coon = nigger and/or niggerlover.

⊠⊠⊠

'Goddamn me if I don't know an insurgent when I see one,' Mike Mazzoni said, flicking his cigarette through the open window, his eye on something, his blood up. He turned off the music. 'And *that* is a fucking insurgent.'

This particular insurgent, a pedestrian, also happened to be an asshole: Jimmy's snivelling younger brother Jimmy Two. When Jimmy Two saw Mike Mazzoni, he shouted 'DOG MAN!'

The kid, who had frequented the Wreck Room back when there

were dogfights to bet on and shout at, scooped up a handful of pebbles and let fly at the driver's side of Mike Mazzoni's armoured vehicle.

'Game over,' Mike Mazzoni said.

The pebbles flew in the open window and bounced off the hood: Chicka da chickety chick. One hit Mike Mazzoni on the nose. Then again, the shout: 'MAZZONI! DOG MAN.' As he ran, he shouted, 'MAZZONI DOG MAN!' over his shoulder again, his elbows and knees flying every which way. He was fast. He turned a corner.

'Gone, no way to make a positive ID,' said Dayton. 'Too quick. Get him next time.'

'Oh, hell no,' said Mike Mazzoni. And gunned the engine.

---

cxl. engine

Clive, that bleeding lovesick fool, tosses and flails on the floor like a wild thing, but the phone's handset cord holds his wrists and ankles tight. You stir within me, ready, even now, to power the nation.

33 In Which Liddell Finally Experiences Regret

At this very window, as she did the dishes, Wafa had once said of the Americans, 'They live as though everything is someone else's fault. They never consider their personal arrogance as connected in any way to the national arrogance that gets them into trouble.'

'But *we're* Americans,' Fatima had protested.

'Used to be. Not anymore.'

Fatima was the one doing the dishes now. Perhaps the American could be helped. Perhaps not.

There was a sudden howl from outside. Something Noura didn't like about a flower, which she dropped, then laughed at, then knelt to recover. She gathered more and more of the tiny red-and-white wildflowers, waved her thin hands in dismay as the new batch flew in all directions, and shouted at some insect not to sting her. She ran. She stopped. She lectured the air.

She was no woman yet, not in bearing, certainly not in her capacity to withstand sorrow or challenge. Yet the structure of her body was changing. That was undeniable. At some point soon, someone would have to have a talk with Noura.

Not a talk about the mechanics of the thing. Noura already knew that part backwards and forwards, and occasionally soliloquized about it in her dreamy, matter-of-fact way.

No. This – what Fatima now had to consider – was the Real Discussion, the discussion that came years after all the talk about where babies came from and how they were placed there. This was a different discussion altogether, one requiring care and tact.

This was the talk about the way men and women either helped each other or destroyed each other. The talk about how love either saves or eradicates, how it has no middle way. The talk about what might be expected from men, about the practical advantages of reinforcing certain restrictions of the faith governing one's encounters with them, about knowing when and how to turn away from them. It was Noura's time.

Ummi knew the Real Discussion needed to take place, yet she was no good at that talk. Baba would have been better at giving these talks than Ummi. When it was Fatima's time, Ummi had only begun the discussion at Wafa's prompting. Ummi had collapsed into evasion and gossip and reverie when she'd tried to conduct the Real Discussion, and the resulting empty, over-told anecdotes about failed betrothals and sorrowful families had only left Fatima wondering what on earth the pauses, the raised eyebrows and the pointed emphases were all meant to convey.

That left Wafa to conduct the Real Discussion with Fatima.

Wafa did this the very morning after Ummi's pointless rehashing of her sister-in-law's broken engagement, which had only led to Fatima rolling eyes. Fast forward to Wafa, strolling with her on the way to buy fruit, her shoulders back and her eyes on the road ahead.

Wafa began with the words 'Now, Fatima, you know it is your time.'

The talk was masterful, encompassing everything. Not merely what elements of one's person must be concealed in public, which Fatima knew, but *why* they must be concealed. Not merely whose hand one may not brush against casually with one's own hand, but *why* it must not be brushed against. What may be expected of men and what may not. How to tell when they believed themselves to be speaking truthfully and when they imagined they were deceiving you.

Wafa's words had been different from Ummi's: insight rooted in an experience the origins of which Fatima dared not attempt to decipher; insight every syllable of which spoke of incontestable personal authority. Fatima's eyes had narrowed, her steps had slowed. Her heart had opened. She had never listened so intently to anyone.

Now Wafa was gone when she was most needed.

Ummi was still useless on such matters, far worse than useless, in fact: a hindrance and an irritation. With Noura still likely to talk about the naked ravings of Crazytown with anything or anyone that moved, Fatima had to begin the Real Discussion. How? When? Who knew how much good it would do?

Noura was edging toward the outer border of the wild, unthreaded tangle she called a garden, pressing toward that dark pool that lay beyond the kitchen window's rectangle.

Fatima rapped on the glass. Noura turned, nodded, and came back.

Noura remembered things that mattered to her. The trick, as ever, was to *make* them matter to her.

A horn honked outside. Fatima pictured her silent, expressionless driver waiting, felt his usual sullen impatience and heard the tough, grim motor of his old grey sedan idling. He never got out.

cxli. silent

Earbuds in.

Even Ringo Starr wrote a song for the *White Album*: Track fourteen was his first solo composition. To 'lose one's hair' is, in Liverpudlian parlance, to be decapitated. Compare 'lose one's hat', which has an identical meaning. Mazzoni's ghastly summary execution at the hands of the terrorist cell is thus foretold at 1:41–1:45. T's more civilized passing, via the Graner Maneuver, is obliquely referenced at 0:19–0:23. I still find myself waiting for his knock on the door, even here. I recall seeing in his eyes the glimmer of settled, indefinable regret. But it was not repentance. It was something else.

No knock at my silent door. Evil men, I think, never willingly admit their criminality.

Fatima stayed at the kitchen window and took a moment to remind herself of something else Wafa said while standing on this very spot.

⊠⊠⊠

Sullivan Hand, whose hips were sound,
whose eyes were clouded,
whose face was round,
Sullivan Hand, who knew the dark,
who liked its descent, who wore its mark,
Sullivan Hand, who made no sound,
save the clicking of keystrokes, with no one around –
young Hand, I say, had just one light.
It glowed from his monitor all through the night.
Sullivan Hand reached out again.
'Why don't you talk to me?'
'Aren't you my friend?'

34 In Which 'Fajr' Is Defined

Having completed fajr and the supererogatory prayers that followed it, Indelible sipped his Darjeeling tea and consulted his various on-line profiles, all of which pointed their messages to ^indelible^@gmail.com. Three emails from muslim&proud@gmail.com materialized in quick succession. Indelible set the cup down and peered in at the screen. None of the three had content in the body of the message. The headings read:

> *Why don't you talk to me?*
> *Aren't you my friend?*
> *Don't forget to pray fajr.*

cxlii. fajr

The Islamic pre-dawn prayer.

A fourth message presented itself, with the heading 'Well?' It had this message in the body: *Salaam. Well? Why don't you talk to me?*

He studied the messages, then ran a simple, if unorthodox, diagnostic.

The messages were tracking from Langley, Virginia. Indelible would create a recommendation concerning whether he should answer them – no, how he should answer them – when he returned from Jahannum.

cxliii. Jahannum

Literally, the internet tells me, a garbage dump! That may be the most apt descriptor after all. Nothing to do with hell. Restless and weary.

⊠⊠⊠

Thelonius said, 'Teach me how to pray for something.'

A prayer right now, with a city of two million or so people calling for his head, certainly wouldn't hurt. Since he was here, since she was out of sorts, he would humour her and pray her way. Whatever way that was.

The Raisin was not as surprised as he'd expected her to be, but she didn't say anything back, either.

'I mean: Would you please teach me how to pray for something. No one ever taught me that before. I have this meeting today at ten. I want it to go well.'

> **cxliv. this meeting**
>
> Track fifteen. No one would be watching them copulating, there in the basement of a prison. And I am supposed to apologize for every ancient indiscretion. Need a nap.

She looked away. He felt the volcano. That was it. That was the part that triggered him. Looking away. Like Becky had.

Stress breath. It was possible she was testing him. Likely.

Stress breath.

'I want to pray to God for help,' Thelonius said. 'For forgiveness of my sins.'

'As you say.' She caught his stare and held it. 'Whenever we are done praying, we are to continue praying. We are to pray to God when we are standing, pray when we are sitting, pray when we are lying down. Impossible, yes? But people are praying even when they don't think they are praying. What are you praying to now?'

He didn't want to try to answer.

'Hmm? To what?'

'I give up. I don't know what I'm praying to.'

'Always our question the same: Does one use free choice to worship the Creator, or to worship what is created? If one worships the Creator alone, one is a Muslim. If one does not, one wanders and strays. A man has only what he strives for.'

'I'm not sure I'm praying right, then.'

The Raisin took a leathery pull on her two unfiltered Pall Malls. When she let the smoke out through her nostrils, she looked like a dragon.

'I think maybe I've just got too many bad things going on in my head to pray for anything,' said Thelonius.

She shook her head. 'Prayer is to worship Allah as though you are seeing Him, and while you see Him not, to be certain He sees you. If you want to pray, say what the Prophet, peace and blessings be upon him, used to say. Say, *Guide us to the straight path – the path of those upon whom You have bestowed favour, not of those who have evoked Your anger or of those who are astray.* Will you say that?'

Thelonius thought of what a lousy Christian he had been whenever Hal and Louise tried to turn him into a Christian. He was about to tell the Raisin he had reconsidered, that he wasn't built for this kind of thing, but something, a trickling feeling inside, stopped him from saying that, and instead he said, 'Give it to me slowly.'

'Guide us to the straight path,' the Raisin said.

'Guide us to the straight path.'

'The path of those upon whom You have bestowed favour.'

'The path of those upon whom You have bestowed favour.'

'Not of those who have evoked your anger.'

'Not … of those who have evoked your anger.'

'Or of those who are astray.'

'Or of those … of those who are astray.'

Just to keep the peace in the cell.

cxlv. peace

Room 209 can't seem to get a moment of peace at the moment. One-thirty in the morning. That makes thirty-seven straight sleepless hours. MotherDaughter refuses to let me go under. Turning up the volume. Kicks within quite vigorous.

35 **In Which I Stand with Difficulty**

Before leaving her kitchen window, Fatima reminded herself of Wafa's favorite proverb: One must enter a house through the proper door. Meaning: Begin all matters properly.

She reminded herself of this proverb with regard to Noura, who was in the wild garden twilling a pleasant-looking weed. The discussion must begin properly. No time for it now. Perhaps when there was the opportunity for a long walk. The proverb was also relevant in regard to Ummi, to whom she owed respect, not resentment.

'Ummi?'

'Yes?'

Probably still in bed.

'Leaving for work now. Noura is in the yard. Will I call her in?'

'Yes, love. *Assalamu alaykum.*'

'*Wa alaykum salaam.*'

Fatima knocked on the window again, caught Noura's glance, waved her hand for her to come inside. Noura came in the back door.

And to that sour driver out there, doubtless drumming his fingers within the sedan he never seemed to leave. The journey with him should begin properly, too.

And even in regard to Thelonius.

Time. Best to go now. Before the driver honks again.

---

cxlvi. Before

Track sixteen. You knew how long I loved you. You knew I loved you more. Yet you lied like all the others. And befouled the years before.

⊠⊠⊠

'I thought smoking was prohibited in Islam,' Thelonius said.

'It is,' said the Raisin, who had just lit the two simultaneous cigarettes permitted to her by mutual agreement. No more before the dhuhr prayer, which was still three hours away. Thelonius knew the timings now.

cxlvii. timings

My body increasingly a battleground. I happened to notice a Tums packet left in my open suitcase. That will calm us. It is now two eleven a.m. Let this work, MotherDaughter, for the love of Mother.

'Then why do you smoke?'

'Because I am addicted.'

'Doesn't count as a sin?'

'Oh, I believe it does,' the Raisin answered. 'Every day, I repent for it and strive to leave the addiction behind. Perhaps today.'

'Surely at this point…'

'I know. I will be dead soon.'

An awkward moment.

'Everybody will be tasting death. Everybody. You. More obvious in my case, is all. Angel Gabriel gave the Koran to the Prophet, peace be upon him, to remind us of this. And of other matters we forget. At this stage, the doctor says I may do as I please. I smoke far less since we made our agreement, you know.'

'You suppose God will forgive all the cigarettes you smoke now because you're smoking less?'

'I pray God will forgive me, not for the outcome, but for the sincerity of my effort.'

'Sounds like a lot of trauma for nothing.'

'It is Jihad. The heart of any religion worthy of practice.'

'That's not what I've heard about Jihad. Jihad is why I had to come out here.'

'There was a listening issue. Jihad means striving. Any striving.'

That possibility circulated in wreaths of smoke.

'Anyway, a lot of work,' Thelonius said, 'quitting smoking while you're…' There was no tactful word.

'Dying?' the Raisin offered. 'What I am occupying myself with now is dying.'

'What I mean is, you might as well take advantage of any way to enjoy yourself.'

Kneeling there, her beads in her hand, blanketed on the floor, the Raisin took a long drag on both her cigarettes, expelled a wave of smoke, crushed one of the embers on her palm, deposited the half-length butt in the can, held on to the other one. She said: 'The chrysalis of the Monarch butterfly shakes quite a bit when it is touched. Some think this is to ward off predators. I wonder if something else is happening.'

Her voice was ragged and slow now. She took a drag on the remaining cigarette. Another plume of smoke went up.

'Look at our cell. Look at our bodies disintegrating. This is Jihad. You and I are Jihadis. We struggle. Struggles and obstacles are gifts from our Lord. Even our faults. Even our losses. Even our weaknesses. What is our intention? Whatever we intend to strive for, that is what we worship. Again: Where are we going? What matters is not whether what we *attain* is just. What matters is whether what we are *striving for* is just. Whether we make an effort.'

She ventured to stand, did not, rearranged herself onto the cot.

'Jihad,' the Raisin said, 'is God-conscious intention and effort in the face of an obstacle. If it is easier for you to be just by saying "intention", say "intention", and don't say "jihad". Whatever you say, or don't say, justice is personal intention and effort. Personal empathy. Personal striving. You must *be* there. It's like pissing. Such a trivial undertaking. But you must do it in person. And with the right intention.'

Morale Specialist appeared at the bars: 'Time.' Thelonius's visitor was waiting in a private interrogation room. The visitor wanted him to know their discussion would not be monitored or recorded.

'Take the Koran with you,' the Raisin said. 'On the windowsill. *Assalamu alaykum.*' The little eyes managed a spark.

He hesitated for a moment, stood with difficulty, then limped to the window, where the morning light made a kind of clearing, despite the clouds and the soot of the city. He took a breath. Then the book was in his hand.

cxlviii. stood with difficulty

As I did just now, before a long, complex and painful trip to the bathroom. That completed, and the door locked, I emerged and tried to lie down on the bed. Couldn't. Ongoing gastric issues. Back at the little desk, I check the time. Christ.

36 **In Which I Experience a Period of Great Restlessness**

At key intersections, the streets were choked with white walkers, all of them gathering for the latest in a series of protests against the anticipated release of the American to the U.S. government. A popular sign held aloft by hundreds of white-clad arms read: *The American Must Die.*

'That's all they ever call him. Maybe you know his real name.' The driver's eyes were uneven in the rear-view mirror.

Not quite a joke, not quite a question.

'Whose name?'

'The American's.'

Fatima looked at him, bit her lower lip. What had made the driver so interested in the details of this case?

Then he laughed and looked back to the road. Fatima resettled her facial veil, which had slipped very slightly when she turned her head to look at him.

'But maybe you do know his name.'

'No,' Fatima lied.

They pulled up. She exited the car and made her way up to Ra'id's office.

Ra'id informed her she was not to worry. Her driver was a relative of his and had passed a background check. Then he told her about the unfortunate leak and about the importance of her meeting with the American today. Time was an issue now.

With less than fifteen minutes to prepare, Fatima passed loathsome, talkative Murad Murad in the hallway, and ignored his casually obscene greeting. She could feel him appraising her body even after she turned the corner. She took a moment in the empty corridor, covered her mouth with her hand and steadied herself.

Distracted – her stomach had nearly rebelled – she made her way downstairs, toward the room she had secured for her private discussion with Thelonius. When she entered it, she sighed and shook her head.

It was, alas, the very same room in which he had been tortured. The only space available. She left, made her way back upstairs and arranged for him to enter it by a different door.

cxlix. alas

Track seventeen. All of what she says is meaningless. Too tired. Turning the CD player off now. Must rest.

cxl. door

Astonishing. Past three a.m., and still you will not calm yourself. I have tried every conceivable position. None permit me any respite from your restless dance. All there is to do is work on this. In silence. Far past weary. I am a door at which you beat, but through which you refuse to walk. Let Mother sleep, good gravy.

37 In Which the Restlessness Continues, and Nothing of Consequence Appears in the Manuscript until Quite Late in the Chapter

'Thelonius, this is your time.'

That voice he knew. That face obscured by its gold cloth, familiar but a matter of imagination now.

The same dreary, windowless basement where he and Fatima had first met – if 'met' was the word. The same smell of stale, damp cement, the same fluorescent hum. The dead guy telling this story attests to the unlikely reality that the fluorescent lights in the interrogation rooms of the Islamic Republic were somehow tuned to the same brittle E-flat hum of the very cell he now occupies at Bright Light. But instead of a board where Thelonius had been pinned like an insect there were now two wooden chairs on either side of a folding-legged card table. Set upon the table were a dozen or so sheets of blank paper and a gold pen. Fatima occupied one of the chairs. When Morale Specialist shut the door, Thelonius limped to the other seat and placed the Koran on the table. She glanced at it.

Thelonius said, 'Hello, Fatima.'

Eyes, icy, right back on him. 'Miss A—, please.'

'And I'm Thelonius?'

'If you want assistance from me, you are, yes.'

He nodded. 'Miss A—, then. Like kindergarten.'

'Like a prisoner meeting with an attorney.'

Already. Irritating him again.

'What's our situation, Miss A—?'

'*Your* situation.'

'Fine. What's *my* situation?'

'We agreed to be honest with each other?'

'Yes.'

'That of a dead man.'

A chill ran through him, settled into his vertebrae. 'Meaning? Worse than yesterday?'

'Much.'

'Why?'

'A story broke this morning in one of the more strident opposition newspapers identifying you as Davis Raymonds, spy, and detailing the murder charges against you. Someone in this building talked.'

'Do you know who?'

'Irrelevant. You are once again topic A in this city. The subtopics are blasphemy and murder. And the assault on my village. Someone named Abu Islam is calling for a march on the U.S. embassy tomorrow. All about keeping you from going home.'

His chest tightened. His fists clenched. Another embassy meltdown. This time about him.

'What do we do?'

Her eyebrows went up. *We?* And down again.

'You repent. I am to type and deliver your signed letters to the families personally. It would be good for us to resolve all of this today.'

'Why today?'

'The people who run the paper that broke this story…'

'What about them?'

'They have unintentionally accelerated your schedule. They call themselves the Defenders of God, and their newspaper is known as *God Defended*. The editors have decided that Abu Islam is the man of the hour. They like to put his image on the front page. A month ago, no one knew who this Abu Islam was. We still don't know who he is, but now he's apparently the "infallible deliverer of the Republic".' When she made quote marks with her fingers, it was like talking to a teenager at the mall.

'He believes you're being held at the U.S. embassy.'

'So much for infallibility.'

'His aim is to surround the embassy with two hundred thousand people tomorrow. The prime minister's office has moved up your court date so it can occur before this demonstration. The trial will take place at four this afternoon.'

Six hours.

'Half of the government, the half that's well connected with itself, wants to avoid any further complications with the Americans. They want you out of the country before that demonstration takes place. The other half, the half that reads *God Defended*, wants you dead this week. Today, preferably. The imam who will be hearing your case is aligned with neither side.'

'Six hours.'

'Yes. These two factions are playing chess, with you as a pawn. I have been assigned to help secure your acquittal. Get you off the board. Alive. Calm down, please.'

He unclenched his hands. 'Less than six hours now, with all our talking.'

She cast a wary eye his way.

He said: 'I'm listening.'

'This imam will convict you of both blasphemy and murder unless you do exactly as I say.'

Thelonius swallowed, rubbed his hands together. Just Get Started.

'Fine. What do I do?'

The blue eyes – they were, again, all swimming-pool blue – settled into a cold, appraising stare. No fear. All business.

'Your employers, those busy men at the Directorate, have identified a way out of all this for you, and it is just clever enough to work. I suppose it was your backup plan. I suppose you already know what it is.'

Thelonius shook his head. 'No idea.'

She glanced again at the little Koran he had brought with him. It sat there on the table, a silent participant in the conversation.

'No idea?'

'I have no clue what they've come up with,' Thelonius said. 'That's the truth. I said I would tell you the truth and I did. Now, what's the plan?'

'Here is the scenario. You send off the three convincing, repent-ant letters that we write here, and your government pays the blood money with the agreement of the families. You remember that part, I think. That vacates the murder charge.'

'Yes.'

'Then comes the clever part, the part your employers cabled to my superior. In court, you make a public statement of remorse and you follow up that performance by reciting the profession of faith, accepting Islam as your religion.'

An odd sensation, the feeling of a trickling, gaining force, of in-evitability, of something nearly bursting under pressure, gathered in Thelonius's chest. By the time she spoke again, it was as though a foot or so of water were surging through open hallways.

'That would clear you of the blasphemy charge you incurred upon admission here. Clever, yes?'

Thelonius felt the waves in his chest rising, rushing harder.

'I said, that's clever, isn't it?'

Thelonius nodded.

'But there's a logistical challenge we would face in implement-ing it, Thelonius. Something none of those clever Directorate men predicted.'

'What's that?'

'I believe,' Fatima said, 'that it would be a mortal sin for me to help you make a false profession of faith. And I am not going to hell if I can help it, Thelonius.'

There was a flickering shadow, and the sound of something pass-ing overhead.

Sergeant USA landed in near-silence on two sets of outstretched boot-toeguards, the great red-white-and-blue Expand-A-Shield strapped to his outstretched left arm. He found his balance with absurd ease, executed a smart forward somersault, curled into a ball and set up secure watch from the corner of the interrogation room, peering over the top of his shield. Fatima pretended not to notice. Morale Specialist inspected his fingernails.

'I would let you die here rather than commit a sin like that,' she said.

The water kept rushing, breaking closed windows now, flattening doors, erasing doorways, coursing down the halls, pounding past everything in its path. It roared and cascaded and drove and pushed its way through every gate and every alley of his heart.

Sergeant USA said: 'Tell her to go straight to hell, kid.'

Thelonius must have fallen silent for longer than he should have, because then she said, 'Where do you want to go, Thelonius?'

His skin tingled. 'I don't know.'

The eyes: *Decide, then.*

The various blues in her eyes softened until certain, tiny compartments of the iris held deep reservoirs of hazel.

'Once you're sure you want to say something, once your intention is good, just say it. Speak Justice. Come what may.'

Thelonius grabbed the arms of his chair with both hands.

'I woke up from a bad dream last night trying to run,' Thelonius said, 'trying to physically run out of my bed, but my legs wouldn't move. I was locked in my own body.'

Fatima whispered something low. It wasn't in English, and he didn't ask her to translate it or repeat it.

'Raghead doubletalk,' Sergeant USA hissed from the corner. 'She's a *machine*. Take her *out*.'

'I think I might be going to hell,' Thelonius said. 'I honestly don't know if I'm a Muslim or not. I might be. I don't know.'

And it was true. At that moment, he didn't. He didn't know anything for sure. He felt only the rushing of a great river in his heart gathering force, a flood getting longer and stronger.

Thelonius said: 'Don't take that veil off, okay?'

Her 'Okay' soothed him, and not just because it reminded him that she was an American. She, too, wanted him to keep his wits about him.

'Keep your mouth shut, kid,' came the voice from the corner. 'Mission-sensitive information stays inside the team.'

'I want to know what happened on Malaika Street,' Fatima said.

'How's it feel to *want*, sister?' said Sergeant USA.

Thelonius drew a deep breath. Let it out again. And nodded.

'Wha–??!' Sergeant USA spun around. 'We've been hit by a LIVING BATTERING RAM!'

As Sarge turned to fight off the Mutant Machines, Thelonius began to talk.

---

cxli. began to talk

Those secrets T revealed were far more damaging than he admits. A second Tums tablet appears to have distracted the insurrection at last. We are calming down again.

38 In Which I Wonder Whether I Have Finally Caught a Break

Mike Mazzoni, having parked outside the alley and used the mounted bullhorn to issue the order to halt, approached the scrawny, terrified motherfucker who had pelted his vehicle with rocks.

The staff sergeant held aloft Hajji, the standard-issue M16 that had MIKE painted on its grip. Hajji fired into the air a 5.56 x 45 millimeter NATO cartridge, an image of which Mike Mazzoni now bore on his right hand, in the same spot the pentagram occupied on his left.

He shouted, 'Enemy fire. Stay in the vehicle.'

Dayton ignored this and followed behind. The others stayed in the vehicle.

'He's scared. That's enough,' Dayton said.

'Fuck you, Bobbler,' Mike Mazzoni shouted. 'On the ground, doggie! Let me hear you bark! Let me hear you say WOOF WOOF!'

The kid did nothing. He only looked back, blank, having reached the old brick wall at the end of the alley. Too sheer to climb, too high to jump.

'Don't do it, Mike.'

Mike Mazzoni came within three paces of the kid and used the muzzle of the rifle to push him downward, onto his knees. The kid seemed empty with fear, light with it, about to float away. His chest heaved. He put his hands on top of his head without being asked to.

'You know goddamn well what I'm telling you to do, bitch. Say WOOF. Say WOOF WOOF, Jimmy Two.'

The kid tried to bark, but his throat was too dry.

'What's my name?' Mike Mazzoni demanded.

The kid said nothing. His lower lip was trembling.

'Don't do it, Mike,' Dayton said, louder this time.

'What's my name, asshole?' And Mike Mazzoni pounded his own

chest and used his face to form a question mark. The kid's expression shifted, as though he finally understood. He nodded. Mike Mazzoni said again: 'Hey, asshole. What's my name?'

'America,' said the kid, his lower lip still out of control. 'America, thank you. Thank you, sir.'

'Wrong, asshole,' said Mike Mazzoni. 'My name is Allah.' And he pounded his chest again. 'Allah!'

The kid's face was pale now.

'No, Mike,' said Dayton.

cxlii. No

No no no no no. I thought we had done it. Thought I had in fact caught a break. I had hoped you were asleep. I even started toward the bed. Now you are kicking again. Four eleven.

39 **In Which You Object to an Insult**

'So what do we do?' Thelonius asked.

'You say what happened and I write it down. I know you don't want a recording. So: You talk. I write, fast as I can. I type it all up and I bring it back to you to sign.'

'About Islam, I mean,' Thelonius said. 'What do we do about that?'

> **cxlii. About Islam**
>
> The manuscript's great moment of betrayal. When I read those words aloud just now, I felt you shudder, as if in protest.

She remained a moment without speaking. Then she said, quickly: 'Well, how much do you know about Islam?'

How much did he know? He breathed. The big current rushed stronger inside.

'I know everything we do can be worship, given the right intention. I know Muslims worship the Creator and not the creation. I know a man will only have what he strives for.'

All he could say. Maybe that was enough. His heart bursting. Water everywhere. His eyes wet. Maybe he would not go to hell after all.

'Do you know what our Prophet, peace be upon him, brought?'

'The Koran.'

She leaned in and studied him. 'Where did he get it?'

'I don't know.'

'No?'

'No. Don't know.' Hard to breathe.

'No?' As though she were talking to a small boy.

'Angel,' he said as he wept. 'It was an angel. Gabriel.' She gave him a clean handkerchief, which he used and pocketed.

She opened the Koran and showed him the part about being guided to the straight path. It was at the very beginning, and everything in the book was in English and Arabic. You could read the English. The Arabic had colours: white with flecks of blue and hazel, like her eyes, marking some of the pronunciation. He looked at the Arabic, then read the English.

She asked him if he wanted to become a Muslim. He said he still didn't know. He really didn't.

He said he knew there were things he regretted in his life.

She asked him if he had had anything to do with the flechette attack on the village of D—.

> **cxliv. attack**
>
> Darling. You and you alone know my troubles. You cannot possibly mean to shred me from within. Let Daughter rest.

He couldn't talk for a time. Then he said:

'Yes.'

He asked her if she would pray for him.

Sergeant USA flung his Expand-A-Shield at a trio of Mutant Machines. The shield skidded across three metallic android metal heads. PLOOF. THWOCK. KA-THOK.

⊠⊠⊠

Fatima said a prayer: *Lord, grant him forgiveness and salvation.*

He told her he was one of twelve people in a working group who had signed off on the flechette plan. He had had misgivings about the target. He had made a note to push the project leader on the accuracy of the intelligence the plan's attack data was based on. He never did that. He wondered now whether he had wanted the project leader to fail. Even if that meant people dying who shouldn't die.

The project leader was a man named Dick Unferth. He knew this man.

Fatima was breathing too hard. She suspected there were tears in her eyes. When she saw him looking at her, she looked down and started writing.

He asked if she would please forgive him for the part he had played in all that. For the death of her sister.

She looked up, searched his eyes, wiped her own, and explained the requirements for repentance. Sincere regret. Intention not to repeat the sin. He considered this, said he accepted both parts, asked her again if she would please forgive him for that.

They should rather pardon and overlook. Would you not love God to forgive you?

'Yes,' said Fatima A—, her voice unsteady. 'I forgive you.'

She asked if he had had anything to do with the desecration of the Koran.

cxlv. anything to do

These clear red pinpoints of light. Their every-minute shift. Four twenty-five. Four twenty-six.

40 **In Which I Wait**

Thelonius saw it from the third floor.

During the city-block-clogging protests that followed the flech-ette attack on D—, Thelonius noticed a serviceman, in the embassy's courtyard, pissing on something. Thelonius looked more closely, re-alized *what* the serviceman was pissing on, considered the sight lines and dashed downstairs. By the time he reached the doorway, the deed was done. Fly refastened, grinning, the idiot met him at the doorway, saluted smartly, and stood at attention.

'Morning, sir. And isn't it a beautiful morning, sir?'

The sergeant's nameplate read: MAZZONI M.

From behind, Thelonius heard a sudden peal of insane laughter, looked around and spotted another marine, blond, shorter and slim-mer than the man who had been pissing. A private.

The private kept up the laughing, more than a little too loud, even considering the crowd. He waved a wad of bills in the air and shook his head in awe.

'Here, you crazy beast. Four hundred bucks. I seriously didn't think you'd have the balls.'

Mazzoni, safely in the compound, grabbed the wad of bills and counted out the twenty dirty twenties, nodded in brisk approval to his companion, then turned to Thelonius.

'Will there be anything else, sir?'

'I should get you both locked up for endangering the security of this embassy.'

A chasm in the exchange, though only the private was intimidated by it. Mazzoni M. was apparently more practised at faking remorse.

Thelonius, who had been in the country for only a day, had a mis-sion to prepare for and no particular inclination to invest precious time filing a report. The crowd outside the embassy gates churned and sputtered, just as before; no one seemed to have noticed the stunt.

A disaster averted. He opted to disengage.

'Witty boys. Witty dumbasses. Keep an eye on each other. Stop covering for each other. You're going to get someone killed.'

'Thank you, sir,' said Mazzoni M.

The private, a blond marine who bore the nametag MAZZONI D, said nothing.

---

cxlvi. nothing

Four straight minutes of blessed calm, of nothing, I swear, and I was on the verge of calling it a night. Then a dark series of unanswered questions: Why such complete quiet? Could there be something wrong? Was it normal for you to be so still, so suddenly? So, like a fool I walked about the room, hoping to produce just a tiny rustle from either of you. And lo, you were awake again, poking me from every interior angle. The gymnastics have begun anew, as though you want to gnaw your way out. Sleep, having taunted me with its close embrace, will not come. Four fifty-nine.

41 In Which the Clock Reads 5:00

'I respect your decision. More important than the name is your intention. Now. The girl and her father, the two who died in the street. What happened on that morning, please?'

Fatima turned the page on her pad, all business. And stared him down. *Here we are.*

The thing was, Thelonius was *supposed* to shoot the man and his daughter. He had been specifically instructed to kill these people. The government of the United States had told him to do that. Dick Unferth had signed the memo.

Thelonius sighted them on Malaika Street. The father held, as promised, a briefcase, in which, according to intelligence assumed to be reliable, was a dirty bomb meant to be transmitted to the United States and activated in Times Square.

That girl, though, was too young to shoot. Her little fist around the man's fingers.

The briefing Thelonius received led him to believe that the father would be accompanied by a teenaged hacker of some kind. This girl, thin and coughing, could have been no more than nine. She clutched her father's hand.

Too young, damn it.

Even on that busy street, the father sensed a hostile foreign presence. He looked over his shoulder, saw Thelonius and widened his eyes.

The father's head snapped forward again. He said a word to his daughter in the native tongue. Probably he was telling her to run.

No time. Shoot the father, let the girl go.

No, kid. No. Orders say take them both out.

The father pulled his hand away and said the word again, whatever it was, louder.

Kid. Take them both out. What if he's telling her to detonate some-thing? A suicide vest? On a crowded street? Follow the orders.

She's too small. Shoot the father, let the girl go.

But the girl refused to run. She coughed and grabbed her father's hand again, turned to look back at Thelonius.

And when she looked over his shoulder, the damnedest thing happened.

Thelonius saw, thought he saw, swore he saw the rat-eyed glare of Dick Unferth.

Sergeant USA said: *Machine. I told you.*

That girl – was she, by some impossible combination of betrayals and infidelities, Dick Unferth's misbegotten love child? She coughed again and covered her mouth and reached up with her other hand. Seeking to be lifted, seeking to be held. Looking back yet again at Thelonius. With Dick Unferth's trademark rodent scowl.

What the hell …?

Unferth's eyes flashed again in the girl's head.

Machine. Machine. Machine.

'Sarge. I can't.'

Follow the orders. Take them both out. Look at those eyes.

The volcano rumbled.

I'm assuming command of this mission, T.

Sergeant USA shot the girl in the head three times. PLOOF. THWOCK. KA-THOK.

The girl fell. That froze the father in his tracks. Then Sergeant USA shot the father in the head three times, too. PLOOF. THWOCK. KA-THOK.

⊠⊠⊠

'When I got to them,' Thelonius said to Fatima, 'the girl on the ground didn't look at all like the person I thought. She was just a dead girl. She didn't have a suicide vest on. The briefcase only had…'

He carried his palms up to his forehead and closed his eyes. He swayed slightly, said to Fatima: 'Someone, somewhere planted bad intel for us. Set a trap. Wanted us chasing our own tails. No dirty bomb in that suitcase. Nothing but a book. A Koran. I don't want to go to hell for that.' He kept rocking back and forth in his chair for some time.

cxlvii. Nothing

Jihadi Queen is raped by committee now in Maximum Security, in a little room she will never leave. You and I will get out of our room, very soon, very soon we will get out of here, and nothing will ever disrespect us again. Be quiet now. 5:04.

42 **5:08**

The facial veil made her a stranger at first, which complicated matters, but she decided to retain it during the hearing, as she had promised Thelonius.

She introduced herself to the youngish imam. He told her, in the native tongue, that he remembered her. He addressed her with respect and concern.

As she had hoped, he chose not to question her again about any of the events she had witnessed at the American embassy, made no mention whatsoever of the event. When she introduced Thelonius, the imam greeted him with exquisite politeness, but shook no one's hand.

He took his seat and said, in uneasy but well-paced English, 'The case is important.'

The two of them sat across from him, on the other side of the card table. Fatima removed her gold pen from its box and prepared her legal pad. Morale Specialist stood and watched from a distance.

The youngish imam listened as Fatima read through her notes of the case. Then he reviewed the signed letters that had been distributed to, and countersigned by, the three families.

'The same notary witnessed all three of the fathers as they signed this?'

'Yes,' Fatima said.

'Is the notary here?'

'Yes. Upstairs.'

Fatima stood and prepared to fetch him. The youngish imam motioned for her to remain seated. He gestured for Morale Specialist to leave the room, and he did.

cxlviii. remain

Five seventeen. No brain cells remain. There is an army within. Somehow, I must quell this uprising.

The imam looked across the table and sized up the defendant, as though Thelonius were an automobile being returned to a rental agency.

⊠⊠⊠

Having recalled a conversation with a typhus patient he knew to be moribund, Indelible returned home at midday to pray alone. On his computer was an email message from Murad Murad: 'Where have you been?'

He typed back: 'Surveilling various localities. Countryside riddled with insurgents.'

⊠⊠⊠

The youngish imam asked Thelonius: 'Were you physically mistreated during your confinement here?' Thelonius peered across the table toward Fatima, who nodded that he should answer.

'Are my remarks confidential?'

'Yes.'

'They beat me. They hurt my leg. It's still giving me trouble. But they've stopped.'

'Have you seen a doctor?'

'No.'

The imam looked at Fatima, who shrugged: *I tried.* He turned back to Thelonius.

'Do you regret your actions on Malaika Street?'

'Yes. I would give anything not to have done it.'

The youngish imam studied him, wrote something on an index card with a pencil.

'You were raised as a Christian, I assume.'

'My grandparents thought so.'

Morale Specialist returned, a little man in a suit in tow behind him. The imam verified that the little man had personally countersigned the letters in question. Morale Specialist led the little man away.

'You seek the forgiveness of your Creator, and seek that the hell-fire should be forbidden to you, and the Paradise should be assured to you?'

'I do.'

'You wish to become a Muslim?'

43 In Which I Do Catch a Break

In the end, Bobbler refused to take the goddamned picture. He just walked back to the vehicle. Mike Mazzoni swore and screamed at him, but that didn't change anything, so he made one of the others come out and take it. It took several shots for the star to show up as big as it was supposed to.

Mike Mazzoni settled back into the driver's seat, grabbed the comlink, and advised HQ that his patrol had been attacked. He called in the location of the body, fired the engine and hit the street.

The rest of the patrol passed without a word.

> **cclix. without a word**
>
> Our body has calmed. I must now attempt the careful navigation of the distance between this desk and my bed. Good night, good morning, MotherDaughter.

In the photo, the dead insurgent's eyes were closed. Mike Mazzoni's pupils caught the flash the wrong way, so it looked like he was a demon or something. Mike Mazzoni thought that was cool. Also cool: him thrusting his too-bright left hand, complete with black star, forward into the face of the viewer. Like an ad or something. Thrusting it forward in such a way that the back of his hand occupied about twenty-five percent of the entire image area of the photo. Neither of the dead insurgent's hands were visible. They weren't cut off or anything, the hands were just out of the frame. The only parts of the dead insurgent that were visible were the shoulders and the head – notable for a large missing chunk that obliterated most of the hairline and looked like it was filled with reddish curdled milk.

The dead insurgent's face had an expression on it that looked almost like a smile. Mike Mazzoni didn't like that smile too much, and he also didn't like the idea of somebody tracing the kid back to that whole mess about the dogfights, so he blurred the face, but he made sure the kid's open skull and the black star from the back of his own left hand still showed. He won Hero of the Week with that photo.

⊠⊠⊠

The same week Mike Mazzoni brought down that insurgent, the ragheads took to gathering spontaneous freak shows in front of the U.S. embassy.

These occurred daily. They really were spontaneous, in the sense that no one appeared to know when they would begin or end. People in white – men, mostly – assembled in their hundreds and then, without warning, in their thousands. They swarmed like insects, acting on some telepathic cue from an unseen queen, once it became 'known' that the 'desecrator of the Koran' was being held ('protected' was the verb of choice employed by the newspaper *God Defended*) within the American embassy itself.

The Americans, the Defenders of God maintained, had taken over the Islamic Republic. Mike Mazzoni didn't think it looked like the Americans had taken over anything.

Mike Mazzoni resolved to add a new star for every kill. He felt less afraid with each new tattoo he added.

cl. new

Rested. Everything old is new again. The headphone jack still fits neatly into its socket, still makes that exquisite little click. I extract the gleaming disc that comprises sides three and four. I settle it into the machine. I hit play. My nipples are wet.

44 **In Which Paul McCartney Celebrates His Birthday**

cli. Celebrates His Birthday

Earbuds on. Press play. Side three begins. In a telling simultaneity, my MotherDaughter's zero-year birthday is likely to take place on my own imminent forty-fourth: August 9, 2006. Note the clear, prophetic alignment of this seditious phase of *Jihadi* with a song that 'happens' to be about (a) birth and (b) synchronicity (e.g., people who 'happen' to share birthdays). CD player on repeat for a bit.

Thelonius said, 'Yes, I want to become a Muslim.'

Sergeant USA leaned in close and muttered in Thelonius's ear: 'Just get us the hell out of here.'

Fatima said, in English, not quite under her breath: 'He has succeeded who purifies her ...'

'Don't you listen to that stuff, kid,' whispered Sergeant USA.

Thelonius closed his eyes tight.

'... and he has failed who corrupts her,' said Fatima.

When he opened his eyes, Sergeant USA was gone.

The imam said, 'Repeat after me. I bear witness that there is no God but God.'

Thelonius bore witness to that. Ninety minutes later, he was on a plane out of the Republic.

⊠⊠⊠

Those who had helped to coordinate the American's exit were advised, in a discreet email from the prime minister's personal account, to stay away from the capital.

'This will pass,' Ra'id said. It would only be necessary for Fatima to avoid the city for the next, say, seventy-two hours. That would be enough time for the grumbling to recede. The White Beast would find some new soap opera, once it realized that this one had concluded.

As she sped through the restless back streets toward the suburbs and the village of D—, her driver's uneven eyes once again flicking glances at her in the rear-view mirror, Fatima was not so sure the soap opera had concluded.

He had been sincere, at any rate. His heart had been sound, and with him gone there was no longer any danger of falling in love with him. She had watched him glance back over his shoulder at her as he was being led away, limping down the corridor of cold linoleum, toward a door that would become a pathway to a waiting car. She had watched him open his eyes wide and smile.

Here we are.

Done with that problem, at any rate.

⊠⊠⊠

Being debriefed is a whole lot like being interrogated. It feels like a continuation of what you just went through, not the end of it.

When word got around of how 'the crisis in the Islamic Republic' had been 'resolved' – two catch-phrases from the media coverage of the period that still make the dead guy writing this story chuckle – most people chose to assume Thelonius and the Directorate had outsmarted the extremists. That Thelonius had only accepted Islam as a legal pretence to get out of a tight spot. That bullshit had carried the day again.

He spent the better part of a day being 'interviewed' – that was the official term – in a brightly lit hospital room. Even though the hospital room was somewhere in Poland, it was really part of America: the Directorate was running the hospital.

During that long session he shared all he could remember about whatever people asked him. Nobody asked about the Raisin. Nobody asked about Fatima. Nobody asked about Mike Mazzoni's piss. Nobody asked about the flechettes. People asked about what had happened to him in the BII compound and how much he had given away.

Thelonius had followed orders and kept his mouth shut. So everyone acted as though his becoming a Muslim was part of a clever trick that made it possible for him to fly out of the Islamic Republic. Which, in fact, it was. Thelonius acted that way too.

As people asked him questions, Thelonius kept thinking about going home.

The truth was, though, he didn't even know where home was now.

Thelonius didn't know all kinds of things. He didn't yet know Becky was pregnant, hadn't yet figured out that Child was missing, had no idea that cats liked to drink toxic puddles of antifreeze. All he knew for sure as he was being questioned was that there was a direction called 'rest' and a direction called 'home', obscure trails that intersected and disappeared into a mist.

As he stumbled into that fog, it was easy to be the person everybody believed he was. To assume, as they did, that he was not really a Muslim and never had been. Every once in a while, though, he peered into the fog and wondered who he would be back in Salem.

He was still wondering about that when he got off the plane in Boston.

He was wondering about it when he made his way downstairs and sat at his dining-room table and stared at a milk carton that vibrated. He wondered when it would pass, this feeling of wandering through the mist, of not being home yet, of being slightly dead.

45 **In Which the Bassist Steps Up**

clii. the Bassist

McCartney's gem – yet another tribute to personal initiative – emerged despite, or because of, one of his bandmates' all-too-frequent, all-too-predictable funks. Starr had announced he was leaving the band and decamping for Italy. (T to a T!) The drummer's tantrum followed an eminently fair request for another percussion take worthy of his, McCartney's, studio time. Genius is everywhere beset with obstacles, and ever in peril of being mislabelled as opportunism … or worse. In such circumstances, one lays down the law or, if necessary, replaces the drummer.

It took some time to rig up the sound system to his satisfaction.

The Bearded Glarers started work on the audio set-up right after fajr, and had the large box speakers in place by noon, but these, according to Abu Islam, produced insufficient clarity. Additional speakers appeared. The Glarers had the microphone ready for him just before one in the afternoon.

At one fifteen on Friday, October 14, 2005, the unseen New Imam, Abu Islam, tapped the mike and began delivering the sermon that preceded a communal prayer taking place in front of the American embassy. He did this from a comfortable, well-appointed hotel room, seated before a bottle of Dewar's to which he made occasional appeals for inspiration.

By his side sat his stout wife, who scribbled occasional suggestions on the hotel stationery.

The boy was nowhere to be seen. Abu Islam had ceased making inquiries as to his whereabouts.

The dead guy telling you this story has no idea exactly how many people showed up for that prayer, but he believes the estimates that put the crowds at roughly ten times the size of the protest about the flechettes that killed Fatima's sister Wafa. That would make it about two hundred thousand people. Technically, this wasn't a protest. It was a religious service that elevated the recent release of the American known as Davis Raymonds to a level of central theological importance in contemporary Islam.

One was obliged from a human standpoint, a moral standpoint, and above all a religious standpoint, Abu Islam insisted, to fight and to kill all of the disbelievers who had launched this insult upon the Muslim people, and to continue the fight until they submitted to his personal authority. His words echoed against five major thoroughfares, into a large public park and through several dozen crooked alleys, all filled to the brim with the White Beast.

Abu Islam continued by pronouncing that any and all members of the government, and any citizens aligned with or supporting the government, whether or not they had direct knowledge of the events leading to the release of the murderer and desecrator of the Koran known as Davis Raymonds, were now to be regarded as infidels. Short of repentance, they were destined for the hellfire. In this world, the world awaiting the Day of Judgement, they were to be killed wherever they were found.

The sound of a bottle of bourbon clinking against a half-full glass echoed through the streets.

(Back in the hotel room, the heavyset woman frowned and indicated silently that she was to do the pouring.)

Abu Islam, calm and even and more voluble with every sip of Dewar's, pointed out that, as infidels, all employees of the government, even someone claiming to have no role or knowledge of the release of the murderer and desecrator of the Koran known as Davis Raymonds, were to be regarded as identical in status to the occupying Americans. Any Americans remaining in the city were also to be regarded as infidels destined for the hellfire. Killing such a person after confirming his or her refusal to renounce all support for the present government was mandatory, and a blessed deed.

Members of the Islamic Republic's armed forces, and their police, and their security forces in uniform, were also to be regarded as infidels destined for the hellfire. However, these individuals were likely to be armed. Killing such a person was a blessed deed, to be certain, but precautions were in order.

First, it was praiseworthy and preferable to kill such a person in collaboration with another male believer. Women at this point were not to carry out such operations without the guidance and approval of a male believer. Particular stress was laid on this point. The loss of women from a family was to be avoided at all costs. They were to remain in the home.

In addition, Abu Islam ruled, it was praiseworthy and most preferable to kill armed infidels in uniform *only* after having consulted with one of Abu Islam's personal representatives. Killing such uniformed, armed supporters was praiseworthy, but had not yet been declared mandatory. It might become mandatory in the weeks to come.

There was more.

Abu Islam ruled next that the murderer and desecrator of the Koran known as Davis Raymonds, whom he had identified in a previous sermon as an infidel destined for the hellfire, was, despite the government's shameful connivance in his escape from the Republic, still subject to Islamic justice. The believer, male or female, who executed this person, acting independently or in collaboration with another believer, acting within the borders of the Islamic Republic or elsewhere, would be assured of Paradise.

In front of the embassy, Skullface, one bony hand on the boy's shoulder, shouted *TAKBEER* into his megaphone.

Two hundred thousand voices responded *ALLAHU AKBAR*.

⊠⊠⊠

Thelonius was now home from the animal shelter, having been released by the police on his own recognizance.

Composed again, he'd asked for Child's remains before they left. The talkative officer had agreed to fetch them, on the condition that Thelonius stay in the back while he did. Thelonius also had to promise the officer that he wouldn't operate heavy machinery for a while, that he would stay off the streets and try to get some sleep.

During the cab ride home, the heavy box in his lap to settle him, he had felt Islamic City recede. His knee, which had caused him pain since his interrogation, had hurt less. Now, standing outside the Salem foursquare where Becky had been born, it ached again.

The Raisin had said: 'Where then are you going?'

Actually the Koran said that.

He placed Child on the railing of the deck, unlocked the door, opened it, retrieved Child, and went in the kitchen.

Chaos surrounded him: puddles of milk from the half-gallon he had smacked around during his argument with Becky, an overflowing garbage pail, a counter full of dirty dishes, debris from breakfast, all of it strewn about, all of it furious. And him, the maddest, biggest mess of all, limping through it, his knee throbbing, the cat's stone casket swaying in his hands. A placid sycamore waved its leaves from the window overlooking the porch.

Both forearms sore, Thelonius set his heavy load down in the middle of the floor.

He did not have to call out to see whether or not Becky was there. He knew she was gone: this silence was quite different from the silence when she was in and not talking. She'd be back. She always came back here. Odd for her to leave a mess, though.

He tidied up the kitchen.

He retrieved Child with an effort, headed upstairs and groaned: the knee throbbing as he made his way up. He kept on, but felt the slightly dead feeling again. He was pushing it too hard, trying to go too fast.

When he reached the landing, he turned. He looked down the stairwell from where he'd just come, then up into a skylight window whose height and width ratios approximated those of a sheet of paper. He saw the dancing leaves of that great sycamore again, colouring itself with autumn. A bird settled onto one of the leaves, blue and grey, its name escaped him. He felt better. He turned, went into the bathroom and placed the heavy box on the floor.

He sat, opened the casket, looked inside it and stared at the rumpled, strangely folded assemblage of fur and limbs that had been his cat.

He began to set Child on the tiled bathroom floor, and then, thinking better of it, laid him with care in the bathtub. There would be less mess if he were washed in there. Child's eyes were empty and sad and finished.

That dead girl's open eyes had looked nothing like Dick Unferth's rat-eyes, nothing.

He wept for a long time.

46 In Which Ringo Starr's Petulance Is Checked

cliii. Petulance

Listen with care to the vocal mix, and you will hear McCartney – now the band's drummer – celebrating rock and roll, celebrating himself and celebrating the ensemble he now leads, as he sustains the count on a critical transition: 'Four! Five! Six! Seven! Eiiiiiight!' Thus the take was held together. Thus the band was held together. Thus we will hold the nation together and be acknowledged as its saviours, when we emerge from the Bottomless Pit.

The dead guy sharing this story recalls that October 14, 2005, was a Friday notable in the Islamic Republic for the New Imam's first public declaration of a Caliphate whose capital was Islamic City, whose head was himself. His wife, of course, had been shouting this in the streets for some time.

October 14, 2005 was also the day Fatima concluded, for reasons she could not have explained, that a strange odour her sister claimed to smell connected to something in the real world.

It was the day Mike Mazzoni made his brother decorate his hand with its fifth star. That happened before breakfast.

It was the day Indelible agreed, via email, to have his first Skype discussion with Sullivan Hand.

It was the day Becky confirmed with a home pregnancy test that she was, in fact, carrying her first and only child, though she knew her body well enough to have suspected as much for some time.

October 14, 2005 was the day Becky devoted her life to acting in defence of that pregnancy.

It was the day Thelonius Liddell found himself staring at a milk carton on his kitchen table. The day he figured out that antifreeze was lethal poison when licked up by cats. The day that all of Becky's past warnings – about cats and toxoplasmosis and foetal deformity and what she would and wouldn't put up with if there were ever a baby on the way – came back to him with special force.

It was the day Thelonius decided his wife was carrying Dick Unferth's baby. He was wrong about that.

47 In Which I Recall Barry Goldwater's Moment of Glory

cliv. Barry Goldwater

Thanks to an exhilarating opening drum fill and various bits of studio trickery, the underlying pace of track eighteen sounds faster, at first, than it actually is. The comparatively moderate tempo is only revealed at the aforementioned percussion break, which cuts in at 0:42 and untangles certain ingenious vocal and guitar effects. Those of us who have been accused of propagating 'extremist' philosophies within certain circles of the Directorate will grasp the great Metaphor to which the *White Album* draws the listener's attention here. We are not going as fast as you imagine. Only as fast as the defence of liberty demands. BG quote here. My feet hurt.

Contingent upon his orders concerning the infidels (Abu Islam told the persistent reporter who had somehow talked his way past the Bearded Glarers) was a precondition.

Of course, he referred to the precondition of lawful Islamic authority, and this, he knew, most people believed not to exist in the Islamic Republic. Until today, there had been ample reason for scepticism. Despite the country's name, he assured the reporter, the present government served only to parody an Islamic state. Indeed, its leaders had up to this point imprisoned all those who called in public for a lawful Islamic state with a single Khilafah. Lacking a Khilafah, they knew, there could be no single voice to speak on behalf of Islam. Abu Islam had resolved this difficulty on the afternoon of October 14, 2005 by proclaiming himself the sole rightful leader of the world's 1.4 billion Muslims, two hundred thousand of whom were now camped out on all four sides of the American embassy on his orders.

Abu Islam confirmed this proclamation, speaking more slowly this time, for the reporter's benefit. He acknowledged that such a step, extreme and necessary in the face of extremity, carried with it personal danger.

He was willing to go to prison. He was willing to die. He was not willing to betray Islam.

He would, however, be out of the public eye for a while.

The reporter asked about an ayat in the word of Allah mandating moderation in daily life.

Abu Islam answered that this verse implied that there were times when moderation must itself be moderated.

The reporter left. There in Abu Islam's private quarters (quite comfortable, despite the earlier protestations against living in buildings) his wife prepared two bourbons.

⊠⊠⊠

There was a window in the hot, stuffy bathroom, and through it Thelonius could see the big sycamore, framed against a darkening afternoon sky. A wedge of Canadian geese flew by, and above them a bank of grey clouds moving slightly slower than the birds, but in the same direction, the sycamore leaning after them in the wind and losing more of its leaves, everything receding, heading south, away from him.

And now the geese were quite small.

He felt the old dead feeling in his chest again, the one that locked him in. Thelonius spun down the knob on the heater, which rattled and went silent. He opened the window.

Becky wouldn't approve, heating the outdoors with all this expensive warm air. But now he could hear the faint calls of the geese as they stretched away towards Florida or wherever.

Cold air streamed through the window. He breathed it in deep, closing his eyes, enjoying the clean feel of it, enjoying the expectation that it was about to rain outside.

He stroked Child once, a slow stroke. The fur was soft and matted in spots. The bathtub's old porcelain surface was cold and white.

He arranged Child as though he were sleeping. Yet his eyes remained open.

Thelonius said out loud, 'He has succeeded who purifies her and he has failed who corrupts her.'

Now what?

He turned the four-pronged COLD handle, nearly as old as the house, then lifted the lever that made water flow through that fake-art deco showerhead Becky had installed last year. When the water hit Child it reduced him in size, but it drew all the filth out of him and straightened the wayward tufts of fur into waves. After enough time, Thelonius shut off the tap and all the water drained away and it was okay.

A HIS towel or a HERS towel: he picked the HIS towel from the rack and dried Child's fur with it, set the towel on the sink vanity, gathered him up, held him in his arms and took a breath.

Should he place the towel in the laundry hamper or throw it away?

He didn't want her touching Child or any part of him. He would come back up and throw the towel away after he had buried Child.

A gentle rain started to fall outside. Just Get Started.

He left the window open. Strong and ready, as though things were behind him, Thelonius walked back down the stairs with the damp corpse along his forearms. The leg slowed him down, and that was fine now.

Favouring the leg, he made his way outside with great care.

With a shovel he procured from the shed, he buried the cat deep in the backyard. The air was cool and open and rainy as he dug. There was a lot of space to work with. The autumn earth smelled damp and alive, and the leaves were shaking with the rain, and when he was done, he looked off toward a hillside that he had always liked, and it looked clean in the rain, cleaner than he could ever recall it looking.

48 In Which a Brutal Edit Evokes a Critical Passage from the Gospel of John

clv. the Gospel

Our new world, our vibrating shimmer within the earbud-pierced CD player, track nineteen, spins. Dark cloud, azure haze: The Great Threat foretold and overcome.

She is on her way. Her Return is prophesied at 3:16 of this piece. Immediately after Harrison's solo, the predictable four-in-the-bar falls apart, and an abrupt edit signals a new phase of consciousness, a new deliverance, a new phase of history. This astonishing pivot-point, 3:16 – whose 'coincidental' (!) timing-mark so clearly evokes the Gospel of John – conveys to the West a message of great comfort: For God so loved the earth that he sent forth his Only Begotten Daughter, that whoever believed in her might not perish, but have eternal life.

Oops. A twinge amidst the kicks. But that's not labour, Dad. That's Braxton-Hicks.

By late afternoon Thelonius, who had been staring at the cat's grave for some time, was wet and a little woozy. It was still raining. His clothes, soaked, stuck to him. It occurred to him that he ought to go inside and pray.

Once inside, though, his leg gave him trouble again, and he thought about trying to sleep that off. But the distance to the couch was intimidating, and anyway he was dripping. He opted to dry his hands and look for some instructions. Must be something about praying in that Koran.

He spent twenty minutes paging through it at the dining-room table, but didn't find any praying instructions. He decided to call up someone. At least he ought to know. So he found a number and called it and asked about how to pray for forgiveness after killing somebody.

The ebullient imam at the Islamic Center of Greater Marblehead spoke with no accent and great enthusiasm, and pretended not to understand what Thelonius had asked. He provided clear, patient and ardent instructions on how to pray: how to find the direction, make an intention, purify oneself with water. All that had to happen before praying. Thelonius wrote it all down. The imam mentioned casually – as though arranging a complex, exciting social event with Thelonius – that if one happened to have committed a major sin, one was supposed to do the purification step and the prayer itself, in an attitude of accountability and repentance. And pray slowly. Would Thelonius come to the mosque that afternoon?

Thelonius said he'd do his best, but he wasn't sure what the rest of the day looked like. He thanked the man and hung up.

Thelonius went back upstairs to the bathroom and did the water thing, which involved saying 'Bismillah' and washing your hands and your mouth and your nose and your forearms and your feet. He figured out which direction Mecca was, made an intention to pray for forgiveness in an attitude of repentance and accountability, and prayed in the bedroom. He wept when he was finished, wept down on his knees. Then he felt angry at Becky.

He decided to do the water thing again.

As he did that, he noticed there was still some black cat-hair in the tub, and heard Becky downstairs. And he felt the anger again and slowed himself and calmed it down and started the water thing once again.

'You're not turning into a Muslim, are you?' she called from below, laughing.

He had left the open Koran on the dining-room table.

He finished, turned off the water.

'That was my idea, you know, that whole conversion,' her voice called. 'You could at least say thanks.'

He dried his hands and feet on a HERS towel. He was okay seeing her face now.

From the bottom of the stairs he heard her call again, closer this time: 'T?'

A note of concern.

'T, you know you have a home here. You'll always have a home here. You aren't going to turn into a Muslim on us, are you?'

A big nothing rested on the stairway after that.

'Are you?'

'Yeah, I was thinking I might,' he called down finally, overloud but at least not angry.

There was another big nothing. The sound of the rain outside. He opened the window all the way, the better to see a new flock of geese trailing away beneath the clouds, the better to hear the unfaltering rain. Over the rain, from behind, came her footfall. He turned. She was standing right there in the doorway, her red hair askew and her eyes tight slits – an expression that had, historically, sent the not-to-be-disobeyed message, *'Don't speak'*. He looked into them now but did not fall in.

'Becky, I let you down.'

She looked at him as she would look at a specimen.

'I didn't know I was letting you down, but I was. That must have hurt you, left you feeling alone. And I am so, so sorry I couldn't give you what you needed.'

Not a twitch of any muscle.

'I assume it's Dick Unferth's baby. I want a divorce.'

Not a blink.

'You and your *secrets*,' she hissed at last. 'You *weak* men with *weak* minds with all your *secrets*. You're not the only ones with *secrets*, you know.'

'I'll leave tomorrow,' Thelonius said.

She went into the bedroom and slammed the door. The rain kept up outside, steady and clean.

He heard familiar music playing from behind the bedroom door.

He took to the couch that night. So far as he could tell, she did not come out. The same album kept playing, over and over.

The next day he started packing and looking for another place to stay. For a direction home. He couldn't reach Dad, but that was normal enough. He called Adelia.

⊠⊠⊠

'Things,' Dayton said right out loud – although there was no way for his brother or anyone else to hear him over the surging ocean of people – 'are happening way too fast.'

The dead guy sharing this story imagines Dayton and Mike Mazzoni as two of the dozen or so marines standing at what was supposed to be attention, but was much closer to shock. Dayton was up on the helipad. His older brother was near the front gate of the embassy.

Although he could barely see his brother's lips move from that distance, Mike Mazzoni also believed all of this was happening too quickly. It had to have been organized ahead of time. The ragheads had come together for the latest Freak Show so hot and so sudden there was no time to call in water cannons or anything else. At twelve forty there had been a few hundred white-robed ragheads, maybe a thousand. At one o'clock it was Raghead Freak Show City.

They were everywhere. All worked up about someone taking a common piss.

It did not exactly fill Mike Mazzoni with warm fuzzies to know that he had been assigned to stand in front of them all like a fucking bull's eye.

By the time the Raghead-in-Chief started his latest prerecorded speech in some damn language that wasn't English, Mike Mazzoni had downed about a fifth of gin from what looked like a water bottle, but wasn't. Hajji dangled comfortably from the index and middle fingers of his left hand. The back of that hand had accumulated a total of seven black tattooed stars: one for the teenager whom he now referred to as Asshole A, and one each for Assholes B, C, D, E, F, and G.

'Getting full,' Bobbler had remarked that morning. 'Just saying it doesn't look so great on a sergeant, maybe. Maybe time to stop adding stars.'

'Oh, hell no,' Mike Mazzoni had said.

He kept the back of his hand facing out now, toward Freak Show Squared.

There it was, right in front of him, a crowd like fucking Woodstock, but all white, shaped like an O that extended out forever, a sea of white surrounding the embassy from every side. The gates around him marked out the hollow of that O, where a crew of armed, uniformed personnel drew together in the courtyard like it was a little mosh pit. On top of the embassy, looking down at that mosh pit, looking down on everything, there was Bobbler, rifle drawn, circling in a constant, slow three sixty, targeting everyone in white and a target to everyone in white. Mike Mazzoni muttered, 'Don't fuck this one up, bro.'

A pinprick in the middle of the O, Bobbler had his own AK-47, not Hajji, nothing with a name, but nothing to be messed with, either. Men screamed themselves red in the face like they were getting paid for it and damned if they didn't dare Bobbler to shoot them. In English.

No way Bobbler could hear that, though.

Crowd or no crowd, it was lonely in the hollow of that O. Who the hell screams at a sniper and waves his hands up in the air, all SHOOT ME SHOOT ME SHOOT ME? These people were in love with death. You couldn't get ESPN or anything worth having in a country based on death. There'd been potential here once, he'd felt it himself in the Wreck Room, he had met a lot of them personally, before the Freak Show began, before this Raghead-in-Chief shit. But once upon a time, man...

Mike Mazzoni wished he had a cigarette. He breathed in a deep lungful of air instead.

Once upon a time you might have seen a mall here and some goddamned satellite dishes or some other signs of fucking civilization. Over the past month somebody had obviously been pumping crap into their heads in the mosques or the madrassas or maybe in the streets, while they were bowing their ragheads to Allah, getting hard-ons over their black box off in Mecca. Someone was pumping this death crap into them. Now they had all gotten on this insane wavelength of just wanting to die.

There was nothing to say to that. So the next lesson would have to be a lesson in respect, and that lesson, if it were ever given, would have to come through families, not through the individual assholes. They were each happy to go down for a dirt nap. But family. Family, they cared about. Family, they would negotiate for. Family was the key.

That, Mike Mazzoni had determined, was the only thing these people took more seriously than death. Family.

Some white-robed idiot tried to climb over the gate.

Over *razorwire.* You could see the stupid son of a bitch bleeding from the hands and forearms. And he just kept on fucking climbing.

Mike Mazzoni called, 'Bobbler!'

Bobbler heard him, or heard something, from the helicopter pad atop the embassy – a brother thing, maybe – and spun around.

49 **In Which the Band Celebrates**

clvi. Celebrates

Track nineteen, checking in at a world-changing four minutes and one second, was laid down in the dead of night in a closet (charitably dubbed an 'annex') at EMI Studio Two. The final version features minimal overdubs, and the 'live' feel of the recording is emphasized by the occasional joyous shouts of the band members celebrating, thirty-seven years ahead of time, your conception.

Ouch.

Motorola was loud and unclear.

There was no internet connection out here anymore. Someone had bombed something. That left Fatima in the kitchen, slicing potatoes. The day off. Time to relax. But Motorola, a small American handheld radio – the only electronic communication of which Baba ever approved – was not relaxing her. Motorola had been a member of the family for years. It crackled an update about the huge demonstration at the American embassy. The static that she loathed, but had come to accept, cut in and out.

God Defended. Peaceful so far. Unprecedented gathering. A slander upon the nation. A quarter of a million people at least. Those following this New Imam. His location unknown. Rumours of a return tomorrow midday. Crowd growing. His clear instructions. A national day of justice. Of reckoning. That murderer and desecrator of the Koran. Intensified. Rage in our hearts. Intensified. A man at the front of the crowd, very near the gate. Some shouts to encourage him.

And so forth.

Fatima put down the knife, washed her hands, ran them wet through her long, black hair, recalled that Baba did that with fingers spread in the same way, missed Baba again.

A national day of justice? Of reckoning? For whom? 'That

murderer and desecrator of the Koran'. A fiction, a composite she knew to be two human beings. Did the nation deserve this demagogue who created such paper villains, who made up the religion as he went along? Had it come to that?

A shriek from upstairs – nothing unusual.

It was a familiar academic shriek. It culminated in a shouted NO. Fatima switched off Motorola.

Noura, unlike Fatima, had always been home-schooled due to socialization issues. Lately, Mother could not get her to focus on her assignments for more than a few minutes at a time. These shrieks had been standard operating procedure for months, but they had become more brash and more common since Noura had smelled the mysterious ripping thing, that invisible, approaching wave of metal and gasoline.

'I want to help with the potatoes! I don't *want* Galileo! I already *know* about Galileo!'

Fatima called upstairs: 'Let her help, Mother.'

Noura padded downstairs, her smile too wide.

'Think you're so clever,' Fatima said.

Noura tornadoed in and stole a hug, which Fatima returned, then eased out of when it became, as most of Noura's hugs did these days, too tight for too long.

'Get to work,' said Fatima, drying her hands on a towel.

Noura took up the knife with glee, set to work upon a helpless peeled potato.

'What do you know about Galileo, then?'

Cornered, Noura grimaced. 'He's boring. I know *that*.'

'Back upstairs, then?'

'No.' Lips tight, eyes set on her moving knife.

'Actually, he's one of the least boring people ever. In the whole history of the world. Oh I do mean it, though. Because. Listen. Because. Galileo found people telling a big lie: The sun goes around the earth. Now, it *looks* like that's what happens. But it's not what happens. Actually the earth goes around the sun. And he proved that with math and telescopes. People thought he was crazy. They were used to the lie. He had to hold on to the truth. No other way out.'

Inspired, Fatima seized a small and a large potato from the bowl, orbited the small one around the large one. Noura stared, rapt.

'Sun. Earth. Got that?'

Noura nodded.

'So. Did he win a prize? For telling the truth? What's the matter? Well, did he?'

'No.'

'No?'

'No. They threatened to torture him. They made him stand up in front of everyone and say the sun went round the earth, made him say the earth didn't move at all. But under his breath he still said, "It moves." Now move the earth.'

'Crazy.'

'Who?'

'Somebody,' Noura said, watching the two potatoes hold still. 'I don't know. All of them. You. Who cares? What was the point?'

Fatima furrowed her brow. 'Earth moves around the sun. Fool. Is the point. No matter what. Whether we're crazy or not. Earth moves. Will you move the earth, please?'

Noura moved the earth around the sun. Fatima ran her hands through her long hair again and stared out the window at nothing.

'That's enough. I'll do the rest. Go get the oil and the pan and an onion. We'll make dinner together.'

Noura spun off. Fatima unplugged Motorola, took it off the shelf and placed it in the little cupboard beneath the sink.

⌧⌧⌧

The lights were all out again, except for his computer screen.

Indelible settled into the same chair in front of the same monitor, connected to the same keyboard, using the same internet connection, with his wife asleep in the same bed. He drank Darjeeling tea from the same cup.

Back on the night the Islamic City dogs took him into custody, Indelible had received two unexpected messages from two unfamiliar email addresses. Tonight, Indelible knew both of those people were Sullivan Hand.

Indelible, whose hacking skills far surpassed those of his new American friend, knew Sullivan Hand's full name. Indelible knew that Sullivan Hand was working in Langley, Virginia, and he knew how long Sullivan Hand had been working for the Directorate, and he knew Sullivan Hand's social security number – all without Sullivan Hand sharing so much as a word about any of that.

In pursuit of a blessed goal – blowing himself up along with as much of the U.S. embassy as possible – Indelible was about to start his very first real-time, voice-to-voice conversation with Sullivan Hand. He took a tiny sip of Darjeeling, thought of a certain typhus patient who had passed in the night, and logged on.

⊠⊠⊠

Sullivan Hand had determined, to his own satisfaction at least, that Indelible was the real thing. He said as much in his report, which was well received by everyone except the dead guy writing this book.

He'd convinced his superior that he was pretty damn good at pretending to be multiple people online, pretty good at figuring out who was who, pretty good at flushing people out of their hidey-holes, pretty good at covering his tracks, pretty good at saving the Directorate money, and so forth.

He was the future. If you didn't believe him, you could ask him.

He was building his fast-track career path in the Directorate, working all hours. All of twenty-three years old, skinny, underpaid, he was eager to continue an affair with an assertive older woman who was reading all his reports, an affair he supposed would keep him on the fast track and keep him sane. Sullivan Hand liked assertive women.

⊠⊠⊠

The dead guy telling this story knows more than he ever wanted to about Sullivan Hand's career. He turned up everything that Sullivan ever submitted to the Directorate, the FBI and local law enforcement. All the sound files, all the memos and the one massive transcript illuminating the process by which fabricated evidence was produced for use in the prosecution and conviction of the Oldburgh Jihadi Ensemble. Three simpletons, it will be recalled, were supposed to have coordinated a complex, scary plot to shoot up a shopping mall and bomb a synagogue, in obedience to the hypnotic death-chants of the Koran.

In reality, the three improvised a scene, two minutes and nine seconds in duration, about three Al Qaeda stooges who spend most of their waking hours smoking pot.

During this impromptu sketch, Al Qaeda Stoner A mentions to Al Qaeda Stoners B and C that he, Stoner A, took the bus out to Watertown's Northway Mall aiming to shoot up the place … but forgot his machine gun. Having arrived at the mall unarmed, he changed his mission, headed to a nearby balcony, and dropped stolen loaves of Panera bread on unsuspecting passers-by. Then, on his way home, he encountered a rasta-obsessed Jamaican rabbi eager to confirm Bob Marley's status as the literal reincarnation of Moses. Having scored from this person an ounce of a particularly potent strain of weed, nicknamed Matzoh-Ball Missile Boy, Stoner A explains how to reach the synagogue in question by public transport.

'Far out, Abdul,' croaks Stoner B, handing an invisible roach to the companion to his immediate right.

'Far out, may Allah accept,' hisses Stoner C on an inhale, taking a long toke from the proffered roach and forwarding it to Stoner A.

'Far out,' say all three Al Qaeda stoners in slow unison, on a communal inverted hiss, to avoid the premature release of precious molecules of THC.

At this point in the recording, Sullivan Hand laughs. Another voice asks: 'Should we record it, Brother Daoud?'

(As a freelance informant for the FBI, Sullivan Hand called himself Daoud Hand for the benefit of his targets. He liked such subterfuge, saw his role as Daoud as evidence of his capacity for upward mobility into the exciting world of espionage. His only mobility, as it turned out, was downward. He ended up tied to a filthy bed, naked, attempting to explain himself to local law enforcement.)

(It might be asked why the dead guy writing this story came to learn so much about Sullivan Hand. The answer is a simple one. He was under orders to find out. Enter Adelia.)

50 **Rishikesh**

clvii. Rishikesh

Regarded (online sources confirm) as the single holiest city of the Indian subcontinent. Terminus of the Fabs' aborted pilgrimage. Site of the Maharishi's ashram, and thus of most of the *White Album*'s composition.

Ouch.

Adelia would not look at Glass, ever, but she led him to it, and she expected him to follow. She said 'Dad will see you now' while she walked, but only as a formality. If she escorted people to Glass, that already meant Dad would see them.

She was stepping fast, as usual, well ahead of Thelonius on the familiar walkway of grey stone that snaked behind the main house and led to Glass.

The nominal maid (and actual Dad-concubine) whom Thelonius followed wore her ebony hair pulled back in a tight bun, obscuring the tiny kinked ringlets Dad was said to favour. Aloofness was a friend of hers. Adelia knew, like her predecessors knew, not to make lingering eye contact with anyone summoned to Glass. Her unseen face, being unseeable now, in the Beige Motel, must, alas, be recalled as a composite. Adelia had the same tawny skin, the same aerodynamically sound facial features, the same light glance, the same avoidance of even the possibility of physical contact with strangers, as those who had come before her. Ryan Firestone had sought and found these traits in a now-uncountable succession of employed mistresses, Adelia the latest of these. The reigning monarch of the Cloisters, she appeared to have at least a few years to go as the representative of her graceful, well-compensated dynasty.

This dynasty's origins were best not probed, but it preceded the attack on Ryan Firestone's wife Prudence by several years.

Glass, the structure to which Adelia led Thelonius, was a private space. Like its occupants, it was not for civilian inspection.

'You've spoken to him today?' Thelonius asked, still well behind her.

The back of Adelia's head nodded.

'You know what this is about?'

The back of Adelia's head shook.

'Any advice?'

Even walking behind her, he sensed the chuckle she suppressed.

'Tell him the truth.'

'I knew that.'

'They all say they know it, then they lie to him.'

'Not me.'

'Up to you, I suppose.'

'Is he better?'

'No.'

They reached Glass.

She stepped aside as he opened the door. She did not look at it. The door closed and she was gone, as the outer world was gone and the time of day was gone. The air was hot and close and things hissed.

Dad preferred this greenhouse for private meetings. Thelonius had suspected for some time this was due to the constant whisper, the vapour and the humid embrace of the perpetual watering system. One emerged damp and changed. Dad seemed to believe that he had created an environment with a plausible liberty from listening devices.

Glass was square and contained eight plant-lined corridors, the central two of which were separated by an empty row. Dad was in a wheelchair directly in the centre of Glass, in a clearing about which philodendrons and wisteria and maidenhair hovered and crawled at a speed undetectable to anyone but Dad. His careworn, ravaged face told all who cared to ask that he was dying.

'Hello, Dad.'

'Yes, you made it back,' Dad said, raw-voiced but casual, as though Thelonius's presence had been a remark in an ongoing conversation. He held up the African violet he'd been inspecting, put it down. 'I am glad for that, and so, so sorry for the trouble we got you into, T. How about a drink to celebrate your homecoming?'

The only feature recognizable from the portrait of Dad that hung in the living room were the warm eyes, eyes that still spoke of possibility, alliance, connection, innovation, shared benefit. They spoke of past excess and present secrets, those quiet old eyes. They were watered, as ever, with liquor.

Thelonius shook his head.

'No? The rumours are true?'

Thelonius nodded.

'Well, with your permission, I will.' Dewar's and a glass and ice from a wooden compartment in the stone, to which he reached down.

The whisky and ice and glass assembled, Dad gestured for Thelonius to sit on the stone bench, which he did.

Dad watched him.

'Hrothgar toasts you,' Dad said, and grimaced as he swallowed, but kept watching. A classicist. Always.

'I'm not Beowulf, Dad. What's this about?' Thelonius asked, trying to sound patient.

'High D as always, just like me. Yes, so we'll get to the point. You're thinking about quitting.'

Always a step ahead of you, Dad was.

'I am. I want out, Dad. I need to do something else with my life. This isn't home for me anymore.'

The warm eyes, saggy and bloated now, behind their grey walls of sunken flesh, said: *Please wait.* Out of respect, Thelonius stood by for the next move.

'Have you ever heard of a fellow named Sullivan Hand?'

'No.'

'T,' Ryan said, sipping his Scotch and placing it on the stone table near his right armrest, 'the lucidity problem has ramped up faster than either of us imagined. She's been cooking up trouble with the FBI. Operating a little sub-unit entirely on her own. Becky has to be brought out of the Directorate.'

Thelonius breathed in a lungful of wet, warm, settling air, took in the green. 'Yes. Of course. That makes sense.'

'And in order to bring her out well and carefully, we have to know what kind of damage she may have caused already.'

Always well and carefully. Not just to do something. To do something well and carefully. And that subtle transition to 'we'.

'Dad. I'm tired. I feel like I'm in jail still. I've felt like that for a while. I wouldn't be much use to you.'

'Oh, that's where you're wrong.' And his patented silence.

'Waiting.'

'The erratic behaviour. The instability in her sleep patterns. The patchiness in her ability to concentrate. You're quite familiar with all that. You know what it leads her to, how she thinks. The various professional networks she's created. You're familiar with those, too.'

'Yes. So are you.'

'You're the one with an axe to grind, though. You're the jilted husband. Ex-husband, I mean. You've got a *reason* to go digging. In the event things ever come into the light.'

'Don't *you* have a reason to go digging?'

'No, T. I don't. I'm above it all.' Dad smiled a weak smile. 'Why you're here: We need you to give us a damage assessment before you quit. Before I let her go. Letting her go will likely be ugly. We need to know what's gone wrong, if anything, and where wrong, and how badly wrong. Over the past year. Just as thorough as you can make it, please. Delivered personally. Not committed to text. Memory, boy. Or if you do keep written notes, keep them in code. You will appear to report to Unferth, who is to know nothing of this. I need all you can get me on what she's got this Hand person doing. Along the way, you may be able to solve that other riddle that's been on your mind.'

Dad smiled.

Thelonius's chest tightened with the pain of not quite being in control, a sensation peculiar to conversations with Dad. Another deep breath.

'What riddle would that be, Dad?'

51 **Postcards from India**

clviii. India

In the *White Album*'s first postcard from Rishikesh, McCartney summarizes the Maharishi's simple theory of enlightenment – 'follow nature'. This is track twenty, a lovely ballad in plain D. Lennon's two explicitly Rishikesh-themed offerings follow.

'I said, what riddle is that, Dad?'

'Well, for one thing, whether it's Dick Unferth's baby growing in that dark place – or somebody else's. Do let me know what you figure out on that front. A man has a right to be curious about who's fathering his grandchildren.'

The bastard had bugged their house. More chest constriction. Breathe again. Look at the plants.

Dad lifted a frail hand to his eyebrow. The little shadow of his movement drew Thelonius's angry stare away from a long row of African violets.

The weathered hand descended, shook. The old man's eyes were still pleading for help, still begging, like someone who had been stranded somewhere, waiting a long time for family to come. But the sandpaper-rough words that came out of his mouth were as firm, as purposeful as ever.

'And actually, T, there's another riddle for us to solve.'

'Is there?'

'I'm afraid so. It's about your most recent trip. I have come to suspect she knows more about what happened to you in the Republic, and why, than we initially thought. You and I need to find out how *much* more. Well and quickly. Before she's decommissioned, you see. To protect all the other soldiers out there. So I do thank you for not quitting just yet. We'll get you out of all this soon enough.'

He poured himself a refill. He took another sip, set down his ice-laden glass. A second or so later, the stacked ice shook and fell.

⊠⊠⊠

'Bobbler!' Mike Mazzoni shouted again, so loud his lungs hurt, pointing at the gate. His brother spotted the bleeding lunatic who'd elbowed his way right through the razorwire. Bobbler looked back for an order. Theoretically, no live shots were to be fired until there was an actual perimeter breach. And theoretically, rounds of tear gas were supposed to prevent any bleeding lunatic from getting as high as this one had, as fast as he had.

So much for theory.

A stone sailed over the gate from some anonymous asshole deep within the Freak Show. The climber Mike Mazzoni had spotted was still moving fast, nearing the top.

Mike Mazzoni nodded.

Bobbler, up on the helicopter landing pad, nodded back and took aim.

'Just wing him,' shouted Mike Mazzoni, though the crowd noise was louder now, and his brother could not hear.

The raghead's face exploded. He pulsed, then sagged like crucified Jesus. He hung there on the razorwire.

Shit.

The crowd howled as one.

There were actually two notes to the big howl it gave out. The ragheads in the very front were all screaming the high note. The larger, deeper crowd was moaning the low note.

Three more white-robed ragheads started clambering up the fucking gate.

Bobbler looked again to Mike Mazzoni with eyes that said *What do I do?*

Mike Mazzoni nodded again, then masked up and called for twenty rounds of tear gas. By the time the smoke cleared, four white-clad bodies, each streaked with red, hung from the razorwire. The crowd tore at itself, and the high note raged over the low note.

⊠⊠⊠

'Brother!'

Well after sunset in the village of D—. Night in her darkened bedroom. Daylight on her computer screen.

One of the videos which bedded, blanketed Fatima now scrolled through on her laptop showed the two and a half chaotic minutes leading up to that afternoon's massacre at the embassy. Shaky and washed out, the images and sounds came from the concealed camera of a BII plant. Ra'id had couriered a thumb drive with a dozen such scenes to her. He had asked her to review them all and call him in the morning. Ra'id was unavailable now, in meetings with his father and his father's circle.

'Brother!'

Rewind.

The video Fatima watched panned across a limitless horizon of shoulders within the uncountable throng that had gathered around the American embassy compound that afternoon. The horizon rocked and churned and shook for its initial ninety-one seconds, gathering its seemingly infinite crowd into itself, very nearly making the close observer nauseous with the constant jostling and shifting of people's white backs. After that roller-coaster ride, the lens settled on the front gate, and the unknown videographer's movement ceased, more or less, for the remaining forty-seven seconds. The audio was intact and clearer than one might have expected.

The shout that rose over the murmurs and prayers trailing through her white earbuds made the hair on the back of Fatima's neck stand up.

Its voice was sharp. High. Male. Angry.

'Brother! Brother!' The rest only half clear, thanks to the crowd noise. Islam? We must what? He is not what?

She clicked the rewind icon again.

She hit play. Increased the volume. Settled her earbuds in.

'Brother! Brother! My dear brother in Islam! We must plan such things! He is not even *in* the embassy!'

Replay.

The same thing. No doubt about any word. Someone had said that.

Once again. Rewind. Play. Watch for moving lips to match.

There.

She had found the face of a small man in the upper right-hand corner of her screen. His face twisted and glared. He called upward to the first man, the one climbing the fence in front of the compound:

'Brother! Brother! My dear brother in Islam! We must plan such things! He is not even *in* the embassy!'

Ra'id needed to know of this remark's existence. She thought of calling him despite his instructions, but concluded that the phones were no longer trustworthy. She would have to go into the city again. Tomorrow. Early.

⊠⊠⊠

Time caves in again, for old time's sake. The dead guy collecting and concealing these stacks of scribbled paper warns her, across time and space, not to call her driver. Oblivious, she calls him anyway.

52 John Triumphant

clix. Triumphant

'Evuhbody Gots Sumpin' 2 Hyde 'Cept Maharishi,' the original title of track twenty-one in its
handwritten foul copy, showcases the highest vocal note of the composition, via Lennon's
deliberately misspelled '2'. The song is structured on this elated vocal climax, which prefigures your
neo-Trinitarian conception by occurring three times in the final recording, at 0:29, 1:10, and 1:50.

A city may be wounded and stagger about in shock, just as a human
being may do, without quite realizing its status as a wounded thing.
Indelible braved a return to the embassy. It was time to evaluate the
patient, acquaint him with his circumstance, speak words of recov-
ery if such could be found. Words of encouragement.

He found his way back toward the scene of the massacre he had,
through the Grace of Almighty God, witnessed and survived. It was
night, and the curfew would be enforced in less than a quarter of
an hour. The streets were almost deserted. The soldiers paired off
on the street corners of the major intersections, a reminder that the
city now operated under martial law. It was past dawn in the United
States, where people roamed as they wished and followed their vain
desires.

The square outside the embassy was empty. Two helicopters cast
spotlights on a few litter-strewn squares of blood-stained pavement.
Indelible found himself in the double beam of that twin spotlight.
He meant to keep walking until he was out of it, but it followed him.

Kafirs in uniform, kafirs with submachine guns, had reasserted
control of the streets surrounding the embassy. Not all kafirs were
Americans: A kafir used his own language now to bark out an order,
Move on, go home, curfew in nine minutes. In the United States,
people were no doubt gathering in orderly fashion for the working
day. They had subways there. And huge highways. They worshipped
Jesus, peace be upon him, there. God forgive us. They filled their

tanks with gasoline and rode the subways and sat in their offices or their shops. They constantly listened to music. Shaitan pissed in their ears.

'Move on!'

Just as the kafir speaking the native tongue put his hand to his gun, Indelible nodded and walked away from the embassy.

Five men had died here. Six at least had been gravely injured. People had fled from the kafirs as they fired. Indelible looked up as he walked. The bodies of the four martyrs who had climbed, without orders, onto the razorwire still hung there on the gate, trophies for the Americans. Lights from the helicopters passed across the men's bodies from time to time.

Another man, a man with only one leg, had died in the tear-gas-driven stampede away from the embassy. Indelible had seen feet crush this man's face and chest as he writhed on the pavement. Indelible had found a safe nook, an angled part of the embassy gate near a dumpster, and watched the crowd's shameful, leaderless, lethally chaotic retreat. He had watched that man die under the feet of his countrymen. His body must have been collected since the attack.

Chaos. The city dying.

In America, people paid to not have such experiences in their cities, and to not know of them when they occurred elsewhere. In America, Indelible thought, people would speak of those outside the gate throwing stones and rubbish, not of the uniformed men firing into the crowd. Or not speak of this at all.

And all for nothing. The desecrator of the Holy Koran had not even been in the embassy.

No one to encourage here. No one in need of encouragement. Only the martyrs, already victorious. He walked faster, and though it was cool tonight, a sweat broke out on his forehead.

There was no compromising with kafirs. Kafirs meant to obliterate everything. A new strategy was in order.

⊠⊠⊠

Not out yet, still working for Dad, dammit. Thelonius kept his mouth shut, signed the auto rental agreement, left the little, grey-carpeted room, warmed himself in the sun and felt stronger somehow, holding the car key beneath the open morning sky.

Having opted not to fly from DC to Salem, having cancelled his ticket in person, he guided the sleek new-smelling rental out of the airport parking lot and threaded his way toward 95. He headed north, but kept an eye out for detours. He wanted to see how long he could make this trip last.

Creative, reckless truckers sped past. They had all defaced the safety-first signs embedded on the backs of their vehicles by contractors and/or employers. Countless variations on the signs, countless variations on the defacements. *HOW IS MY DRIVING? CALL 1–800–9,* and the rest of the plastic burst away in shivers. *WE ARE PROUD OF OUR PROFESSIONAL FLEET OF DRIVERS – TO COMPLIMENT THEM, CALL US AT* – what?

On some signs, the number was entirely obscured with black paint or ink. On others, only certain carefully chosen numbers were transformed: from a 3 to an 8, or a 4 to a 9, or what might have been an 8 to a black void. On one such sign there was no text at all, only grey paint where the message should have been. Men – he had yet to see a female trucker – who were unwilling to be traced, men unwilling to be held accountable. All those numbers had been rendered useless for the identification of excess. Whenever they settled into their vehicles, these men reserved to right to conduct their journeys according to their own guidelines. They hurtled around him, as though he were one of them, but slow to catch on.

He stopped whenever the leg said to stop.

At a gas station, he avoided looking at the skin magazines and lottery tickets and cans of beer, none of which would be missed, and bought a compass and a dense comb-bound road atlas. These came in handy: he took many byroads that branched off 95.

From Baltimore onward, he aimed to reach the oddest real town names he could find listed on that map. He made a point of buying gas and praying in places with strange names, names he never would have come up with.

Double Trouble. Fearnot. Little Heaven. Disappointment. Burnt Chimney Corner. Othello. Fair Play. Hot Coffee.

Once he had visited, bought gas from, prayed at and written down the name of one of these places, Thelonius pulled out the atlas, consulted it, put it back, gunned the engine of his rented Accord and found 95 again. He obeyed the speed limit. It was good driving in the right lane, under the speed limit, good to be passed, all the restless truckers well ahead of him or well behind him.

Big, disarming, half-plausible road signs for what claimed to be genuine tourist attractions swam past him. Marketing. The signs appeared every twenty miles or so, fleeting hallucinations beckoning him in gaudy colours. Thelonius started recording them too. Bates's House of Turkey. America's Largest Humidor. The World's Largest Chair. Turtle Built from 2,000 Tire Rims. Motel in the Shape of a Giant Elephant. Everything Elvis Ate. Nuclear Waste Adventure Trail. And so forth. He never stopped at any of these places.

After a while, he was able to laugh out loud at each one he passed. So much bullshit.

Each of these places did in fact exist. But just because they existed didn't mean he should go visit them.

The sun blanketed a far hillside with bright golds and greens that seemed to have nothing to do with the surrounding buildings. The perfect colours coexisted with a warm feeling in the centre of Thelonius's chest. He'd been chanting *ALLAHU AKBAR*. Much of the last day had been about chanting. He was fine until he had to stop chanting.

53 **Maharishi**

clx. Maharishi

'Maharishi, You Little Twat.' So began one 'sexual', sadistic rewrite of the third postcard from India. By the time a disillusioned Lennon strummed this initial version, he had already begun spray-painting graffiti (as it were) upon the abandoned guru's image. Yet Thelonius still did Dad's bidding.

The cell phone rang.

Thelonius did not want to talk as he drove. That was unsafe and (in Delaware, anyway) illegal. He pulled into a rest stop and answered the phone without saying a word.

'Hello, Thelonius,' the voice said anyway.

Sawdust and sucrose. Advice about to be shared if one wasn't careful. A sceptical vibrato. It was Dick Unferth.

'Let's have lunch. Hey, where the hell are you, anyway?'

Stress breath. Not her, using his phone. But him. Him. Stress breath.

'I'm still somewhere in Delaware,' Thelonius said. 'I left Maryland yesterday. I've been taking a lot of back roads.'

'Yeah. Okay. Maryland. Okay. I'm from Baltimore. Did I tell you that? Hey. Watch out for the Maryland State Police out there. Turn on your radar detector, okay? Well. Welcome back from that long strange trip. You're the man of the hour around here, did you know that? You should see the party we have planned. Anyway, I got an email from Adelia. Did you see that? Maybe not. I guess we'll be working together.'

On his left, a truck hurtled by the place where Thelonius had parked.

'So. We'll have lunch and sort stuff out, Thelonius. Crazy, crazy trip you just wrapped up, huh? Crazy. Maybe lunch tomorrow? Everyone will be happy. Okay. Hey. I heard you guys were going through a rough patch. If you need a place to stay, let me know. Okay?'

A bad pause. Thelonius heard himself filling it with that ridiculous Unferth word 'okay'. Which he did not mean.

'Okay,' said Dick Unferth. 'You take care of yourself, okay?'

There was the sound of someone who had been listening for a while hanging up.

Thelonius drove out of the rest stop, the grey concrete of which had set his teeth on edge. A valley appeared along the driver's side window. Sunlight streaked through it and made it buttery. The valley conceded its place to a shopping mall, abandoned and boarded over. The dead shopping mall was buttery, too. A few cars had parked inexplicably in its vast, otherwise empty lot, which vanished and yielded to the harsh, rhythmic, man-made thrum of a long sequence of paved edges. Bordered by some Jersey barriers on his right, Thelonius kept his eyes ahead.

Dad had asked him to figure out whether Unferth was the father.

Which meant there was someone else.

Which wasn't supposed to matter now.

But who then?

He still had the phone in his hand. It reminded him of Unferth, so he put it down. He kept on driving north. The sun gilded another hill. He started saying *ALLAHU AKBAR*, but half an hour later, he had still not quite dug himself out of the hole, and he wanted to call someone. It had been some time since he'd wanted to call someone.

Thelonius pulled over, called Carl Arnette, his best friend and fellow hostage at the Directorate, and asked if he could stay with him for a while.

'Yes, sure, T. Of course.'

Carl didn't say anything else, which was nice. Thelonius thanked him several times to fill the blank spot in the conversation and tried hard, as hard as he had ever tried to do anything, not to say something he didn't mean. He wanted to describe what he liked about the trees in the distance as the sun set. Nothing came out of his mouth. But at least he hadn't said anything he didn't mean.

He thanked Carl again and, after Carl said he was welcome, hung up.

Then before he knew it, he was driving again and it was maybe half an hour before dark. You could combine the prayers when travelling, the man at the mosque had said. Uncertain what to call home, Thelonius assumed he was a traveller. He passed a sign for a storefront called 'Women Women Women A Gentleman's Club'. More marketing bullshit.

A mile or so down the line, he saw a sign for yet another town with a weird name – Shortly – and found a gas station. He made his ablution there and prayed, using the chapter of the Koran he had learned, the one that had the line about 'whoever honours her flourishes, and whoever defiles her fails'.

And felt better when he hit the road. Like there was something glowing in him again.

Able to drive whenever he felt like it, or stop if he felt like it, he felt ready for whatever was waiting for him. The road he chose went through a rural area with no billboards, and his headlights cut right through the night. He was wide open with possibility, like the night and the straight, open road. The road seemed to say: *Soon enough. Soon enough.* It was straight and full of dark trees but very beautiful, utterly free of bullshit.

He smiled.

54 **White Metal**

---

clxi. White Metal

Having heard a rumour that a forthcoming single from The Who would stand as the rawest, most intense rock recording in history, Paul McCartney summoned his three colleagues to a meeting. They would (he announced) accept the challenge of outdoing that work. They would record the rawest, greatest rock song ever. He overruled all debate. Cue track twenty-three. As a direct result of that historic band meeting, McCartney launched the genre of White Metal, writing lyrics that identified, repeatedly and without ambiguity (0:09–0:13, 1:52–1:56) the Bottomless Pit from which America's elite will derive safety and respect during the inevitable religious wars of the End Times.

Ouch.

'Your last session closed unexpectedly. Press OK to restart.'

Mike Mazzoni's computer kept saying that, on the table next to the cribbage board, but it wouldn't restart, so a lot of the time he might otherwise have spent online looking at calming pornography was spent looking at that stupid message. If you turned it off and turned it on it said the same thing. You couldn't press OK. Bobbler kept saying he could fix the thing, but Bobbler had not taken Freak Show Out of Bounds well. He would tighten up his face a lot and then pretend he hadn't.

'What was the first time you killed someone out here?' Bobbler asked, when he should have been playing a card.

'I said Go. Count is twenty-six, in case you forgot.'

Bobbler just winced.

'I didn't want to see that picture, you know.'

Mike Mazzoni had snapped a photo of that jawless idiot who'd first tried to climb the fence. He was too far up, though. You couldn't stand next to him.

'There must have been a first time you did it, Mike.'

'Yeah. I killed a guy for spacing out during a cribbage game. No, wait. That's five minutes from now.'

Nothing. Staring at the cards like they would tell him what to do next. It was like he didn't want to relax.

'I just think maybe Mom would want us to look out for each other out here, Mike.'

'Yeah? What if I'm sick to death of looking after you? What if I've already got a job out here?'

They stayed quiet until Bobbler put down all the cards.

'Maybe we ought to talk about what happened is all I'm saying.'

'All right. You shot a guy in the face is what happened. I'm not going to second-guess you. I didn't say you fucked up. Pick up the cards and play one, for Christ's sake. Count is twenty-six.'

Bobbler stood up and moved the sides of his face around like he had eaten something with his ears and he was trying to get rid of it. He shook his head. 'My head hurts, Mike.' he said. 'I can't seem to sleep right lately. This weird thing in my jaw making noise. I'm going for a walk. I don't feel like cribbage.'

'Play out the hand.'

'I *hear* something. Like in my jaw. I don't know what it is. Something cracking.' And he left the tent, holding his head in his hands.

'You still haven't fixed my *computer,* bro.'

He heard that. He just didn't call back.

Two days of R&R, and he had been like this the whole time. Only one day left. Things were getting kind of crowded on the back of Mike Mazzoni's hand. Tonight he would ask Bobbler to work his way up the forearm. One for each raghead on the razorwire. Once he calmed down.

Mike Mazzoni lit up a Marlboro and glared at the computer that now topped the long list of Things That Pissed Him Off. He stood, got a running start, and kicked the tabletop hard. The computer fell over onto the ground and clanged around a little, but the screen still said the same damn thing.

55 **The Bottomless Pit**

clxii. The Bottomless Pit

In the Bottomless Pit, an underground Death Valley hideaway chosen for its inaccessibility, a select few from the nation's respected corps of leaders will escape death in the impending religious apocalypse with the Muslims. It will indeed be awkward and uncomfortable there for a time. But you and I will emerge from it to reclaim our barren homeland and awaken it to glory.

Once the ever-well-dressed Ra'id stepped inside the car, which smelled of some new dousing of pine air freshener, Fatima knew that what she had to speak of now should not be spoken of in front of the grey, cockeyed figure who seemed bolted into the driver's seat. No smile, or at least none affecting the driver's eyes, greeted them from the rear-view mirror.

In the back seat beside her, Ra'id reached forward and patted the sour man's shoulder. Some kind of signal: The car's idle engine stopped. Ra'id leaned back again and smiled a familial smile out toward the driver.

'You can relax, Fatima. If anyone is with us, my uncle is. What have you found?'

Ignoring such a direct request seemed reckless. She opened her laptop, passed it over. Ra'id hit play. He watched the clip.

'*What* did he say?'

Fatima, who had anticipated this question, handed him a sheet of handwritten paper. Her tiny, neat handwriting spelled out the words: 'Brother! Brother! My dear brother in Islam! We must plan such things! He is not even *in* the embassy!' The word 'in' was underlined with precision.

Ra'id's face darkened. He hit play again and watched the clip a second time.

'Forgive my asking. Is there any chance you shared the prisoner's location with anyone? Even inadvertently?'

Fatima shook her head, no.

'You're quite certain.'

'Yes.'

Ra'id played it again. He looked more closely at the screen. The video concluded.

'It's fortunate you didn't email me about this,' he said. 'There was an attack on our email system last night. I'm not sure we've repaired it.' He pursed his lips as he played the video a third time. When he was through, he closed the laptop.

'If you ever have difficulty reaching me, Fatima, please call Nada, my assistant. She can be reached at any time of the day or night. You have her number? Yes. What you've found presents a number of problems. The first is the security breach itself, quite a serious one. Another is its cast of characters. I recognize this man. He is one of Murad's informants. High in value. Or so we were led to believe. We call him Indelible.'

'Indelible.'

'Indelible. His own chosen codename.'

The driver's eyes met Fatima's in the mirror, monitored her for a moment, then glanced away.

'Important that we plug the leak,' Ra'id said. 'Where he got this information, I cannot tell yet. Murad, for all I know. He may have gotten it from the Americans. There is a special etiquette for dealing with triple agents, you know, Fatima. One kills them.'

The grey driver caught Fatima's eye in the rear-view mirror once again. He did this with the more penetrating of his two wandering eyes. A newer, darker malevolence in his wrinkled stare told Fatima it was time for her to get out of the vehicle.

Don't be ridiculous. His uncle, after all. Grow up. You've seen grey skin on people. He's a smoker. That's all it means.

But he would not look away.

'Where do I take the young lady today?' the cockeyed driver asked, too loud, as though speaking to Ra'id, as though no awkward moment had passed between them, as though he were not still staring at her.

This question changed the nature of the vehicle, caused it to darken and shrink.

A sensation of not being present passed through Fatima, and the adrenaline rose in her veins. She thought of Noura, and she found within her own sudden, shortened breath an intense unwillingness to leave Noura and Ummi to fend for themselves.

Fatima tried to attract Ra'id's attention, but he was reading something. She returned to the grey man's oblong eye reflection. The interior of the back seat of the car shrank again, became still darker, grew into a conspirator, an entity aware of her thoughts and dangerous to her.

There emerged a deep necessity of movement.

'I'm so sorry,' she said.

She let no more time pass, but announced, louder than the driver had spoken, that she had urgent business in the city for which she was overdue already. Before even receiving Ra'id's approving nod, she opened the passenger door and stepped out.

The instant her foot hit the gravel of the police station parking lot where they had stopped, she heard an electric mechanism grasping from deep within the car's grey door. She heard the mechanism failing to catch, as though someone had attempted, too late, to lock all the doors at once.

She slammed the door and walked away – somewhat faster, it was possible, than she meant to.

She heard the car start. Heard it speed away. Chose not to look back.

Something – instinct – told her to speak with no one, interact with no one on the way out of the city.

It took her three and a half hours to reach Wafa's house, her house, on foot. Long miles. She entered, saw Ummi reading to Noura, gave her salaams, found Motorola, put Motorola on the kitchen table, plugged it in, switched it on, listened and gasped.

56 **Cold and Hot**

clxiii. Cold and Hot

Track twenty-three of the *White Album*'s cycle of thirty, the product of that great band meeting, bears a sacred title. It carries not only the meanings of 'confused' or 'confusedly', but also – this is critical – serves as the name of a kind of English amusement park slide. The slider picks up speed as he, she or it, tumbles downward. This clash initiating the 'hot' war – a term we use to distinguish that which is imminent from the current 'cold' war against Islam – lies at the apex, the tumbling-point of that slide. This downward slide cannot begin before the ninth of August of this year. A date somewhere near the end of the present decade appears most likely. So damn dark in here now. After a nap it lightens up.

Skullface sat in the darkest, noisiest corner of the restaurant, gesturing toward the lit screen of an open laptop.

Indelible studied the PowerPoint presentation that had secured the New Imam's approval. He asked for permission to take written notes, but this permission was denied.

Under the cover of the restaurant crowd's animated discussions, Indelible repeated certain important event sequences and dates in a low voice until both he and Skullface were convinced they had been memorized. Then Skullface reformatted the hard drive and scheduled the next rendezvous.

⊠⊠⊠

'Now, full disclosure,' Dick Unferth said as they made their way, ahead of the waiter, to what looked like his customary table in the nice restaurant he had chosen for their you're-working-for-me-now discussion, 'I took Becky to this very place once, while you were stuck in the slammer over there. Two red wines, please. Give us a minute, thanks. Once. Took her here once. Because she begged me to. Nothing happened. Scout's honour. So. You're the hero now, eh? Have a seat.'

Wary, Thelonius settled into the dark, stately, wooden chair.

'To be perfectly honest with you, she was a little over the top that night. She may have had a few too many.'

He stared at Thelonius, as though Thelonius were the one who was supposed to explain himself.

'Possible,' said Thelonius. 'She's been in her cups. Out of curiosity, did she happen to mention anything to you about the source of the intel on my mission?'

'What? No. Oh, no. That wasn't her lane. Even drunk. No. The records are bad on that, I'm afraid. But no.'

Too insistent on that point, Dick was, and too willing to stop talking having made it. Ride the silence out. Make him talk next.

But he didn't, not until the waiter came with the wine, at which point Dick Unferth ordered the baby lamb chops and asked Thelonius what he wanted. Thelonius didn't feel much like eating, but ordered a salad and sent back the wine just to establish that he was there, in a restaurant, with Dick Unferth. Who buttered a piece of bread. 'I am working on that, you know, T. Obviously a major malfunction.'

Thelonius put the bread down on the plate. 'And when, if I may ask, did you last sleep with her?'

The rat-eyes had eyebrows, and they arched upward.

'Dial it down, T,' Dick Unferth said, without missing a beat, his focus narrowed on his prey. 'Dial it down.'

'More than a month ago?'

'What? Why?'

'Why do you think, Dick?'

A look of genuine surprise played across his features: a rare crack in the facade. She hadn't told him.

The waiter rematerialized, bearing a platter with two big glasses of iced water. He set them down carefully and Dick stared at his, as though doing so would make deciding what facial expression to display next a little easier.

The waiter left. Dick continued to commune with his water glass. Thelonius checked his watch and said, 'Maybe I shouldn't stay.'

Dick raised his hand, as though he were expecting Thelonius to count the fingers.

'You know, T, sometimes women come at you like a ton of bricks, and if that happens when your guard is down, they see you like a deer in the headlights and you get knocked out of the park.' He re-examined his water glass.

'Mm,' said Thelonius, drinking from his.

'But, for the record, well more than two months ago.'

'For the record.'

'Yes, and I tell you that because you know what, with some time on the clock under our belts, under our rug, under the bridge, I mean, and working together, now, at this particular juncture, you and I can make some impactful things happen if we want to. We don't have to like each other, but we do have to respect each other if we are going to get any truly impactful work done. Which is why we're here. To get impactful work done. And I do respect you, T. Now, you know and I know we respect each other.'

'Am I supposed to say something now? Agree with that, I mean?'

Unferth sipped some wine, his rat-eyes fixing Thelonius.

'So, fine. We've got a history. Let's just not make a federal production out of any of this, is all. Let's get over this little speed bump, all right, because if we both behave ourselves and dial it down and play for the team and keep the conversation focused on business, you will shine here. Okay? I swear that to you. Now the principle you and I have to bear in mind here is a pretty simple one, T. The last team standing wins the game. Keep the team standing and you will shine here, that's my promise. Deal?'

He hadn't known she was pregnant. Important, then, if any more data of consequence were to emerge from this discussion, that it appear to Dick that Thelonius's aim was to shine. Important not to be seen as having had an affair with Dad's daughter. And in exchange for that: *You will shine here.*

'Deal,' Thelonius said. 'So what am I working on?'

57 **A Message to Comfort the Faithful**

> **clxiv. Message**
>
> In track twenty-four, George Harrison takes a chord structure lifted from *Blonde on Blonde* and turns it into a public service announcement for the deathless Divinity of the Eternal Woman I carry. The song is anticipatorily phrased in my voice and from my perspective.
>
> Ouch

With Ra'id's head flung upon the iron grating of a gutter outside the American embassy; with a YouTube video of the bloody ovoid spinning and landing on the opening to the sewer, its ghastly, disastrous red eyes open and askew, and then receding as the car filming it sped away; with that video having drawn four hundred thousand views in the two and a half hours before it was taken down; with the city and the nation in the profoundest turmoil, Fatima conceded, definitively, the validity of her misgivings concerning the driver.

A group, Defenders of God – perhaps connected to someone at the newspaper of the same name, perhaps not; perhaps large, perhaps small; perhaps new, perhaps old – had claimed credit for the murder of the prime minister's son, and for 'the blessings accompanying such actions'. And demanded the withdrawal of all American forces.

And announced the instalment of the New Imam as head of state.

And forbade women from public places, including the mosques.

Calls to the prime minister's office, calls to Ra'id's assistant Nada, calls to the police – all essential, all impossible. The land lines were down. The cell lines were down. The country was in the midst of a seizure. Only one link to current events remained.

Through the usual thick waves of white noise, Motorola announced the military's 'patriotic intervention': the city under martial law, the prime minister 'escorted' to an unspecified location, where he would remain 'safe from terrorist threats' while grieving the passing of his son. A brigadier general would be making a public statement 'of the gravest national importance' that afternoon. An interim director of the BII had been named: Murad Murad, a 'veteran intelligence analyst and seasoned administrator'.

Fatima found Ummi and Noura in the back, trimming weeds. Without telling them why, she ordered them indoors, demanded they move far away from all windows. In saying these things, she employed a tone of voice that she had never heard herself use.

Neither of them questioned her use of that voice. They did exactly as she said.

The driver of that grey car, or someone else connected to Ra'id's murder, would be coming back, intending to kill her as well. And possibly her family. Sooner, rather than later, instinct said.

Because of what she knew about Indelible. Because of her ability to tell the Americans what Indelible looked like, share that video, alert the Americans that he was not to be trusted. Whether she should harbour any intention to do so now was irrelevant. Fatima had to protect Noura and Ummi.

She found her sheathed machete, brought it with her to the base of the large tree that marked the edge of Wafa's property line. She clasped the cloth-covered blade with her teeth, set her foot upon the trunk and her right hand upon a limb, and climbed. Three-quarters up, she crouched on one of the broad, leafy arms and carefully set the machete in a little nook in the tree.

She changed positions as necessary, combined her prayers in a seated position from the limbs of the tree where she hid. There was legal precedent for this.

Just before sundown, she saw the familiar double headlights of the grey sedan approaching.

Fatima unsheathed her machete.

⊠⊠⊠

The night after the members of the Oldburgh Jihadi Ensemble were arraigned, Sullivan Hand's mentor showed him her appreciation for all his hard work on the case.

She did this by taking him to a nice hotel in Marblehead, turning on a little video camera, tying him to a bed, taking his clothes off, and having rough, loud sex with him as she talked to him about his future in the Directorate.

She knew she was ovulating and mentioned this frequently – over a dozen times – during coitus. She was eager, for some reason, not only to document the sex act on video, but to demonstrate her own willingness to be impregnated. Having taken what she wanted, she flipped over, lay next to Sullivan, hugged her own knees close to herself, stayed motionless in that position for some minutes, then received or pretended to receive an important text message.

(The dead guy telling this story found that video on Becky's computer. He was performing intel work for Dad.)

(Dad is a dead guy now, too.)

Becky put away her phone, showered, dressed, said goodbye, took the camera, shut it off, and walked out of the hotel room, leaving Sullivan Hand there tied to the bedposts. He liked that sort of thing: being dominated.

The last thing one heard from Sullivan Hand on this video was him imploring Becky to untie him and let him use the toilet.

Sullivan Hand was, as usual, full of shit.

58 Something about Time Running Out

clxv. Time Running Out

Track twenty-four's continual references to an exceptionally long span of time attain a certain epic dimension, thanks to Harrison's attenuation of an already glacial 6/8 meter, which then morphs into an unorthodox, raga-esque 9/8. This time-stretching effect – more at home in the world of jazz than on a rock-and-roll album – juxtaposes itself with his equally inspired decision to insert a measure-long instrumental riff in the gap following each two bars of vocal melody. The mournful organ notes represent the long centuries preceding your rebirth.

Ouch

As he drove into the glare of the late-afternoon sun, Skullface took another small, white pill to calm his heart. He drew these from a grey case, which he opened and shut with the word *Bismillah*. After he took each pill, he said *Bismillah*, too.

He told the boy, who was in the back seat, that the pills were nitroglycerine, that he was taking them to treat the bad heart condition he had inherited from his father. He said that he was ready to face his judgement before Allah at any point in time that Allah should choose to take him. The boy said nothing, but wondered if anyone could really take nitroglycerine without exploding, wondered what kind of doctor would tell someone to take such a pill.

The dead guy scratching out this manuscript wondered about this when he was a kid, too. He found out, when he was in Oregon, that lots of doctors prescribe nitroglycerine to calm down people's hearts. He drew a comic book about a doctor who thought he was helping people with heart conditions, but who was actually blowing all his patients up.

He called this comic book *Sorry!*

59 **Certain Obscure Pronoun References in Track Twenty-Four Clarified**

> **clxvi. Pronoun References**
>
> For 'you' in Harrison's lyrics, read Prudence. For 'I', read me. I really don't think that was labour per se.

The cockeyed, grey-skinned driver stopped the car earlier and further from the house than he usually did, parking directly beneath the tree. He opened the driver's-side door and got out to survey the property before approaching Fatima's home. In his hand was a revolver. Had he looked up, he would have seen Fatima tensing her limbs, a cat before the great forward leap upon her prey.

Had he listened more carefully than he was listening, he would have heard her tiny whisper before the leap: *Bismillah*.

Over the prone body, she said this verse:

Whoever honours her flourishes
Whoever defiles her fails.

60 **The Third Side Concludes, the Fourth Side Begins**

clxvii. the Fourth Side

John Lennon insisted – in 1968, mind – that track twenty-five, his farsighted, explicitly political condemnation of Islamic extremism, should be the band's next single.

Ouch

At the end of their brief period of shared R&R, Mike Mazzoni and his brother received separate duty assignments. This parting of the ways, which seemed temporary to each man at the time, came at Dayton's request.

Mike Mazzoni never knew that. He thought of this as HQ imposing a much-needed break from someone he was close to, but who had been getting on his nerves. He didn't have a good history of dealing with such people.

After only a day or so, it felt like it had been his own idea, not seeing his brother. It felt like running away, as indeed his own enlistment in the marines had felt at first. This flinging away of himself from his old life, the one he didn't want. It was how he functioned.

For as long as he could remember, Mike Mazzoni had been running away from home. It was probably too late to change that now.

⊠⊠⊠

Fatima's face was unveiled, but her gold headscarf still covered her hair and throat. A red bruise ran across her nose where she had been struck.

Her face was contorted now in what might have been agony, or might have been a lover's grimace in a moment of passion, or might have been the deep expression of purpose found on the face of a woman at war issuing a death blow. It was, at any rate, a private face, not one meant to be shown to the world, and if you happened to be imagining it, as you scribbled, for longer than absolutely necessary, as you suspected you might be, you felt a little guilty for doing so.

You wonder from time to time whether you loved Fatima. 'I love you,' you sometimes say out loud, to her, but also to the walls of your personal suite at the Beige Motel. You are never quite sure how it sounds. Saying it doesn't seem like home.

61 **Lennon's Demand**

Far away from embassy duty, on his own, and no longer even in Mike's unit, Dayton did not have to take orders from his brother. He was no longer Bobbler.

He disliked the nickname, made the best of it, as he had made the best of things back in Little League. The coach and everyone else had adopted 'Bobbler' out of obedience to the sheer mass and volume of his older brother's personality. Not having to answer to that was like waking up without a bad tooth.

Dayton was the best sharpshooter in his new unit. He was probably the best American sharpshooter in the Islamic Republic, but he didn't like talking about whether or not this was the case. This morning he was on his own in the sunlight, pretending to guard a perfectly safe police station that was far from any hot spot and needed, so far as anyone could tell, no guarding. He had just stepped outside for a smoke, hoping to get rid of the little click in his head, when he saw a boy emerge from the shadows and say something that sounded like 'HELP'.

62 Hips Still Killing Me

> **clxix. Killing Me**
>
> Before the virus took him, Thelonius and I were on a path to reconcile, to salvage and shelter our family, our people, our nation. To prepare for the Inevitable: The great Conflict to come. YOU BASTARD, leaving me alone to sort all this out. Worse than Granddad even. Who blew his brains out in the bathtub and left the family to clean up the mess. Worse than him. Betraying the White Nation to fragmentation and disgrace. You heartless, traitorous, niggerloving, all-but-literally-motherfucking bastard. You deserved everything you got

After she had reassembled time, it occurred to Fatima that she had never before seen the driver outside the confines of his vehicle.

The cross-eyed, grey-haired assassin had made almost no noise as he died, just a little, damp exhale sound as she opened his throat from behind in perfect surprise. He had been crook-backed. He lay on his side now in a kind of C shape.

Immediately after dispatching him, a physical convulsion had seized Fatima. This was a convulsion of a powerful nature, one she felt uncomfortable even considering discussing with others. It was not a new thing to her, just not to be spoken of. Such convulsions had occurred a few times before in the state just before sleep, as one's mind wandered. If one happened to begin dreaming of men. They woke one up and made one move one's hands away from one's body.

Ummi had locked Noura in her room as ordered, thanks be to God, and the neighbours were sheltered behind their tightly closed night blinds, which meant Ummi was the only person now alive who could have seen that fierce, shameful shuddering. But it had been dark. Perhaps Ummi hadn't actually seen the shuddering at all, only heard the shout.

This had been the strongest such wave she'd experienced. She had lost her footing with the fierce compulsion of it, having to clutch a limb of the tree for support. Shameful. The man there on the ground bleeding out. She had shouted out, 'Don't look at me!' She had tried shouting it twice but the words would not come out.

A curtain had closed in front of her mother.

Five minutes might have gone by for Fatima like that, in shameful convulsions. As though her body were gloating as the old man emptied out.

Once she recovered, she dragged the corpse out to the pond and left it there. It sank beneath the surface, but she knew it would still be visible in daylight to anyone who knew where to look. Not a proper burial. It would have to do until she could find someone to conduct a formal funeral ceremony.

In the far corner of the pond she washed her hands quickly and did not think of this act as carrying any special significance or symbolism. She washed the machete, too. With a clean blade she went back and cut away the bloodiest patches of grass near the tree. These slippery, broad threads she threw into the pond. She washed her hands once again.

⊠⊠⊠

In the house, she gave in and wept.

Ummi's hand brushed against her cheek.

'You are a good girl, Fatima, and a patient woman, and a true believer.'

⊠⊠⊠

The three of them – Ummi, Noura, Fatima – required protection now, and the sooner the better. A conversation with Ra'id's secretary was imperative. None of them knew how to drive, however, and even if Fatima had known, the laws of the Republic prohibited women from driving.

No neighbours answered when Fatima knocked. The options were all unappealing. Taking the grey sedan across the city limits would have been an invitation to jail time (if she attracted the attention of the authorities) or far worse (if she attracted the attention of the zombies).

Fatima was unwilling to risk either possibility. She would eat something for strength, walk back to the city and meet with Nada, Ra'id's assistant, to explain her family's situation. They needed either to be relocated or to have an armed guard of some kind.

Having showered, having dressed, having prayed, with her hunger assuaged, she reminded Ummi to keep Noura locked in her room, then made for the straight, tree-lined road that led out of the village.

But Noura begged for release so piteously and with so many promises to behave that Ummi relented.

'Only if you sit right next to me the whole time, Noura. Only if you sit with me on the couch until your sister returns.'

Ummi unlocked the door.

⊠⊠⊠

An hour or so passed, during which time Ummi had been sewing and Noura had been reading or pretending to read a book. For no apparent reason, Noura thrust her nose in the air.

With a speed and intensity that gave Ummi gooseflesh, Noura exhaled sharply, leapt up, dashed to the living-room window, opened it, and bellowed, 'It's a trap! He says to smell the air! He says for you not to come back in the house!'

63 **Wait a Minute**

clxx. Wait a Minute

That was a bang on my locked door. Local law enforcement, proclaiming its solemn need to pose those stereotypical 'few questions'. I stood by the door, silent, armed with the grey-handled steak-knife. The retreat of steps. That cursed motel phone started ringing. Let it ring.

Ouch

AC is out, beastly hot now

They were parked behind a warehouse. The boy was in the back seat.

Skullface sat in the front and craned his neck, checking every angle. It looked like he was waiting for something or someone, but whatever or whoever it was never came. After a long wait, and for no reason the boy could understand, Skullface said, 'Now we will get out.'

He stood the boy behind the vehicle, motioned for him to be still. The boy was still.

Skullface went to the back seat, extracted the box and brought it behind the car to where the boy was. He untopped the box and removed the vest.

'Arms up,' said Skullface. The boy put his arms up. Skullface settled him into the vest.

'Arms down.' The boy complied.

'I am about to hit a button at the base of the back of the vest, Godwilling, that will arm it. Say Godwilling.'

'Godwilling,' said the boy.

Skullface reached around and the boy heard a click.

'Tell me with your mouth, not by moving your hands, where the button is that detonates.'

'Over my right shoulder, with the angel who records my good deeds,' said the boy.

Skullface pointed toward an alleyway that traced the back of the warehouse. 'You see that little street?'

The boy nodded.

'Follow it to its end and you will come to the police station. Are you ready?'

No answer.

'Are you ready? TAKBIR! What do you say?'

'Allahu Akbar,' said the boy.

'If I get in that car and drive away, will you go down the alley?'

The boy nodded.

Skullface smiled, then said it was time to put a jacket on over the vest. He grabbed a boy's jacket he had set on the ground and said *Bismillah*.

Before he could put it over the vest, however, a wave of grey passed over his face.

Skullface dropped the jacket. His eyes widened, he clutched at his chest, as though searching for something lost there, and then he fell forward. He lay motionless in the dust.

The boy studied him, but did not lean over to touch him, for fear of setting off the vest.

A plane passed overhead through the blue sky. It was an American plane.

Leaving Skullface behind, the boy turned and made his way down the alley toward the police station.

64 Keep Typing

clxxi. Keep Typing

Track twenty-six. Pru stirs.

She likes a simple foxtrot.

WATER BROKE, fetching towels

The alley was long and cold, colder toward the centre where he walked because the mid-morning sun did not penetrate it at all there. The boy looked behind once and saw Skullface still sprawled out face-down on the gravel. Then he followed a bend in the alleyway and when he tried to look behind he could not see the gravel anymore.

He kept walking.

The shadows increased and then receded. He saw the police cars lined up in front of the building and he saw officers in blue, as well as Americans in green, going in and out.

The boy stopped and stared, still in the shadows, hoping he could not yet be seen. He looked for a policeman with a kind face.

The word to say to the Americans if you were ever lost in front of them, she had told him, was 'HELP'.

The word to say in front of Muslims was 'SALAAM'.

An American with what looked like a kind face stopped in front of the police station and lit a cigarette. The boy felt good about the man's face but kept watching it to be sure. He watched from the shadows as the man stepped away from the policemen in blue, watched as the man found his corner and stared into the blue sky, watched as the man released the smoke in a relaxed way.

The boy stepped into the light and said, loud and clear enough for the man to hear, 'HELP.'

65 **Whatever**

According to Dick Unferth, Thelonius was supposed to track down any connections that might have existed between certain terrorists Becky had helped to put in jail and some other terrorists operating in the Islamic Republic.

Dick Unferth set great store by connections.

Thelonius didn't find any connections. What he found was Sullivan Hand.

66 Two Rotten Teeth

clxxii. Two Rotten Teeth

Hips bad again. Track twenty-seven. Harrison wrote this to commemorate Eric Clapton's chocolate addiction, plucking his lyrics from the ingredients listing of a box of chocolates. The chorus, which insists on the imminence of tooth extraction, prefigures the arrest of Fatima Adara for murder and the extraordinary rendition of Ali Liddell to undergo questioning for an indeterminate period. The song predicts, that is, their extraction from the body politic. Two rotten teeth. Internal reference to earlier *White Album* track at 2:06; 2:06 also predicts Liddell's death. When Fabs foretell such things, not functioning as vehicles of any kind of predestination. Like town criers. We control our fates. We do. No one else. We are not locked away in the nuthouse by fucking MEN and their SECRETS.

ok that Is a contraction

That kid was wired to explode.

'VEST! C4!' Dayton called at the top of his lungs. 'CODE RED! TWELVE O'CLOCK!'

Nine green uniforms appeared, one of which handed Dayton a rifle. He dropped his cigarette, crushed it imperfectly with his right boot, raised the rifle and pointed it at the boy.

'STOP WHERE YOU ARE!' Dayton said in the native tongue, his eye at the gunsight.

The boy stopped. His forehead was in the crosshairs. A red dot wavered on that forehead.

'GET YOUR HANDS UP!' Dayton said.

The boy babbled something, firm, with purpose, but beyond the scope of Dayton's five or six memorized phrases. He kept talking. Not scared, insistent. Was that good or bad? Well, if the vest hadn't gone off yet…

'Get one of the natives,' Dayton told a nearby captain, technically his commanding officer. 'Get one of the policemen out here. Find out what the hell the kid is saying.'

The captain obeyed. The deformed, half-smoked cigarette, which Dayton had not quite extinguished, smouldered on the ground near his feet.

Considering how close he was to blowing out the brains of what looked to be an eight- or nine-year-old boy, Dayton Mazzoni felt he was handling the situation pretty well. He wasn't shaking at all. He smelled the nearby tobacco smoke, but didn't dare attempt to stub it out again, didn't dare divert the smallest measure of his attention from the target.

Procedure said that whenever you positively identified an individual wearing a vest like that, whenever you had clear visual confirmation, as in absolutely no ambiguity, and the subject was over twenty yards away from any other person – as this kid was – then you were to shoot to kill.

Procedure didn't say anything about making an exception if you happened to be engaging with a kid who clearly didn't speak your language and who had eyes that locked on yours, eyes that looked, even from that distance, like they wanted out of this situation as bad as you did.

Dayton did not want to shoot the kid. So if anything went south here, Dayton was pretty much on his own as far as procedure was concerned. Then again, he was pretty much on his own no matter what happened.

Dayton's red laser sighting dot moved in tiny jags, in alignment with the movement of his own pulse.

The nine green uniforms were kneeling, but none of their scopes were lit up. Good, Dayton thought. They didn't want to confuse him.

'Your call, Bobbler,' said one of the green uniforms. Dayton now assumed everyone had the kid in the crosshairs. 'Do what you need to do.'

'HOLD FIRE. Where the hell is that policeman?' Dayton shouted. Being the first one to take aim at the kid had given him a certain authority that even he didn't quite grasp, but it was imperative that it be used well now, so he used it.

The captain reappeared, with a slim, blue-uniformed teenager in tow. Using peripheral vision, Dayton sized him up and was unimpressed. This 'policeman' had a peach-fuzz moustache. It wasn't a policeman at all. It was police boy.

Police Boy was the one member of the Islamic City Police Force stupid enough to have stayed in the vicinity just because the Americans had said to. Everyone else had run as soon as someone translated the word 'vest'.

You play the cards you've got.

'He keeps saying something,' Dayton barked, never taking his eyes off the boy. 'Tell him to say whatever it is he's saying again, from the start, so you can understand it.'

'Slower please,' Police Boy said. 'Slower. My slow English.' His face was tight and grim and his slim hands were trembling.

'Make him talk, Police Boy. Slow. Translate.'

And that came out too fast. From the corner of his eye, Dayton saw the terror on his translator's face, winced.

'I'm sorry. I shouldn't have called you that. What's your name?'

'Abbas.'

Still staring at the boy in the vest: 'What's it mean?'

This question appeared to startle the young man, but once he grasped it, his face loosened up just a little.

'Lion,' he said.

'Abbas, you're our lion. You're going to be brave. You're going to make him talk. Okay?'

Abbas nodded. He made a verbal request in plaintive tones to the boy, whose hands were now raised, and who was still babbling. The boy began babbling more slowly. A good sign, Dayton thought. Following instructions.

'He says someone put the vest on him, and he wants help taking it off.'

'Bullshit!' one of the green uniforms shouted.

'HOLD FIRE GODDAMMIT. Abbas. Tell him if he moves without permission, I'll shoot him and make it hurt, but he won't die. Tell him that. Ask if he understands.'

Abbas shouted something, and his voice squeaked as he did so.

The boy nodded. Second consecutive instruction followed.

'Tell him he needs to hold absolutely still for a count of twenty.'

Abbas relayed the message.

Everybody watched everybody else while Dayton counted to twenty, silently.

'Ask him to tell me whether his arms are feeling tired.'

Abbas posed a question. The boy answered.

'He says they do.'

Fourth consecutive instruction followed.

'Tell him to *slowly* put his hands right up on top of his head. *Slowly*, Abbas. He can rest them there.'

The boy received his instructions and complied. Five consecutive instructions followed.

'Ask him if he knows how the vest works.'

The boy listened and gave a reply.

'He says,' the quavering voice translated, 'that there is a button that makes it go off. He was told to push it but he doesn't want to. He wants help taking the jacket off.'

'Bullshit! Don't you believe it, Bobbler!' came a voice from a green uniform. Even though he knew Mike Mazzoni was sleeping off a hangover, eleven miles away, Dayton said:

'Shut up, Mike.'

Everything got quiet.

'Ask him what disarms it.'

This one sentence from Dayton marked the point at which things began to fall apart.

⊠⊠⊠

Much of what the dead guy sharing this story still has left to relate would not be there for him to tell if Dayton had not, while talking to Abbas, used the unfortunate word 'disarm'. If he had used some other word, like 'stop', in its place.

Or if Abbas had known what the hell 'disarm' meant.

If only Dayton Mazzoni had said, 'Ask him if he knows how to turn the damn bomb off,' the rest of this dead guy's book could have led in a different direction, a direction that steered well clear of the multiple disasters to which this particular conversation led.

If it hadn't been for a single word that lay beyond Abbas's woefully limited English vocabulary, Dayton Mazzoni and his brother might still be playing cribbage somewhere.

Ali Liddell (that's me, that's the dead guy writing this book) might not have landed in Bright Light.

Fatima might not be locked away in her own cell somewhere in the USA.

Fatima's sister Noura and her mother Salma might still be alive.

And so might Abbas and the boy wearing the suicide vest whose true name the guy telling this story chooses not to repeat.

But Dayton did the best he could with the words he knew. The rest was not up to him.

clxxiii. cry

and back

track twenty-eight

cry ali cry

67 **Revelation 9:9**

clxxiv. Revelation 9:9

And they had breastplates, as it were breastplates of iron; and the sound of their wings was as the sound of chariots of many horses running to battle.

'Ask him what disarms it.'

Abbas, fearful that even a moment's pause might result in someone shooting him, had decided to start talking, even though he did not quite know what the English word 'disarm' meant.

He supposed it meant 'destroy'. It sounded like 'destroy'. As in, to take one's arm off one's body. The guy telling this story acknowledges that it does sound like that. If you wanted to destroy something terrible, wouldn't you think ripping off its arm would do that?

Abbas translated what he thought Dayton wanted to know into the native tongue. Because he wanted to show Dayton that he was doing what he was told, he made his request over and over again.

'What button sets off the bomb in the jacket?'

'How does one explode the jacket? Tell him.'

'He wants to know how one sets off the bomb, you see. That's what he's asking. What makes the bomb explode?'

And so forth.

'The button above my right shoulder,' the boy said.

'He says the button above his right shoulder disarms,' Abbas said.

When Abbas was nervous, he talked a lot. So he repeated this point in several ways. The idea here was to convince Dayton Mazzoni that he knew what he was talking about. Which he didn't.

'Tell him I'm going to walk toward him. Tell him that when I get close to him, I'm going to want him to put his hands back up in the air. Way up high.'

Abbas translated. The boy said something.

'Don't do it, Bobbler,' said one of the green uniforms.

'He says the vest is very heavy,' Abbas offered. 'So heavy that he is afraid it will make him fall down. He needs help.'

'Don't fucking do it, Bobbler,' the voice said again. 'Shoot him. Then we call in the pros to deactivate it.'

Bobbler put his rifle down.

'Let's take a look,' he said, and walked toward the boy, grabbing Abbas and bringing him in close, too. In case the kid said anything else.

'Wait,' Abbas said, as though he wanted to go back. But Dayton's grip was strong.

The kid made direct eye contact. Dayton got a visual on the button.

'Wait,' Abbas said again.

'Why?'

Abbas had no answer.

Dayton looked back at the kid in the vest, who looked back at him. The kid was still doing exactly as he had been told.

'Tell him I don't want to hurt him.'

Abbas translated. Accurately.

Dayton nodded at the boy in the vest, who kept his hands on his head and nodded back. The nod said, *I don't want to hurt you, either.*

Dayton hit the button on the kid's shoulder.

Three one-hundredths of a second later, bits of broken nail and barbed wire made a THWOCK sound as they ripped through everyone within a hundred-foot radius.

'Wait,' Abbas wheezed. Like the boy in the vest, like Dayton, like nine green uniforms standing within that hundred-foot circle, Abbas was focused on dying.

68 **all right**

> Pain when she stirs now
>
> Number these later
>
> Not on the desk, not on the bedside table, not under the mattress. Has to be in here somewhere. It was low on charge, too

By the time Fatima reached the BII compound, her legs were screaming a deep, silent ache.

She showed the armed guard her ID and made her way through the big interior steel-and-glass gate with no problem. The gate closed behind her. Once past it, she saw a young man at a reception desk. He smiled at her. Behind him lay a bank of elevators she had been visualizing for at least five miles.

The helpful guard informed her that the phones and the elevators were out of service until further notice.

She made her way toward the stairs. Her smile had worn away two hours ago; she felt as though she had been walking all her life. Once she coaxed her sullen, aching, but obedient legs up the stairwell, up to what had been, only yesterday, Ra'id's ample third-floor office, Fatima found, not a new ally named Nada, but a locked door.

A large, precise sheet of grey paper was taped into place over the pane of glass set into that door's top quarter.

If you had seen Fatima, it would have looked to you as though she were trying to read that sheet of paper with her cheek and the flat of her palm. But there was no writing on the sheet and no mystery as to what it conveyed. The paper taped onto the glass was there to obscure the letters of Ra'id's name. Those letters, once visible in broad block print, once painted large and neat for all to see, were never supposed to be read again.

Fatima had walked thirty long miles in less than twenty-four hours. She almost tore the brown paper off the glass, but she opted to save her energy, pull her hands back and make her way back downstairs to the reception desk. Her legs groaned and her feet creaked with each step. Nowhere to sit yet, though. She told them to mind their manners, to cultivate patience.

The helpful young man at the desk informed Fatima that Miss Nada was no longer employed by the BII. Miss Nada's resignation had been accepted yesterday. That was all he knew.

Her eyes and the bridge of her nose were the only portion of Fatima visible to the young man. That, at least, was an advantage.

Was there anything else he could do to help her?

Fatima's troubled legs insisted in plaintive tones that she lean in against the reception desk. She disagreed and quieted them again.

She took a deep breath, closed her eyes, opened them again, and asked whether he would please inform Murad Murad personally that Fatima A— was waiting at the reception desk for him. If the young man would emphasize that Fatima was extremely eager to see him, she would be grateful.

69

Wish I hadn't cut the handset cord from the room phone. Getting dark in here.

Visual search for cell phone continues after a break

Break time is over

No phone. Next contraction imminent

He asked the Directorate, in good English, for one hundred thousand American dollars. The moment Indelible did that, on Skype, Sullivan Hand got physically excited. His trousers strained with it.

Here, at last, was a live lead. On the ground. In the Republic. With contacts in the insurgency. And not only that: Motivated by what appeared to be serious financial problems, rather than religious drama. This was something the Directorate could work with. This would once again win Becky Firestone's favour, impress her more, even, than the Oldburgh sting had.

Indelible told Sullivan Hand that he had the names and recent confirmed locations of five – five! – insurgent leaders, and that he, Indelible, was willing to share that information. If it was of interest to the Directorate. If that would help them build up trust together. If he could get the cash immediately.

And so forth.

While this was going on, what was Becky doing?

That very evening, Becky sent Thelonius a text message: 'One warning and one warning only. Are you respecting my privacy?'

Thelonius chose not to respond, preferring to destroy the phone and replace it with one bearing an entirely new number.

70

And back. I have some time now. Twelve minutes apart. Could last for hours, stage one, but I do need to call hospital

'Call Dad? What are you talking about, call Dad?' Dick Unferth said. 'Close that door.'

Thelonius closed the door. 'These Oldburgh fools trusted us. We sold them out. Sent them to prison. So Becky could win at something. And you knew all about it.'

'Sullivan Hand was acting as liaison on a legitimate FBI operation, T. Sit down, please.'

Thelonius sat.

'*We* were paying him,' Thelonius said. 'He's *our* guy.'

'So? It's still an FBI sting. If the Bureau screwed up, that's the Bureau's problem. We're not FBI. We don't do domestic. You do know that, right?'

'He was *bait*. This was entrapment. For headlines. It's going to blow up on us. Becky's going to go to prison for it if we're not careful. So is Sullivan Hand. So are you. You have a right to know that. So does Dad.'

Instead of responding to something he didn't like hearing, Dick Unferth would remove his glasses, wipe them, replace them and look at you like it was still your turn to talk. Thelonius didn't fall for it.

'We don't *know* they were set up,' Dick Unferth said. 'It's a complex case.'

'Have you heard the audio? Have you read the transcripts?'

'I read the summaries.'

'The summaries are bullshit. Do you know what actually happened?'

'What actually happened is what we say happened. I think you need some time off.'

'They're innocent.'

'Not our lane, Thelonius. We don't do innocent and guilty. We do good guys and bad guys.'

Thelonius stood and leaned into Dick Unferth's space. 'I want you to declassify that audio. I want you to send it to the defence attorneys and the judge who sentenced them. And I want you to fire Sullivan Hand. Now.'

'Hell, no. Now sit down.'

'No. That kid is a loose cannon. Get rid of him. Then we can move on to the next problem. She's got obstruction of justice and perjury and entrapment on her hands now – and so do you – until we clean this up.'

'You're not *listening*, T. That's all *domestic*. It doesn't apply to us…'

'Yeah, well, it's *going* to be international the minute some reporter connects it back to the Directorate. You don't think the families are going to push? You don't think this is going to get out?'

'Not if you don't *put* it out. And you're not going to do that. You're a team player, T. Last team standing wins, remember?'

The afternoon traffic went past outside the big window. Rush hour. People going home.

'Here's what we've got. If you don't fire him today, *Dick,* I'm calling Dad. And I'm heading to court tomorrow morning and making a motion to have my wife declared mentally incompetent.'

Dick stood up.

'I wouldn't do that if I were you, T.' Dick Unferth gave him a dark look. 'She warned me about you, you know, even before you left for the Republic. Warned me you'd try something like this. Cast aspersions on her. Try to undercut her if you came back.'

'*If* I came back?'

Dick Unferth flinched, lost himself in conjectures, then put his boss face back on and said: 'Just get out of my office.'

'I thought you said she had no role in setting up that mission.'

No reply. Thelonius felt his knees giving way beneath him, then steadied himself.

'Okay, T. I am calling Security.' But he didn't reach for the phone.

'Dick. Believe me. I'll leave. For good. Once you fire Sullivan Hand.'

'I can't.'

'Why not?'

'Because,' Dick Unferth said, with what may or may not have been actual remorse, 'he's on to something big now. Please don't call Dad. Please.'

71

At least ten minutes before next one. Clothes off, constricting me. Dead Clive getting an eyeful. Closed the blinds.

The first thing he felt when he heard the news was not sadness at all, but the leftover dry throat and raging skull of a sick hangover he thought was finally receding. It returned as the words hit him. The first thing he felt was the insult of his own body waking up.

The generalized, overwhelming sense of being disrespected that spread through Mike Mazzoni with each throb of his head connected to everything that sucked in the Republic. After they woke him, stood him up, and told him Bobbler had been shredded by waves of nails and barbed wire and bits of sharpened aluminum, the disrespect of having his brother taken out by a raghead mingled with the disrespect of having that ache in his skull, and the disrespect of not being able to speak, and the disrespect of not being able to focus his eyes properly, and the disrespect of not being able to get rid of the sweating.

Fiercely dehydrated, hearing too many things at once, none distinctly, and all too loudly, sensing that someone right behind him might just be going at his head with a small ball-peen hammer, Mike Mazzoni may not have had the capacity for deep grief. What he was capable of, however, was updating his list of Things That Piss Me Off to include this new, transcendent item, which took its place at the very top of the list.

He was pissed off at everything, pissed off at a cellular level. At being woken up. At not having been there to stop this. At being the one left to explain to everyone, to his mother, *why* he had not been there.

At ragheads who got away with shit by blowing themselves up, in particular.

Some raghead, somewhere, he swore wordlessly in his underwear, was going to feel justice.

Once the two officers had left, Mike Mazzoni grabbed a virgin bottle of tequila, hid it in a paper sack, and staggered out to the latrine, his head pounding, his chest heaving. He held the paper sack close to his chest with his left hand, lowered his shorts with his right hand, and pissed – aiming, more or less, for the little son of a bitch who had done this. He did not wash his hands and did not shave. He dressed, banged through the door, still clutching the sack without having cracked the bottle's seal, and commandeered a vehicle.

They brought it on themselves, the ragheads. They always did.

⊠⊠⊠

Thelonius was driving his rental car to his friend Carl Arnette's place after work. He wasn't driving home. He still didn't have a home to drive to. The rush-hour traffic had gotten worse. Dad still hadn't answered his calls.

'Drive to Salem instead,' Sergeant USA said. 'Look. You can take Route One. It will be quicker than this damn parking lot. Then, when you get to Salem, we can take her out. Once and for all. Gun it. Hurry.'

'I don't think so, Sarge,' Thelonius said.

'Machine, kid.'

Thelonius opened all the windows so the traffic noise could come in, but it wasn't enough to drown out Sergeant USA. He just amped up his own volume to compensate.

'*Machine*. You hear me? *Machine*. We should have taken her out years ago. Hey. Let's take the exit for Route One, that exit, it's coming up. Look. It's wide open. Put the pedal down, kid. Pick up some speed. Then let's take her out.'

Thelonius clicked on the radio. A country music station was playing. Thelonius turned it up as loud as it could go.

Sergeant USA glowered.

Thelonius inhaled deeply through the nose, then exhaled through the mouth. The radio sang:

Why we break each other's hearts, I swear I just don't know.

'Machine!'

'It's time to shut up now, Sarge.'

'Not on your life!' Sergeant USA bellowed over the music. 'Hit that accelerator. That's an order, kid. There's a kitchen knife you can use. It's on that wall magnet doohickey where she hangs everything up. She's an android, kid. I swear. You saw that text, didn't you? "One warning and only one." That's evidentiary threatening. That makes it self-defence. *Machine.* You'll see. *Machine.* Turn. There. That's the exit. Right there. Right –'

Thelonius raised his arm and delivered a sharp, lethal upward elbow strike to the tip of the masked man's nose.

The blow shattered Sergeant USA's ethmoid bone and drove its fragments through the cerebrum, all the way through to the hypothalmus, the ancient lizard brain.

Sarge bled out from the face. Thelonius, who knew what it looked like when someone bled out, looked over and checked him from time to time as the traffic eased up. Somewhere in Saugus, after Thelonius got to the Hilltop Restaurant, but before the exit for Carl's place, the body vanished.

72

This was not a good idea. Get out.

A grunting heard. And another grunting. This was the room where she had been shown Thelonius's possessions. Yet something different now about the design of it: a silver row of gleaming, straight, newly installed coat-hooks protruding from the rear wall. Fatima counted them. There were five of them. In his new capacity, Murad expected important visitors.

'Shut the door.' And grunting again.

No salaam. No eye contact. A bad start? She would sit, rest her legs when the chance came and then leave if necessary. How they ached.

73

Final seconds (3:02) of previous track. A spat between producer George Martin and his flunky, Alistair Taylor. Two men arguing over a bottle of claret. The great conflict to come. Might be end of one song. Might be beginning of another.

Fatima shut the door. She stood before his desk, behind the chair set in the middle of the room. Her fists were clenched, and her forearms close to her hips, but this was invisible beneath her loose garment. Remember to breathe.

Behind his desk, his back to her, uniformed Murad Murad was grunting, working out. In each hand was a heavy miniature dumbbell, each a formidable gold-painted hand-weight, each with a handle across, for the convenience of the sweaty grasper. He moved these weights to and fro in rhythmic patterns. No earbuds drove his grunting. This was his own private symphony, playing for himself and for Fatima as he stared out the first-floor window.

The window was lined with one-way glass. Pedestrians a foot or two away had no idea how minutely they were being evaluated by the Interim Director of the BII.

'They are still (grunt) preparing my office upstairs,' he said, without looking at her. 'But this place will do for now. (Grunt.) The joke in the newspaper is that I did not kill Ra'id, (grunt) but I did not stop him being killed, (grunt) and that I threw a party after he was killed. (Grunt.) I arranged no such party. (Grunt.) You believe what they say about me?'

(Grunt.)

Murad Murad's fat ass jerked and twitched beneath the khaki as he moved the dumbbells. He still would not turn and look at her.

She sighed, low, and looked to the ceiling.

'I know who killed Ra'id.'

He turned from the window at last, his sweaty face set in an attitude of purposeful confusion. 'Who is this? Hm? To whom am I speaking?'

She met his eyes. 'You know who I am.'

'No, no, not with certainty.' He looked away. 'Not with clarity. You could be the New Imam. No one knows where he is now, you know. No, no. I know nothing with certainty about you. These are dangerous times. One must know something about you. Remove the facial veil.'

Fatima felt a sour taste at the very back of her throat.

'I'd rather not.'

'Strangers among us. Not everyone is to be trusted. I'm unsure.'

'Listen to me. I have information. Important to you. Something Ra'id knew, something that you should know. That's why I'm here.'

'No. You are here because you need protection. You and your family. That's why you came. The only possible reason to talk to a man you swore never to talk to again would be protection. Remove the facial veil. Then we can speak more comfortably together.'

And he smiled his weak little smile and glanced at her again, a little insect, briefly there and then gone.

'Be seated. Then show me your face. As a gesture of goodwill. The past being the past. And so forth. Do understand my position. I must confirm your identity, you know, if we are to discuss your information. And I do so want to discuss your information.'

Technically, this is a workplace. Nothing in the Sunnah against it. Very well. The offer, at least, must take place. If he declines, he declines.

Instinct said, *don't.*

Her legs screamed, *sit.*

She ignored instinct, supposing she was doing so for Noura and Mother.

74

Back again. Contractions still twelve minutes apart. Eradication of Islam (crescent moon) is predicted in the first few seconds of the momentous track twenty-nine (0:01–0:23), a critical passage that establishes the spoken 'nine' motif, which recurs at (checking notes) 1:47, 3:48, 4:20, 6:23 and is there one more? Have to listen again.

Fatima took her seat in the chair, which welcomed her and soothed her legs immensely, but she noticed it had been bolted to its spot, directly in front of his desk. There was no wheeling the chair backwards a pace or two, a fact that made her uneasy.

Instinct said, *Too close. Leave now.*

No. Noura. Mother.

Instinct said, *Leave now.*

Fatima ignored instinct.

She removed her facial veil.

With a heavy mini-barbell in each of his plump hands, Murad Murad stepped around the desk to inspect her more closely, as one might inspect a hanging cut of meat.

Too close.

75

Difficult – in places, impossible – to make out, some JohnAndGeorgeBabble begins at 0:50 and continues intermittently until 6:50. The opening phrase has been variously transcribed: 'Then there's this Welsh/welch/Walsh rabbit/rarebit/rabid, wearing some/sun brown underpants.' The two Fabs appear to be reciting and improvising around bits of newspaper and magazine articles encountered in or brought to the studio on June 20, 1968, when this portion of the track happens (!) to have been recorded. The day following Mother's mortal wounding in Venezuela.

Fatima leaned back in the chair.

Curious as a fish, Murad Murad did not shift away, despite her obvious discomfort, but continued evaluating her – leaning forward slightly, in fact.

'Good. It has almost healed. I felt badly about giving you that bruise. I so wanted to tell you how badly I felt. One regrets an action like that, a bad overreaction, I should say, when it affects a person one cares for.'

Too close. His breath stank. The beginning of an edge of nausea. Everything had happened today. Now this.

Just Get Started.

'Respected Interim Director, there is a mole in your informant network. I know this mole's identity. I can describe him. I have video of him. He is working for a group affiliated with the Defenders of God. The man who killed Ra'id knew this mole's identity as well. You will want to arrest this man, I assure you.'

He sniffed, stepped back, sized her up once again. Then, without taking his eyes off her, he dropped both barbells on the surface of his desk. They fell with a heavy clanging sound.

'Ra'id had you placed on some interesting assignments. Where is this video?'

'At my home. On a thumb drive.'

'Why didn't you bring it?'

'I didn't feel safe transporting it. Didn't want it to be seen prematurely.'

'Prematurely.'

'Yes.'

He smiled another limp half-smile.

76

'So. You came here to bargain with me.'

'I came here to bargain. It turns out I am bargaining with you.'

He walked behind her. To turn while remaining seated was impossible. The chair bolted. The casters disabled.

The options now: Stay seated, or stand and signal a desire for conflict.

Stay seated. Look at the ceiling.

'You think I am worried about these people,' Murad Murad said. And laughed. 'About this White Beast. Worried enough to negotiate with a woman. But you see I have them on my payroll. And there is only one thing I will negotiate with a woman. I will tell you something, it is not the White Beast. They are a minor irritant, these people in white. In their thousands. In their tens of thousands. I don't care. I will tell you something else. At the most they are forty percent of this country. Thirty-five, more likely. So. What are we to make of this thirty-five, forty? Are we to lose sleep? They are more vocal than the majority. That is all. More willing to identify themselves. Easier to pick off in a gunfight, if it comes to that. I tell you something else: The sixty, sixty-five percent I work for wants it to come to that. These are schoolboys, these men in white robes. I could have a hundred moles. I will still beat them all down. This is not what I'll negotiate, Fatima. With a woman, I will negotiate something else. You are concerned for your sister. For your mother. For yourself. Say yes. It's true. You are concerned for them. You want to protect your home.'

Breathe. Still time to engage him in the trade you came to make.

'Yes. We need protection. Now listen. This man I am talking about. I believe a major operation of some kind is under way. I believe he's been researching it, preparing it. Someone tried to kill me so that I could not interfere with it.'

He made a tsk tsk tsk sound.

77

A woman's laughter – 1:35, 1:42, 1:44, which transitions seamlessly into the cooing of a baby at 1:48. Order established. She was not killed and will not die! She brings Order to the Nation!

'Go back to "Yes". Go back to "We need protection".'

He was standing directly behind her now. His voice too close again.

She looked up over her right shoulder.

'Very well. We do need protection, my family and I. And so do you. Now I believe you have a decision to make. The BII has a decision to make. What is your decision?'

With a few soft, fat taps of his feet, he was invisible again. He could move quickly.

'These are dangerous times we live in.'

Well, he is much further away now. Either good or bad that he's moved away.

She heard the little click of the door: *He has locked me in.*

Very bad.

The soft, fat taps of his gait returning. And he was close again behind her, unseen: 'As I have told you already, Fatima, my dear Fatima, there is a thing I am willing to negotiate with women.'

The sound and smell of him directly above her, whispering, almost, to the top of her head. The foul breath again. His forearms on the high-backed chair, stressing it. She felt his forearms there without touching them.

The room fell still.

Without moving, the room seemed to ask her what she planned to do next. A mistake to come here. *Yes,* the room agreed, *but what now?*

She had been chased out of her body. She hovered above it, above her own body, above sweaty Murad Murad, above the bolted chair, above everything. Time skittered like a top. It spun down, kicked around, and bounced itself dead into a corner.

78

As the second section begins (1:51), there is a sudden transition away from instrumentation and toward crowds/choirs.

The wrong place to be, but there regardless.

It was instinct that set time spinning again. Instinct said, *Stand up, claim your ground. Purify yourself.*

Fatima felt herself descending, felt time coursing back into her body. A sense of her life being brief and sacred possessed her.

While she was still seated in that high-backed chair, while her eyes and spine and feet reformed, while her heart opened and closed, at the first hint of her movement, she felt a blow at the top of her skull. She felt knuckles and knives at the point where time had reawakened. The room wobbled.

Then three of his untrimmed fingernails cut right through the thin fabric and into her scalp, two left, one right – and one of his hands pulled the covering from her head while the other pulled the blouse from her chest.

Abomination. As she reclaimed her body. Sudden, unforeseen, indefensible, animal force. To eliminate the border of her modesty. Abomination.

Safety pins flying through the air. The topmost part of her garment torn. The sudden pain from three deep, bleeding gash-lines in her scalp, each imparted by what she imagined, at the moment of the Abomination, to be the claws of a beast. Her right hand instinctively rising to her throat to hold her torn jilbab in place.

A tidal wave of shame engulfing the room.

79

The choir (2:33 etc.) represents Western (i.e., white European) civilization; it is challenged by mongrel (i.e., Islamic) terror/chaos at 2:30, 3:15, 4:02 and 4:20. But this will pass, and she will emerge victorious from the Bottomless Pit.

She was bareheaded now, clutching the shreds of her jilbab about her, in a locked office, before a man. Not a close blood relative. A non-mahram. A non-mahram with bad intent.

Stand or crouch and cover?

Instinct saw the two pathways, too, and demanded this decision from Fatima: *Stand.*

Fatima stood as she had been ordered to by instinct. She did not turn to reveal her face to her attacker. Instinct had not told her to do that. The chair, bolted in place between them, served as a kind of barrier for her as she spoke.

'Open that door immediately or by God Almighty, you will regret the consequences.'

'Fatima,' he whispered again from behind, his lips too near her ear. 'Fatima. Certain words feel so good to say. The end of all the secrets today. Dark hair, then, quite long, quite straight, inclining to auburn in places. Let me be your father. You need not say anything.'

Murad Murad made a *shhh* sound, very close to her ear. Then, with practised ease, he stepped back a pace or two and placed his left hand on his belt buckle. He began to unfasten it. When he did that, the metal components of the belt struck against each other and made the sound of an alarm pronouncing danger.

When instinct heard that sound, it spoke to Fatima again, advising her of Murad Murad's new position in the room, and ordering her to undertake a certain course of action. She obeyed without hesitation.

80

At 4:50, the piece transitions abruptly into its third section, with violent, muttering rabble replaced by cheering Islamic masses, imagining they have won the day.

She scanned the desk that was now in front of her. She found the two gold hand-weights lying near the centre of the desk, and she took up her weapons, one in each hand.

She shut her eyes, gathered the two weighted hands together into a single projectile, positioned her arms as instinct instructed and spun around towards Murad Murad with all the speed and momentum her body could summon.

At the lethal point where the twinned weights caught him, just below his left cheek, the iron missiles spun Murad Murad's head abruptly sideways. Fatima heard his neck crack with the force, but because her eyes were closed, she did not see his body fall backward against the rear wall and then hang there.

She dropped the two gold hand-weights and heard them thud and clatter, low-toned against each other and the floor. The dark kiss of gravity.

'Bismillah,' she said. In the name of God.

She opened her eyes.

81

And back. Just played 4:54–5:10, and pausing there: Someone's wife informs him that he must now wear yellow underwear. This section foresees T's detention at Bright Light, fluorescent yellow garments being issued to all inmates.

The leftmost coat-hook had punctured his temple, impaling him with its four rigid inches of stainless steel. Murad Murad dangled, on display, unconscious, twitching.

Fatima approached him with slow steps, breathing hard. She looked him over. A thick rivulet of blood ran from his nose, wound its way down his cheek and onto the shoulder-pad of his khaki uniform. His eyes stared at everything and nothing, and then rolled back into his head.

He gasped and then stopped gasping.

Short of breath herself, she grabbed his wrist and felt for a pulse. Nothing. The question of what to do next was now moot. Instinct had removed the threat.

Her breathing, already hoarse and raw, became more frequent in the certainty of his death, and she heard herself moan and wheeze with it. Something shuddered again inside her, the roaring and coiling from the very core of her, and she staggered backward with it. The chair held her, though it was bolted in the wrong direction, so as to only afford her its back. She gave it her armpits, slung herself there, heaving with it. He was dead, with certainty he was dead, so she did not attempt to prevent the shuddering.

The thing writhing inside her swung in and out of itself from all angles, like a pot boiling over from beneath its lid, sputtering and stopping, sputtering and stopping. It was stronger than last time, even, and it bent inward with each new heave it demanded of her. It kept up that inward bending and heaving for the longest time. She clutched her torn garment, held her upper body tight. Instinct was content with this arrangement. It had its own momentum.

There was no shame in her following where the writhing led. When the spasms had passed, when she had returned to herself, she asked instinct 'What next?' and listened for the answer.

Having been granted permission, she returned to the corpse that hung by its hook on the wall. She repeated *Bismillah* and fought back the urge to spit into its face. That would have been shameful. She found a loaded pistol in a holster on Murad Murad's hip. She took that pistol.

She retrieved her torn scarf and facial veil from the floor, found three of the four pins. She worked them back into place as best she could. She sat for a brief rest. Her hair, forehead and lower face covered again, her jilbab pinned acceptably, she remembered Thelonius.

Just Get Started.

She stood, retrieved the two gold hand-weights, covered her eyes with her left hand and hurled the hand-weights toward the grey window.

They sailed right through its one-way glass. There was a tremendous crash and whine and clatter. Gold afternoon light flooded the room.

The danger past, she removed her left hand from her face. Her eyes were safe.

She ignored the alarm that sounded. She kicked free the loose shards of glass in the corners of the frame, and walked calmly into the late-afternoon rush of Malaika Street on her numb, obedient legs.

82

You are rumbling again, in anticipation of 5:36.

'Getting some wheels now?'

Sullivan Hand joked that, with all the money he had just transferred to Indelible's bank account, Indelible could afford to buy a new car now if he wanted. They both laughed at that.

Indelible laughed exactly the same way Sullivan Hand laughed. He acknowledged that he might be buying a Lincoln at some point, but said that, right now, he had to pay off some pressing debts. During all of their conversations, Indelible made frequent reference to desperate financial straits.

In reality, he had no pressing debts. As soon as the conversation concluded, Indelible arranged for the money he'd secured to be delivered, in the event of his death, to the trustees of the refugee camp known as Jahannum.

Indelible emailed Sullivan Hand the names and locations of five insurgents. These five men had agreed to be martyred in order to help Indelible build up a bridge of trust with Sullivan Hand. Sullivan Hand didn't know that.

During their next call, Indelible told Sullivan Hand that he had recently been appointed the New Imam's personal physician. He hadn't, really. Sullivan Hand didn't know that, either.

In his cubicle, Sullivan Hand maintained his fatherly tone as he said 'Oh.' Then he punched his silent fist in the air. It felt to him as though he had just won the Super Bowl. As though Becky Firestone were, at any moment, about to walk in the work area, strap him down to something solid, his desk, say, and have at him, as though he were immortal.

83

Gunfire @ 5:36 signals global religious war. The conflagration that will follow Her rebirth and send the elect to the safety of the Bottomless Pit

Late that night, Thelonius phoned Adelia and asked to speak to Dad. When she recognized Thelonius's voice, she said she had been meaning to call him and asked whether he was sitting down.

84

And back. A coda begins at 6:47, culminating in the voice of a WOMAN WHO GETS THE LAST WORD at 7:44. Babies are of course born naked. Peace possible only through the establishment of Order, and Order in the nation only possible through revering Her.

This was like running patrol, only all alone. This was like hunting, and like looking for a new black star to tattoo, and like pinning disrespect itself in the laser sight. This was like getting down to business at last.

The drive had helped Mike Mazzoni to even things out a bit. He took another hit from the fifth of Cuervo, which was beginning to undercut that headache. Hair of the dog. Good for whatever ails you. Have to remember that when time to call Mom rolls around. Women a lot more likely to overreact to things.

He wasn't ten minutes from the base when he spotted her.

Damn.

Some fool raghead girl. Thirteen, fourteen. Stark naked. In a pond. Splashing herself between the legs. He slowed. Either she hadn't heard the vehicle or she had heard it and not cared. He pulled the vehicle onto the shoulder on the opposite side of the road. Peered through the window. She was visible from the road through a parting in the trees, no problem. She was *facing* the road, in fact. And she was spending way too much time washing her goods.

Which looked fine and clean and free of distracting stubble and open for business to Mike Mazzoni.

Cold water or no cold water, she certainly seemed to be enjoying herself. Her face. Damn. He killed the engine, swigged some more Cuervo, got out, stepped around quiet to the border of the asphalt, and stared at her. A little rosebud blooming.

Damn.

The broad grey road between them. Forty feet away, maybe.

And she was *still* trying to work something out down there. What the hell kind of water was she cooking with? How long would this go on? This long, anyway.

Damn.

Then the moment died. The girl heard something, abandoned her half-crouch, stood straight, met his eyes. Her forehead wrinkled and her face went dark. She screamed something he didn't understand. Like she was calling him a name. Warning him off.

When he didn't move, she raised her two hands like two paws with claws and howled at him like a cat. Loud as she could. Now a meow. A howl. High, then low and rumbling.

Then she covered her little teenybopper titties. Turned and splashed her way out of the pond and ran her little teenybopper butt cheeks back into the brush.

Oh hell no.

Something about the way she had looked at him, something about the cat thing, pissed him off in a way he couldn't quite translate.

Bitch.

Things That Piss Me Off. His go-to topic, and, in a sense, his only topic. Prominent on the long list of Things That Pissed Mike Mazzoni Off were any and all stunts pulled by people who had the intention of humiliating him. That was what the raghead teenybopper had just done: tried to make him look like an idiot by howling at him like a cat. Like she could kill him just with a look.

That ridiculous claw gesture, that dying howl, might not have raised his blood in quite the same way on any other occasion, but on this afternoon, the afternoon he learned of his brother's death, and greased his throbbing head with tequila, her howl became the latest entry on the list of Things That Piss Mike Mazzoni Off, and clicked into place somewhere right at his foundation.

He went back to the vehicle for Hajji, and for a grey steel container he had, the day before, filled with gasoline. They felt familiar and ready in his hands.

85

At 7:48, we return to the present day, to an American (!) football game. A metaphor (see next note) and also an in-joke, as Mother was and is a huge Redskins fan

Walking what might have been the fourth mile away from BII on her numb legs, the late-afternoon traffic coursing all around her and hours to go before she reached home, Fatima's debate about what she would and would not tell Mother was interrupted by a smell.

The smell of that ripping thing.

It hit her. The overpowering stench. Not sweat. Not steel. Not petrol. All three at once.

She spent five minutes attempting to wave down a car. Any car. Finally one stopped. A black cab. The driver, a high-pitched fast-talker with sunglasses to fight the glare, demanded to see her cash before he let her in. She showed it to him. He nodded. She got in the back.

She gave her address and promised him double if he made his way around the traffic somehow. He hung a right onto a side street that she otherwise wouldn't have believed in. The cab rushed forward all at once, pushed her like a lover into the dark embrace of her path. She wept for Noura.

86

> At 7:57, as the clock winds down and the players tense for the final snap, we are urged to block
> a kick. The metaphor of the football game. Defence = defence of White America, last remaining
> bastion of Western culture
>
> dark in here

From the same discreet airstrip that had welcomed Thelonius into the Islamic Republic the month before, the five flying killer robots prepared to take off.

Each was quite expensive. When you turned them on, they made a steady, unyielding, high-pitched whirr, precious metal birds gone insane.

Sullivan Hand had recommended UAV strikes on the five insurgents Indelible had identified for him. Dick Unferth approved those UAV strikes.

The acronym UAV stood either for Unmanned Attack Vehicle or Unmanned Aerial Vehicle, depending on the people you talked to. The dead guy telling this story wants you to know he used to call them Unanticipatable Airborne Vasectomies. They're also known as drones. UAVs are flying killer robots. They're all the rage these days.

All five of the men the killer robots targeted were prepared to die. They each knew with certainty, and accuracy, that death was coming. They had each been talked into believing that their dying would hasten the arrival of the global Islamic Caliphate and ensure the forgiveness of their sins. And forgive the sins of their near relatives who had passed on. And forgive the sins of their children. And so forth.

Dick Unferth believed that these kills, which were confirmed, proved the viability of Sullivan Hand's new contact, Indelible, as a source of invaluable intel within the senior leadership of the terrorist network operating in the Islamic Republic. Dick Unferth told everyone that Sullivan Hand's actions were the future of counterinsurgency. And so forth.

87

Stuck here at the desk for a bit. Hips bad. Need to make that phone call. The room darkening again, had to brighten the screen up to maximum. At 8:12, chaos recedes once and for all, and the longest track in the band's oeuvre comes to an end.

Dad was dead.

Adelia, calling at just after midnight, refused to say anything more about it over the phone. Using a series of private codewords only she and Dad and Thelonius understood (the relevant words here being 'rare water', a phrase Thelonius never imagined he would hear her say) she went on to intimate that she had something she had to give Thelonius. ('Improving'.) She wanted to give it to him in person. ('Eyes'.) He had to come out to the Cloisters as soon as possible. ('Sunny'.) She would wait for him. ('Sleepy'.)

After Adelia said these words, a deep sense of not knowing where he was predominated. For a long moment Thelonious could not establish his position. Wait. Carl's apartment. Yes. Thelonius was in a bed there, at Carl's place. That half-open door. Through it, there would be stairs leading down to Carl's front door. Beyond that, to the right, there would be a kitchen, with a window that opened onto the street. Cats, two of them, one orange and small, one tortoise-shell and a bit larger, liked to sleep near the heat vents in Carl's kitchen.

Adelia hung up. Thelonius placed the cell phone on the bedside table.

Assume the best. Assume the simplest. Assume the least twisted. Assume the normal. Old men, sick men, do die. Adelia, it was true, was not known for overreactions in emergency situations, but no one, not even Adelia, was *incapable* of overreacting. In all likelihood, she was overreacting now, having lost the man in her life. Loved ones do leave a hole in you when they die.

Sleep was impossible. He would have to leave a note for Carl.

⊠⊠⊠

Thelonius took the next available flight. Upon arrival at Dulles, he hustled himself and his two carry-ons off the plane, navigated a familiar maze and planted himself in front of what he knew to be the only open rental option at that hour, Budget. The sole unclaimed vehicle on the Budget lot was a green Siena.

What the hell.

The thought of driving it worsened the fluttery, empty feeling in his stomach. His heart pounding, he nevertheless told the acne-cursed counter teen, Brace, that he wanted the Siena. It made no sense to waste any time fussing in order to avoid a Becky-related memory built into the structure of the moment.

Brace was sorry the Siena was all that was available.

He gave Brace, who reminded him of TV's Eddie Haskell, his credit card. He signed the necessary paperwork, received a copy of the rental agreement, grabbed the keys, strode with five minutes of deep purpose to T-19 (the location scrawled helpfully on the agreement), and stared at the doppelganger Siena for a moment.

He pushed thoughts of Child aside.

The rental key in his hand, confirmation that there was actually nothing serious to worry about less than twenty minutes away, Thelonius made a point of edging out of spot T-19 slowly, checking both mirrors for oncoming vehicles as he did so.

What kind of a name was Brace?

He knew the route: muscle memory. He did not bother turning on the Siena's GPS. He claimed his exit without cutting anyone off. Hardly any traffic. Cautious, careful, steady, he guided the Siena toward Dad's house. Impossible to think of the Cloisters as anything but Dad's house. Impossibility everywhere. He couldn't seem to stop blinking.

Focus now. No need to complicate things. Safe trip. Road ahead.

He obeyed the speed limit. He stopped for traffic lights. He used his turn signals when changing lanes. His drive was uneventful.

By the time he made it to the Cloisters, it was a little before dawn. He worried he might wake Adelia, but her text as he parked his car in the open garage read, *Come to the back of the House.*

They both still knew to capitalize House.

Not even a hello. A nod. Which was fine. It was time for him to pray. She said that was fine and pointed him toward a spot just outside the House. Level moss. Cool. Which way was northeast? Did she happen to know?

She did. Did he need a carpet or anything?

He did not.

He prayed.

⊠⊠⊠

'They're flushing the town water system this morning,' she said when he was done.

'Okay.' Good to speak of something other than Dad.

'It's not supposed to start for a half an hour. The old machinery bought by the city fathers back in the day had to be replaced. It collapsed and left every drop in the water tower contaminated with rust. We've been on bottled water in the House. They have to dump the whole thing this morning and then refill it. Don't be surprised when you make your way back to your rental.'

There was no more *we* to be on bottled water. But it seemed cruel to point that out.

He looked at her, with an expression that asked, *what happened?* Adelia only nodded again, still all business, and said, 'Let's go in.'

Like Dad, like Thelonius, she knew Glass to be a safe place to speak.

She led him down the familiar pathway, which was lighted with the high-angled beams of the security lighting Dad had installed just after Thelonius entered the family. Those lights had lit many wanderings toward Glass. Once more, following the back of that graceful, tawny neck. That kinked, tightly bound hair. Adelia's existence emerged as a sober, comforting reality he could cling to, the closest graspable fact in a sea of bobbing uncertainties. But he wasn't really walking toward Glass, wasn't really following Adelia at all. He was swimming through the waters bordering a bleak, cold shipwreck: Dad Gone.

⊠⊠⊠

Adelia was both the last keeper of Dad's secrets, and the culmination of a private theory that Thelonius had nursed for some years. All of Ryan's known mistresses had been black. Thelonius had always wondered whether this sensual preference of his had been some kind of declaration of independence to Prudence, whose family boasted at least five generations of white supremacists from various South Carolina and Georgia elites.

And after Prudence's passing, was he also making some kind of statement to Becky?

Who knew? Dad never brought it up. Thelonius never brought it up. There were many topics one never brought up with Becky. Her barefaced, apparently immovable refusal to accommodate herself to the dark, high-cheekboned women who always guarded Dad's House, to the open secret of her father's string of elegant, bronze concubines, was simply never discussed. This silence was non-negotiable.

There were several jokes that had helped to make Becky a laughing stock within the Directorate. One of these, in which Thelonius never indulged, ran as follows: *How do you end a conversation with Becky Firestone? Ask her whether or not Dad likes dark meat at Thanksgiving.*

⊠⊠⊠

The whisk of the doorway. They stepped into Glass. A warm embrace of moist air met them. Adelia closed the door and locked it behind her. Thelonius had never seen her in here.

In the centre of the crystal-walled terrarium: Dad's empty wheelchair. Tendrils and buds and leaves, too close to it already, surrounded it from every angle of the structure, gave every impression of being prepared to claim it as their own.

'They collected the body late last night. You will want to stay in motion, I think.'

'Stay in motion?'

'The last official decision Dad made was to confirm your spot as the keynote speaker at the Freedom Banquet. The White House signed off on that last night, just after seven p.m. That's not going to be revoked. But if I were you, I would skip the banquet.'

'Why?'

'You've had an adversary since before you left for the Republic. We both have. I suspected as much, but I couldn't prove it to Dad's satisfaction. And now Dick Unferth is interim Director. So. Leave the country for a while, I think. That's what I'm going to do. Keep moving.'

Thelonius's heart folded into a tiny square.

Steel in her eyes, Adelia handed him a thumb drive.

'Becky killed him,' she said. 'He died around midnight. While I was sleeping. They had an argument in the House. This is the audio of it. You deserve to hear it. I would destroy it afterwards, though.'

Impossible. All of it.

The lush green tangle of the place had a familiar slow throb. It pulsed and edged out toward the empty wheelchair, toward them. She held the back of Thelonius's head with both hands. She kissed him on the cheek. That was impossible, too. She opened the door to the greenhouse. The air changed again, chilled and collapsed. He followed her out. The sun was up now, somewhere behind those clouds.

He left her, went back to the garage and stared at the Siena, wondered where on earth it would take him.

Before he could bring himself to press the key-button that un-locked its doors, a gurgling and roaring sound from the street outside. He went down to investigate. As she had promised, the gutters were rushing, about to overflow their banks with red liquid.

Everything impossible was happening now.

88

The dream past, the nightmare past, Prudence opens her eyes and sees Victory. A singer of lullabies approaches to soothe the Chosen One and rock her to her well-earned rest.

The eyes had not been cool.

It wasn't like in the movies, where dead equals closed eyes.

But not thinking about that anymore.

Mike Mazzoni drove someplace else, he didn't much care where, and he listened to a name circling in his head instead of music, which he didn't feel like turning on. The name circling in his head was 'Kelly Deane'. His mom's maiden name.

The house screamed smoke and ragged flames behind him. He saw the flames in the rear-view mirror and drove straight until it disappeared.

He said his mother's first name, 'Kelly', out loud, so he could hear what it sounded like. It sounded okay.

The tank said he had four hours of fuel. Plenty of time. Eager to get that burning out of his mirror, he pulled a left, and then another, and then went for several miles on a road that admitted no turns.

After a time he took a left anyway, found himself upon a broad stretch of desert, which worked well enough, hit the gas, grabbed the bottle of Cuervo and took a pull from it. The Cuervo was for survival. You couldn't survive out here the way you survived in other places.

He took a long pull on the bottle and started wondering what this was all coming to. Maybe the house would just burn everything to a crisp and that would be the end of it. Or maybe not.

Hadn't counted on the mother being there. That would complicate it. Mothers always complicate it.

Mike Mazzoni pulled another hard left turn into nothing, hit some kind of sandrut, felt the gravity angling on him, saw the sharp and sudden arc of the moon spin by on his left and wasn't anywhere at all.

⊠⊠⊠

The Islamic City police reported that after her rape, the lower part of Noura A—'s body, from her navel down to her feet, had been set on fire. The flames eventually spread to a carpet that bordered the kitchen where she had been attacked, and the smoke and flame issuing from the kitchen window alerted neighbours to inspect the scene. One neighbour, an elderly woman, recalled: 'That poor girl. I was close to her family. They brought me food. She was beautiful before this. To leave her there, with her one leg stretched too far and the other bent away, to expose her. Shameful.'

Firefighters arrived, drew a crowd, doused the inferno, and made their way inside. They removed the bodies. After approximately three hours, personnel from a nearby U.S. checkpoint arrived to secure the location.

The captain – Mike Mazzoni's captain, as it happened – made a statement to the restless locals who had gathered. He insisted that Islamic extremists had perpetrated the tragic events that had taken place there, the arson, murder, rape and so forth.

With a bullhorn, a paid translator relayed his words, but they were not well received. The captain waited in vain for the crowd to disperse.

To the contrary, people accumulated.

In the middle of the night, the captain called in heavy equipment. He planned to use it to flatten the remaining structure, which he deemed a safety hazard. Carrying out his orders proved difficult, however. Thirty or so of the locals, all men, most wearing white, linked arms and somehow got in front of the Caterpillar D8 in time to keep it from razing the house. The yellow monster rumbled and groaned and spat exhaust and did not retreat.

A standoff.

A tense half-hour passed. There were now something like fifty men with linked arms. One of the men in the middle of the link blocking the Caterpillar D8 shouted, 'Barricade! Takbir!'

His fellows responded, 'Allahu Akbar!'

Fatima watched all of this from her tree.

89

The last page of the young imam's letter read:

I close by noting a disturbing trend of which I must assume you are unaware, the heretical tendency of certain of your followers to perform the prayer directly before your photograph. This practice violates every known ruling on the matter within the past fourteen centuries of Sunni jurisprudence. A public rebuke is in order, and may I assume you will deliver this in your next communiqué?

Yours very truly,

And here the youngish imam signed his name. Behind him, an intruder advanced.

The intruder, a beefy zombie, followed Abu Islam's orders verbatim, approaching the imam from behind and slitting his throat from ear to ear with a box-cutter.

A moment later, the zombie encountered the youngish imam's wife or daughter. He wasn't sure which it was. She entered the room on soft, quiet feet. He looked her in the face, and, unmoved by the horror there, spun her around, following to the letter these instructions, too. He opened her throat without looking her in the eye.

⊠⊠⊠

Fatima had climbed her tree on instinct's orders, which she'd chosen not to disobey, after seeing smoke issue from her house. Just a few seconds later, the grey shadow of a U.S. soldier had flashed past what had once been her living-room window.

There is a way certain people walk, a loose-limbed disregard for the prerogatives of others, that radiates danger. The arms flip about, the elbows flail, the arrogant hips command each other in turn, the feet stray into paths not designed for them. This had been the physical signature of the man who had walked from her burning house.

It was the man who had pissed on the Koran. No mistaking that walk.

From her tree, through the window, Fatima had seen the corpses of her mother and sister.

She had trained the pistol on the man's skull.

Yet even though she had had the target in her sights, Fatima could not bring herself to pull the trigger.

Certainty: the enemy of justice.

By law, she needed a second witness. And she needed a name.

She had lowered the gun and watched him disappear into his vehicle, an ugly thing, and saw it spin a U-turn that was as arrogant as the man's walk had been. She had heard it roar away, smelled his scent receding, saw the flames extending from the house.

Fatima wanted now only to become part of the tree, to be its steady, strong limbs. She prayed to stay there, but instinct told her what to do next.

⊠⊠⊠

At a Starbucks similar in ambience to the one he had frequented those queasy few days after he learned of his wife's infidelity, Thelonius nursed a latte. He set it down. He plugged the thumb drive into his computer. He settled himself into his earbuds.

He hit play.

The following dialogue, between a near voice and a distant voice, coursed through his head.

(Near.) – What a surprise. Sit down, Becky.

(Distant.) – No, I don't believe I will, Dad.

– Flair for the ugly now? No need to make things ugly.

– Already beyond ugly, Dad. Once you set my husband to spying on me, it spun right past ugly.

– Is this what you flew up for? Well. No time for drama. Sorry. Look,

*I do have to make my way back to the main house and get my medica-
tion. Then I have some calls to make. I wish you had phoned.*

– I'm sure you do.

*– I understand you're expecting. I've always dreamt of a grandchild.
Boy or girl, do you think?*

*– If you had the vaguest flicker of strategic insight, you'd be asking my
forgiveness right now. Our forgiveness.*

*– Asking you what? I'm sorry? You know, sometimes I feel the best
thing to say to you is nothing at all. That's the right thing to say more
often than not, I've found.*

(A pause of over four minutes, during which time Thelonius
made out the intermittent hissing of mist within the greenhouse.)

– You would, wouldn't you?

– Would what, dear?

*– You would just sit there. Do nothing. Nothing. You would. Just
watch them. Watch it as it all falls apart. Watch the Muslims and the
secularists and the mulattoes destroy our civilization. Issue press releases
about regret. To win favour with them.*

(Another pause, eighty-four seconds.)

– Say something.

*– Well, you see, it is precisely this kind of puerile, ideologically driven
fantasia that … ah. Ah.*

*– That's what? That's led you to what? End my career? Sabotage me?
Cut my throat, take my hat off? As you wanted to take Mother's hat off?
This was how you were going to finish the sentence?*

*– Ah. Becky, dear Beckystone, stand aside and let me out of here. I'm
past due for a pill. I really can't miss my timings. Ah.*

*– You've already missed your timings. Dad. You would sit in this
hothouse and WATCH as Sharia law wrapped its filthy hands around
the throat of this nation? You would DO that? You would hand over our
PRIVATE research materials on the OJE case to JUSTICE? And make
us feel SHAME? We have dug beneath you, you know. We have dug beneath you, dug beneath both you and T at two hundred feet, and blown
you into the sky. He went away out of control, you see, and I made damn*

sure he could only come back in one of two ways, Daddy: in a box, or as a hero. And the thing about heroes, once they're done being heroes, they have to do as they're told.

— Rebecca.

— You can't take our hats off. Can't possibly take our hats off now.

— We are not going to continue this discussion. Stand aside. Ah.

— Did you think I wouldn't know your medication schedule? Or Brown Sugar's sleeping schedule? Hm? Did you think I wouldn't use due diligence, when I chose where to engage with you? The one place in all of the Beltway, with no possible inbound or outbound communication? The one place you haven't bugged? And wasn't this where you betrayed her? With your first niggerwoman, I mean? After she took care of you? Oh, you made our blood just burn.

— Now, Rebecca. If you don't step aside and open that door for me, this wretched twitching I am feeling just now will expand to a heart attack. I am past the timing for my medication. I was due when you walked in, you. You see. You. Rebecca. Ah.

— Yes, due when I walked in, Daddy, past due, really, half an hour late, as usual. Perusing your African violets. Monitoring their growth. Jotting the figures on your little clipboard. Distracted. Collecting more data. Verifying it. While the time passes. While the country suffers. I was monitoring YOU, Daddy. You see, sometimes you just have to step beyond the data, Daddy, and follow your GUT.

(A full nine minutes and twenty seconds of silence, punctuated at intervals by hissing and the sound of a man gasping. Then the sound of a woman walking away, the sound of a door opening, the sound of a door closing.)

The audio ended.

Unsafe in his little rearmost booth at Starbucks, Thelonius stared at the computer. He lost himself in it, unaware what time zone he was occupying, what day it was, what country he was in. There was only the media player's dialogue box on the screen.

Playing the audio exchange again seemed impossible. Closing the window seemed impossible, too.

Everything seemed impossible. He did not dare drink his latte.

Then a new dialogue box popped into existence, right over the media player that had hypnotized him, paralyzed him:

Fatima A— has asked to be added to your list of Skype contacts.

90

Strings just too damn syrupy on this track. I said come in.

Mike Mazzoni was never prosecuted. The events at Wafa's house accrued instantly to unidentified wayward insurgents, their motives obscure and suicidal.

Having spun around in the flatlands, having run out of gas, having radioed in for help, the man who sped away from the burning house that held the bodies of women found himself retrieved, sobered up and returned to active duty. He stank. Even after a shower, there was a strange smell on him. His colleagues picked it up. Metal and gasoline and something else maybe, something you didn't want to know.

A big part of the reason Mike Mazzoni was rushed back into duty as quickly as he was – despite still being technically eligible for bereavement time – was the trouble bubbling up in the village of D—, near the base where he was stationed. The ragheads were getting antsy out near the supply road, according to Captain X. Boots on the ground were in order.

⊠⊠⊠

The New Imam's Community Leadership Council, mindful of the village of D—'s recent history as the site of the disgraceful flechette assault masterminded by the kafireen, requested all available brothers to assemble at that village. Their presence was necessary to prevent the imminent bulldozing of the structure where the rape of the nation itself had taken place. A grand and obedient march from the sick heart of the city followed, on the urging of a heavyset woman who led it largely by scowling.

She rode in a dark vehicle, an American convertible, driven by a

Bearded Glarer. She faced backward in it and grimaced at the crowd as it edged forward. From time to time she shouted at them.

Evidence had already been removed from the site of the atrocity. Word of that much had reached her. What remained was subject to the judicial proceedings of the Islamic Caliphate, and not to be tampered with or destroyed, not by the Americans or anyone else. Kafirs, she had heard, had sworn to build a Christian church on the spot.

The brothers from Islamic City arrived and reinforced the local brothers who had been staring down the bulldozer.

Well ahead of the Americans in number, the White Beast's thousand hands set to work and joined in the assemblage of a great and ever-expanding wall of debris around Wafa's house.

This was a wall of fortuitous bits of garbage and basement-clearings, all fitted together like masonry. Surrounding the charred scene of the crime, rising beyond every new high point it established, the wall protected the sacred soil it enclosed from the corrupting hands and feet of Americans. It consisted of stray planks and bicycles, of appliances and milk crates, of rubber trash bins and once-discreet briefcases now open to the world, of discarded tyres and cracked computer monitors, and of the heavyset woman's black convertible, upended and set on its side near the base at her instruction. If you happened to be a bird flying above that wall, you saw that it formed a great inverted U around a half-burned-out shrine where the improvisers who built it now worshipped, bowing in synchronized awe and reverence, a few dozen at a time, toward the cracked, kicked-out kitchen window, where a flattering photograph of Abu Islam had been nailed.

The top of this U was guarded now by a line of hundreds of severe men in white, their arms linked, all bearded, all glaring.

They chanted, 'No church, no church, no Christian church here.'

⊠⊠⊠

The night after his desert rescue, bleary-eyed Mike Mazzoni put his very own boots back on the ground and rejoined the ranks of the American soldiers, committing himself to the cause of pulling down a building that presented a significant hazard to public safety.

But the wall around the burned-out house was still growing. It was nineteen feet high at its topmost point, which rose above the base of the U.

Mike Mazzoni didn't understand what the hell the men were chanting, but he was impressed at how fast they were chanting it. Half of them were out front, staring his unit down, and the other half were busy throwing stuff to each other. They kept working as they chanted, fitting their space heaters and their dead radios and their baby carriages into the wall.

91

bang bang bang fine you've got the warrant ok get in here

cant get up legs locked

The walk to the city was over. She thanked God for that. Her dead legs ached beneath the table in the rear of the dark, noisy internet café she had found on the borders of the city. She looked down at her own feet, imagined them without their shoes. What a journey they had pursued, those feet. So long, the path. So long.

Open all night. A booth all to herself. She thanked God for that too. Time to work. She began with a question: Was it possible he had a Skype account? It was.

Working on the paired theories that Thelonius would use his beloved comic book as the starting point for his screen name (plausible, but not certain) and that he was unlikely to broadcast his whereabouts (almost certain), it had taken her less than half an hour to identify all the candidates. Skype featured less than four dozen accounts bearing some variation on the name Sergeant USA. Of these, careful examination had confirmed that only six were located in undisclosed locations. She sent each of the six a contact request.

One came back immediately.

She clicked the icon and initiated a video call. They would need to see each other's faces, tired and bloodstained as hers was – that blow across the bridge of her nose that simply refused to heal. As the call connected she felt a shiver of embarrassment, then fought it down. This was not a courtship. They had business to conduct. Not a good world to bring children into anyway.

His face appeared.

His eyes, as tired as hers, said through the looking-glass of the computer screen, *Here we are.* She felt her own eyes say, *Here we are* in return.

Then he said:

'Assalamu alaykum.'

Odd that the phrase translating *peace be with you*, easily memorized by anyone, should have so completely dispelled any doubts about him. She believed he meant it.

⊠⊠⊠

Indelible made a request. Would he be permitted to meet face-to-face with an American contact? Within the American embassy? In order to discuss his deep desire to attain American citizenship and set up a plan for doing so?

Back in his cubicle in Langley, Sullivan Hand stared at his glowing screen and smiled.

He had never held a conversation like this before. If he had, or if he'd had the sense to work with someone who had, he would have known that confidential informants working within war zones are unlikely to ask for face-to-face meetings in environments densely populated by surveillance cameras. Cameras tend to make them skittish. Unless of course they are planning, in short order, to detonate themselves.

Working all on his own, Sullivan Hand assumed Indelible's enthusiasm on this point was a positive sign. He thought giving the people in the embassy a close-up look at Indelible was a damn good idea. He also wanted to position himself with Indelible as a nurturing parent, as his mentor had instructed. Last but not least, he wanted greater visibility among the half-dozen or so important Directorate people he knew to be based in the embassy. He intended to surprise them all. He wanted to be there. In the embassy. To welcome his asset.

So he said yes. And said he would be there in person to shake Indelible's hand. Becky set up the flight and arranged the clearances.

⊠⊠⊠

'We have business to conduct, you and I,' Fatima said. She looked down, gave herself half a smile, looked into the camera again. 'That is. I need help from *you* now. I have information to offer in return for your help. I mean to say: This is to be a transaction.'

'How did you get this Skype address?'

She waved a hand in dismissal. As though she meant, but didn't care to say, *please*.

'We are here to discuss justice. Then other matters, if you wish.'

He nodded.

'I live,' she said, 'in a republic ruled by madmen. Do you understand?'

Thelonius did. He said: 'It's not much better over here.'

Through the screen, she laughed. He laughed, too. Even though it was only a tiny laugh, it felt good to laugh with someone again.

The laugh subsided.

'My family is gone,' she said. 'I have been expelled from my home and banned from my mosque. The only publicly permitted form of worship involves praying toward a picture of this demagogue, Abu Islam. They actually place his picture on the street corners. Thugs roam the public places and take down the names of people who object to worshipping his photograph. Under such circumstances, one is forced to constitute one's own authority. A frightening time in one's life, to be the only member of one's own private nation.'

'Yes,' Thelonius agreed. 'It is frightening.'

'My mother and sister were murdered. The man who did this was an American. A marine.'

Although he could not see her hands, she might have placed them on the edges of the table from which she spoke, the better to steady herself.

She continued: 'I intend to execute this man without making him a public spectacle.'

Her eyes closed, firm against the world, she said:

'I am my own republic now.'

He felt his heart rising. As though to protect her. To bring justice. Another impossibility.

'I do recognize this man,' she continued, eyes open again, rimmed with tears. 'The man who destroyed my family was the same man you observed desecrating the Koran. Legally, I need confirming testimony from another person before I can execute him as an enemy of the state. I want you to confirm my certainty in his identity. I want his name, and I beg you, Thelonius, to tell me the truth.'

92

Whatever he said now, it sounded like he was ready to shoot somebody.

Some idiot was blasting 'Purple Haze' from a boom box. Mike Mazzoni demanded that it be shut off, and silence followed.

One might have imagined, from the tone of his voice, that he was taking a principled stand for greater discipline on the night watch. Or that he was fixed with some particular grim purpose on the five hundred or so bearded, poorly lit men who stood before him, the human barrier protecting the narrow, and only, gap in the wall. Or that their eleven elders, spotted by airborne surveillance, had become visible to him, that he had seen something untoward, some kind of movement or decision from those eleven shadows moving behind the barrier, casting some spark that might define the obscurity before him.

None of that was happening. His head hurt more when the music played. The more his head hurt, the more he remembered that he hadn't slept enough. That was all.

They all had to stand watch, all had to surround the damn thing and the greybeards inside it. Waste of boots, guarding this tower of crap, if you asked him. It was twenty-four feet high now, the wall, with a goddamn Lincoln convertible set into its base. It had been growing from the inside for hours, the wall, but he was pretty sure now that they had finally used up everything that could be flung or hoisted.

Plastic chairs, white, about a dozen of them, some with messed-up legs. A big metal fan-blade that looked like it once belonged to a factory or a warehouse ventilation system. A manhole cover. Some kind of entertainment centre, but without any of the equipment, just the wooden frame and the glass, which somehow hadn't broken. A bookshelf. A rake with plastic teeth. A piano. Upright, not grand, but still, how the hell they got a piano up there, which neighbour's house it had come from, how they had managed to levitate it to the peak of that wall of crap, he couldn't guess. Wasn't music supposed to be illegal to these people?

Aerial images showed that, once the marine guard had settled into formation, eleven ragheads had opted to stay seated in a circle on the ground, well behind the wall, in tight, near the remains of the house, near what would eventually be the strike point. Like they knew that was the best place to be if you wanted to die.

No one had thrown anything up over the top of the wall for more than an hour now. The betting was it wasn't going to get any higher unless they started throwing bodies up there.

There were voices from inside, old men within the U who could be heard but not seen, arguing or something. Sounded important.

The birds made a weird chirring sound as they flew over. These were photo birds. Not bomb birds. The bomb birds made a different sound. Higher.

Time to flatten this fucking place.

Every fifteen minutes, Mike Mazzoni, his hand home to thirty-nine black pentagrams, his face set taut against any truce or parley with ragheads, recited a lengthy foreign phrase out loud, into a bull-horn, its syllables set down on an index card. If he recited them correctly, the syllables were supposed to mean: THIS PROPERTY IS NOW UNDER THE CONTROL OF THE UNITED STATES MILITARY. EXIT IMMEDIATELY IN AN ORDERLY FASHION OR ACCEPT RESPONSIBILITY FOR ILLEGAL TRESPASS.

He recited the words so poorly they didn't actually mean anything.

93

> better make hospital 1st stop
> come in dammit
> theres the phone
> finally
> left it on the floor beneath the bed
> i see it
> have to call hospital
> cant get up

'This is to be a transaction,' Fatima's screen image said. She wiped her eyes. 'Men and women must come to terms. I have information I am willing to share with you in return for this confirmation. There is a mole, quite dangerous, working both with your people and with the BII. A zombie. Your superiors would reward you for identifying and imprisoning this man.'

A long silence passed. Thelonius, lost as a compass without a pointer, said: 'There are American channels for prosecuting …'

She waved her hand again in dismissal. Again, she did not have to say it: *Please.*

His chest strained again.

'I knew you were in danger. I knew it.'

Her eyes flashed.

'Not a good time to fall in love, I don't think, fool,' she said. 'Time to speak. Yes or no?'

Thelonius tried to form a word, but nothing came out.

'You knew I was in danger? Should I stop thinking because you knew that? Fool. Say yes or no.'

'This is treason.'

'So? Yes or no?'

There was an awful stillness as she stared at him. He felt naked.

'It will pass, that fear. Speak. And it will pass. In this world, no condition is eternal. No danger. No safety. We are in God's hands. If the condition is painful, pray for patience, because it will change. If the condition is pleasurable, pray for staying unattached, because it will change. And in either case speak justice.'

'You want me to say something when I don't know what to say.'

'No. Speak *justice*. Every moment. Every condition. That's the only permanent place, the only way we can live. In our speaking. Our only nation now. That's home. Sura Six, verse one fifty-two: If you speak, speak justice.'

'And I'm supposed to know what's just?'

She moved her hand. *Please.* And then the screen was dark and she was gone.

He put his hand to his mouth, then lowered it again and typed out a message: 'Call me tomorrow, same time. Please.'

Thelonius's latest cell phone, which should have received texts from no one, buzzed with a raw droning sound. This sound sent a wave of adrenaline through his veins. He pulled the phone from his pocket. The text was from Becky:

Why did you kill Dad?

He shut it off.

94

A day's delay, then. Fatima's plan now was to step over the border once
again and find a place to sleep that was free of the city. A warehouse
she remembered passing seemed promising. A large open window
there. She replaced her facial veil, paid her fee for the use of the computer and stood. Her scalp still ached, and it hurt to stand again.

Her legs bone-weary, she exited the internet café. The street was
busy, busier than it should have been after midnight. A television
set in a shop window was tuned to a station broadcasting a bulletin
about Wafa's ruined, blackened, barricaded house. The burned-out
structure was pictured from the queasy viewpoint of a helicopter.

Fatima felt heat rushing through her body.

She saw the single word 'standoff' in the headline, saw the crowd
gathered around the glow of the television, so easily hypnotized by
it. Men. All men.

As she walked north toward the city limit sign, a wave of rage
against the people standing in front of the shop passed along her
insides and would not recede. So much lost. Everything gone. All
because of them. Because of men.

A tightness as she walked. Her fists clenched. The blood was up
now, but it would pass, it would pass, it had passed yesterday, once
she thought of Baba and made ablution, and a person's breathing
could –

'Out late at night, sister. Against the Sunnah.'

She spun around, locked eyes with a white-clad zombie.

'My father was in an accident. Family emergency.' Both state-
ments true.

'We must keep the city safe,' the zombie said. 'Men may have cause to wander at night, but not women – unless they are selling something. State your destination, sister?'

Zombie eyes glared at her, and she fought down the urge to glare back at them, to reply to the insult with an insult of her own, or with a blow, or with something worse.

'Your destination?'

The clear difference between instinct and rage. No justice in rage. She was armed now, with Murad Murad's pistol, and with her own machete, each hidden away in the loose folds of her garment. She would no longer navigate the streets of the city without both weapons. But this was a case of stupidity, nothing more. Not a case of justice.

'Home,' Fatima said. 'Home, brother.' And nodded from behind her veil in solemn thanks for his attention.

And turned. And kept walking. No idea where that was now, though. Home.

'Khilafah!' the man shouted to her turned back. A test. As though no prostitute would dare utter the word.

'Khilafah, brother!' she shouted back, without looking at him, careful to mirror his tone and cadence. And raised her right hand with the index finger pointing upward.

And he applauded. Left her to walk alone toward a home that no longer existed, his loud clapping echoing through the alley. She followed it through to another, better-lit street, a street that led out of the city.

With the arrival of the real possibility of revolution in the Islamic Republic, she had heard it claimed by such loud men as these, that those leading the movement to overthrow the prime minister were comparable in character and motive to the companions of the Prophet of Islam, peace and blessings be upon him.

They dared to call themselves scholars. Loudmouths, rapists and sycophants. Imagining themselves entitled to every adolescent girl they could kidnap.

These loud men aimed to eliminate from the ranks of both leadership and followership anyone actually willing to think. 'Islam as a system of knowledge is already complete,' one of them had intoned during a sermon she heard echoing, amplified, through the morning streets today. 'No addition to it or subtraction from it, from science or any other source, is possible.' He was defending the use of textbooks whose lessons had not changed in four hundred years.

Fatima had long thought of stupidity as a violent contagion in her country, a threat to both political and moral well-being, and a crime against a faith whose Prophet had instructed his followers that the seeking of knowledge was obligatory upon every Muslim, male or female. She realized now, and with some alarm, that stupidity had already had its triumph here. The contest was over. Stupidity had assumed a deep centrality in the travesty of Islam that ruled the city. This stupidity had brought out the worst in non-Muslim and Muslims alike. Stupidity had taken both Ummi and Noura. Stupidity was now obligatory.

Despite the Prophet's specific, categorical objection to it, stupidity had become both required and fashionable in most nominally 'religious' circles since the grand marches had begun. Influential gatherings were not in the least shy about promoting distrust of anyone seeking knowledge that was not already categorized. Faith in stupidity was a way of life, a sign of honour in the new regime.

She wrote such thoughts in a small gold journal she carried everywhere, an indefensible folly. Yet she was afraid she, too, would begin to see practical advantages in stupidity if she failed to write such things down. Would lose her way. Would never make it home.

⊗⊗⊗

Why did you kill Dad?

The text meant he was a wanted man, a man wanted by the Directorate. It meant Becky had been tracing Adelia's calls. It meant the Patriot Act had come into play.

He had chosen to remain in motion. In the rented Siena, he maintained a careful, steady northeasterly course, always a few miles below the posted speed limit. He threaded his way through an underground tunnel too brightly lit with fluorescents for his tastes. Above him the Atlantic Ocean. Below him concrete, and then more Atlantic Ocean. Around him, circular patterns of harsh lighting that made unpleasant blinking patterns as he drove, as if they meant to shake the foundations of the continent.

The tunnel, which had been humming for quite some time, felt like something he was falling through endlessly. Eventually, it was supposed to release his rented green Siena near the Eastern Shore of Maryland, an iconoclastic, rural-feeling corner of the state that might, if he switched on his phone, signal multiple intentions on his part. For instance: a desire to proceed north on 95 toward Boston; a desire to check back in at Langley and submit to questioning; a desire to return to Washington, where the Freedom Banquet would be held, and where he was still listed as the keynote speaker.

Even, perhaps, a desire to flee the country. Rock Hall, Maryland, was a functioning harbour.

Forward, forward, forward. The tunnel kept on humming. In a long stretch like this, one felt almost stationary. Was he driving too slow now? He checked the speedometer. No. Fifty-eight. Just fine.

Should he give her Mazzoni's name?

Uncertain whether he would, or should, take any action at all on her behalf, whether there was any point to any of this, the dead guy who now called himself Ali Liddell felt, for the first and last time, deep anger toward Fatima. It came on him quickly. A kind of heat passed through his body, made him want to stomp down on the accelerator.

On the seat beside him rested the Raisin's Koran. He put his hand on it. Things slowed down again. Waiting for him inside it was the verse from the Surah of the Sun he had now memorized:

Qad aflaha man zakkaha / Waqad khaba man dassaha
Whoever purifies her flourishes / Whoever defiles her fails

He kept heading northeast. Thelonius passed out of the artificial light of the tunnel and found himself dazzled by the break of mid-morning daylight.

95

finally – what is that a piledriver. ram

or something. bring it on boys

'Damn fine work,' said Captain X, inspecting the wall at close range.
A stand of portable lights from behind him illuminated it. 'Not an
edge of it out of place. Flat, almost. Even close up. Straight edge
meeting straight edge. Crates. Doors. Tyres. Shopping cart up there.
Look. But one more or less even surface, all the way around. How
many people dragged stuff out here for this party, do you think?'

Mike Mazzoni, eyes wide, occupying a point far beyond sleep,
said, 'A few hundred, at least. Caravan. See the cars? All from the
city. The neighbours brought crap from their basements.'

'Mm, *mm*. What happened to that opening they had?'

'Closed up. Bunch of milk crates stuffed with some kind of grey
metallic shit, steel wool, looks like.'

'It's not a U anymore,' Captain X said. 'It's an O now.'

'Yeah, don't think they're planning on coming out.'

'We'll see about that. Tear gas.'

'Still don't fucking think they're planning on coming out.'

The captain, not used to being contradicted in such terms, pursed
his lips and scanned Mike Mazzoni's face.

'You are tore up from the floor up, son. Been a rough week for
you, I know. Almost done here. We are going to clear this area. Then
we are going to get you home. Don't you worry. I have friends in the
Directorate. They've been covering for us here. Making sure we take
down this particular safety hazard.'

Mike Mazzoni sniffed twice, cocked his eye toward the wall, and
chose not to tell his commanding officer he wasn't going home.

Captain X stepped back a few paces, into a clearing beneath a
tree, saw a tiny wet patch of red on the grass.

'What the hell …'

He kneeled down to inspect it.

A shot rang out from somewhere within the wall.

The captain's head flew backward with the impact. Mazzoni saw him gazing solemnly upward, into the air, as though he were reading it.

'Man down!' Mike Mazzoni shouted, although his commanding officer was not down at all, was still perched on one knee.

His own arms spread wide, Mike Mazzoni, who had dropped his weapon, was not down either.

Everyone else hit the dirt. He walked toward the wall.

⊠⊠⊠

In the warehouse, Fatima had a dream that she was on a sidewalk that was crumbling beneath her, and that only by moving forward, in a straight line, toward what appeared to be a kind of sun, could she secure her footing.

⊠⊠⊠

Indelible recorded the video message he planned to send Sullivan Hand. He knew it was quite possible Sullivan Hand would survive, and even in the event that he did not, Sullivan Hand's superiors certainly would, and could be expected to examine the email correspondence closely.

In the video, Indelible explained to Sullivan Hand that he did not want any money or cars, that he had given away all his money. He expected to secure forgiveness for all of his sins as a result of his actions today.

Indelible edited the video to remove some dull spots at the beginning and end, saved it, then timed its delivery so that it would reach the Directorate's servers at a certain predetermined point in time. When he had finished, he used duct tape to apply explosives to his body, with the help of his wife. That done, his wife dressed him, handed him his Thermos of Darjeeling tea, and turned away.

⊠⊠⊠

He could only come back in one of two ways, Daddy: in a box, or as a hero. And the thing about heroes, once they're done being heroes, they have to do as they're told.

As he recalled these words, Ali's chest was doing strange things.

He pulled over, picked up the phone, and speed-dialled Carl Arnette. He had a favour to ask. Some research he was unable to conduct properly while on the road.

⊠⊠⊠

Mike Mazzoni took long, direct strides toward the wall, intending to dare its occupants to shoot him.

As he approached it, a black mongrel, so large it almost seemed a parody of a dog, leapt toward him, hurling itself like a missile from the barricade it had scaled.

Growling, snarling, seething with what appeared to be rabies, it landed on its back with a yelp, then found its feet and surveilled its former owner.

The beast paced, a deep-howling, red-eyed, lunatic guard on watch before a mountain of repurposed rubbish.

Mike recognized the dog, his last champion. Abandoned by a grey road. No name. He must have been adopted and snuck in by one of those goddamned cowards inside the wall.

The moment they made eye contact, establishing some unspeakable common purpose, the insane dog stopped pacing, settled into its hind legs, and sprang forward.

⊠⊠⊠

96

Fatima made her ablution with clean dust, permissible when no water is readily available. In the warehouse, she made her Sunnah prayer, then she made her obligatory prayer, then she made the prayer one makes when one is about to embark upon a major undertaking and one asks God to remove the commitment from one's path if it does not bring benefit in the afterlife.

⊠⊠⊠

Indelible, surrounded by an overcoat, stayed within two or three blocks of the American embassy compound, walking a crazy zigzag path that assured him he was not being followed. He never got too far from the target. If for some reason the situation required acceleration, he was prepared to accelerate.

⊠⊠⊠

The leaping dog had a distance of just under six feet to cover before its maw reached Mike Mazzoni's proud, exposed neck.

From the left, there came a pop and a whizzing sound. A bullet from the rifle of a marine caught the black dog in midair with a wet thud.

The dog dropped to the grass at Mike Mazzoni's feet.

A hand grabbed him by the back of his shirt-collar, and a voice – he did not know whose – called him a dumb motherfucker, berated him for risking somebody else's life besides his own, told him they all had to fall back now. They were heading back to the base. Drones were on their way in.

⊠⊠⊠

He was in another Starbucks, waiting for another call. When the computer screen announced her, there was fear in each chime. It chimed once, then twice. Then a third time. The fear got worse each time.

Just Get Started.

He clicked on the stylized green image of the phone receiver. She appeared in her headscarf again, without her veil.

There was the same little pause, which he found now that he enjoyed. But staying on too long put her in danger. So he said, out loud:

'You were right. It was him. The name is Mazzoni. M-A-Z-Z-O-N-I. A sergeant. First name Michael.'

She wrote on something off screen.

'I'm so sorry you met me,' Thelonius said.

She looked upward, smiled. Shook her head, 'No.'

'The mole you are looking for,' she said, 'has been codenamed Indelible by BII. Here comes a video of him. In the video, he's the man shouting at the fellow climbing the fence. I hope it helps someone. I hope it helps you. I hope it helps the country.'

He nodded as the file transferred, looked into her eyes once more, tried to make out the colour for the last time, but the lighting was unfavourable. He saw bits of gold, nothing else, before she said, 'Assalamu alaykum.'

The window was dark. He emailed the file to Dick Unferth, who opened it, then deleted it.

⊠⊠⊠

There was a dispute among the eleven elders who had taken a stand behind the wall. One of them suggested that they refer the matter to the New Imam.

When the representative of the elders finally reached the New Imam on the phone, it was two o'clock in the morning. The New Imam listened patiently, and without apparent prejudice, to both sides of the disagreement.

One party was of the opinion that that those fathers and heads of households who wished to stay at the location should be permitted to remain through the entirety of the inevitable American drone assault.

The contrary party held that men with wives and children should be excused, whether they wished to leave or not, because of the market for human flesh that existed in the poorer quarters of the city. Such martyrdoms, martyrdoms that left women and children without protectors and supporters, were to be avoided, they argued, because of the possibility of defeat.

Which view should prevail?

'Defeat?' the New Imam asked. 'You believe you face defeat?'

He pronounced in favour of the first group. He instructed the emissary to inform those in the second group that their position flirted with apostasy.

They obeyed. An hour later, a distant propeller, not unlike the buzz of a bee, was heard. Presently they were all dead, all the men with wives and children and all the men without, and the house Wafa had meant to be a mother in was reduced to chunks of smouldering rubble.

⊠⊠⊠

Take a look at this sketch. You see from it that there is a restroom on the first floor of the American embassy, near the metal detector at the front entrance of the building. This room is reserved exclusively for the diplomatic corps and, by extension, for the spies pretending to be them or work for them.

Sullivan Hand, who had recently arrived in the Republic by means of the same discreet runway Thelonius Liddell's plane had once used, had regarded his admission to this sacred space, and his use of it, to be a confirmation of his own inevitability within the Directorate. He was planning a party that evening, even though there was no one out here he knew by name yet. That was no obstacle. He would damn well meet some people and introduce them and toast the day. He had a right to toast the day. He was, officially, not a desk jockey anymore. He was in intelligence. He was working in the field, about to meet, in mere minutes, an asset he himself had cultivated. Face to face.

Right after he finished dealing with the problem of his own stool.

The stool, which was somewhat smaller in size than usual and tapered distinctively, and which had struck its issuer as structurally impeccable when subjected to a cursory visual inspection, was proving problematic. Owing either to its unique, aerodynamically evocative shape, or to the design of the commode's bowl, or to some complex interplay of the two factors, a single flush had been powerless to make it vanish. So had a second flush. And a third. And a fourth. Having watched the fifth flush fail, too, Sullivan Hand studied the stool's compact, insolent, implausibly resilient form, floating in the bowl, mocking him. It was as though his own faeces had begun speaking to him, proclaiming that it had found its place and was unwilling to yield it to anyone.

Sullivan Hand regarded the bowl philosophically. Leaving a turd suspended for other members of the embassy staff to discover seemed like a poor career choice for a prominent new arrival. He wondered why no one had thought to place a toilet brush in the supposedly elite stall he now occupied. He might be able to break the thing up with a toilet brush. Perhaps there was one in an adjacent stall.

Before he could resolve this problem, however, there occurred, more or less simultaneously, a hoarse ripping sound and a flash of light.

⊠⊠⊠

That afternoon, when Mike Mazzoni reached the point where he refused to communicate, they walked him, saucer-eyed, ramrod-straight and sleep-deprived, into the infirmary.

The doctor, who was not at his best either, took only five minutes to examine him and hand over the prescription. Like the rest of the base, he was on edge with the news from the embassy.

This physician, a jittery premature grey-hair who suspected, correctly, that he was about to be ordered to work triage, had been up for a while. He had worked the previous night's shift, then been told not to sleep. He was to prepare to get on the helicopter that would take him to the city. The carnage at the embassy was said to be epic. He wasn't looking forward to classifying it.

He had no remaining reserves of patience or ingenuity for what seemed like a garden-variety PTSD onset. He watched Mike Mazzoni swallow both tablets, roughly sufficient in narcotic capacity to take down a horse.

Premature Grey confirmed to his own satisfaction that he had done his job well enough, then confined the sergeant to quarters, where he was to be left undisturbed until morning.

Mike Mazzoni, however, would not be confined to his quarters. After his escort left, he made his way over to the Wreck Room, where he pulled out the last hidden bottle of Jack.

⊠⊠⊠

She went just after nightfall, her face covered. Sidestepped down the hillside, the least evident route. Slipped through a narrow, but adequate, hole in the untended chain-link fence, a gap she had identified from a distance that afternoon. Entered the little shack, which was unlocked and unguarded. The entire base seemed, and indeed was, close to empty, most of its occupants having been assigned to deal with civil unrest, which had broken out once again in the city.

He was not dead, or anything close to it, when she found him sprawled face-down on the floor. He was semi-conscious, a circumstance that suited the purpose and made the pistol she was carrying unnecessary.

The name on the dogtag: MAZZONI MICHAEL R.

She knelt down, inspected him closely, took his wrist, let it go. The pulse was steady, the face that of the criminal she had seen walking from the house. The position of the body was not optimal, so she stood and straightened the arms with firm movements of her right foot.

After these repositionings, she knelt down again and loosened the man's shirt, the better to expose the neck.

Her hand brushed against his cheek and ear as she did this.

Face down, he stirred at the unexpected tenderness of that touch, the apparent compassion of it, twisted his prone head to one side and then the other, opened an eye, and mumbled a single word: 'Bitch.'

His palms went to just below his shoulders, as though he were preparing to do a push-up.

She stood quickly. Instinct said *now.*

A critical concern in any beheading is the sharpness of the blade. A weak, dull blade causes undue pain in the criminal and virtually ensures the necessity of multiple strikes, both of which are violations of the Sunnah of the Prophet, peace and blessings be upon him.

Fatima had sharpened her blade that afternoon.

97

On the other side of the world, as you slowed your green Siena to manoeuvre your way out of the passing lane where you knew you did not belong, there came a twinge in your chest that signalled full complicity. And you felt, to your relief, fine with that twinge.

98

When the two most recent Heroes of the Week found his cot empty, when they came to the Wreck Room to investigate, when they saw the small, quivering figure backing away from the flow, they didn't notice the machete.

They assumed her shuddering was the shuddering of trauma, thought she was a fearful teenaged girl unused to the sight of blood. They were wrong. It was not that kind of shuddering.

They found the machete in a far corner of the room. It was in its green canvas case, but it bore red streaks when one withdrew it.

99

> contracs 8 min apart .here they come door down Ok
>
> Hitting save
>
> gnight wverybody WE SHALL PREVAIL

Standing room only. The bright hall was packed. You showed up at the last possible moment.

Dad, although dead, had old friends in the Secret Service. He had placed you on some special list. You waited in the wings. The speaker scheduled right before you, a Ph.D. from Harvard, was concluding some remarks that established the moral superiority of drone warfare over all previous military technology.

UVAs, it turned out, were more flexible. They were safer. They were more precise. They had the potential to substantially reduce civilian casualties, though they did carry certain public relations risks. And so forth. When the Ph.D. finished, with a flourish, on the word 'freedom', the Important People at the banquet applauded until the stage was empty. It remained empty for a time.

As you took your place at the rostrum, the commander-in-chief, who had apparently been briefed on your status as a returning hero, stood up bravely and clapped loud, beginning a personal standing ovation that was dutifully imitated by everyone else in the room.

'So,' you began, keeping your tones slow and measured. 'So. We have a big problem with terrorism, and we mustn't be afraid to say that much right out loud.'

There was another slow swelling of applause. The idea of getting up and starting a whole new standing ovation, even though one had just finished, might have started at the front of the room, at the commander-in-chief's table, but it was hard to tell. Wherever it began, everyone was soon standing again.

'Yeah,' the dead and guilty guy you had become said. 'Yeah. Thank you.'

You waited until things quieted down.

'So. There's a news story that's just breaking. I didn't break it. It broke itself. Probably the Defenders of God broke it. Anyway, you're all going to read about it, hear about it, see videos about it on all the various internets.'

The commander-in-chief's face went a little sour for a microsecond, then returned to its 'smile' setting.

'So. This story's going to be about a marine who snapped. He snapped all the way over there in the Islamic Republic. Where I was. He did something terrible. It's going to be big, this story. Lots of people will tell it. I can guarantee you one thing about this story. Most of the versions we hear are going to use the word "tragedy".'

There was a rustling at the edges of the great hall, just beyond your field of vision, as though, to the far right of you and the far left of you, barely seen men were receiving instructions from their earpieces, and preparing to position themselves.

'So. When we hear that word "tragedy", and repeat it over and over again, most of us are going to file this episode in the exact same place we file stories about bus accidents when the brakes go out. As just one of those terrible things that happen. That's what we've convinced ourselves tragedy means. Random awfulness that happens to be extremely severe. But that's not what a tragedy is.'

The palms of your hands, which had been pressed against the sides of the podium as though it were about to fly away, fell to the sides of your body.

'So. Tragedy is not a snapped brake cable that no one could have foreseen. Tragedy means someone makes a mistake, and then comes to regret that mistake from the soul and pays for that mistake in a painful way, a way that everyone else can learn from. That way the mistake doesn't repeat.'

Another silence passed. A stirring at the table of the commander-in-chief suggested low, ongoing conversation.

'So. I suppose you want to know how I feel about terrorism. I'm a terrorist. I shot a little girl while I was over there. Shot her dad, too. Shot them dead.'

There was a gasp from one of the tables. You tried to make eye contact with someone in the audience – anybody would do – but the lights made this all but impossible. Behind the commander-in-chief's table, there were only dark silhouettes of bodies, male and female, seated and standing, in the shape of suits. No faces.

'So. We're all going to say that was a tragedy. What a tragedy it was, those dead people over there. In that faraway place. And we're going to use that word "tragedy" like a kind of shield. But the point is, it shouldn't have happened.'

All still and soundless. Your stance still straight. Your hands by your sides.

'So now we're all out to make this look like some kind of bus accident I was in. That's what we're doing here tonight, really. Fast-forwarding over what I did. What he did. And I think maybe we're all just a little ill. Mentally ill, I mean. Everyone in this room. Because these are actual mistakes we made, and most of us can't see or feel that yet. Can't even bring ourselves to say what happened clearly.'

This remark caused heads to lean to the left and to the right, and to whisper, at the table of the commander-in-chief.

'Personally, I think we all went too damn fast for our own good for a while. I think we all just need to slow down.'

You took a drink from a glass of water that had been placed at the podium for you. You replaced the glass with care. The water within the glass made little ripples consistent with its having been set down.

'So. What do I think about terrorism? Terrorism is killing civilians, on purpose, in order to fulfill a political agenda. Like installing a theocracy. That's a political agenda. Or defeating an insurgency. That's a political agenda, too. And I think terrorism has to stop, and it's not going to stop as long as we are so ill we don't even realize what we're doing. We're lost. And I think if we don't slow down, we're looking at nothing but war, all of us, for a very long time to come.'

The commander-in-chief put a closed fist to his mouth, cleared his throat and looked around the room.

'Nothing but war,' you repeated.

Every light in the hall came on. An extended, piercing two-note squeal assaulted the banquet room, then repeated itself, and repeated itself, and repeated itself, and gave no sign of ever wanting to stop. Someone had set off a fire alarm.

'Please clear the hall in an orderly manner,' an invisible man's bass voice ordered. Chairs and tables made scraping noises. Above those noises, the endless two-note shriek continued.

The commander-in-chief allowed himself to be ushered from his table. Others followed his lead. A steady stream of well-dressed people marched toward the exits, which were brightly marked. Most of the people walking away from you had their hands over their ears.

'So. It's not like we've never *been* lost,' you continued. 'We get lost all the time. Slavery. Interning the Japanese. Charging people money at the polls to keep them from voting. What do we always do fifty years after we screw up like that?'

A silent wall of suits assumed its formation against the back wall. Before he exited, the commander-in-chief looked back over his shoulder and made a gesture toward someone standing in that line. Then the commander-in-chief was gone, an index finger in each ear.

'So. Fifty years later, we look back and we say, "Was that us? Did we do that? Did we buy and sell people? That wasn't America. Not really." But it was. It was us screwing up. "Sorry." Well. If the "sorry" is real, if it hurts, fine. But we're not sorry about this yet. This should hurt a little more than it does.'

The two-note siren's onslaught continued. It made your ears throb. Fleeing it, half the attendees had already made their way through the exits, and the other half were on their way out, their hands clapped to the sides of their heads.

One of the black suits mouthed an unhearable phrase and pointed directly toward the stage. The mike cut off with a pop.

'Having wiped out three thousand civilians with flying killer robots,' you went on, 'have we got more terrorists to worry about? Or fewer? More suicide bombings? Or fewer? Is what we're doing really protecting the people we love? Or is it driving them insane? It's not working. We have to go back to an empty space. To nothing. From nothing, who we are is the possibility of justice.'

The siren grew louder, which you didn't think was possible. The man in the darkest grey suit approached the stage.

You leaned into the podium and shouted your final question toward the back of the hall.

'Will one of you please take care of my wife?'

There were only men in dark suits in the hall now. One of them came up from behind you, assumed ownership of your right arm, twisted it behind your back and hustled you off the podium. When you got offstage, Dick Unferth was waiting for you there in the wings. Dick nodded to the man in grey, a black hood swept over your head and you heard a voice that definitely belonged to your wife say:

'We are quite capable of taking care of ourselves.'

⊠⊠⊠

It has been one of the questions on your mind – you know you are not the first to ask this – whether or not the universe is a moral place.

Even though no one chose to hear your final questions, even though you are not certain anyone will ever read this, even though you will die here, you are inclined to believe, with the preachers, that it is, and that it simply has a very long arc, an arc that tends toward justice. That there is something that lasts. That what matters – you have no idea how, but you sense that it matters deeply – is whether one makes an effort along such an arc.

Your death is likely to come at your wife's hands, probably within the next session or two. She keeps asking you the same questions: Was any recording made of her final discussion with Dad? (Yes.) Who received it? (You didn't give it to anyone. You destroyed the thumb drive.) Who received it? (No one.) But who received it? A name, please. (No one.) Where is Adelia? (You don't know. You're glad you don't know where Adelia is.)

These answers she finds unpersuasive. You've accepted that. You're getting out of here, though. You're going home.

Last time you checked, the Islamic Republic had achieved, not democracy, not theocracy, not secular dictatorship, but the cursed state of wavering forever among these three possibilities.

Fatima (the gossip says) ended up in a maximum security prison somewhere in the States. In addition to convicting her of killing Mike Mazzoni, which she did, they convicted her of firing an anti-aircraft missile at an American plane, which she didn't.

They didn't have to convict you of anything. They just disappeared you. They do things like that now.

They took your Koran away last week. Without it, you turn mentally to some verses you have already memorized, and you get ready to leave this place. These days, you turn to chapter one hundred of this book you have written, this book of struggle and striving, which you hope Becky gets to read carefully one of these days. You read chapter one hundred a lot.

You have a nickname for Becky now. It's a loving nickname, the name of the first wife of the Prophet of Islam. The only woman he loved, as long as she lived. The woman he thought he was going to spend his life with. The woman who took care of him when his life seemed to be falling apart. The woman who strove with him during his darkest days. The woman who made his life's work possible.

Some might expect you to be angry at Becky, but the only emotions you feel for her now arise from the spectrum of sorrow: countless shades of regretful blue on the wing of a butterfly, blues for the loss of a love that you cannot now describe. You wrote this book for her. Perhaps someone in the Directorate will read it, and having read it, decide it's time to take care of Becky now.

Even here, in the Beige Motel, you never forgot her many moments of patience and compassion with you, never really stopped loving her. This is a love story. Your mouth bleeds red and your heart aches white, until you think of her awakening to herself, shaking free of her chrysalis, guided by the light of a glow from neither the east nor the west, greeting you in Paradise.

100

قِيلَ ٱدْخُلِ ٱلْجَنَّةَ قَالَ يَلَيْتَ قَوْمِي يَعْلَمُونَ
بِمَا غَفَرَ لِي رَبِّي وَجَعَلَنِي مِنَ الْمَكْرَمِين

Qeelad-khulil-Jannah. Qala ya layta Qawmee ya'-la-moun.
Bima gafara lee Rabee wa ja-'alanee minal-mukrameen.

It was said, 'Enter Paradise.' He said, 'I wish my people could
know of how my Lord has forgiven me and placed me among the
honoured.'

36:26–27

Acknowledgements

Grateful acknowledgement goes out to Karen Sullivan, Bob Diforio, West Camel, Mark Swan, MacGuru, Richard Gibney and Safie Maken Finlay, none of whom ever gave up.